FATAL FLAW

"You really are scared," Michael said, "aren't you?"

"Ragnorson's never quite rational about women," Prataxis replied. "And there are so many women involved this time that I can't pretend to predict his behavior.

"Nepanthe. Mist. Inger. Kristen. Sherilee. Each pulling Bragi in a different direction, and each a danger. Nepanthe cost us Varthlokkur's help. Mist nearly killed Bragi during the coup, then went away, taking that source of support. Queen Inger has turned like a mad dog. Kristen's scheming to have her son designated crown prince. And this—thing—with Sherilee has him completely distracted at a time when every minute has to be devoted to keeping the kingdom on a steady course."

Michael nodded. "And now there's Yasmid, pulling him into the desert."

Prataxis dropped into a chair. "What are we going to do?"

GLEN COOK

AN ILL FATE MARSHALLING

A TOM DOHERTY ASSOCIATES BOOK

AN ILL FATE MARSHALLING

Copyright © 1988 by Glen Cook

First printing: January 1988

A TOR Book

Published by Tom Doherty Associates, Inc.
49 West 24th Street
New York, NY 10010

ISBN: 0-812-53379-8
Can. No.: 0-812-53380-1

PRINTED IN THE UNITED STATES OF AMERICA

0 9 8 7 6 5 4 3 2 1

AN ILL FATE MARSHALLING

Prologue;
Year 1013 After the Founding of the Empire of Ilkazar: Castle Greyfells in Duchy Greyfells, in Northern Itaskia

THE COLONEL STALKED through the quiet corridors, each step charged with the nervous energy of a caged panther. Servants got out of his path, turned to watch after he passed. His tension surrounded him with an aura of danger.

He reached the door of the chamber to which he had been summoned. He stared at it, rose onto the balls of his feet, settled back. He was afraid of what might lie on the other side. This was more than the portal to a room. It was a doorway to tomorrow, and he didn't like the smell of it.

Something was afoot. He had come to the castle last evening, and had found it infested with tension. The Duke was planning something. His people were scared. All the recent Dukes had become involved in schemes that failed, and each failure had brought violence down on the family and its retainers.

The Colonel steeled himself, knocked.

"Enter."

He stepped inside. Six men were seated along the sides of a long table. The Duke himself sat at the table's head. He gestured, indicating the seat at the table's foot. The Colonel sat down.

The Duke said, "Now I'll end the speculation. Our cousin Inger has received an offer of marriage."

One of the others asked, "That's why all the whispers and night messengers? Pardon me, Dane, but that seems a little. . . ."

"Let me expand. You'll see why it's a matter for the highest family councils.

"Our cousin nursed in a hospital during the siege of the City by Shinsan's forces. She became romantically involved

1

with a patient. Rather a torrid affair, I gather, though she was understandably reluctant to part with details. When the siege broke and the war moved southward, she thought it was over. She heard nothing from the man. The usual story. Used by a soldier who moved on.

"But four days ago she received a proposal of marriage from the man. She thought it over, then came to me for advice.

"Gentlemen, the gods have smiled on the family at last. They've handed us a golden opportunity. Our cousin's suitor is Bragi Ragnarson, Marshall of Kavelin, who commanded the allied armies during the Great Eastern Wars."

Dead silence held the room for half a minute. The Colonel didn't even breath. Ragnarson. Blood enemy of the Greyfells for a generation. Responsible for the assassination of one Duke and the bloody abortion of half a dozen family projects. Probably the man most hated by everyone in the room, saving himself. He was just a soldier. He didn't hate anyone.

He began to sense the shape of the shadow and didn't like it. It was in the tradition of Greyfells schemes.

The six all started talking at once. The Duke held up a hand. "Please?" He waited. Then, "Gentlemen, if that news isn't enough to excite you, consider this. Those fools down there are going to make him King. They couldn't find anybody else willing to take the crown. Do you see? This is an opportunity not only to avenge ourselves on an ancient enemy, it's a chance to steal the crown of the richest and most strategically placed of the Lesser Kingdoms. A chance for us to move our base out of Itaskia entirely and free ourselves of the miserable nuisance of a perpetually inimical Crown. A chance to seize the most important counter in the conflict between east and west. A chance to recoup the greatness we've lost."

The Duke's excitement communicated itself to the men at the sides of the table. The Colonel was less intrigued. Here was more Greyfells dirtywork, and he had a feeling he would be asked to carry part of the load. Why else was he here?

The Duke said, "The simple, basic question is, should we let our cousin accept?" He smiled. "Or, do we dare *not* let her? It would be a sin to ignore an opportunity like this. Eh?"

No one demurred. Someone said, "But we couldn't just let it go and hope."

"Of course not. Inger would be the lever. The foot in the door. The distraction. Right now she just wants to see her leman again, but I imagine we can get her to be the family's agent. For insurance, and to take charge of the day-to-day details, I suggest we send the Colonel here."

The Colonel kept his features rigidly controlled. So there it was. And it stunk. There were times when he wished he didn't owe this family a debt of loyalty.

The Duke asked, "Can anyone propose a reason why we shouldn't pursue the policy I'm suggesting?"

Heads shook. One man said, "Something as good as this, you needn't have asked."

"I wanted unanimity of purpose going in. Carried, then? Pursue the possibilities, at least till we see some insuperable stumbling block?"

Heads nodded.

"Good. Fine." The Duke's voice was silky with pleasure. "I thought you'd like it. That's all for now. Let me look into it further. Let me see if there are pitfalls. I'll keep you posted. You can go now." He leaned back. As everyone neared the door, "Oh. Don't discuss this with anyone. Anyone at all. Colonel, yes, I want you to stay."

The Colonel had risen but not left the table. He seated himself again. He rested his forearms on the tabletop and stared at a point over the Duke's right shoulder.

Once the door closed, the Duke said, "Actually, we're farther along than I admitted. Babeltausque put me in touch with some old friends from the Pracchia days. They've agreed to help." Babeltausque was a sorcerer in the family employ. The Colonel loathed him.

"That's a strange face you've got there, Colonel. You don't approve?"

"No, My Lord. I don't trust the wizard."

"Perhaps not. They're a slimy, slippery breed. Nevertheless, we seem to have adequate resources for the project. We have but to convert the woman and send her on her way."

"I see."

"I really do get the feeling that you don't approve."

"I'm sorry, My Lord. I don't mean to appear negative."

"Then you'll take the mission? You'll go to Kavelin on our behalf? You'll be away for years."

"I am yours to command, My Lord." And how he wished he were not. But one had to pay one's dues.

"Good. Good. Make yourself free of the castle. I'll keep you posted on developments."

The Colonel rose, bowed slightly, left the room smartly. A soldier doesn't ask, he told himself. A soldier obeys. And I, sadly, am a soldier in the Duke's employ.

1

Year 1016 AFE;
Rulers

BRAGI GROANED. Inger shook him again. "Come on, Your Kingship. Get up."

He cracked a lid. One glassless window stared back with a cold eye. "It's still dark out."

"It just looks like it."

He grumbled as his feet hit the chilly floor. It was one of those ice-bottom days, going to turn hell-fire come afternoon. He gathered the bearskin round him and told himself there had to be a point to rising.

It was springtime in Kavelin. The days were hot and the nights were cold. The weather was foul more often than not.

Bragi yawned, tried to rub the sleep from his eyes. "It raining? My head feels like it's packed with wool."

"I wouldn't argue with that. Yes. One of your steady Kaveliner drizzles."

He said what everybody always said. "Be good for the farmers."

She completed the ritual. "We need it." She posed. "Not bad for an old broad, eh?"

"Pretty good. For a wife." There was no heart in his jest.

Her too-small mouth fashioned a pout. "What do you mean, for a wife?"

His grin was as grey as he felt. "You know what they say. That old grass always looks greener."

"You grazing in somebody else's pasture?"

"What?" He heaved himself to his feet, stumbled round looking for his clothing.

"Last night was only the second time this month."

He gave it the light treatment. "I'm getting old."

Something inside cawed sarcastically. He was fooling himself, not her. A nasty black chasm yawned at his feet. Trouble was, he did not know if it was waiting for him to try

5

jumping over or if he was on the other side looking back.

"Is it another woman, Ragnarson?" There wasn't any kitten in her now. She was all bitch cat. The habitual brittle smile had left her lips.

"No." For once he was telling the truth. He didn't have a single little round-heel on the string. The soft curves, the warm mounds, the humid thighs did not set the fires roaring these days. They seemed more a distraction than a reasonable interest. They irritated more than excited.

Was it symptomatic of age? Time was an implacable thief.

Ragnarson's growing indifference worried him. The departure of the drive to collect scalps left a vacuum like the loss of an old friend.

"You're sure?"

"Absodamnlutely, as friend Mocker might have said."

"I wish I had met him," she mused. "Haroun, too. Maybe I'd know you better by knowing them."

"You should've known them. . . ."

"You're changing the subject."

"Honey, I haven't had no strange in so long I wouldn't know what to do. Probably just stand there with my thumb in my ear till the lady cussed me out."

Inger whipped a comb through her hair. Blonde rat's nests grabbed it. She was wondering. He had come tagged with a reputation, but had not lived up to it.

Maybe he was too busy. Kavelin was his extramarital lover. She was a demanding mistress.

He eyed this woman who was both his wife and Kavelin's Queen. She was the one gift the wars had given him. Time had done well by her. She was a tall, elegant woman of brittle beauty and even more brittle humor. She had the most intriguing mouth he had ever seen. No matter her mood, her lips seemed on the verge of a sarcastic smile. Something about her green eyes magnified that foreshadow of laughter.

First glance said she was a lady. Second might suggest an earthy soul. She was an enigma, an intriguing creature hiding inside a shell that betrayed a new mystery each time it opened. Bragi thought her as perfect a Queen as a King could ask. She had been born for the role.

That secret smile came out of hiding. "You just might be telling the truth."

"Of course I am."

"And you're disappointed, eh?"

He did not answer that one. She had a knack for caging him with questions he did not want to answer. "Maybe you'd better check the baby."

"You're ducking the issue again."

"Damned right."

"All right. I'll let up. What's on for today?" She insisted on being a full participant in royal affairs. He was new to the kinging business. Coping with a strong-willed woman complicated his task.

His circle of old comrades agreed. Some had strong opinions about Inger's "interference."

She returned from the nursery. She carried their son Fulk. "He was sleeping like a rock. Now he wants to be fed."

Bragi slipped an arm around her. He stared down at the infant. Babies were still a wonder to him.

Fulk was his first by Inger, and her first ever. He was a lusty six-monther. Bragi told Inger, "I'm having the whole mob in about Derel's message this morning. After lunch I'm supposed to play Captures."

"In this weather?"

"They challenged. It's up to them to call it off." He began lacing his boots. "They're good mudders."

"Aren't you a little old for it?"

"I don't know." Maybe he *was* past it. The reflexes were going. The muscles could not take it the way they had. Maybe he was an old man with one hand desperately clamped on an illusion of youth. He did not enjoy Captures much. "What about you?"

"Terminal boredom. And it won't stop till the Thing adjourns. I feel like a governess."

He forbore reminding her that she had demanded the right to entertain the delegates' women.

Commencement for the spring session was a week away, but the wealthier members were in town already, sampling Vorgreberg's social possibilities.

Bragi said, "I'm going to get something to eat." He was an informal King. He had no patience with pomp and ceremony, and very little with the luxuries his position afforded. His was a warriorly background. He strove to maintain a spartan, soldierly self-image.

"Don't I get a kiss?"

"Thought you'd be kissed out."

"Never. Fulk too!"

He kissed the baby, left.

Maybe Fulk was the problem. He pondered it as he descended the stair. The battle had begun during the name-choosing. He had lost that round.

It had been a difficult birth. Inger wanted no more children. He did, though he did not consider himself a good father.

Too, Inger was worried about Fulk's patrimony. He was born of Ragnarson's second marriage. Bragi had three older offspring, and a grandson named Bragi. The latter might as well have been his own child. His father, Ragnarson's firstborn, had perished at Palmisano.

The King's first family lived at his private house, outside Vorgreberg proper. His son's widow managed the place and youngsters. He had not visited them in weeks. "Have to get out there soon," he muttered. His inattention to his children was one of the few guilts he suffered.

He made a mental note to solicit a legal opinion from his secretary, Derel Prataxis, as soon as the man returned from his mission.

Ragnarson had led a charmed life. He thought his luck overdue to change. It was part of that fear of growing old. The edge was going. The reactions were slowing. The instincts might not be trustworthy. His mortality was catching up.

Maybe he could negotiate some succession understanding during the Thing's session. They had not made the kingship hereditary when they had dragooned him into it.

He approached the castle's main kitchen. Strong smells and a loud voice emanated from its open door.

"Yeah. That's no lie. Yeah. Nine women in one day. You know what I mean. In twenty-four hours. Yeah. I was a young man then. Fourteen days on a transport. I never even saw a woman, let alone had one. Yeah. You don't believe me, but it's the truth. Nine women in one day."

Ragnarson smiled. Someone had Josiah Gales cranked up. On purpose, no doubt. He was a one-man show when he got going. He grew louder and louder, flinging his arms around, dancing, stomping, rolling his eyes as he underscored every statement physically.

Josiah Gales. Sergeant of infantry. Bowman supreme. Minor cog in the palace machine. One of two hundred soldiers and skilled artisans Inger had brought as dowry because her cadet line of Itaskia's Greyfells family had fallen into genteel poverty.

He smiled again. They were still laughing up north, thinking themselves rid of an unruly woman cheaply, while gaining a connection with a prized crown.

The unseen sergeant whooped on. "Fourteen days at sea. I was ready. How many women you had in one day? I wasn't showing off. I was working. Yeah. That seventh one. I still remember her. Yeah. Moaning and clawing. She's going, 'Oh! Oh! Gales! Gales! I can't take anymore.' Yeah. That's the truth. Nine women in one day. In twenty-four hours. I was a young man then."

Gales repeated himself over and over. The more wound up he was, the more he did so, mouthing every sentence at least once to everyone within hearing. His audience seldom minded.

Bragi approached the duty cook. "Skrug. Any chicken left from last night? I just want something to snack on."

The cook nodded. He jerked his chin in Gales' direction. "Nine women in one day."

"I've heard this one before."

"What do you think?"

"He's consistent. He doesn't make it bigger when he retells it."

"You were at Simballawein when the Itaskians landed, weren't you?"

"It was Libiannin. I didn't run into Gales. I would've remembered him."

The cook laughed. "He does make an impression." He produced a tray of cold chicken. "This do the job, Sire?"

"That's plenty. Let's sit over here and watch the show."

Gales had an audience of serving people come to town with the advisers and assistants Bragi was to meet later that morning. For them the sergeant's stories were fresh. They responded well. Gales undertook further flights of whimsical autobiography.

"I've been all over this world," Gales declared. "I mean, everywhere. Yeah. Itaskia. Hellin Daimiel. Simballawein.

Yeah. I've had every kind of woman there is. White women. Black women. Brown women. Every kind there is. Yeah. That's no lie. I got five different women right now. Right here in Vorgreberg. I've got one, she's fifty-eight years old."

Someone catcalled. Everyone laughed. A passing palace guard leaned in the doorway. "Hey! Gales! Fifty-eight? What's she do when she goes down? Gum you to death?"

The group howled. Gales flung his arms into the air. He let out a great wail of mirth. He stomped and shouted back, "Fifty-eight years old. Yeah. That's right. I'm not lying."

"You didn't answer the question, Gales. What's she do?"

The sergeant went into contortions. He evaded answering.

Ragnarson dropped his chicken. He was laughing too hard to hang on.

"Low humor," the cook growled.

"The lowest," Bragi agreed. "Straight out of the gutter. So how come you can't wipe that grin off your face?"

"If it was anybody but Gales. . . ."

The sergeant's audience trampled his protests. They buried him in questions about his elderly friend. He reddened incredibly. He bounced around, roaring with laughter, vainly trying to regain control of the group. "Tell us the truth, Gales," they insisted.

Bragi shook his head and murmured, "He's a wonder. He loves it. I couldn't stand it."

Soberly, the cook asked, "But what's he good for?"

"A laugh." Bragi stiffled a chuckle. It was a sound question. Inger's dowry-men had proven useful, but he often wondered what their presence signified. They were not loyal to himself or Kavelin. And Inger remained an Itaskian at heart. That might prove troublesome one day.

He munched chicken and watched Gales. His military adjutant came in.

As always, Dahl Haas looked freshly scrubbed and shaved. He belonged to that strange fraternity who could walk through a coal mine in white and come out spotless. "They're ready in the privy audience chamber, Sire." He stood as rigid as a pike. His gaze darted to Gales. Disgust flickered across his face.

Bragi did not understand. Dahl's father had followed him

for decades. The man had been as earthy as Gales.

"Be there in a minute, Dahl. Ask them to be patient."

The soldier strode out as though he had a board nailed to his back. Second generation, Ragnarson thought. The others were gone. Dahl was the last.

Palmisano had claimed many old friends, his only brother, and his son Ragnar. Kavelin was a hungry little bitch goddess of a kingdom, eager for sacrifices. He sometimes wondered if it didn't demand too much, if he hadn't made the biggest mistake of his life when he had allowed himself to be made King.

He was a soldier. Just a soldier. He had no business ruling.

Vorgreberg shivered with gentle excitement. It was not the great dread-excitement foreshadowing dire events, it was the small, eager excitement that courses before good things about to unfold.

There had been a messenger from the east. His tidings would touch the life of every citizen.

The magnates of the mercantile houses sent boys to loiter by the gates of Castle Krief. The youths had strict instructions to keep their ears open. The traders were poised like runners in the blocks, awaiting the right word.

Kavelin, and especially Vorgreberg, had long reaped the benefits of being astride the primary route connecting west and east. But for several years now there had been little exchange of goods. Only the boldest smugglers dared the watchful eyes of Shinsan's soldiers, who occupied the near east.

There had been two years of war, then three of peace occasionally interrupted by furious border skirmishes. Easterner and westerner perpetually faced one another in the Savernake Gap, the only commercially viable pass through the Mountains of M'Hand. Neither garrison permitted travellers past their checkpoints.

Merchants on both sides of the mountains railed against the never-ending, knife-edged state of confrontation.

Rumor said King Bragi had sent another emissary to Lord Hsung, the Tervola proconsul at Throyes. He was to try again to negotiate a resumption of trade. The whisper had raised almost messianic hopes among the merchants. No heed was paid the fact that past overtures had been rebuffed.

Warfare and occupation had shattered Kavelin's economy. Though the kingdom was primarily agrarian and resilient, it had not yet come all the way back in the three years since liberation. It needed resumption of trade desperately. It needed a freshened capital flow.

The King's henchmen had gathered. Michael Trebilcock and Aral Dantice stood at the foot of a long oak table in the gloomy meeting room, chatting in soft voices. They had not visited in months.

The wizard Varthlokkur and his wife Nepanthe stood before the huge fireplace, silent. The wizard seemed deeply troubled. He stared into the prancing flames as though studying something much farther away.

Sir Gjerdrum Eanredson, the army's Chief of Staff, paced the parquetted floor, smacking fist into palm repeatedly. He was as restless as a caged animal.

Cham Mundwiller, a Wesson magnate from Sedlmayr and King's spokesman in the Thing, puffed on a pipe, a fashion recently introduced from far southern kingdoms. He seemed engrossed in the arms of the former Krief dynasty hanging over the dark wood of the chamber's eastern wall.

Mist, who had been princess of the enemy empire till she was deposed, sat near the table's head. Exile had made of her a quiet, gentle woman. A knitting bag lay open before her. Needles clicked at an inhuman pace. A small, two-headed, four-handed imp manipulated them for her. Its legs dangled off the table's side. One head or the other muttered constantly, apprising the other of dropped stitches. Mist shushed them gently.

There were a dozen others. Their backgrounds ranged from sickeningly respectable to outrageously shady. The King was not a man who selected friends for appearance. He made use of the talent available.

Sir Gjerdrum mumbled as he stalked. "When the hell will he get here? He dragged me all the way from Karlsbad."

Others had come farther. Mundwiller's Sedlmayr lay near Kavelin's far southern border, at the knees of the

Kapenrung Mountains, in the shadow of Hammad al Nakir, beyond. Mist, now Chatelaine of Maisak, had descended from her fortress eyrie in the Savernake Gap. Varthlokkur and Nepanthe had come from the gods knew where; probably Fangdred, in the impenetrable knot of mountains known as The Dragon's Teeth. And pale Michael looked like he'd just returned from a sojourn in shadow.

He had. He had.

Michael Trebilcock mastered the King's secret service. He was a man largely unknown personally but his name was a whisper of dread.

The King's adjutant entered. "I just spoke with His Majesty. Stand by. He's on his way."

Mundwiller harumphed, tapped his pipe out in the fireplace, began repacking it.

Ragnarson arrived. He surveyed the group. "Enough of us are here," he said.

Ragnarson was tall, blond, physically powerful. He had scars, and not all on the flesh, to be seen. A few grey hairs peeped through the shag at his temples. He looked five years younger than he was. Captures kept him fit.

He shook hands, exchanged greetings. There was no majestic aloofness in him. King he was, but here just another of a group of old friends.

Their impatience amused him. Of Sir Gjerdrum he asked, "How do the maneuvers look? Can the troops handle the summer exercises with the militia?"

"Of course. They're the best soldiers in the Lesser Kingdoms." Eanredson could not remain still.

"Youth and its fury of haste." Sir Gjerdrum was yet in his twenties. "How goes it with the beautiful Gwendolyn?"

Eanredson growled something.

"Don't worry. She's young, too. You'll outgrow it. All right, people. Gather round. I'll only take a few minutes."

There were more henchmen than chairs. Three men ended up standing.

"Progress report from Derel." Bragi placed a ragged sheet of paper on the distressed oak tabletop. "Pass it around. He says Lord Hsung accepted our proposal. Subject to approval from his superiors."

A soft ripple swept round the table.

"Completely?" Sir Gjerdrum demanded. His scowl became one of incredulity. Mundwiller sucked at his pipe and shook his head, refusing to grant belief.

"To the letter. Without significant reservations. Without much dickering. Prataxis says he barely looked at our offer. He didn't consult his legion commanders. The decision had been made. He knew his answer before Derel got there."

"I don't like it," Eanredson grumbled. "It's too dramatic a turnaround." Mundwiller nodded and puffed. Several others nodded, too.

"That's what I'm thinking. That's why you're here. I see two possibilities. One is that there's a trap in it. The other is that something happened in Shinsan during the winter. Prataxis didn't speculate. He'll be back next week. We'll get the whole story then."

He surveyed his audience. No one wanted to comment. Odd. They were an opinionated, contentious bunch. He shrugged. "They've given us the runaround so long. Demanding impossible tariffs and arguing over every word of any agreement, but suddenly they're wide open. Gjerdrum? You have a guess why?"

Eanredson flashed his scowl, his adopted expression of the day. "Maybe Hsung's legions are up to strength again. Maybe he wants the Gap open so he can run spies through."

Ragnarson said, "Mist? You shook your head."

"That's not it."

Varthlokkur gave her a venomous look that startled Ragnarson. She caught it, too.

"Well?" the King asked.

"It doesn't make sense that way. They have the Power. They don't have to send spies." That was not entirely true, Ragnarson knew it, and she knew he knew. She amended the remark. "They can see whatever they want to see unless Varthlokkur or I shield it." She exchanged glances with the wizard, who now seemed satisfied. "If they wanted an agent physically present they would send him in over the smugglers' trails."

Something had passed between sorcerer and sorceress and Ragnarson was aware of that fact only, not what. Puzzled, he chose to let an explanation wait. "Maybe. But if you kill that reason what do you do for one that makes sense?" He glanced around. Dantice and Trebilcock looked away.

Ragnarson was uneasy. There were undercurrents here. Mist, Varthlokkur, Dantice, and Trebilcock were his most knowledgeable advisers in matters concerning the Dread Empire. They seemed unusually disinclined to advise. They looked like people with their fingers on a pulse both shifty and strange, unwilling to commit themselves to an opinion.

"I'm not sure." Mist's gaze flicked to Aral Dantice. Though Dantice had no official standing he was a sort of minister of commerce by virtue of his friendships with the Crown and members of the business community. "Something is happening in Shinsan. But they're hiding it."

Varthlokkur nearly smiled.

Bragi leaned forward, cupped his chin in his right hand, stared into infinity. "Why do I get the feeling that you do know but that you don't want to tell me? It doesn't cost anything to guess."

The woman stared at her knitting. The wizard stared at her. She said, "There might have been a coup. I don't feel Ko Feng anymore." Her tone became cautious. "I did have a few contacts with old-time supporters last summer. Something was in the wind, but they refused to be pinned down."

Trebilcock snorted. "Tervola, no doubt! Wizards always refuse to be pinned down. Sire, Ko Feng was stripped of titles, honors, and immortality late last autumn. They practically accused him of treason because he didn't finish us at Palmisano. He was replaced by a man named Kuo Wen-chin, who had been commander of the Third Corps of the Middle Army. Everybody who'd had anything to do with the Pracchia or Feng got transferred to safe and obscure postings with the Northern and Eastern Armies. Ko Feng vanished. Kuo Wen-chin and his bunch are all younger Tervola and Aspirators who had no part in the Great Eastern Wars."

Trebilcock steepled his hands before his pallid face, looked at Mist as if to ask "What do you think of that?", then shifted his attention to Aral Dantice. His expression was tense. He hated groups and loathed having to speak out in front of them. Stage fright was the one chink in his armor against fear.

Trebilcock was a strange one. Even his friends thought him weird and remote.

Bragi said, "Mist?"

She shrugged. "Apparently my connections aren't as good as Michael's. They want to forget me over there."

Ragnarson glanced at Trebilcock. Michael responded with a tiny shrug.

"Varthlokkur. What do you think?"

"I haven't been watching Shinsan. I've been preoccupied with matters at home."

Nepanthe stared at the tabletop and blushed. She was eight months pregnant.

"If you're convinced it's important I could send the Unborn," the wizard suggested.

"Not worth the risk. No point provoking them. Cham? You're quiet. Any thoughts?"

Mundwiller drew on his pipe, belched a blue cloud. "Can't say as how I know what's happening yonder, but your occasional smuggler's rumor crosses my path. They say there's been riots in Throyes. Hsung maybe wants to shift the yoke so he can head off a general uprising against his puppets."

The King's gaze flicked to Trebilcock again. Michael did not respond. As a gesture of good faith Ragnarson had instructed Michael to stop supporting Throyen partisans and to break with their leaders. Had Michael defied orders?

Michael had genius and energy but could not be broken to harness completely. The espionage service had become too much his fiefdom. But he was very good, very useful. And he had a knack for making friends everywhere. They kept him posted. Through Dantice he used Kavelin's traders to gather more intelligence.

The King scanned the group through narrowed eyes. "You're a moody bunch today." No response. "All right. Be that way. If you're not going to talk to me there's nothing else till Derel gets home. Meantime, think about what's happening over there. Check your contacts. We have to hammer out a policy. Gjerdrum. If you think you really need to keep an eye on Credence Abaca go back to Karls-bad. Just be back here when Prataxis gets in. Yes? General Liakopulos?"

The general was on permanent loan from the mercenary's guild, helping improve Kavelin's army.

"Not to the point of the meeting, Sire, but important. I've had bad news from High Crag. Sir Tury is dying."

"That is sad news. But . . . He was an old man during the El Murid Wars." Musingly, "I first met him the night we broke out of Simballawein. Gods. Was I only sixteen? . . ."

He drifted away on a memory-cloud. Sixteen. A refugee from Trolledyngja, where a war of succession had devastated his family. He and his brother, with nowhere else to go, had enlisted in the Guild and almost immediately had been thrown into the boiling cauldron of the El Murid Wars. They had been dumb kids then, he and Haaken, but they had earned names for themselves. So had their friends Reskird Kildragon, Haroun, and the funny little fat man, Mocker.

He turned his back on the company. Tears had come to his eyes. They were gone now, those four, and so many more with them. Reskird and his brother had fallen at Palmisano. Haroun had vanished in the east. Mocker. . . . Bragi had slain his best friend himself.

The Pracchia had used its hold on the man's son to turn him into an assassin.

I'm a survivor, Ragnarson told himself. I got through all that. I lifted myself up from nothing. I hammered out an era of peace. The people of this little wart on the map made me their King.

But the price! The damned price!

Not only had he lost a brother and friends, he had lost a wife and several children.

Everyone in that room had lost. Loss was one of the ties binding them. He brushed his eyes irritably, thinking he was too sentimental. "You all go on now. Keep me posted. Michael, wait up a minute."

People began to file out. Bragi stopped General Liakopulos briefly. "Should I send someone to the funeral?"

"It would be a mark of respect. Sir Tury was your champion in the Citadel."

"I will, then. He was a great man. I owe him."

"He had a special feeling for you and Kavelin."

Bragi watched his people go. Most had not spoken at all, except to exchange greetings. Was that a portent?

He had a bad, bad feeling down deep in his gut. He was headed for a season of changes. Fate was marshalling its forces. Dark clouds were piling beyond the horizon.

2

Year 1016 AFE; Conversations

"THERE GOES A long-term problem in the making," Michael Trebilcock observed. "But you've got time to head it off."

"What?" the King asked.

"There were what? Twenty people here today? The insiders who make Kavelin work. Hold up a hand. Count the natives. Gjerdrum. Mundwiller. Aral. Baron Hardle. That's all. Who wasn't here? The Queen. Prataxis. And Credence Abaca. That's one more native, and Abaca is only Marena Dimura."

"What are you trying to say?"

"Undue foreign influence. Nobody worries about it now. We've got Shinsan on the brain. Suppose this deal goes through? We cuddle up to the Dread Empire. Trade turns the economy around. When people stop worrying about making it, and about Shinsan, what's left? Us. They haven't lost their ethnic consciousness. You could end up in a tighter spot than the last Krief."

"College boy," Bragi grumbled. But Michael had a point.

Kavelin was the most ethnically mixed of the Lesser Kingdoms. Four distinct groups contributed to the population: Marena Dimura descendants of ancient natives, Siluro descendants of the civil managers of the days when Kavelin had been a province of the Empire of Ilkazar, Wesson descendants of Itaskians the Empire had transported from their homeland, and Nordmen descendants of the people who had destroyed the Empire. Friction between the groups spanned the centuries.

"You might have a point, Michael. You might have a point. I'll think about it."

"Why did you want me?"

"Got a Captures game this afternoon. I'm playing right point. I want you as my side."

Trebilcock grunted in disgust. He disliked games and loathed any exercise more strenuous than his morning rides with friends. Captures was demanding. It could go on forever if the teams were evenly matched. "Who are we playing?"

"The Charygin Hall Panthers."

"The merchant boys. I hear they're good. There's money behind them."

"They're young. They have staying power. But not much finesse."

"Speaking of young. Aren't you getting a little old for Captures? Meaning no offense, of course."

Captures was a Marena Dimura game originally played over vast expanses of forest. They settled inter-village squabbles by playing—though the dirth of rules left casualties all over the woods.

The citified version was played on more limited ground. Vorgreberg's "field" covered one square mile north of the city cemetery. There were forty players to a team. There were rules intended to make the game fun.

Everyone cheated.

Captures resembled Steal the Flag. The teams tried to capture balls from their opponents and carry them to their own "castles." Each started with five oxhead-sized balls. Each tried to prevent opposing players from seizing its own balls, or to recover them once stolen. The game was played in two forms. In the short the first team to convey all its opponent's balls to its own castle won. In the long, the winner was the team which acquired all the balls. The long could continue for weeks. Round Vorgreberg they played the short form.

"I don't have the wind I used to," Bragi admitted. "And the legs get tired faster. But it's the only fun I have anymore. It's the only time I can get off by myself and think. There aren't any distractions out there."

"And on the point there's no one to listen if you want to have a little heart-to-heart with your side?"

"Even the walls have ears here, Michael."

Trebilcock groaned. He did not want to waste an afternoon running through the woods. . . . He grinned. He could get himself thrown out of bounds. A player could not return to the game if his opponents ejected him in front of a judge.

That was the crucial point. A judge had to witness any infraction. Creative cheating was the soul of the game.

"Meet me out there," Bragi said. "We drew the west castle. Try to show up by noon." He smiled. He knew how Michael felt about Captures. "Wear something old."

"Your wish is my command. Can I go?"

"Head out. We'll talk there."

Trebilcock slouched away. Bragi watched him go. The tall, lank spymaster looked like a caricature of a man. His skin was so pale it seemed never to have seen the sun. He appeared to be a weakling.

Looks were deceiving. Trebilcock was all wire and stubborn endurance. He had carried out several harrowing missions during the Great Eastern Wars. His successes had won him a reputation as a super-agent. Some of the inner circle were more awed by him than were the enemies he watched and hunted.

"Michael," Bragi murmured, "are you one of the problems I'm going to face down the road?"

Trebilcock was one of Ragnarson's most competent people. He had a strong, fatherly affection for the youth. But Michael was prone to go his own way, within his shadow world. He was an embarrassment occasionally.

Ragnarson settled at the table. For a while he wandered memories of the events that had led him to this moment, this place, this position. He reiterated his losses. . . . He shook like a hairy old dog after swimming a creek. Enough of that! A man could go whacky worrying about what he should have done differently.

"Got to see the kids tonight," he muttered. "If I don't come in too sore to drag over there."

Michael coaxed his mount out the castle gate. He slouched in the saddle. The drizzle pasted his hair to his head in strings.

Guardsmen rendered indifferent salutes from the gatehouse. "That one is a real spook," one whispered.

"Looks like he's late for his own funeral," another observed. "Who is he?"

The first shrugged. "One of the King's people. Don't see him around much anymore."

They would have recognized Trebilcock's name. His reputation burned into the deep shadows. The belly side of society watched for him over their shoulders. He was tight with the wizard Varthlokkur, whose creature the Unborn looked into the darks of men's minds. The plotters of great crimes and treasons invariably caught Michael's eye. Then the pitiless hammer fell.

Trebilcock had extended himself to create his nasty image.

Aral Dantice met him on the cobbled way linking the castle with the surrounding city. They turned their horses into the parkland encircling the palace. Cherries and plums were in bloom.

"Late start this morning," Michael observed. For years they had ridden the park when they could. Usually they shared the bridle trails with others from the castle. This morning they were alone with the drizzle.

"Would have been nastier earlier," Dantice replied.

They talked out old times and finished gossiping. Now they grew guarded.

Aral was a squat, wide man in his middle twenties. He looked more street thug than prominent merchant. Before his father's death he *had* been more the former than the latter. Since, he had turned his father's nearly bankrupt caravaneer outfittery around. He had become a major supplier of tack and animals to the Royal Army.

"I suppose." Trebilcock swung a hand. His gesture took in their surroundings. "I'd like to redesign this. At the Rebsamen I had this adviser. His hobby was landscaping. Whoever did this didn't have any imagination. It's nothing but a damned orchard."

Aral looked at him askance.

"I'd move all these fruit trees out. Scoop out a lake. Make a reflecting pool. Put a line of poplars down each side, yea and yea, to frame the castle. Maybe put some shrubs and flower plantings in front for spring and summer color. See what I mean?"

Aral smiled. "Be interesting to see what you could do." He scanned the castle. "You'd either have to knock down

Fiana's Tower or build another one over on the left. To give the palace balance."

Trebilcock looked puzzled. "Balance? What do you know about balance?"

"What's to know, Mike? Stands to reason, don't it? You don't want it to look lopsided. What did he want, anyway?"

"What did who want?"

"The King. When he had you stay behind."

"You won't believe it. I still don't. He wants me to play side to his right point in the Guards' Captures game this afternoon."

Aral studied him, one cheek crinkling questioningly. "Really?" He laughed. "That's right. It's the Guards and Panthers today, isn't it? Battle of the undefeateds. The old fox is trying to sneak in some better players." Dantice leaned, punched Michael's bicep. "Put your money on the Panthers, Mike. Charygin Hall recruited the best men money can buy. Nobody will beat them for years."

"What're the odds? Is there a spread?"

"You can get five to one if you're stupid enough to bet Guards. Two goal spread. You can get ten to one if you bet the Guards to win."

They rode another fifty yards before Trebilcock mused, "Think I'll have my bankers cover a couple hundred nobles. On the Guards."

Dantice and Trebilcock went way back. It was Aral's opinion that Michael was a fool with money. "What the hell for? It's your money, and you've got more than you could throw away, but why the hell waste it?"

"Your class chauvinism is showing, Aral. The Guards are undefeated too. Remember who's on their team when you make your bets. The King don't believe in losing."

Michael felt Dantice studying him. He felt the question in his friend. Had he meant more than he had said?

"Mike?"

"Uhm?"

"You still messing around with those Throyens? I got the feeling he was sniping at you."

"Maybe he was. I keep in touch. I don't want to burn any bridges. Situations change. We might need them next year. What are you into, Aral?"

"Me? Nothing but the sutler business anymore. I'm not sure why he had me come."

Trebilcock nodded. This had become a duel of half-truths and outright evasions. "Maybe he wanted you to pass the real story to your friends. About the Gap maybe opening. So the rumors don't get too crazy."

"That's all I could figure. How long you going to be in town? I was thinking maybe we could get down to Arsen Street some night. Remember the Fat Man's? They've done the place over. Gone class. Got in some girls from the coast. We could go tear the joint up some night, like old times."

"I don't think I've got the energy to keep up anymore, Aral."

"Come on, hey? You can't live forever. Might as well have fun while you can. You've got to come out of the shadows sometime."

"I'll be around till Prataxis gets back. I'll let you know." They had ridden halfway round the palace. Michael said, "If you did it right, you could lay out lakes in each direction. Like the arms of a cross."

Dantice could be infuriatingly practical. He asked, "What are you going to do for fresh water? You'd have to run it in steady, wouldn't you? Else your lakes would go stagnant or dry up."

"Damned! I'm just dreaming out loud, Aral. You want to cut me down with practical, make me tell you who's going to pay the workmen."

"Hey! Mike. I was only joking."

"I know. I know. I'm too touchy. My people tell me all the time. I don't want to come here in the first place, then the King drafts me to play Captures. I hate Captures."

"Why didn't you beg off?"

Michael just looked at Dantice. That hadn't occurred to him. The King would not have asked had there been no need.

"What do you hear out of Hammad al Nakir, Mike? You got anybody reliable down there?"

The question sounded almost too casual. Trebilcock snapped, "Why?"

"You *are* testy, aren't you? Because I've got a long-term arrangement for remounts with one of Megelin's generals.

Because I've been hearing whispers about El Murid maybe trying a comeback. They say Megelin hasn't turned out. They say he's getting more unpopular every day."

"Then your sources are better than mine. All I hear is how the honeymoon is still on. I've got to run. I want to get some bets down before I head for the woods. I'm staying at the palace. I'll be riding mornings. Send a message if you want me to wait on you."

Aral smiled. "Don't forget about the Fat Man's. I think you'll be surprised."

Michael brushed the rainwater off his forehead. He hated hats. Sometimes you had to pay for your quirks. "I'll think about it."

Ragnarson was crossing a courtyard to the stables when he spied Varthlokkur atop the castle wall. He shifted course.

The man was staring at the east as though it might bite. And he'd behaved strangely earlier. "Is it something you can talk about?"

"What? Not really. It's nothing concrete. Something in the east. Not entirely with the flavor of Shinsan."

"You didn't mention it this morning."

"Nepanthe. She's lost too much. I wouldn't want to crucify her with a false hope."

"Oh?"

"It's Ethrian. He might still be alive." Ethrian was Nepanthe's son by her first marriage, lost during the Great Eastern Wars.

"What? Where is he?" Ragnarson owed his godson a huge debt. A cruel fate had compelled him to slay the boy's father.

"It's just a touch of a feeling I get sometimes. I can't track it down."

Ragnarson babbled questions. The wizard didn't respond. He thought Bragi overly romanticized his one-time friend, Mocker, and the events surrounding the man's death. Bragi had had no choice. It had been kill or be killed.

Ragnarson mused, "We never saw any proof that Ethrian died. Is there anything else?"

"Anything else?"

"Something you didn't want to bring up before. Everybody was hiding from everybody else. Your claim to be preoccupied was unconvincing."

Varthlokkur turned slightly, shifting his gaze from the distance to the man. The corners of his eyes crinkled in amusement. "You grow bold. I recall a younger Bragi who shook at the mention of my name."

"He didn't know that even the mighty are vulnerable."

"Well said. But don't bet your life on it."

Ragnarson grinned. "I'm going to try this conversation some time when you're less in the wizardly mood. When you're ready to answer questions." He nodded slightly, left the wizard to his meditations.

Josiah Gales was a frustrated man. He could not cut the Queen out of her herd of courtly matrons. Even once she was aware of his need she could not disengage herself easily.

The moment arrived at last. She stepped into a curtained alcove, beckoned. That mocking, tormenting smile danced across her lips. He ducked in after her.

"What did they talk about, Josiah?" No one else called him Josiah.

"Practically nothing."

"They had to talk about something, didn't they?"

"They did. It wasn't worth me skulking around through a lot of dusty passageways, my Lady. A lot of 'Hello, how are you, long time no see.' Some 'How come Prataxis scored so easy this year.' A little 'What the hell is going on in Shinsan these days.' Then His Majesty sent them on their ways. He says they'll get together again when Prataxis gets back. He's got me wondering if maybe he isn't some suspicious."

"He's always suspicious, Josiah. He's got good reason."

"I mean more than your everyday suspicion. It was something he said."

"Which was?"

"He had Trebilcock wait till the others was gone. Told him to come play Captures with him. That's when he said it."

"Said what?" A wrinkle of frustration danced across the Queen's brow. She peeped round the curtain. Her flock had not yet missed her.

"That even the walls have ears."

Inger's smile vanished. "Uhm. That bears thought. Thank you, Josiah."

"I'm your slave, Lady."

She left the alcove wearing a curious little frown. Her charges would find her a less gracious hostess than before.

Gales nibbled his lower lip. Had he spoken too boldly? Had he betrayed too much?

Josiah Gales was a victim of love. It was a hopeless love. There was no chance it would be consummated in any manner more intimate than what had just taken place.

He had resigned his head to the limits long ago, before Ragnarson ever entered his lady's life. It was his heart that would not admit there were insuperable barriers between a lady of quality and a middle-aged foot soldier.

He let imagination run with the moment just fled. Fantasy chided him for not having been sufficiently daring.

3

Year 1016 AFE;
Captures

KAVELIN'S KING INTERRUPTED his ride at Vorgreberg's cemetery. He had left the city early so he would have time before the game.

He first visited the mausoleum of the family Krief. They had ruled Kavelin before him. He leaned over the glass-faced sarcophagus of his predecessor and former lover. Queen Fiana's clay had been cunningly preserved by Varthlokkur's art.

"Sleeping beauty," he whispered to the cool, still form. "When will you waken?" Imagination insisted that her chest was rising and falling slowly. His heart wanted to believe it. His mind could not conquer the lie.

He had loved her. She had born him a daughter he had hardly known. Little Carolan lay interred nearby. This jealous kingdom had pulled them down. . . .

There had been fire in their loving. It had been that once in a lifetime perfect physical match, where all the needs and likes had meshed to perfection. The remembered heat of it made him doubt his commitment to Inger now. He was a little afraid to let himself go, to owe this latest woman completely. Fate had a way of striking down everyone for whom he cared.

He kissed the glass over Fiana's lips. For an instant imagination supplied a ghost of a smile.

"Be patient with me, Fiana. I'm doing the best I can." After a minute, "Trying times are coming. They don't think I suspect. They think my head is in the clouds. They underestimate me. Like they underestimated you. And I'll go on letting them think I'm just a dumb soldier till they fall into the pit I'll dig for them."

She seemed to nod her understanding.

They worried about him in Vorgreberg. He did not come

here often, but they thought it strange that he visited the dead at all. They thought it stranger still that he spoke to the dead.

He let them think what they would. This was one of his away places, his thinking places, his refuges for those moments when he had to be alone.

He went outside and sat on the moist grass near a freshly filled grave. The rain had stopped. For a time he did nothing but sit and chuck the occasional soggy clod at a nearby headstone. It had begun to add up. To what he did not yet know, but a whisper here, a rumor there, and news of something strange from beyond the mountains. . . . It all meant something.

As a boy he had made one passage reeving with his father. They had sailed from Tonderhofn with the ice floes, and had been one of the first dragonships through the Tongues of Fire. A few days into the ocean they had become becalmed. The sea had taken on the look of polished green jade. The crew had been in no mood to man the oars. Mad Ragnar had taken the opportunity to teach his sons a bit of his philosophy.

"Look around, boys," said the man called both Mad Ragnar and The Wolf of Draukenbring. "What do you see? The ocean's beauty? Its peace? Its serenity?"

Not knowing what was expected, the young Bragi nodded. His brother Haaken refused to go that far.

"Think of the sea as life." Ragnar seized a maggoty chunk of the pig they had sacrificed before hazarding the treacherous currents of the Tongues. He drove a spear through it, leaned over the gunwale, swished it through the water. Then he leaned against the ship's side, meat poised inches above the glassy sea. He waited.

Soon Bragi saw something moving through the green glass. Another something passed beneath the dragonship. A fin cut the surface fifty yards away.

Something exploded out of the deep. It took meat, spear, and very nearly Ragnar as the sudden jerk yanked him against the rail. The water boiled, then became still. Bragi never saw what took the rotted flesh.

"There," Ragnar said. "You see? There's always something down there. When it's calmest is when you've got to watch out. That's when the big ones hunt." He pointed.

A vast dark shape drifted past the dragonship, too far down to be discerned as anything but a shadow in the green. "That's when the big ones hunt," Ragnar said again. He began kicking and cursing his men. They decided rowing was less unpleasant than their captain's tireless sound and fury.

Bragi flipped a clod at a weed stalk left from last year. Luck made a contact. The stalk went down.

He rose. "When the big ones hunt," he murmured, and began walking across the hill.

He went to a rank of graves. They contained his first wife and the children he had lost in Kavelin.

Elana had been a special woman. A saint, to have followed him through his mercenary years, to have born him a child a year, to have endured his wandering eye and affection without protest. She had been the daughter of an Itaskian whore, but she had been a lady. She remained stamped upon his soul. He missed her most when he was troubled.

There was some barrier in him that prevented his sharing with Inger that way.

Fiana had been both passion and a symbol of commitment to a greater ideal. Elana had been solid, simple, family, perhaps representing that tightest, most intense and basic of human allegiances.

Strange, he thought, staring at the line of headstones. He had not given either woman his all. He was giving Inger nothing he had given them. How vast were the resources within one man?

He was not sure what he was giving his wife-queen. Something, to be sure. She seemed satisfied most of the time.

He stood there a long time, remembering his years with Elana, and the friends who had given their days that special touch.

All that was gone. He had come to the grey days, the soft, colorless days, to which his acquaintances contributed little.

Maybe he *was* aging. Maybe, as you grew older, the highs and lows and color faded away, and it all got so oatmealy you just decided it was time to lay down and die.

He glanced at the sun. Time had stolen away while he stretched himself on the rack of his yesterdays. Best quit fooling around, he thought. Wouldn't do for the King to be late for his game of Captures.

He encountered the Panthers on the road. Had he been anyone else, they would have ragged him mercilessly about the Guards' chances. The Panthers were young and exciting and on a hot streak. They were the darlings of the sweet young things who devoured winners and scorned losers. They expected to be on top for years.

One bold lad suggested as much.

Ragnarson grinned. "And you might be in for a surprise, boy. Us old dogs know a few tricks."

Youth received his assertion with its usual disdain.

Was there ever a time when I was that young, that self-certain, that positive about my world and my answers? he wondered. He did not remember being that way.

They parted to go to their respective castles.

The opening minutes of the game would be free of irregularities. The judges assembled the teams at their castles. They counted heads and took names. They sounded horns when the teams were ready, and winded them again to signal the opening of play.

The stretching of rules generally began after the teams spread out to defend and attack.

Bragi's team had cheated ahead of time. It brought to Captures some of his tricks of government. In preparation for the Panthers, a hot-blooded, round-heeled spy had been deployed.

Bragi was late. He gave the judges his name and joined Trebilcock, who clung to the edge of the gang. The youth wore a hangdog look. The others were intent on their spy's boyfriend.

"They're gonna bull it. They're gonna punch up the middle with everybody," the man said. He was team captain. His friends called him Slugbait. "They're gonna hold a deep defense of like six guys two hundred yards from their castle. The rest are gonna swamp us, then just march back with our balls. They figure they gonna hoo-miliate us on account of we're a bunch of old buzzards and we won't be able to keep up. We got a couple ways to go. I figure the best is we go them one better. We don't guard our castle. We all of us go over there, swamp their defensemen, grab their balls. We have five guys sneak their balls around the flanks. All the rest of us jump them while they're coming back. Pile on and take our balls back away. Snakeman? What you jumping about?"

"They're going to know they been tooken when they don't find nobody in our castle, Slug. So all we're going to do is turn the field around. Then they start running us. They'll wear us down. Then it's good-bye ballgame."

Ragnarson said, "Slug's on the right track. But so is Snake. I say play the turnaround. Only all the way. I'm thinking we could use a variation on a Marena Dimura trick to shift the odds. When we come to their defensemen, we pick them up and carry them over to the castle judge and fling them out of bounds. That puts them six players short. Then we take their balls into the woods and bury them someplace. Then we play the strong defense on their castle. It'll confuse hell out of them. Whenever any of their people get through, the deep line can grab them and throw them out of bounds too. We just put a few strikers out to watch our balls till we get a whole bunch of them out of the game."

"You're talking too much running," Michael grumbled. "I won't get out of bed for a week."

"You're younger than me."

The men liked Ragnarson's suggestion. It was a different angle. It would put the Panthers off balance.

A judge demanded, "You people going to piddle around all day? Let's play Captures. We want this over by sundown."

"Go ahead and blow them horns," Slugbait cried. "We try it the King's way to start," he told his team.

Michael groaned.

Bragi told him, "I'm not so fond of it either. I counted on sitting most of this one out."

The horns honked and snorted like drowning geese.

"Out to the sides!" Slugbait growled. "We don't want them to see us."

A half hour later Ragnarson and Trebilcock had established their defensive position. Their backs were toward the Panther castle. "Guess they got a little cold-footed," Bragi gasped. His lungs ached. They had pushed hard. The Panther defenders had struggled valiantly while being thrown off the field. "Leaving ten men instead of six."

Trebilcock was sour. "They suckered you. They knew that girl was a plant. They sent five people to your castle. The rest were out in the rocks and trees seeing where their own balls were hidden. They'll snatch them and hide them somewhere else."

A grin spread across Ragnarson's face. "You'd do that, Michael. But these are kids. They don't think they have to be sneaky." He looked around, making sure they were free of unwanted eyes and ears. "Give me a rundown on what you're doing and what you know. And I want more than generalities."

Michael's expression soured even more.

"Mike, you're a good man. One of my best. But things can't go on this way. I can't go to Hsung and make promises when my people won't do what I want. I can't make plans if you won't tell me what the hell is going on. I didn't give you the job so you could play hide and seek. Here's the word. Either you play with the team, or you're off it."

Trebilcock stared at Ragnarson. He seemed startled.

"I mean it. Suppose you tell me about Hsung's plans. You know what's going on in the east. And tell me how you know."

"How?"

"I don't just judge information. I judge the source, too, Michael."

Trebilcock sighed. He appeared upset. "Part of the deal is, I can't expose him. He's on Hsung's staff. He has access to conferences and documents."

"Shinsaner or Throyen?"

"Does it matter?"

"It matters a whole hell of a lot. I don't trust snakes, and I don't trust anybody from the other side of the Pillars of Heaven."

"Shinsaner. But he's trustworthy."

"Why? They don't commit treason."

"Not against the empire. They'll betray leaders they don't like. We came up with proof that he was trying to set Mist up for a comeback. He'd be dead in a minute if we let Hsung have it. Hsung is Kuo's brother-in-law."

"Blackmail?" Ragnarson studied Michael. "Nu Li Hsi and Yo Hsi were brothers. They spent four hundred years trying to kill each other. How do you know the man is feeding you good information?"

"He's right every time."

"You've got checks on him, then."

"No." Michael stared at the leafy earth like a school kid getting it from his teacher.

"Has he told you anything important? Anything we wouldn't have found out anyway? You going to recognize it when he feeds you the big lie they want you to believe?"

"Yeah. He told me *why* they're giving Prataxis what he wants."

"Well?"

"They expect war with Matayanga this summer. The Matayangans have been getting ready since Escalon fell. They're as strong as they're going to get, and the legions are still weak. They're going to have to fight someday, so why not get in the first punch? They've got the Tervola worried. They don't want trouble anywhere else, so Hsung is going to be the best friend you've got outside of Kavelin. He had to give up his reserve legion to the Southern Army. Kuo is stripping the whole damned empire so he can stiffen his southern posture. The only army he didn't hit is the Eastern Army. Nobody can figure that because there isn't anything east of them."

"That's more like what I want, Michael. Why couldn't you tell me before? Why do I have to get you mad to pry anything out of you?"

Trebilcock did not respond.

"How far can we push Hsung?"

"He has orders to get along, but they're filled with ifs, ands, and buts. Don't push him. He has the proconsular power. He just can't invade Kavelin without Kuo's okay."

"Meaning he can stir up all the trouble he wants if he doesn't use his own troops, eh?"

"Meaning exactly that."

"Sounds like your friend is sending a message saying leave us alone and we'll leave you alone."

"You could look at it that way."

"And you're still provoking the Throyen partisans."

"No. I'm maintaining contact. And that's all. We might need them someday. They give me information because they hope we'll support them. They set up my inside man for me. Whatever else they do, they do on their own."

There was the slightest of tremors in Michael's voice. Ragnarson did not think it was anger. Trebilcock was holding back.

He shifted tacks. "What's this about Mist?"

Trebilcock sensed that his interest was not casual. "It won't amount to anything. That sort of thing's gone on since she got here. There'll always be cliques that want her for a figurehead."

"Wanting and getting aren't the same thing. She'd never settle for anything less than the imperial power. What did you think of the wizard today? Behaving a little strange?"

Trebilcock stared at the woods. "When isn't he strange?"

"Out of character. Throwing scowls around at people. Like trying to intimidate. Like saying if you open your mouth I'm going to give you a case of the miseries to last you the rest of your life."

"You'd have to ask him about it. I did catch something between him and Mist."

"I talked. He didn't have anything to say."

Michael shrugged.

"Reason suggests a problem would not be political. Varthlokkur doesn't get into those games. It would be something personal. And with him personal means Nepanthe. His great obsession."

Centuries ago the child who would become Varthlokkur had watched his mother burn at the command of the wizards of Ilkazar. The child fled into the Dread Empire and learned sorcery at the knees of Shinsan's then tyrants, Yo Hsi and Nu Li Hsi. He had come forth from the shadow a man of vengeance and had pulled the old empire down. And when he was done he had discovered he had nothing more for which to live. Nothing except a presentiment that one day a woman would be born that he would love. If he would wait.

Waiting had become more agony than joy, for the woman, when the time came, fell in love with another man. A man who, as the fates snickered, proved to be Varthlokkur's own son by a brief earlier, loveless marriage.

The woman was Nepanthe and the man Mocker, and they, before Mocker's death at Ragnarson's hand, had brought into the world a single son, Ethrian, who had fallen into the hands of enemies during the Great Eastern Wars and not been heard of again, except as the lever by which the Pracchia had compelled Mocker to attempt assassinating Ragnarson.

Ethrian. It was a name accursed.

The man who had fathered the wizard had been named Ethrian and he had been the last emperor of Ilkazar. The woman had named her child for the father, though he had shed the name upon entering the Dread Empire. And he, in his turn, had named his son Ethrian, though the child was but a babe when carried off from his parents and did not know he bore the name till later years, when he had borne the Mocker sobriquet too long to change. . . .

Varthlokkur had, at last, attained his dream after Mocker's death and the fourth Ethrian's disappearance, four centuries of patience rewarded. He was obsessed with the woman, and dreadfully frightened of losing what had been so difficult to obtain.

And she? Perhaps she loved him. But she was a strange and closed and lonesome person even in a crowd, even with sworn friends, for the winds of doom sweeping the world had stolen from her everything she cherished. The last of her many brothers, Valther, Mist's husband, had fallen at Palmisano. And the war had claimed her only son. And now she had a second child on the way and her mind was filled with a poisonous dread of what price fate would now demand. . . .

Very softly, Michael Trebilcock said, "There is only the hint of a ghost of a rumor. My source in Throyes speaks only of matters concerning his own goals, not of Shinsan's greater tribulations. But there is something happening in the far east. Something that has drenched the entire Tervola class in dread yet which they will not discuss even among themselves. It seems to be something they fear as much, or more, than war with Matayanga. Yet the only token of it I have been able to unearth yet is a name or title. The

Deliverer. Don't ask! I don't know."

"But that's what has the wizard all cockeyed?"

"I don't know that. But I suspect it."

"And he and Mist know more than they are willing to say."

Trebilcock let one of his rare chuckles escape. "We all know more than we are willing to tell. About anything. Even you."

Bragi considered ways to pursue the matter, possibly to dig out something Michael did not know he knew, but a grand hoot and holler broke out about a quarter mile away, somewhat toward the Guards' castle.

"Damn!" Bragi swore. "Know what they did? Decided to stick to their plan. Come on." He charged through the woods. Michael bounced along in his wake. In minutes Ragnarson was puffing like a wounded ox.

They joined several teammates atop a grassy slope overlooking a free-for-all. Twenty-five Panthers surrounded the Guards' balls. A dozen Guards were trying to break their formation.

"Everybody get down," Bragi told the half dozen men around him. "Out of sight." He heard teammates floundering through the brush. Those idiots from the deep line had left their positions. "We'll hit them when they get up here." He flung himself down in the grass.

Black patches swam before his eyes. He could not breath deeply or fast enough.

The ruckus rolled closer. Bragi peeked. Not long. More men joined him. "Wait till I go," he told them. "Give me a couple steps, then follow me."

The Panthers had formed a wedge. Guards whooped around them like puppies yapping at a herd of cattle.

A few feet more. Now. Bragi flung himself forward, rolled into the shins of the leading Panthers. He took a half dozen down.

He heard Michael howl. He watched the lean, pale man sail into the pack. Panthers began flying out of the mob.

Bragi writhed and cursed. Somebody was twisting his arm. There was a boot under his chin. The cord of thrashing limbs atop him was growing higher.

He heard Slugbait's ecstatic haroo. "I got one!" A portion

of the melee thundered back downhill and into the woods, the Panthers baying like bloodhounds.

Two Panther ballcarriers broke loose and raced for their castle. The main whoop and holler headed that way.

Ragnarson slithered out of the pile and tackled another ball carrier. Michael grabbed his burden and did a quiet fade into the woods. Bragi yelled at and pummeled his teammates, trying to get them to eject a few more Panthers from the field.

The hulabaloo died away. Both teams faded into the woods. Panther victory horns sounded twice despite their being down so many players. From the Guards castle there was nothing but a dreary hoot indicating that one Guard ball had found its way home.

There was a lot of derisive noise from the Panther end, where their ousted players waited under the watchful eye of the goal judge.

Ragnarson and Trebilcock returned to their positions. Michael said, "Your strategy might be better suited to long Captures."

"I think you're right. Credence Abaca suggested it one time. Only he says when the Marena Dimura play, they tie and gag people and hang them up in the tall trees where nobody will find them. He says sometimes both sides get so busy doing that that the balls get forgotten and all of a sudden there's not enough players to move them around."

"You think he was stretching it? If it came to that point, you'd have people in the trees so long they'd starve to death."

"Where are we?"

"Two zip. Panthers. And me with two hundred nobles on Guards to win."

"Two hundred? Gods!" Ragnarson forgot his questions. "What are you? Some kind of fool?"

"I thought you'd come up with an angle."

"I did, but it might be too late. Go on with what you were telling me. Anything more about the east?"

"Hsung's Throyen puppets might occupy the Kotsüm coast of Hammad al Nakir. A put-up, so Hsung can pose a naval threat on Matayanga's flank."

Ragnarson smiled gently. "What *is* happening in

Hammad al Nakir? They wouldn't sit still for that, would they?"

"I don't see what anybody could do about it. El Murid is hiding in Sebil el Selib. He has almost no followers now. He don't seem interested in anything but opium. Megelin is such a clumsy king that people are just ignoring him, hoping he'll go away."

"That's sad. Really sad. Haroun's son. I thought, how could he be anything but good? He's his father's boy."

"Your friend didn't teach him much but how to fight. They say he's a devil when there's a war on, but if it weren't for el Senoussi and Beloul his government would fall apart. I hear his officials are more corrupt than El Murid's were."

"Probably the same people. Without the restraint of religious righteousness."

"Whatever. The west can declare the threat of Hammad al Nakir a dead issue. The sleeping giant isn't snoring anymore. He's belly up and the maggots are about done with him."

"That's not good. If the Itaskians stop worrying about Hsung and El Murid, we'll be out a lot of military aid. You have people in Al Rhemish?"

"Two good men."

"And in Sebil el Selib?"

"One of my best people."

"Send in someone else. Someone independent. Double check. I don't believe a word you're telling me. Maybe somebody is lying to you."

"Sire! . . ."

"Watch your temper. Michael, I trust you when you do it yourself. Still, you're a devious type. Maybe too devious for your own good. I think people lie to you and you believe them because you've gotten them to lie to somebody else for you. Damn! I lost something. I'm not even making sense to me. What am I trying to say here?"

"I think I understand. And maybe you're right. I get too involved in the game side, and underinvolved with the people. It's true. Just because I enlist them doesn't mean they're going to be my faithful eyes and ears. I can think of three or four who probably don't know whose side they're on themselves."

"What about the rest of the world?"

"Aral could tell you more than me. I use his trader friends in the west. I get the feeling he edits everything before it gets to me."

Ragnarson stared at the moldy forest floor. That had been, at best, an evasion. It might be an outright lie. Michael had scores of foreign contacts. His family's business acquaintances. Old school friends. People met during the war. All glad to keep an eye on this or that for him. Some of the things he had deigned to pass on could have come from no other source.

Bragi let it slide. "How about here in Kavelin?"

"Your enemies are keeping their heads down. They'll keep on that way as long as Varthlokkur and the Unborn wander through once in a while. They figure the only thing to do is wait for you to die."

"Nobody planning to hasten my appointment with the Dark Lady?"

"Not that I've heard of. It's a waste of time watching anymore."

Ragnarson rose. He said, "There's a couple Panthers trying to sneak past us in that gully down there. They've got one of our balls. Act casual."

Trebilcock glanced once. He saw nothing. He had heard nothing. He believed his eyes and ears were better than the King's. "Are you sure? How could you know?"

"When you've been playing these games as long as I have, Michael, you smell the tricks before they happen. If you get to be my age, you sit on a rock somewhere with somebody your age and think about that."

Trebilcock gave him a funny look. Ragnarson knew he was wondering exactly what had just been said. "Maybe you made the right bet after all. The one this morning. Experience counts for as much as energy and enthusiasm. You've got the energy here, so you slide down behind them and run them to me. I'll bushwhack them."

Michael nodded and faded into the woods. His face was paler than usual.

Bragi watched him go. Had he made his point? Friend Michael was walking a tightrope. It could end up knotted around his neck.

Michael did not look lucky enough to pull off a big one. He looked like a man with the seal of doom stamped on his forehead.

Ragnarson didn't want anything to happen to Michael. He was fond of the man.

"Damn you, Kavelin," he murmured as he slipped into his ambuscade. And, "Michael, for gods' sakes get the message. It's almost too late."

He crouched and remembered Sir Andvbur Kimberlin of Karadja, a young knight he had known during Kavelin's civil war. Another man he had liked. Sir Andvbur would have become one of Kavelin's great men had he not been too idealistic and impatient. Instead of lying on goosedown, he lay in his grave, his neck broken by a rope.

"Just don't start thinking you've got the only answer, Michael. You're all right as long as we can talk."

A twig cracked a few feet away. He gathered himself for his charge.

4

Year 1016 AFE; Family Life

IT WAS A weird sunset. There were pastel greens in the clouds scattering the western horizon. Green was rare. Ragnarson wondered why.

The old man had to shout twice to get his attention. "I'm sorry. What did you say?"

"Was you out to Captures today?"

Ragnarson laughed. "Was I? Was I ever." Every muscle in his body ached. They would need a hoist to get him off his horse.

"What was the score? Fellow told me the Guards won. Why would a guy lie that way? I want to know on account of maybe I beat the spread."

"Who'd you bet?"

"Panthers by three. That was the best I could get."

"Hope you didn't bet the daughter's dowry, Pops. You're hurting."

Dismay—yea, even despair—blackened the old man's face. Ragnarson could not stifle a bark of laughter.

He felt good, not being recognized. For these few minutes he could be just another man. The old-timer didn't expect anything of him.

"You wouldn't lie just to see an old man squirm, now would you?"

"I don't want to ruin your evening. But you did ask. It was five to three. Guards."

"That's impossible."

"You know how it goes. The Panthers got too cocky."

"The King played, didn't he? I should have known. King's luck. He could fall in a cesspool and come up wearing gold chains."

Ragnarson faked a coughing spasm to keep a whooping

laugh from busting loose. He? Lucky? With everything that had happened to him?

He rode toward his home in Lieneke Lane, thinking he should have brought presents. Some little guilt offering for his kids.

He was passing the park when the man in white stepped into his path. He yanked his sword from its scabbard, looked round for the other two. The Harish always worked in threes.

The man held a lantern to his own features. "Peace, Sire." He had a gentle, priestlike voice. "No dagger has been consecrated with your name." The Harish were assassin devotees of the fanatic religion El Murid had brought forth from the barren womb of the deserts of Hammad al Nakir. In its youth the sect had spread across east and west with the wild violence of a summer storm. It had declined as the charisma of its Disciple faded. Today it had few adherents outside Hammad al Nakir, and even there its followers were dwindling.

"Habibullah? Is that you?"

"It is, Sire. I was sent by the Lady Yasmid."

Ragnarson had not seen the man since before the wars. In Fiana's time he had been Hammad al Nakir's ambassador to Kavelin. In those days El Murid had ruled the desert kingdom. Haroun had been alive. His son Megelin had not yet donned the crown and led Royalist armies victorious into Al Rhemish. Haroun's wife, El Murid's daughter Yasmid, had come slipping into Vorgreberg, hoping he would help her end the bitter strife between her men. He had sent her to her father with this same Habibullah, then had heard nothing more.

Ragnarson scanned the gloaming again. El Murid's fanatics had tried to kill him before. He saw no sign of treachery. He swung down. His pains seemed to have deserted him. "Into the park, then." He did not sheath his blade.

Habibullah settled crosslegged in the shadow of a bush, his hands palms up on his knees. He waited patiently while Bragi rambled around prodding bushes. He seemed to accept this as perfectly rational behavior.

Satisfied of his safety, Bragi sat down facing the man in white. "You might have to help me up if I get stiff."

Habibullah smiled. "It was a vigorous contest?"

"That's putting it mildly. What's on your mind?" He knew Habibullah wouldn't mind a blunt approach. Too damned many ambassadors danced around things and euphemized. One couldn't be sure what the hell they wanted. Habibullah was more direct.

He reckoned the man had something worth saying. A man didn't sneak through so much unfriendly territory, and make a contact carefully calculated to go unnoticed, just to be sociable.

"The Lady Yasmid sends greetings."

Bragi nodded. He had known El Murid's daughter, though not well, since her childhood.

"Then, she's bid me explain the present situation in Hammad al Nakir. She wants you to understand how and why things have changed since Megelin's victory." Habibullah went way back, to the day when Yasmid had come to Bragi begging for help. He picked the tale up there. It was a long one. He bore down on the fact that the followers of the Disciple, defeated, now holding on only in the holy places of Sebil el Selib and along Hammad al Nakir's rich eastern seacoast, had begun to despair. He said, "The Disciple himself has given up. He just sits and dreams opium dreams about days gone by. He doesn't know where or when he is anymore. He talks to people who have been dead for twenty years. Especially to the Scourge of God."

"Which leads up to you telling me what?"

"To my stating the obvious. The Movement is no longer a danger to Kavelin or any other western kingdom." In a confidential voice, "It's barely a danger to the heretic on the Peacock Throne, and that only because the Harish still consider him their prime target."

"Maybe. But I don't think the Disciple has changed his ideas. He'd be a danger if he could."

"The point is, he can't. He won't be able, ever again. On the other hand, the heretic might well be."

Bragi had a notion where the man was going, based on Michael's report. Intuition told him he'd best give Habibullah a full hearing. "Go on. I'm interested."

"The threat to the world today—your world and mine —centers in the east. In Throyes, specifically. In Lord

Hsung. He's a determined and treacherous man. He sent
ambassadors to Sebil el Selib. They offered to help us
recapture Al Rhemish. The Lady Yasmid exerted her influence and had them driven out. There were those who didn't
agree with her, but her doctrinal arguments were irrefuta-
ble. The lamb does not lie with the lion. The Chosen cannot
walk hand in hand with the minions of the Evil One."

"Yeah. I didn't know she had that much pull."

"She has a lot more. . . . If she cares to use it. She's still
the Disciple's designated heir."

"I meant push, I think. Drive. Off-your-ass."

"I see. Yes. She has been lacking in initiative."

Ragnarson   pricked   up   his   ears.   Something   in
Habibullah's tone suggested that times had changed.

Habibullah became confidential again. "Our agents in Al
Rhemish say Hsung sent ambassadors to Megelin at the
same time he sent them to us. The Tervola doesn't care who
he enlists. And indications are, he got a more sympathetic
hearing there. Megelin now has a wizard stashed in the
Most Holy Mrazkim Shrines. A master of the Power, not
some feeble native shaghûn."

"Uhm." Bragi saw one of Habibullah's unstated arguments. If Shinsan had people in Megelin's court, then
Kavelin and El Murid had a sudden congruence of interest.
Imagine that. After all those years of enmity. "You're
suggesting we ought to get together on something?"

"Exactly. If Megelin has an arrangement with Hsung,
then, obviously, he's no longer your friend. He's sold you to
the Dread Empire."

"How do I make a deal with an old enemy? Can you see
me trying to sell it to my people? On the evidence available?
The older ones are still as scared of El Murid as they are of
Shinsan."

"As I said, the Disciple isn't much interested these days.
He is, in mathematical terms, not part of the equation."

"Ah? Meaning?" Ragnarson had a feeling they were
getting to the heart of it.

"The Lady Yasmid. . . . Shall we say she's considering
finding some initiative?"

Ragnarson's laugh was hard, barking, and bitter. "She's
going to overthrow him?"

"Not overthrow. Not exactly. More like take charge in his name. If there's any point."

"Any point?"

"What point in trying if you're caught between royalists and Shinsan and haven't a friend to help? A grain of wheat between millstones would have a better chance. It would be better for the Faithful, in the long run, if they weren't led into certain destruction."

A very muted appeal, Bragi thought. She would let the collapse continue unless he offered some hope. And if the collapse did happen, Hsung and his Western Army would have access to the southern passes through the mountains. Hsung could march west through the desert and hit the western kingdoms from the south instead of east. He harkened to his intuition again. "Tell her to go ahead. I can't promise an actual alliance, understand."

"I understand. No iron commitments. Just a hope. And only the three of us to know we're in contact, please. I'll inform the Lady and return as soon as I can."

Ragnarson nodded. "Habibullah, you're better than you were when you were ambassador. Much more efficient." Much had been said here, and a lot in words never spoken.

"The Lady Yasmid has led me into a more mature path."

"Good for her." Bragi groaned as he struggled to his feet. His muscles had set like mortar. "I won't be able to move tomorrow." He backed away, not turning till he was outside throwing range. A sensible man took no chances. The Harish were masters of the knife.

He continued his interrupted journey, puzzling the way things were turning around. So much was becoming inverted to the traditional.

This making a deal with Yasmid. . . . Something told him it was right. He had a feeling the day would come when he would need friends as desperately as she did now. And the people of Hammad al Nakir, of whatever religious or political persuasion, could be as hardy in friendship as they were steadfast in enmity. Hadn't Megelin's father, Haroun, twice surrendered his chance at the Peacock Throne so that he could help friends? Wasn't that very friendship the reason a boy now sat on the Peacock Throne, going off in his own strange direction?

What about Michael? His testimony supported Habibullah's, and vice versa. So unless there was a plot. . . . "Damn!" He was getting *too* paranoid.

He should get the two men together. But Habibullah wanted the thing kept below the horizon for the time being. Probably more for Hsung's benefit than anything. I can't go working against Haroun's son, can I? But if I don't, I'm abandoning his wife, and she's more dear to me than the boy. . . .

"Is a conundrum, as Mocker used to say," he muttered. Mother and son were at war, and he had an obligation of friendship to each.

"Guess in a choice like this I have to go with self-interest." Meaning his intuition had been right all along. He would have to stick with Yasmid.

Bragi pulled the bell cord. Behind the door, someone grumbled about the time. An old man opened up, ready dagger in hand. No one trusted the night.

"Hello, Will."

"Sire! We weren't expecting you."

"That's all right. *I* don't know what I'm going to do half the time."

"Yeow!" a girlish voice shrieked from the rear of the house. "Daddy's here! I hear Daddy!"

He got three steps inside before a whirlwind of pigtails and flailing arms hit him. His son Gundar also ran in, but became a stately, manly twelve the moment he was on stage. "Hello, Father."

"Hello, Gundar." His daughter-in-law appeared. "Hi, Kristen. They giving you too much to handle?" Could she be just nineteen? She looked so damned old and wise.

"Father." A smile seized the girl's taut lips. Now she looked her age. "They haven't been any trouble."

"Where's my boy? Where's Bragi?"

"Into mischief, probably. Come on in. Let's get you comfortable. Find you something to eat. What have you been doing? Wallowing with the hogs? You're filthy."

"Playing Captures, huh Dad?" Gundar asked.

"I was. And we beat their pants off, five to three." He was

getting high on the victory. Maybe he wasn't quite ready for the midden heap.

"The Panthers? Dad!" The boy's voice rose to a wail. "What did I do?"

"You were supposed to lose," Kristen said. "He bet against you."

"What kind of family loyalty is that?"

"But Dad. . . ."

"Never mind. I've been hearing it all day." In a half-serious tone, he added, "I hope Kavelin's friends don't start thinking that way. We'd be in big trouble."

"How's the baby?" Kristen asked. Her voice trembled.

Bragi rubbed his forehead, hiding a frown with his hand. Didn't take her long to get to it, he thought. "Healthy as a wolf cub. Eats and howls like one, too."

"That's good. Sometimes when there's a hard delivery. . . ."

He was tempted to take Inger, Kristen, their brats, and Gundar, shake them up in a sack, then set them all down together and explain that only he had been made King. There had been nothing in the deal for his offspring. And if he had the opportunity to choose his successor, he probably would not pick someone of his own blood. He would pick someone whose skill and judgment he had seen at work, someone whose qualities he knew fit those Kavelin needed in a king.

There was a definite potential for trouble here, and someday he would have to get off his duff and straighten it out.

But there was time. Plenty of time. He had a lot of good years left, didn't he?

He realized he had fallen into a habit of vacillating, of letting things work themselves out. Was that another sign of aging? Developing a more passive, accepting nature? A greater store of patience?

Fifteen years ago he would not have waited to see what was developing. He would have jumped in, flailed around, and would have *made* things happen. And the results might not have been positive.

Then, too, it might be the "luck" the old man had

mentioned. That knack for intuiting the right course. It might be telling him to lay back in the weeds and wait this time. There was too much potential for fireworks in the apparently unrelated elements he had identified so far.

Got to be patient, he thought. Got to let it take shape. The things I think I see might all be false clues. There might be more Habibullahs waiting in the wings.

"You're very somber tonight," Kristen said.

"Uh? Oh. It was a tough game. I ran enough for two fifteen year olds."

"If you're that tired, maybe you'd better stay here tonight."

He scanned what he could see of the house. Kristen had made it bright and cheerful. She had remarkable taste for a Wesson soldier's daughter, he thought. Elegant, yet simple. "I couldn't. There's still too many ghosts for me."

Kristen nodded. His first wife and several of his children had been murdered here. He could not make peace with the house. He had slept there only a few times since.

"No," he said again. "I want to visit Mist tonight anyway. Maybe I'll stay there. And watch that smile, little lady. There ain't nothing between me and her, and there never will be. She's too damned spooky for me."

"I didn't really think so. If she's got a thing going, it's with Aral Dantice."

"Aral?"

"Sure. He's out here all the time whenever she's in town. Saw him this morning."

He frowned, became thoughtful.

"For heaven's sake, sit down," Kristen said. "I'll have them get something cooking. You kids better head for bed. It's past time. Tell Bragi to come say hello to his grandfather."

There were cries of protest. Ragnarson wanted to keep them there himself, but kept his mouth shut. He had abdicated his child-rearing responsibilities to Kristen. He wasn't going to tamper with her routine or discipline.

He had made that mistake only once. She had told him what she thought. She had a spirited tongue when she was right.

And, obviously, she wanted to talk without little ears being there to hear.

Curious, he reflected. I hardly ever really *talk* with anybody anymore. All my real friends, male friends, are dead. Or have drifted away somewhat, like Michael, so there's a chasm between us. It isn't just Inger I can't open to. It's everybody.

Not long ago, coming up Lieneke Lane, he had been wondering if what he needed was a lover. Not just some woman to tumble. One he could fall for head over idiotic heels like he had Fiana. Now he realized he wasn't just missing a lover. He lacked friends, too. To-the-death, put-up-with-anything friends like those he had brought to Kavelin for the civil war. His circle now consisted of people bound by common interest. The common interest seemed to be diverging with the decline of direct survival pressure. Tomorrow's defeat might be hiding behind yesterday's victory.

Derel Prataxis was the closest friend he had these days. And that might be only because *he* was Derel's abiding interest. The Daimiellian scholar was writing the definitive modern history of Kavelin, from the inside.

Bragi wondered if he could manufacture a crisis to force a closing of ranks. . . .

Michael. Was that his angle? Had he seen the consequences of a too secure peace? Was he stirring the pot in response? What had he said about a problem in the making?

Sounded like a good possibility. It reflected Michael's kind of thinking.

"Has something happened?" Kristen asked. "You're not just tired."

"It's not anything I can put a name on. Just a feeling that something is wrong. A resonance. People I've been talking to, they feel it too. It feeds on itself." He glanced around. The children had made their retreat. Little Bragi apparently wasn't interested in his grandfather tonight. Nor was Ragnarson's youngest boy, Ainjar, interested in his father. He had not made an appearance either. "Forget it. Let's talk about what's bothering you."

She took him from the blind side. He was mustering the

troops for a squabble about the succession, and she said, "I'm not getting any younger. I don't want to spend the rest of my life being Ragnar's widow."

His first reaction was a startled "Hunh?" He stared. The muscles in her neck were taut. Tension stiffened her body. She was pale. She was milking the fingers of her left hand with her right.

"I'm nineteen years old."

"Over the hill for sure."

"Come on. I'm serious."

"I know. I'm sorry. You have a different perspective on nineteen when you're my age. Go on."

"I'm nineteen. Ragnar has been gone a long time. I don't want to spend my whole life being his memorial."

"I see." This was a problem he had not foreseen. Different backgrounds, he supposed. Kaveliners had customs he would never understand. "Why are you telling me? It's your life. Go ahead and live it."

She relaxed a little. "I thought you would. . . . I thought you might. . . ."

"You found somebody you're interested in?"

"No. Not that. I wouldn't do that. It's just. . . . I feel locked up. I don't mind keeping this place, and taking care of the kids—in fact, I love it—but that isn't all there is, is there? All of my friends are. . . ."

"I said it's your life. Do what you want. You're a sensible girl. You won't make you or me any problems we can't handle."

The tension left her completely. So completely she looked limp. Am I that intimidating? he wondered.

"I was so afraid you'd think I'm some kind of traitor."

He snorted. "Crap. The gods didn't make pretty girls to waste on dead men. If I wasn't old enough to be your father, and if you hadn't been married to Ragnar, I'd be out here chasing you myself." He stopped there. That wasn't quite the way he should say it. Too much subject to misinterpretation.

She knew his style well enough to accept it in the spirit in which it was meant. "Thanks. It's good to hear I'm not an old hag yet."

"You've got two or three good years left. Speaking of your

friends, what ever happened to that tiny little one? The blonde. Sherilee. Something like that."

Kristen smiled saucily. "Interested?"

"No. I. . . . Uh. . . . I haven't seen her around. I just wondered."

"I've seen the way you look at her. The game you're thinking about doesn't have anything to do with running through the woods."

He grinned weakly, unable to articulate a protest. The woman in question had stricken him speechless the few times he had encountered her. He did not know why. That is, he understood his glandular response, but not why the particular female should have initiated it.

"I'm not shopping, Kristen. I just wondered. She's your age, after all."

"Be twenty-two in a couple months. Don't let Inger see you looking at her like that. She'll cut your throat. Yes. She's still around. I see her maybe once a week. You just haven't been around much. She's a little scared of you, you know. You're so quiet and broody, you make her nervous."

"I'm that way because she makes *me* nervous," he admitted. "I'm supposed to be old enough that women don't affect me that way. I shouldn't even notice them when they're that young."

"I'm not going to say anything. Just keep talking yourself in deeper."

"Don't laugh, either. It's not funny to me. You said Aral comes to see Mist when she's in town. Tell me about it."

"You're changing the subject."

"You noticed. You're too damned smart for a female. Can't put anything past you."

"All right. I'll back off. All I can tell you is that he goes to Mist's house every day when she comes to the city. I saw him go by this morning. He was pretending he was interested in the park. I recognized him anyway."

"He doesn't seem to be sneaking, though, eh?"

"I don't know."

"He wouldn't just ride out Lieneke Lane if he was, would he?"

"I don't know him well enough to guess."

A servant signalled Kristen. She led Bragi to the kitchen,

where he devoured most of a chicken. "Been eating so much chicken lately, I'm going to turn into one. Guess I'll have to see Mist for sure. Find out what the hell is going on. Going to be embarrassing if they're just playing a little push-me pull-you."

"She's ten times as old as he is!"

"She doesn't look it. And Aral's still that age where he does most of his thinking below his belt."

Kristen gave him an arch look. "Do men ever outgrow that?"

"Some. Some of us take longer than others. Old Derel probably outgrew it when he was twelve. Which reminds me. He should be back by Victory Day. We're going to have a wingding Victory Day night. I'll send a carriage for you. . . . It don't seem possible that it was that long ago. You must have been a snotty-nosed kid in pigtails."

"I remember. Mother and I went out to meet you coming back from Baxendala. To meet Dad, really. You were all so dirty and ragged, and . . . glowing, I guess. I remember my father broke ranks to grab me and squeeze me. I thought he was going to break my ribs. It's still hard to believe. We beat the best they had."

"Not without luck. Should I send that carriage?"

"If I can find something to wear."

"Good. I'd better go if I want to catch Mist before she goes to bed."

But before he left he toured the bedrooms, to look at his sleeping children and grandson. He ventured into the Vorgreberg night feeling better about his role as King. It was for such as they he was struggling. Yesterday's little ones were today's Kristens and Sherilees. Today's children needed their chances too.

Mist met him in her library after keeping him waiting twenty minutes. She didn't apologize. "You're out late."

He scanned her quickly. She was as cool as ice. He wondered why her beauty didn't demolish him the way it did so many men. He was conscious of it, but never overwhelmed or intimidated. "I was at the house. I wanted to see you. Thought I'd save a trip and do it now."

"You look exhausted."

"I had a rough day. Excuse my manners. They may not be what they should."

"What's on your mind?"

"I'm curious about what you and Aral are up to."

"Up to?"

"I see some things coming together. Thought I'd get an explanation before I jump to conclusions."

"So?"

"There's an exiled princess minus the tempering effect of a husband who fell at Palmisano. A young merchant of wealth and influence. And on the staff of Lord Hsung's Western Army, Tervola who remain supporters of the exiled princess." He watched closely, saw no reaction. She was good.

"It's curious that these ingredients should come together just when it looks like there might be war on Shinsan's Matayangan border." Again, he awaited her reaction. This time she seemed a little twitchy.

She seemed to go off somewhere inside herself. He spent several minutes trying to decipher the titles on the spines of her books.

Finally, "You're right. I've been in touch with people inside Shinsan. A traditionalist faction displeased with Lord Kuo. They think I can restore stability and traditional values. It's just talk. Nothing will come of it."

"Why not?"

"These groups don't have enough power or influence."

Bragi steepled his fingers under his nose. "What's Aral's part?"

"The trading climate would improve if a friend ruled the east. He's been trying to gather financial backing."

Bragi stared at the books. Her explanation sounded plausible. As far as it went. Was she yielding two-thirds of the truth to mask the remainder?

"Sounds like a good idea to me. It would benefit Kavelin, surely, if the historical inertia of Shinsan could be shifted. Otherwise it doesn't matter who's in power."

Again she made him sit through an extended silence. He did not let it distract him.

"What are you saying?"

"That I wouldn't be averse to a scheme. But I want an understanding up front. You're Chatelaine of Maisak. I don't want to worry about my hold on the Savernake Gap."

"I see. You want guarantees. What did you have in mind?"

Bragi smiled. Her attitude betrayed her thinking. "Not now. Not here. We need time to think. And I want witnesses. Varthlokkur and the Unborn."

"You don't trust anyone, do you?"

"Not now. Not anymore. Why should I? Your scheme is just one of my problems. I'm going to walk light and careful till it's all under control."

She laughed. He responded with a smile. She said, "It's too bad you were born a westerner. You would have made a great Tervola."

"Possibly. My mother was a witch."

She seemed startled. She started to say something, but was interrupted by a servant who announced, "My Lady, there's a gentleman here looking for His Majesty."

Bragi looked at Mist and shrugged. "Send him in," she said.

Dahl Haas bustled through the doorway. He still looked fresh. "Sire, I've been looking all over."

"What is it?" Bragi had a bad feeling. Haas looked grim.

"An emergency, Sire. Please?" He gave Mist a meaningful glance.

What is this? Bragi wondered. "We'll talk later," he told Mist, and followed a frantic Dahl out of the house. "Come on. Spill it, Dahl."

"It's General Liakopulos. Somebody tried to kill him."

"Tried? He's all right?" Kavelin's army was the foundation of Ragnarson's power. Liakopulos was one of his most important officers.

"He's in bad shape, Sire. I left him with Doctor Wachtel. Doc said he didn't know if he'd make it. That was three hours ago."

"Let's ride, then. Who did it? A brawl?" The General frequented rough dives. He had been warned, but warnings did no good.

"No, Sire. Assassins." Haas kicked his mount into a trot beside his King. "He was riding outside the palace. They ambushed him in the park. He got one of them, but they cut him up pretty bad. Gales found him and brought him in."

"Who was the dead man?" Wind streamed past Bragi's ear. It bore a smell of rain.

"Nobody recognized him. There wasn't anything on him to identify him."

"Harish?"

"No. He was fair. Possibly from the north."

"Find Trebilcock when we get back."

"He was with the General when I left, Sire." Haas kicked his mount again. The animal had been pushed hard for a long time. Bragi recognized its fatigue and eased the pace. Dahl added, "He seemed to take it personal. Like it was an attack on him."

"Good." Bragi eased the pace even more. It had been a long day for his animal, too.

And this long day was not over yet. Not for him.

5

Year 1016 AFE;
Mystery Attackers

RAGNARSON PUSHED INTO the room where General Liakopulos lay. The Guildsman was as pale as bone china. "How is he?"

Doctor Wachtel, a grisled old man who had been Royal Physician forever, replied, "He's resting."

"Will he make it?"

"It could go either way. He lost a lot of blood. The wounds aren't that bad. Nothing vital injured. But when you've been cut so many times. . . ."

"This the dead man?"

"The assassin? Yes."

Ragnarson lifted the linen covering. He saw an unprepossessing young man of medium height, slightly overweight. He tried to imagine the man on his feet, moving around. He reminded himself that they looked smaller and meeker when they were dead. "Where's Trebilcock?"

"The General came to an hour ago. He described his assailants. He'd cut the other two. Michael went looking for wounded men."

"Uhm. You talk to Varthlokkur about this?"

The doorway sentries stirred. Wachtel shrugged. "He may know. I haven't told him. Didn't see any need."

"Maybe he could give you a hand."

The old man scowled. "Am I incompetent?" He was the best physician in Kavelin, and jealous of his reputation.

"Guards. One of you get the wizard. He's in the brown guest suite." To Wachtel, Ragnarson added, "Who better to question our friend?" He indicated the dead man.

"Uhm." Wachtel put a world of disgust into his grunt. He and the wizard had collaborated before. He had a profound loathing for sorcery in every form, though he grudgingly admitted that Varthlokkur was a master of life magicks, and

56

occasionally offered hope when his own science failed him.

He did not protest much. He was a truly good man, incapable of a spiteful or wicked act. If there had been no other hope for Liakopulos, he would have summoned the wizard himself.

It would not have occurred to him, though, to yield the corpse to the sorcerer. He only concerned himself with the living.

He was quite civil when a sleep-fuddled Varthlokkur arrived. He quickly accounted the locations, depths, and severity of his patient's wounds. He controlled his scowl as Varthlokkur ran his hands over the General, making another examination.

"You've done all you can? Hot broth, and so forth? Herbs for the pain?"

Wachtel nodded.

"He ought to recover. Might have trouble using the one arm, and there'll be scars. No point me getting involved."

Wachtel's scowl lapsed into a somber smile. He turned it on Ragnarson.

"Check this one," Bragi told the wizard. "This's the man Liakopulos killed."

"One of the assassins?" Varthlokkur peeled back a lid and stared into an eye.

"Presumably." Of the room in general, Ragnarson asked, "There couldn't be any mistake, could there?"

"The General identified him while he was conscious," Wachtel replied.

Varthlokkur looked at Bragi, said nothing. Ragnarson's skin felt crawly. "The Unborn?" he suggested softly.

The wizard nodded. "That's the easiest way. Down in one of the closed courts where we won't disturb anybody."

"Guards. One of you find your sergeant. Tell him I need four men and a stretcher."

Four Guardsmen came. One was Slugbait. He gave Ragnarson a big grin and rattled a pocket filled with coins before assuming a more businesslike manner. He was a soldier here, not a Captures captain. He and his companions rolled the corpse onto the stretcher and awaited instructions.

"The back exercise court," Ragnarson told them. "Just

take him down and leave him."

Their eyes went to Varthlokkur, slid away. The color left their faces. They had guessed what would happen.

"Did anyone interrogate Gales?" Bragi asked.

"Trebilcock," Wachtel replied. "I didn't pay attention. Varthlokkur. Does his breathing seem easier?"

The wizard bent over the General. "I think so. He's definitely past the worst. He'll make it."

Ragnarson and the wizard followed the stretcher-bearers. Bragi said, "I saw Mist tonight. I'd stumbled across a couple things I was curious about. She answered my questions, but she was evasive."

"And?"

"She's involved in some scheme to get her throne back. She claims a group of Tervola approached her, but nothing would come of it. She's in deeper than she'll admit."

"And?"

"You're not contributing much."

"What do you want me to say?"

"Your best guess about her. Is she really involved? Can she do anything if she is? What would the consequences be, from my viewpoint? Both if she pulled it off and if she lost out."

"Is she involved? Of course. Once you attain a throne, you don't give it up without a fight. She felt constrained while Valther was alive. Now she doesn't. Consider her viewpoint. There's nothing here for her since Palmisano. There once was there. Her need for a feeling of self-worth will make her grasp for what's hers by right."

"She's vulnerable, though. Through her children."

"Aren't we all?" Varthlokkur sounded sour. "They're hostages to fortune."

"Can she make a comeback?"

"I wouldn't know. I don't know what's going on in Shinsan. I don't want to. I want to ignore them, and have them ignore me."

"But they won't."

"Of course not. Which brings us to consequences. My feeling is, it won't really matter if she wins or loses. Shinsan is Shinsan, and always was and will be. When the moment comes, it won't matter who rules there. You and Kavelin have earned special attention. Be it tomorrow, or a hundred years from tomorrow, a blow will fall. I think it'll be a while coming. They have to recover from a devastating couple of decades. They have to survive external threats. They have to preserve their new frontiers. They'll be hopping like the one-legged whore the day the fleet came in."

Ragnarson chuckled and looked at the wizard askance. That was not a Varthlokkur metaphor.

"Excuse me. You mentioned Mist. That reminded me of Visigodred, which made me think of his apprentice, Marco. I heard Marco say something of the sort once."

Visigodred was a mutual acquaintance, an Itaskian wizard who had helped during the Great Eastern Wars. He was a long-time friend of Mist. His apprentice, a foul-mouthed dwarf named Marco, had perished at Palmisano.

"Marco. That's funny. Every damned conversation today leads to somebody who died at Palmisano."

"We left a lot of good people there. A lot of good people. Victory may have cost us more than we could afford. It took the good people and left the blackguards. They'll start their power games before long."

They were in the back exercise court now, standing over the body. The soldiers had beaten a hasty retreat. Bragi said, "Maybe they've already started."

"Maybe. Move back. You don't want to be too close."

"I don't want to be in the same province," Ragnarson muttered. Nevertheless, he seated himself on some steps and waited.

Varthlokkur did not do anything flashy. He just stood there, head bowed, eyes closed, concentrating. Neither he nor the King moved for twenty minutes.

Ragnarson felt it before he saw it. He stiffened. His right hand strayed to the sword he always carried. He grimaced. As if mere steel could avail against the Unborn.

He hated the thing. Created by one of the Princes Thaumaturge, it had been insinuated into the womb of his Fiana. It had grown there, and grown there, and its coming forth had killed her.

Varthlokkur had delivered that child of evil, had made of it a terrible tool, and had turned the tool upon its creators. It drifted over the east wall, looking like some new, bizarre little moon. It glowed softly, palely, the color of the full moon soon after rising. It bobbed gently, like a child's soap bubble drifting on the breeze.

It settled toward Varthlokkur, becoming more defined as it drew nearer. A luminescent globe about two feet in diameter. Inside, something hunched and curled. . . . Up close, clearly a fetus. Humanoid. But nothing human. Far from human.

Its eyes were open. It met Ragnarson's gaze. He battled a surge of hatred, an impulse to hack away with his sword, to hurl a rock, to do something to destroy that wickedness. That *thing* had killed his Fiana.

Varthlokkur had used it to terrible effect during the war. It kept the Tervola east of the Mountains of M'Hand even now. It was the one weapon in the western arsenal capable of intimidating them. They would find a way of destroying it before coming west again.

It made Ragnarson secure on his throne. At Varthlokkur's command it would drift through Kavelin's nights routing out every treachery. It could do countless wicked and wonderous things, and was almost invulnerable itself.

Ragnarson compelled himself to remain seated. He forced his eyes away from the bobbing globe. He did not want to see the mockery in that tiny, cruel face.

Varthlokkur beckoned his creation down, down, till it hovered over the dead assassin. He murmured. Bragi recognized the language of ancient Ilkazar. He did not understand it. It was the tongue of the wizard's youth. He used it in all his sorceries.

The dead man's skin twitched. His legs jerked. He rose like a marionette on uncertain strings. Once upright, he sagged against whatever force it was the Unborn used to support him.

"Who are you?" Varthlokkur demanded.

The dead man did not reply. A puzzled look did cross his face.

The wizard exchanged glances with Ragnarson. The corpse should have responded more positively.

"Why are you here? Where is your home? Why did you attack the General? Where are your comrades?" Every question elicited an equally uninformative silence. "Wait a minute," the wizard told his creature.

He sat down beside Ragnarson, elbow on knee, chin in the cup of his hand. "I don't understand," he grumbled. "He shouldn't be able to hide from me."

"Maybe he isn't."

"Uhm?"

"Maybe there's nothing there to hide."

"Everyone has a past. That past is stamped on body and soul. When the soul flies, the body remembers. I'll try something else." He stared at the Unborn, his face intense.

The dead man ran in circles. He leaped. He jumped an imaginary skip-rope. He turned tumblesaults. He did push-ups and sit-ups. He flapped his arms, crowed like a rooster, and tried to fly.

"What's all that prove?" Ragnarson asked afterward.

"That the Unborn does have control. That this is a man."

"So maybe he's a hollow man. Maybe he never had a soul."

"You could be right. But I hope not."

"Why?"

"He would have to be a created thing, then. Something brought to life full grown and devoid of anything but the command to kill. Which means an accomplished enemy. Probably one we thought already destroyed. The question is, why would he go after the General? Why attack the lion's paw and waste what could have been a telling blow to the head?"

"You lost me. What the hell are you babbling about?"

"I think we've been laboring under a mistaken presumption of death."

"You're not telling me anything." The wizard had a habit of orbitting in on a subject, circling as a moth circles a flame. Ragnarson found it irritating.

"We accounted, directly or indirectly, for all the Pracchia but one. We assumed his body was lost in the heaps at Palmisano." That climactic battle had been hard on every-one. Insofar as Ragnarson knew, the other side had lost every captain but Ko Feng.

He scratched his beard, listened to the hungry rumble of his stomach, wished he were somewhere snoring, and made several false starts at trying to unravel the riddle the wizard had posed. "Okay. I give up. Who are we talking about?"

"Norath. Magden Norath, the Escalonian renegade. The Pracchia's chief researcher and monster-maker. We never located a body."

"How do you know? I never met anybody who knew what he looked like."

Norath had been a wizard with a difference. His tools had not consisted of incantation and the demons of night. He had shaped life. He had created men and monsters every bit as dangerous as anything Varthlokkur, Mist, and their ilk, were able to summon from Outside.

"Can you suggest a better candidate?"

"You're making a hell of a long jump to a conclusion," Ragnarson said. "Even giving you the benefit of the doubt, why attack Liakopulos? You're spinning a nightmare out of moonbeams."

"Maybe so. Maybe so. But it's the only hypothesis that fits the facts."

"Find some more facts. Try another hypothesis. Say the man had his soul erased before he was sent. Whoever wanted the General dead would assume his people would cross your path, wouldn't he?"

"Possibly. I don't think an erasure could be done without destroying the brain completely. Let me try something else."

Varthlokkur rose and strolled over to the Unborn. He rested one hand on the thing's protective globe. He closed his eyes. His body became as slack as that of the dead man. He and the corpse leaned together, two drunken marionettes buoyed by the Unborn.

Ragnarson struggled against the encroachment of sleep. He stood and stretched his aching muscles. He wondered what Trebilcock was doing. The materialization of assassins must have been a tremendous blow to Michael's pride. He would be savage in his effort to unearth something.

The wizard's tall, spare figure slowly straightened. Color returned to his face. He batted a hand before his eyes as if to scatter a cloud of gnats. He tottered toward Ragnarson, his gaze still unfocused. After a moment, he said, "I went inside him. It's amazing how little there is to him. The skills and cunning a killer needs, but without the background, without the years of growth and training. . . . He's maybe a month old. He came from somewhere to the west. He remembers crossing the Lesser Kingdoms to get here, but isn't clear about directions or geography. There was someone with him and his brothers. That someone knew what was going on and told them what to do. He has a vague memory of his father having lived near the sea. His sole purpose was to eliminate Liakopulos."

"Ah. Put that together and it sounds like a blow by the Guild against one of its own."

"What? Oh. I see. High Crag is west, and it overlooks the sea. No. I think my stab in the dark hit closer to the mark. He remembers his father. Or creator, if you will. The memory fits what's known of Norath."

"Why Liakopulos?"

"I don't know. Usually you ask who would benefit. In this case I can't think of a soul. The General has no enemies."

"Somebody was willing to make a big investment in getting rid of him."

"The obvious conclusion would be Shinsan. But they're trying to get along. They're flashing the hand of friendship. And assassination isn't their style."

"Somebody trying to frame them? Somebody who doesn't want peace?"

Varthlokkur shrugged. "I couldn't name a soul who would be ahead by maintaining a state of tension."

"Matayanga. Michael's rebel friends in Throyes."

"I doubt it. Too much risk in the backlash if they got found out. And he did come from the west, not the east."

Ragnarson shook his head. "I'm getting groggy. I can't get anything to add up. Liakopulos just isn't that important. Valuable to me because he's a genius at training soldiers, but that don't especially make him a threat to anybody else. . . . I can't go on with this now. It's been a brutal day. Let me sleep on it."

"I'll have this taken back to Wachtel, then have Radeachar find its brothers and master. Check with me tomorrow."

Radeachar was the wizard's name for his creature. In the tongue of his youth it meant The One Who Serves. In the days when Ilkazar had been great, *Radeachar* had been the title given wizards who served with the Imperial armies.

"All right. Damn! It's going to take five minutes to get this old carcass of mine moving."

As Ragnarson turned to leave, a shadow in the courtyard gateway withdrew. The silent observer had remained unnoticed even by the wizard's servitor. He vanished into the Palace halls.

Ragnarson took a couple of steps, paused. "Oh. I been meaning to ask you. The name, or title, or whatever you want to call it, of The Deliverer mean anything to you?"

Varthlokkur started as if stung. Stiffly upright, he faced the King. "No. Where did you hear that?"

"Around. If it don't mean anything, how come you're acting like. . . ."

"How I act is my concern, Ragnarson. Never forget that. Forget only that you ever heard that name. Do not speak it again ever, anywhere near me or mine."

"Well, excuse me, your cranky-assed wizardness. But I got a job to do around here and anything that might affect Kavelin is damned well my business. And you and seven gods aren't going to tell me different when I think there's something I got to do."

"The thing you mentioned, whatever it might be, has nothing to do with you or Kavelin. Expunge it from your mind. Go, now. I have nothing more to say."

Bemused, Ragnarson forced his weary legs to carry him toward the kitchens. What the hell was with the wizard these days? The old grouch knew a damned sight more than he wanted to let on.

Concern began to fade. His stomach nagged. It was a hollow pit demanding something more before the body was permitted its rest.

He was trudging down a poorly lighted hallway, still frowning and slithering around thoughts about Varthlokkur's weirdnesses, when something crinkled beneath his foot. By night the castle was lighted only by a few fat-fueled lamps. One could barely see. One of his little economies.

The odd sound registered late. Bragi stopped, turned back, spotted the wrinkled piece of paper. Penstrokes marked it. Paper was a scarce commodity. It did not get wasted. Someone must have lost it. He picked it up and carried it to the nearest lamp.

Someone had written names in a terrible hand. Bragi could scarcely decipher some. The author's spelling wanted something, too.

LICOPOLUS with a check mark behind it, and the mark scratched out. ENREDSON. ABACA. DANTICE. TRIBILCOK. In another grouping, as if set aside, were the names Varthlokkur, Mist, and others of his supporters. The names of the three soldiers all had stars in front of them.

He leaned against the wall, sleep forgotten. He smoothed and folded the paper and slipped it into a pocket inside his jacket.

His three top soldiers first. Why? And why was his own name not on the list?

He thought about taking the paper back to Varthlokkur, decided it could wait. He resumed his stalk of the kitchens, muttering, "Bet the old spook-pusher doesn't find anything. The man running them was right here in the castle."

Something began nagging him. It took him a minute to recognize the crabbing of his survival instinct. That note! It could indict him as easily as the next guy. It could have been left for him to find.

He got it out, opened it again, stared, started to stick it into the nearest torch. Then he had an idea. He tore out the names Trebilcock and Varthlokkur and burned the rest. He would let Michael and the wizard follow up on their fragments.

The cooks had nothing but more cold chicken. He sat in a brooding silence, eating slowly.

Somewhere in the halls, approaching, a voice. "She said, 'Oh, Gales, you can loan me a crown. You got a good job.' I said 'Shit.' Yeah. I ain't lying. They know you got one penny. . . . She said, 'Gales, loan me a crown.' I said, 'Ain't this some shit.' Yeah. Young woman, too. Fine looking woman. 'Gales, you got a *good* job.' I said, 'Ain't this a bitch.'"

The sergeant stalked by the doorway. Accompanying him was a young Guardsman wearing the look of a man hard pressed to keep from laughing *at* someone.

"Yeah," Ragnarson murmured. "Ain't this a bitch."

6

Year 1016 AFE;
Victory Ball

THE MUSICIANS MADE their instruments tinkle and whine and moan. Couples swept across the floor of the great hall, dancing. Ragnarson ignored both music and dancers. Derel Prataxis had come home, and had dashed from his quarters to the Victory Day festivities as soon as he had freshened up. Every chance he could, Ragnarson murmured with his emissary.

"He's absolutely sincere," Prataxis said of Lord Hsung. "He wants peace and friendship. He has that way about him. Meaning every word he says. Tomorrow he may say the opposite, and with the same fervent sincerity. It's a rare talent. It pulls you in and makes you one of his intimates. It makes you feel like he's letting you in on big things. It works so well he can trap you even when you know what's happening."

"I knew a man who did that with women," Bragi murmured. "They bought it even when they knew what he was after."

Ragnarson had briefed the wizened scholar about the strange things that had happened in his absence, finally asking, "You hear anything over there about somebody called The Deliverer?"

"I heard a whisper. Nothing more. Something that has the Tervola gritting their teeth and shivering. But nothing even a little concrete. Associated with the far east. Of Shinsan. I believe."

"Curious. How might it involve Varthlokkur?"

"You'd have to ask him."

"I did. He wouldn't talk about it."

Prataxis was more intrigued by Varthlokkur's inability to locate the master of Liakopulos's attackers. The matters of Mist, Dantice, and Trebilcock he dismissed as predictable restlessnesses. He was even more interested in the contact with Yasmid's agent, which Bragi shared with him despite Habibullah's admonition.

"That's interesting. Because Hsung has a plan which meets the spirit of his orders but also forwards Shinsan's ancient urge toward western dominion."

Bragi held up a finger. He made a brief show of interest in the celebration. Inger was out mingling with Kavelin's noblest Nordmen ladies. She awarded him one of her remarkable smiles. He winked back. "Okay, Derel."

"Hsung has made Throyes the complete vassal state while pretending otherwise. His notion is, he can send Throyens out to do Shinsan's work, then disavow them when the protests start."

"So?"

"So he's going to send them marching down the eastern littoral of Hammad al Nakir. The Throyens have claimed the territory for ages, same as Hammad al Nakir claims Throyes. Hsung wants control south as far as Souk el Arba. Farther, if the Throyens can manage."

"Michael told me. He thought Hsung wanted ports for coastal raids on Matayanga."

"A good secondary reason. And a good mask. But the Throyen staff is more porous than Hsung's.

"The truth is, he wants access to the passes through Jebal al Alf Dhulquarneni. The one near Throyes, and Sebil el Selib both. Did Michael tell you Hsung had ambassadors in Sebil el Selib and al Rhemish both? Both delegations offering alliances?"

"Michael isn't well-informed about Hammad al Nakir. I did know Hsung had agents in Sebil el Selib." Bragi shifted his attention to the festivities without bothering to concentrate on them. Derel's news filled a few gaps.

"Clever," he said. "He can pull it off in broad daylight and we can't squawk. He'd just claim he was meeting his treaty obligations. If we try to stop him, we're the aggressors."

"Exactly."

"What can we do?"

"Several things. We can let it run its course and hope it fails by itself. We can ignore the opprobrium and launch a pre-emptive attack if the Matayangan situation deteriorates. Or we can play Hsung's own game. We don't have the resources, but we have the minds."

"Those first two choices aren't squat. Tell me what you mean about having the minds."

"You have some very intelligent and byzantine associates. Take Michael. He can be devious. He can be merciless. He's more intelligent than he pretends. And the people he's recruited are the best. Your greatest strength, though, is possession of a legitimate pretender to Shinsan's throne. That should be exploited. Then you consider Hsung's disadvantages. He has to garrison the whole Roë Basin. Western Army is down to five legions. The best are at Gog-Ahlan, guarding the Gap, and in Throyes. One is at Argon. There's another at Necremnos. The fifth is scattered among the smaller cities."

"That's still thirty thousand of the best soldiers there are, Derel."

"Sure. A lot to you. But not so many when you consider the population of the Roë Basin. What they become then is a symbol of the power of Shinsan, not the power itself. They'd disappear in a general uprising."

"They'd do a lot of damage."

"Certainly. But they'd be overwhelmed anyway."

"I've been on Michael not to roil things up. Now you're saying I should stir the pot."

"Hsung won't back off poking at you. Don't let him get away with it. Poke right back."

"Then he hollers foul."

"Don't involve your own people. Not directly. There'll be nothing he can do. He operates under constraints, too. He has a peace-loving image to maintain. That means putting up with provocations. What it boils down to is, you play their game, only nastier. Because of the trouble with Matayanga, they're in a tighter spot than we are."

"When you back off and look at it, Derel, it all seems kind of pointless. What difference will it make a hundred years from now?"

"Maybe none. Some of my colleagues subscribe to a futility theory of history. Even so, there are turning points.

They're usually invisible except in retrospect. One of the great moments in Kavelin's history took place in Itaskia. We're still feeling the consequences."

Ragnarson grinned. "You're zigging when I'm zagging, Derel. You lost me that time."

"The day you left your homestead to complain about a little trouble you'd had. You'd barely heard of Kavelin. Six months later you were leading Fiana's army. Now you're King."

"By that reasoning, Haaken and I changed history by running out of Trolledyngja instead of fighting the Pretender."

"Absolutely. You'd be twenty-five years dead if you'd stayed. Other men would be alive. The El Murid Wars would have had a different shape. Something different could have happened in Freyland. Duke Greyfells might have become Itaskia's King. Kavelin's civil war could have gone the other way. There might have been no Great Eastern Wars at all."

Prataxis's talk made Ragnarson nervous. It made not only life but history itself sound fragile. He had been taught differently as a boy. Trolledyngjans were determined believers in fate. "We're getting away from the point."

"No, we're not. Not from mine. I want you to understand that, every time you make a move, you're shaping tomorrow. You shape it even when you don't do anything. Your best chance to shape this the way you want it is to stay aggressive. There'll be more ramifications. Some might be exploitable."

"Okay. I get the message. I'll get out there and keep the cauldron boiling. We don't want your thesis getting dull."

"Sire! . . ."

Bragi grinned. "I couldn't resist. You take yourself too serious sometimes." Ragnarson rose, surveyed the gathering. Hundreds had come. This was the biggest turnout since the war. Most of the Thing and their women. All of his own clique, except Michael and Mist and Varthlokkur, who avoided all functions. Many of the old Nordmen nobility, who now called themselves the Estates because they controlled the largest landholdings. Influential members of the merchant class. Representatives of the silent, seldom-seen,

and absolutely essential Siluro civil servant class. Credence
Abaca and a clutch of Marena Dimura chieftains who
formed a human stockade in a corner. They reminded
Ragnarson of cattle in winter, standing nose to nose, their
tails turned to the wind. Drink might bring them into the
exchange of thought these functions sometimes precipi-
tated.

He looked for Trebilcock. Michael still had not shown,
and had not been seen since the attempt on Liakopulos's
life. Ragnarson had begun to worry. He wanted to talk to
the man.

They were still arriving. The hall was getting crowded. If
all the invitations were accepted, he would have trouble
packing people in.

Mist arrived, escorted by Aral Dantice. The effect of her
was like a numbing gas spreading from the doorway. Men
stopped talking. They stared in awe or hunger. Women
stared in awe, envy, and outright hatred. The woman's
impact was incredible. Even the musicians faltered.

And how well she carried off her act of being unaware of
the effect she produced!

Behind Mist and Aral were Kristen and several friends.
His daughter-in-law had been free with the secondary
invitations, he saw. Each of her guests was unattached and
lovely.

That startled him. He dropped back into his seat. "Derel,
I just noticed something."

"Sire?"

Bragi folded his hands under his chin. Thoughtfully, he
said, "There are a lot of unattached women these days.
Good-looking women. That's unnatural."

"Adopt the marriage laws of Hammad al Nakir."

"What?"

"Let a man have more than one wife."

"Gods! One is trouble enough." He glanced round the
room. He saw a lot of unmarried younger women. Most
were the daughters of guests. Each had a huntress's gleam in
her eyes.

"The war claimed a lot of young men," Prataxis observed. "Kavelin's single females probably outnumber single males five to one."

"What am I doing married?"

"Definitely a tactical mistake, Sire. Michael appears to be prospering. But it's a game with few survivors. The huntress knows how to net her prey."

"It's something I never really thought about. An imbalance like that is going to have effects."

"Absolutely. It'll strain the traditional mores. What you have to do is make the girls having illegitimate children all have boy babies. After a while there would be husbands to go around, though they'd be a little young."

Bragi gave Derel a sour look. That was a Prataxis joke.

"It's not a problem unique to Kavelin. One way or another, one place or another, the west has been at war since the Scourge of God broke out of Hammad al Nakir. We're into our second generation of sexual imbalance. One more and the die-hard guardians of the old morality will be gone. Changes in female attitudes will accelerate. . . ."

"I've got a question, Derel."

"Sire?"

"Do you have a lecture for every topic?"

Prataxis looked bewildered, then a little hurt.

"Just joking. Every time I notice something, you already know about it. And you go on forever about how it happened and why, how and why it works, what it means. . . ."

"I'm a don of the Rebsamen," Prataxis replied stiffly. "I was taught to observe and reason. There's nothing mystical about that. You do it yourself, though on a less premeditated level. That's why you make correct decisions more often than not."

"I didn't mean any offense, Derel." Why was the man so damned humorless and touchy? He had asked to come live among the barbarians. . . . No. Derel would object to the wording. Insufficiently precise. He would prefer something encompassing self-righteous ignorance.

"Father?"

He glanced down. His daughter-in-law stood at the foot of the dais supporting the party thrones. "Kristen! You found something to wear. And I thought you weren't going to make it."

"Liar. You knew I'd be here if I had to come mother

naked. These are my friends." She indicated the girls still with her. "It's okay, isn't it?"

"The more the merrier. I'd rather look at them than bald old men with beards. But maybe you should show a little respect for your King in front of people." He smiled. Kristen's girlfriends had performed their deep curtsies immediately.

"Oh. Yes." Flustered, she bent a leg.

"Good enough. Now. Who are all these beautiful ladies?"

Kristen pointed. "Anya. Tilda. Julie. And Sherilee. You met Julie and Sherilee before."

The girls nodded shyly. Except the tiny blonde. She looked him in the eye. But her hands were white and shaking. She clasped them and continued looking at him. That look did not read invitation, but neither did it contain disgust.

"Enjoy yourselves, ladies. Kristen, would you honor an old man with a dance?"

The request surprised her, but only momentarily. "Not that old, I think." She glanced at the blonde. "All right. If it's a Royal command."

His smile declined to a ghost. "It is." He left the dais, caught Inger's puzzled look from the corner of his eye. He wasn't a dancer.

He quickly proved it. He could not follow the steps. "Ah, hell," he gasped. "I just wanted to talk, anyway. Come over here and taste this fizzy wine Cham brought from Delhagen. He tells me it'll become a big export item."

"Talk?" Kristen's eyes sparkled more than did the wine.

"You said something to that Sherilee."

"I? Father!"

"She's young enough to be my daughter."

"I thought men liked women young and fresh. The Krief was fifty years older than Queen Fiana."

"I'm a married man. A king. Whatever. That's a trap I don't need to get into."

"Sounds like you're convincing you."

He grinned half-heartedly, glanced across the hall. The girl was watching through breaks in the crowd. Her timorous look made her more appealing. "So I've got to convince me first. So what? Honest, Kristen. Don't push it. It's too much temptation. I don't know about her, but *I* couldn't handle it."

Kristen's amusement faded. "You're serious, aren't you?"

"Yeah. Really. I can tell just by looking at her, and from what I know about her, and about how I work inside, that I'd fall like a rock. I'd make a complete fool of myself. That's fun once in a while, but I don't have the time now. I can't handle two mistresses at once. My main lady is headed for some hard times, I think."

She asked her question with a raised eyebrow.

"Kavelin."

"Oh. You think there's going to be trouble?"

"Maybe. I'm trying to head it off. You'll get a feel of it tonight. Listen to what people are talking about. The big subjects this year aren't crop yields and mine production."

"Does it have anything to do with General Liakopulos?"

"It may. Sic her on Michael, why don't you?"

"She's not interested in Michael."

"Damn you. What did you have to say that for? Excuse me." He glanced at Sherilee again. So tiny. Like a toy. And every curve and line of her a match for a fantasy-lover's template. He shook his head viciously. "Damn me, too." He left Kristen looking bemused.

Inger joined him on the dais. Her perpetual mocking smile had shrunk to a minimum. "What was that about?" She did not like Kristen. They were both mothers of candidates for Kavelin's throne.

"Household allowances. She wants a separate tutor for Ainjar and Bragi. She tried her jolly-the-old-man-along approach."

"Grasping little witch. It never fails. The commons. . . ."

"Inger?"

"Hmm?"

"Hold my hand."

She reached over. Her smile returned. He squeezed once, gently, reassuring himself. "Inger. Don't take this as a shot. But you're holding the hand of a common foot soldier who did a lot of grasping. And you married him."

"What do you mean?"

"I don't think it makes much difference who our parents were. We all take what we can get. Switch a Marena Dimura baby with a Nordmen child and when they're adults they'll act like the people who raised them. Blood doesn't have anything to do with it. Be quiet, Derel."

He and Prataxis had had the blood versus environment argument before. Derel was perfectly willing to take either side. Argument was a game with the scholar.

Inger said, "I try to believe in what you're doing, but it's hard. The most you can make out of a peasant is a peasant in pretty clothes."

"What about his children? It's the children that interest me. And the peasant himself, for that matter." Before she could reply, he added, "I'm indifferent to the quality of a man's speech and table manners, dear. It's what's up here that counts with me." He tapped his temple. "And how well he does his job."

"Like Abaca?" Her sarcasm was thick. She loathed Credence Abaca.

"Exactly. He has a foul mouth, abominable habits, and the best tactical mind I've ever seen. Ever. Given time, I think we can housebreak him."

"*He* doesn't even have the qualities of a peasant. Those disgusting people eat insects. . . ."

"Dear, if blood counts for that much, you and me, we're headed for a heap of trouble."

Her eyes narrowed. Her fighting smile vanished. She leaned forward. A string of blondeness fell over her left eye. "What do you mean?"

"You've got the Greyfells blood. The Greyfells have been traitors, treachers, murderers, and rebels since my grandfather was a pup. If blood tells, then I'd better have you watched by my fifty most faithful men."

Her face lost expression. The color drained away. She surged to her feet. Crimson replaced her pallor. She sputtered in anger.

"Sit down, darling. I was just trying to show you the hole in your argument."

"I don't think that was a very nice way."

"Maybe not. But I think you'll have to concede."

She looked at him hard. "I suppose. If I don't, I might end up sharing my life with your cronies from the Captures team. The Baronness Kartye wants to see me. I'll be back."

"You didn't change her mind," Prataxis said.

"I know. We open the Thing tomorrow. Anything you want to tell them?"

"The discussions were fruitful. The legion in the Gap will allow passage of traders beginning two weeks from tomorrow. Transport and sale of weapons won't be permitted. Caravaneers will be allowed customary defensive arms. Western caravans won't be allowed east of Throyes. Dealings with Argon, Necremnos, and their tributaries have to be handled through Throyen intermediaries. And we're advised that trade with Matayanga is contingent on the daily military situation."

"Don't sound all that unreasonable to me."

"There'll be squawkers. It's weighted toward the Throyens."

"In this country somebody is always crying about something. Their caravans will be in the race to get through the Gap anyway."

"Anyone who can afford to assemble a caravan has one put together already. They'll trample each other when I say the magic words."

"Then I wasted a lot of people's time, having them hang around to talk to you."

"There are thoughts to be aired. Viewpoints to share."

"They weren't sharing anything with anybody last week."

"Let me make them mad. They'll say what they're thinking."

"I don't. . . ."

Women screamed near Abaca's Marena Dimura group. Men shouted angrily. Ragnarson heard steel meet steel.

He flung himself off his throne. "Get the hell out of my way!" he roared as he pushed through the crowd. Taller than most of his guests, he saw the surge as the Guards moved in. Good. They had been on their toes. He had not expected to get through the evening without at least one fracas. "Will you get the hell out of my road?" he snarled at a heavy old matron. She promptly threatened a faint.

The Guards had the men separated when he got there. One was Credence Abaca. The other was a young gentleman of the Estates, the son of a baron in town for the Thingmeet. The Baron himself was shoving through the crowd.

Abaca and the youth both shouted accusations. "Shut up!" Ragnarson snapped. "You first." He indicated the younger man.

"He made improper advances to my sister." The young noble was sullen and defensive. It was an attitude increasingly common to his class.

"Credence?"

"I asked her to dance, sir." Abaca had regained his aplomb. Perhaps he had not lost it. He was a tactician in more than the military sense. He was a master manipulator and could be as heartless as a spider. There was no apology in his manner.

"That's all?"

"On my honor, Sire."

"You have no honor, you. . . ."

"Shut your mouth, boy," Ragnarson snapped. "You're in up to your ears now." He looked for the woman in question. Her father had driven her away from the confrontation. The man wore a thin smile of anticipation. Ragnarson wondered if it hadn't been Abaca who had been maneuvered this time. The Estates remained mortally offended because a Marena Dimura had been appointed second in command of the army. Only the most trustworthy Nordmen were permitted to participate professionally.

Ragnarson turned to the youth. "You dared draw a blade in the Palace? Against one of my officers?"

The Nordmen would not keep his mouth shut. "Somebody has to teach these . . . these . . . animals their place. I challenge!"

"You don't have a right to challenge," Ragnarson told him.

"I'll accept anyway," Abaca said. He was a small, lean, olive man. He had big black mustachios and deep lines in his face. His dark little pupils were flakes of obsidian.

"Credence!" Bragi said. "That's enough." Abaca stepped back, relaxed. He had superb self-control. "Good." Bragi faced the youth. "Son, you committed a felony. The Estates are allowed their weapons in the Palace, but you don't have a right to use them." He indicated the Marena Dimura group. Only Abaca was armed. "That's an honor, not a right. You abused it. You forfeited your right of challenge when you broke the law. It's a capital offense. I could have you hung." The youth blanched. "But it would be a shame to do that. The real crimes here are stupidity, arrogance, and a bad choice of parents. Sergeant Wortel," he snapped at the Guardsman nearest Abaca.

"Sire?"

"Take the boy outside. Give him twenty lashes. Just hard enough to make him think next time his mouth threatens to override his common sense."

"Yes, Sire." Wortel was pleased and did not hide it. An older man of Wesson stock, he had grown up to the crack of Nordmen whips.

Ragnarson ignored the departure. The youth did a lot of yelling and threatening. When he realized that he would actually get the whipping, he became silent, pale, and scared.

Bragi faced the young man's father.

There was a new order and a new law. The Estates no longer rode roughshod over the land. Nothing had to be said. The Nordmen knew they had to pay when their old habits got the best of them.

Nevertheless, Ragnarson wanted to make a point. He asked, "Would you rather have him dead?"

The Baron croaked, "Dead?"

"He'd be dead now if I'd let them fight."

The Baron sneered. "A Marena Dimura kill him? That's ridiculous."

"Lie to yourself if you like. Baron, I considered your son's age. He's not old enough to know better. I did what I had to to save him." A cry echoed in the courtyard. Murder flared in the Baron's eye. "I'd let *you* fight Credence, though. I figure you put the boy up to this, so it's really your battle. Credence. Choose your weapons."

"Knives, Sire. They don't like knives, the gentlemen of the Estates."

How can such a small mouth stretch into such a big grin? Ragnarson wondered. "My Lord Baron? Are you ready?"

The Nordmen reddened, sputtered, looked for support from his peers. Any he may have seen existed only in his own imagination. He drew himself up, said, "That's hardly the way gentlemen. . . ."

"What gentlemen?" Bragi asked. "This mess came up because you won't accept Colonel Abaca as a gentleman. Why expect him to change now?" Not wanting to pour it on too heavy, Ragnarson added, "One of the bases of the law, Baron, is that we *all* have to face the consequences of our actions. Birth doesn't grant you immunity anymore. It only allows you limited privilege. In return, you're supposed to protect and guide the people of your fief. It's all set forth in the traditional oath of fealty, which goes all the way back to Jan Iron-Hand. You yourself swore that oath three times. Before the old King. Before Queen Fiana. Then before me. All I've ever asked of the Estates is that their lords fulfill that oath."

He thought he was getting through. The Baron had begun to squirm. "Let's drop the whole business, shall we? Send your family back to their quarters. Wait for your boy. I'll have Doctor Wachtel attend him. Credence, confine yourself to barracks for the night. I'll have more to say to you later. Derel, let's put some life back in this party."

When they were out of earshot of the Baron, Ragnarson asked, "How did I do?"

"Pretty good," Prataxis replied. The scholar had indulged in his own form of intimidation. He had written down every word spoken. The Nordmen had an almost superstitious fear of the magical recall of his notes. "Do you know him? Is he likely to hold a grudge?"

"I don't think so. He's just impulsive. He survived the civil war. I haven't had to hang him since. That's about the best you can expect from the Estates. Take a couple notes. Have the old noose hung out. The one we used on Lord Lindwedel, Sir Andvbur, and the Captal. As a gentle reminder. And ask Varthlokkur to have the Unborn show himself. That should do it."

Ragnarson paused to obtain wine for Prataxis and beer for himself. "It's so damned depressing sometimes. Here I am, the third consecutive monarch to bust his ass to make this a good country to live in. And if you get more than a bowshot from Vorgreberg's gates, you're up to your ears in the same old hardheaded, completely irrational bullshit the old Krief met head-on when he was crowned."

"This is a feudal state, Sire. Rigidity is one of that form's characteristics. And it's a positive characteristic, considering the forces which act to create feudal societies. The structure has a place for every man, with his responsibilities and privileges clearly defined. The weakness of the form is its inflexible response to novel ideas. It's been rocked by too many of those during our lifetimes, dating back to the Scourge of God, who did not fade from the field at harvest time. Now it wants to make like a turtle and pull its head in till the worst blows over. Only the storm won't go away. So the mossbacks strike back. Civil strife is one result."

"You trying to tell me something?"

"Change will be slow and painful in a kingdom like Kavelin. You can push too hard. Reaction will be like a recurrent boil. You lanced ours once, by winning the civil war. Now it's rising again."

"And there's nothing I can do about it?"

"To pursue the medical analogy, use poultices to keep the swelling to a minimum and the pain short-lived."

"For instance me a poultice."

"A conciliatory message, in private, might help with the Baron. You don't want him thinking you humiliated him maliciously. Press the lifesaving point, and agree with his prejudices without saying so in so many words. These illiterates have a great awe of the magic of reading and writing. He'll be tremendously impressed because you took time to do a letter."

Ragnarson whistled silently. "I wanted to humiliate him. I wanted to hang him out to dry. Sometimes the Estates make me want to cry like a baby. Yes. Write me up one of your classic little notes. I'll rewrite it in my own hand and have Dahl sneak it over."

He bumped into someone. Hard. Wine splashed against his side. He looked down.

His daughter-in-law's friend looked up at him. She did a quick, flustered, apologetic curtsey. "I'm sorry, Your Majesty. That was clumsy of me." Her voice was high. It contained a tiny squeak. It wasn't her normal voice. He had heard that at the place in Lieneke Lane. She was nervous. And the fright was alive in her eyes.

"My apology, Miss. It was my fault. I wasn't watching where I was going."

He walked away wondering. Was she afraid of the man? In awe of his Crown? Or afraid of herself?

Damn you, Kristen. You've got a big mouth.

Derel was chattering again. He told himself to pay attention. When Prataxis ran down, he said, "Send out the word for Michael to get in touch. We need to talk."

7

Year 1016 AFE;
Decisions

RAGNARSON SAT WITH one leg sprawled across a small, square table. His eyes were closed. He was daydreaming.

To his left sat Varthlokkur. The sorcerer's tongue-tip protruded from the corner of his mouth. Slowly, he forced a quill to produce a drawing. "The memories are clear enough," he told Prataxis, opposite him. "But I'm no artist."

The drawing betrayed that. It was of a man's face. But of whom?

"Maybe charcoals, that you could erase," Prataxis suggested.

"Better would be an artist who could work from my descriptions."

The two were toying with an illustrated history of the Fall. Varthlokkur was the last living participant. The major extant record of the epoch, *The Wizards of Ilkazar*, consisted of impassioned anti-Empire propaganda. Whenever his path crossed that of the sorcerer, conservator Prataxis teased forth memories and committed them to paper. The Fall was western history's crucial crossroad. Prataxis believed the perpetuation of old lies to be a sin.

Ilkazar's last king had slain Varthlokkur's mother. Varthlokkur had crushed the Empire in revenge.

"I can't capture the real feel of the man," the wizard grumbled. "Wish I could impress a thought directly onto the paper."

Ragnarson snorted like an old boar hog being wakened by a pig farmer. "Why not? I hear tell a good sorcerer can think pictures into one of those seeing bowls. So think your memories of those old-time wizards and kings. Let an artist draw what he sees." He sniffled, sneezed, searched for a handkerchief. There had been another rainy day game of

Captures, a rematch with the Panthers, that had been long and savage and had left him with a murderous cold. The Panthers had won, five-four, on a disputed goal. The judges themselves were still arguing.

Varthlokkur and Prataxis exchanged looks. Derel said, "Wouldn't it work?"

"Maybe," Varthlokkur grumped. He awarded the King a foul look. His was the ire of a professional being taught to suck eggs by a layman.

The door opened. Dahl Haas stepped inside. From a rigid attention, he announced, "Sir Gjerdrum Eanredson, Your Majesty." A slight scowl crossed his face. He was not pleased with his King's inelegant sprawl.

"Herd him in, Dahl."

Sir Gjerdrum took the remaining chair. His handsome Wesson face looked perplexed.

Ragnarson sat up. "That's all, Dahl. Look around to see if we're getting any unusual attention."

Haas withdrew, clearly piqued because he had not been invited to stay.

"What's up?" Eanredson asked.

Ragnarson began paring his nails with a small knife. Prataxis wrinkled his nose. "Some odd stuff has been piling up. I figured it's time we did something."

Eanredson ran a hand through his hair. The room was hot.

"It's this way. I spent a lot of time thinking. I decided you're the only ones I really trust right now. So we powwow. We decide where we're going." He wiped his knife on his trousers. "Okay. Questions."

Baffled, Gjerdrum asked, "What kind of problems? I thought we were in pretty good shape." He paid little attention to politics.

"It's a long list, Gjerdrum. I clogged it all together into three groups, then rated those by how many people they'd affect. So. First area. Mist, Aral Dantice, and their cohorts, are probably plotting to get Mist her throne back. If they make it, problem number two might disappear.

"That's Hammad al Nakir, where some strange things are going on. Mainly, Hsung's machinations. Seems he's trying to round our flank by making a puppet of the Peacock Throne.

"Third general problem. The succession. It doesn't look important right now. I'm healthy. But somebody could stick a knife in me, like they did Liakopulos. Then what? Civil war? Gjerdrum, if I croak tonight, what will the army do?"

"I don't know. That isn't something we've been worrying about. Support whoever the Thing elects, I guess."

"What if that somebody was from the Estates? Somebody from the old school. Would you put up with that? Would Credence? The Marena Dimura have to be taken into account."

"I don't know about me. Credence would take to the woods. He'd fight."

Varthlokkur said, "One of your sons would be the logical candidate, even though it's not in the law."

"But I have three sons. And a grandson. Which should it be? My grandson is the firstborn of my oldest, if you like that theory of succession. Gundar is the oldest surviving son. But Fulk's mother was Queen when he was born. Elana was just a soldier's wife. Ainjar don't count because he's the farthest away."

Prataxis observed, "They're all under age. That means a regency."

"I know. Meaning more worries. Mainly, about trust. All my worries are about trust. What about those Itaskians of Inger's? Are they a foreign fifth column? Inger could become regent. How about Michael? What would he do? Then there's Abaca. And the Estates. And Dantice, Mundwiller, and that crowd. And whoever tried to kill Liakopulos, and dropped the list I found. There are people with stakes we don't recognize. I want to set up guidelines for dealing with everything. Then, even if I'm gone, there'll be a path to follow."

"We're going to be here a while," Eanredson said.

"So be it. Derel, you and I have been over this some. You've had time to think."

"The problems are interrelated. If you solve one, the others will soften."

"I know. So let's pick an area and hammer away."

"The succession, then. Hsung's doings aren't pressing. They're a sideshow. Shinsan is preoccupied elsewhere. He won't do anything but tinker. He'll have to stay free to help Kuo if the Matayangan thing goes bad. And Mist will be around a long time."

"There'll never be a better time, Derel. Shinsan is in big trouble. Once they drop the hammer on Matayanga, Kuo is out of the woods. He can cover his ass. I want to smack him while he's vulnerable."

Prataxis shrugged. "You're King. But really, an established line of succession, including a designated regent, would do more good."

"Gjerdrum?"

"I'd be more comfortable if I knew who'd take over. Hammad al Nakir? That's Michael's area."

"What about Mist?" Ragnarson's mind was set. He was disappointed in his people. They wouldn't see the importance of weakening Shinsan. Not even Derel, who so recently had advised him to play Hsung's game.

"How would she change anything?" Gjerdrum asked. "Sorry. The Chatelaine is your friend. But there's no reason to believe that she could or would alter Shinsan's historical imperatives."

"Historical imperatives? College boy. Varthlokkur?"

"I don't like Shinsan." The wizard examined his fingertips. "Lord Kuo is an enigma. His supporters are unknowns too. Mist we know."

Prataxis started to protest.

Varthlokkur snapped, "Wait, will you? I think I'm speaking from a more knowledgeable viewpoint."

Prataxis subsided. Ragnarson sat up straighter.

"When I couldn't find the man responsible for the attack on the General, I started making daily divinations. I've been spending so much time at that that my wife claims I'm neglecting her. I'm trying to do what I can while I can. Her time is close. I won't be able to help much longer."

Prataxis said, "Tell us why you're not worried about the succession."

"Did I say I wasn't? I don't think so."

"We don't expect you to neglect Nepanthe," Bragi interjected. "You were talking about divinations."

Varthlokkur unleashed one of his classic intimidating frowns. Any man in the street would have fainted. Ragnarson just grinned, though his stomach did flutter.

"Divinations. The damned things are as unreliable as ever. I put in a hundred hours on them this week. . . . Well, twenty-five or thirty. I didn't find out much, but I can tell you the King will still be around five years from now. It was only a glimpse, but a solid one."

Derel's eyebrows rose. "You're sure?"

"Didn't I just say so?"

"Easy," Ragnarson said. "Damn, you're getting touchy. So I'll live another five years. That's good to know."

"That don't mean they'll be happy years. Just that you'll survive them."

"Will they be bad, then?"

"I don't know. The divination just showed you with a sword in your hand on a summer day five years from now. There were dead men around you. Your sword was bloody. You were wearing that wolf grin you get during a fight. Your helmet was banged up. A lot of grey hair hung out from under it."

"And I know who's going to give it to me. That satisfy your reservations, Derel?"

Prataxis tugged at his chin. "I want an artist to paint that scene. If we'll be at war. . . ."

Ragnarson muttered, "Gods, deliver me from. . . ."

"There might be details that would help us prepare. . . ."

"Derel. Answer me yes or no. Will you go along with me on Mist, knowing I'll be around for a while?"

Prataxis sputtered. He hemmed and hawed. He mumbled, "Yes, Sire."

"All right. That didn't hurt, did it? No. I'm going to ask Gjerdrum now. Wait your turn. Gjerdrum?"

"I'm minded that divinations are treacherous, sire. During the war everybody was looking for that Spear of Odessa Khomer that kept showing up in the divinations. And the damned thing turned out to be a guidon some kid from Iwa Skolovda used because he didn't have anything else."

Ragnarson's fist hammered the table. Varthlokkur's inkwell flipped. Ink poured across oak. King and wizard became entangled as they tried to right the well. The spill spread. Ragnarson growled, "Goddamnit, why can't anybody give me a straight answer? I know all the goddamn arguments. It's worrying about that crap that keeps us from getting anything done. We've got to say the hell with it, decide to do something, then do it. Gjerdrum, I want a yes or no. Understand? Do we work on Shinsan? Can I count on you and the army?"

Gjerdrum sighed. "All right. But. . . ."

"But me no buts. Not now. That's what I wanted to know. I'm going to find Dahl. Play with the ifs, ands, and buts while I'm gone. We'll hash out a program when I get back." He rose. Scowling, he said, "I'll send for ink and paper." Prataxis had salvaged his notes, but his blank paper had been ruined. "I want this nailed down quick."

Bragi stepped into the hallway. "Dahl? Where the hell are you? What happened to Haas?" he asked the guard.

"He was here a minute ago, Sire. He couldn't have gone far. There he is."

"Sire? You wanted me?"

"Yes." He told Haas what he wanted done. While he spoke, Josiah Gales left a doorway down the hall and strode purposefully away.

Bragi turned to the guard. "What's Gales doing up here? Does he have the watch?"

"I don't know, Sire. No. Sergeant Wortel has it. Gales has the six to midnight this week."

"Curious. Dahl, get going." He sent the guard for ink and paper, then checked the room Gales had departed. He found nothing unusual.

Kristen's legs ached from crouching behind the hedge. How long would this take? Sherilee had been over there for an hour. It wasn't fun anymore.

The blonde's face popped through the hedge surrounding Mist's estate. She looked up and down Lieneke Lane, burst into motion. She joined Kristen an instant later. "They had a Tervola in there!" she gasped. "Kris, he had a voice like a devil. Kind of like a nasty wind blowing through old dry leaves. Like he was dead, or something."

"What did they talk about?"

"I don't know. It didn't make sense. About how the King

was going to help them. . . . Ouch!"

Kristen yanked her down hard. "Somebody is coming out."

A coach came around the house and waited for an older, well-dressed, heavy man. He puffed a pipe and surveyed his surroundings lazily before entering the vehicle.

"Who was that?" Sherilee asked.

"Cham Mundwiller."

"The one from Sedlmayr? That helped the King during the civil war?"

"Yes."

"How could he change like that?"

Kristen laughed softly. "People do. I used to know a girl who was *so* in *love* with a guy named Hanso. Then she developed a crush on a married man."

"Kristen! I did not."

"Whatever you say, love. Let's run to the house. Gundar can write down what you remember. One of the servants will take it to the palace."

Ten steps away, Sherilee suggested, "I could take the letter. I have to go to the city anyway."

Kristen put an arm around her friend. "Somehow, I thought you did."

Gales rambled through the palace halls, mumbling to himself. "Gales. Going to be rich someday. Yeah. Rich. Going to get out of this fool's business. Yeah, rich. Gales, you ain't nothing but a fool." His gaze seemed fixed on the floor three steps ahead, but his eyes moved in quick little glances. He rounded a turn and tramped toward the soldier outside the door to the Queen's apartments.

"Got a letter for Her Majesty, Toby," he said. "Just came in from the north." He produced a large leather wallet closed with straps and buckles and heavy wax seals.

"Right. Hang on a minute, Sarge." Toby tapped on the door. A woman answered immediately. They exchanged a few words. The soldier pulled the door shut. He wore a slightly bewildered expression.

"What's up?" Gales asked.

"I don't know. She wants to tell the Queen before she takes it."

Gales made a gesture of defeat. "Women. You ever seen anything like a woman, Toby? A man's got to be a pure fool to put up with them. Yeah. A pure fool. And you know what, Toby? I like it. Yeah. Ain't that a bitch? A man *wants* to be a fool. Yeah."

Toby grinned. "There ain't no better way to go, Sarge, that's what I always say."

Gales grinned back. "You gotta do like me, Toby. Yeah. Be a fool, be a fool all the way. Yeah. I got six women right now. That's no lie. Six women."

The door opened. Toby turned too quickly to catch the changes in Gales' eyes. He whispered with a woman, became more perplexed. He told the sergeant, "The Queen wants you to hand it over personal."

Gales sighed dramatically. "Do a good deed," he muttered, just loud enough for Toby's ears. "And me with the nightwatch. All right."

Toby opened the door. Gales stepped through, followed the woman to the chamber where the Queen awaited him. She sat behind a small writing table, clad in a dressing gown of deep green. Gales thought the color became her.

"Your Majesty." He bowed.

The Queen told the lady, "You may go, Thelma."

The woman's eyes grew huge. "My Lady?"

"Leave us."

"But. . . ."

"You heard me. Scat. Sergeant, you have a letter for me?"

The woman closed the door behind her. Gales asked, "Is this wise?"

"He doesn't pay attention to what I do anymore. He'd as soon I went back home." She tossed the despatch case into a chest. There was nothing in it.

"I'm Your Ladyship's man, of course, but I think you misjudge His Majesty."

She made a placatory gesture. "Sorry, Josiah. I guess it's the pressure." She gave him one of those melting smiles. "What did you find out?"

"I couldn't make sense of everything, but it looks like the King wants to act against Shinsan."

"How?"

"By helping the woman Mist reclaim her throne."

"That's it? Why was he so sneaky about this meeting, then?"

"There was some discussion of the succession. Then the wizard said he'd performed a divination that guaranteed His Majesty would be around for years. They talked about Hammad al Nakir, too, and where Michael Trebilcock might be."

"I wonder that myself, Josiah. He's a dangerous man. He deserves closer observation."

"All right. When we locate him again."

"This business with the east. It'll complicate things, won't it?"

"Some. It'll probably get them pulling together again. Which might be his plan."

"Then we take it more carefully. We've made some serious mistakes. We've been lucky. Let's don't repeat them and trap ourselves."

"It's too late to stop. . . ."

"I know. We'll have to live with the risks."

Gales bowed slightly. Reluctantly, he started backing from the room.

That smile crossed Inger's lips. "Was there something else, Josiah?"

Was she daring him to make a fool of himself? "Uh. . . ." He thought fast. Better to be a small fool than a big one. "When last we spoke, you accused His Majesty of having a mistress. It isn't true. I checked."

Inger laughed. "Oh, thank you, Josiah. Thank you. You're precious. I didn't mean it that way. His mistress is this ridiculous little country, not some tavern slut. You'd better go before Thelma decides we're worth gossiping about. Don't forget Trebilcock."

"I won't, My Lady."

When Josiah Gales used that tone there was no doubt he meant what he said.

8

AFTER HE HAD viewed the dead assassin and questioned the injured general, Michael went walking in the park surrounding Castle Krief. During two long circuits he reviewed everything he knew, thought he knew, and suspected. His memory was virtually perfect. He seldom had to consult the small staff he employed to keep records.

A finger pointed. It was a shadowy finger, and its thrust lay in a strange direction. He had no evidence harder than intuition. He couldn't take that to the King.

He had a good idea where evidence might be found. If it existed at all.

He didn't return to the castle. He thought his best course would be to disappear. He had to handle this personally. It was that touchy. It would be best if nobody knew a thing till he had something concrete.

He walked into the city, to an apartment he seldom used. The owner lived on the premises. He was a veteran and a reliable man. His connection with Michael Trebilcock was a secret shared with no one else. He would gather the necessary resources and equipment. Michael would begin his journey there.

Trebilcock had made up his mind while questioning Liakopulos. There was no point searching for the assassins. There was no cross-contact between his people and their masters. He would have had prior warning if there were.

He was that sure of his organization.

He assumed the guise of a post rider. Two days later he crossed the border into Tamerice. Two days later still he reached the home of a wartime acquaintance, a merchant named Sam Chordine. They traded favors regularly.

Michael's system was based on the trading of favors and

his ability to convince people that what he wanted was right and necessary.

Chordine laid on a spread, though it was the heart of the night. He asked no questions till Michael was thoroughly stuffed, and then only, "How long has it been?"

Michael belched. "Sorry. Right after Palmisano?"

"No. Must have been later than that. I remember you in the Gap."

"Then in Kavelin, sure."

"Yeah. I remember. King Bragi's coronation."

Trebilcock grinned. "Don't bring that up. Just remembering makes my head hurt. I'm still finding out things I did that night."

"I'm not too clear after the crowning. I remember you and that chunky friend of yours—Karal, was it?—trying to take me some place called the Fat Man's."

"Aral. Aral Dantice. You didn't go. The King had to have Prataxis bail us out." Michael chuckled at the memory. "You haven't seen scorn till you've seen it on the face of a Rebsamen don."

"What brings you to these parts?"

"Wish I could say just a friendly visit, but that'd be a lie. Put on a few pounds, haven't you?"

"A few too many. I don't get much exercise. Business is too damned good. I can afford to eat stuff I like. And that's what I've been doing. What do you need?"

"You have anything going into Hammad al Nakir? Headed for Al Rhemish?"

"We run a train through the Pylons every week. Luxury goods. You want to send something in, or bring something out?"

"Somebody. Me."

"Uhm!" Chordine closed piggish eyes and pursed thick lips. Michael waited. After a time, Sam asked, "Any point me asking why?"

"You can ask. I won't guarantee I'll answer."

"That's the way of it, eh? All right. I'll see what I can do. I do hire people sometimes. Megelin's men don't take much notice."

"I appreciate it, Sam."

"You'll pay for it, too. Old Sam will come collecting someday."

"Seems to me you're one up on me already."

"That spot of business with the woman? Hardly the same thing, Michael."

"It was a lot of trouble convincing her she should move west instead of having a talk with your wife, Sam. She squealed and squawked all the way. My man nearly ended up getting hung. Not to mention the expense."

"Seems as how I recall footing that bill, Michael." Chordine grinned. "But thanks anyway. I suppose we're even if I help you."

"Till your next girlfriend finds herself in a family way."

Chordine picked through the wreckage atop the table, snatching tidbits overlooked first time around. "Hope you're in a working mood, boy. You'll have to do your share. And you'll have to come back out with the same caravan."

Michael closed one eye and raised the opposite eyebrow. "You've got a heart as black as Hell's gate, Sam."

Chordine responded with mock surprise. "Me? What on earth do you mean?"

"I read you like a book. Right now you're figuring how many weeks pay for a guard you'll save. Once I'm out of sight, you'll wring your hands in glee."

Chordine responded with a huge, deep chuckle. "And run down to my strongroom and worship my sacks of gold. So it goes, friend Michael. So it goes. I'm getting fat in more ways than one. Let me show you your room again. Anything you need? I have a little scullery maid you'd find tasty. Not too bright, but what the hell? She makes up for it with enthusiasm."

"We'll see, Sam. Don't send her. Just let our paths cross. We'll see what course nature takes."

"You're a man after my own heart, Michael. A man after my own heart. Explain to me why I ever did a fool thing like get married. Common sense told me to stay away from that damned altar, but would I listen? Hell no. Had to have that woman, and that was the only way. She acted like she was sitting on a gold mine. I've been paying gold rates ever since. For pyrite. If I was young and single like you, you bet your sweet ass. . . ."

"How are your kids?" At war's end Chordine had had seven, including two sets of twins. All daughters.

"Ah, Michael, they're my despair. They'll be the death of me. A man has eleven daughters, and the older ones blooming, every rogue in a thousand miles darkens his door. What's the world coming to? Don't the young think about anything else? It got so bad I hired guards to protect my little string of pearls. What happens? I have to run the damned guards off."

"You should have hired amazons."

"Yeah." Chordine grinned. "Plump little gals about five feet tall. Redheaded and randy."

Michael smiled. "Think I'll turn in, Sam. Let's solve your family problems tomorrow."

Trebilcock liked Chordine—in small doses. Waiting for the caravan would have driven him to distraction had he not diverted himself with the scullery maid. Chordine's older daughters did not make the waiting easier. They shared their father's appetites, and were not the least bit shy.

He sighed relievedly when he joined the southbound caravan.

At his request it travelled more briskly than was customary, or good for the animals, all of which carried skins of wine. Wine brought a premium in a land where it lay under religious interdict.

The drink was bound for Megelin's crowd. Chordine got it past customs by paying a nominal "contraband tax," which found its way into the purses of the inspectors. The train entered Hammad al Nakir a day ahead of schedule, and reached Al Rhemish three ahead. Michael figured that would give him three extra days to poke around.

He had been into the desert on occasion, but never to its capital. His first glimpse stunned him.

Al Rhemish lay at the bottom of a great craterlike bowl surrounded by broad, barren vistas. After all that waste, it was a shock to crest the ringing hills and see so much green.

Al Rhemish itself stood on an island surrounded by a shallow lake. One stone causeway connected the holy city to the mainland. The inner slopes of the bowl boasted citrus orchards, pastures, olive groves, and countless little truck farms. An irrigation canal began at the wall's highest point and spiralled lazily down to the lake, making three complete circuits of the bowl.

Michael stopped and gaped. He mopped sweat from his sunburned face. He was an unnaturally pale man. His fairness served him poorly in the broiling desert sun.

"Keep moving," the master caravaneer growled. "Look all you want after we get there."

"Where does the water come from?"

"There's an aquaduct comes down from the Kapenrungs. El Murid built it. In my father's time this was desert too. Megelin wanted to bust up the aquaduct. He wanted to wreck everything El Murid did. The priests said they'd put a curse on him. His generals said they'd desert him." The caravaneer indicated a stand of monuments on the bowl's far rim. They were barely discernable from where Michael sat his horse. "He did start wrecking the Stellae of the Immortals, but Beloul and El Senoussi made him stop."

"What were they?"

"Obelisks. Graven with the names of people who died for El Murid's movement. They surround the graves of his wife and son. They say there's another stand at Sebil el Selib called the Stellae of the Martyrs."

"Uhm." Michael urged his mount forward. He knew most of this already, of course, but hearing or reading about the wrack of history was not the same as actually seeing it. He remained beside the caravan master down the long slope to the causeway. "Any suggestions?" he asked.

"Not many, son. I don't know what you're up to. I'll tell you this. Keep your head down. And watch what you say. These people aren't very tolerant. Megelin is running scared. He doesn't have much popular support anymore, so he comes down hard on critics. Try to mind the law. They don't accept ignorance as an excuse. Guess that's a holdover from El Murid's time. That old boy was a tough nut."

Michael had heard his King reminisce about the El Murid Wars. He admired the idealistic El Murid of twenty-five years ago. He was himself too young for clear memories of those days. "It's a pity the man went mad," he said.

The caravaneer's eyebrows rose. "El Murid? He was always batty. What you mean is, it's a pity he got hooked on opium. That's what ruined him. Yeah. He wasn't all bad.

Not for the desert. Too bad he wanted to convert the rest of the world."

They reached the causeway. Michael saw fish in the water below. On the island side, some of the landscaped inlets still survived, with their patches of water lilies and the tiny, colorful gardens surrounding them. Many of those gardens had become weed patches. Stately homes, in a unique blend of western, desert, and Imperial architectures, spotted the waterfront. Michael supposed they had belonged to the Disciple's more influential followers, and had fallen into the hands of Megelin's when El Murid had been driven from the holy city.

"You're in here pretty regular. What's your estimate of Megelin's survivability? Where will he be going the next few years?"

The master smiled thinly. "Son, you've asked me that question six different ways the last couple days. Why don't you just back off, make up your mind to ask what you want to know, then come at me with that? Ain't no guarantee I could answer, or that I would if I could, but this beating around the bush ain't getting you nowhere. Be cautious with *them*. I'm on your side."

Michael considered that while the caravan cleared the causeway and began wending through snaketrack streets. "All right. I came to find out a couple things. Most of it I can get by observation. One thing I need to know for sure is if a mysterious wizard, maybe named Lord Norath, has attached himself to Megelin."

The caravan master turned slowly. He studied Michael through narrowed eyes. "Lord North."

"I heard one brief mention from a friend. A panicky mention, maybe three months back. Then nothing. Just a protestation about having a too active imagination."

"I see."

A sudden chill ran down Michael's spine. The master had changed. He had become cold and remote.

Had he made a fatal mistake?

After a time, the caravaneer said, "Son, don't ever say that name. I've never seen any such person. Neither has anybody else. Like you say, a few months ago there were rumors. They stopped. Bam! People who said that name tended to disappear. Maybe no such man exists. But if he does, it's safer to pretend he don't."

"I see." Trebilcock relaxed a little. His hand drew an inch farther from the hilt of his sword. "Back when there were rumors, did anybody say where the creature does his non-existing?"

The caravaneer smiled. "You're getting the knack. Best not to talk about it at all, though. And now you've named the name, best you don't show your face on the street at night. That's when the talkers disappear."

"Then there's no night life here?"

"I didn't say that. There's plenty for them as haven't said a certain name, or don't care who sits the Peacock Throne. Those as stands against Megelin also have a way of disappearing."

"Nice trick. Would you say there's a hint of wizardry in the air?"

"Me? No. I wouldn't say anything that foolish. If there was, it might come down on me."

Michael smiled. He now had most of what he wanted. And he could have learned it in Tamerice. If only he had thought to ask his questions there!

What he wanted to know now, though, he could learn nowhere but here. What was the connection with Liakopulos? The learning process looked more dangerous than he had expected.

"Does Sam's place here have a room with doors and locks? I assume the men sleep in a barracks."

"They do. You'll have to ask Mister Chordine's brother if you want locks. He runs the show here." The master guided the caravan into a side street, and soon into a staging compound of vast size. It was structured as a small fortress, with only one gate penetrating its twelve foot adobe walls. Stables lined the walls inside, and in the center of the compound stood several three-storey buildings, back to back, like a group of men facing out toward their enemies. Michael went and presented his letter of introduction to Sam Chordine's brother.

Three days passed. Michael learned almost nothing. The people of Al Rhemish were tight-lipped and grim. They spoke to one another less than they did to foreigners. Most vigorously pretended that their King did not exist.

Michael saw little evidence of Megelin's presence, other than the ubiquitous fear. Few Royalist soldiers patrolled the city. They seemed unnecessary. Then, too, Megelin's army was still scouring the wastes for El Murid's followers. The little Michael heard indicated the King was having no luck. Hammad al Nakir was vast. There were too many places where guerrillas could hide. The Scourge of God had proven that a generation ago, during El Murid's sweep to power.

Night had fallen. Michael lay on his pallet, staring at the ceiling, wondering how he could penetrate the veil surrounding Norath. One candle wanly lighted his room. He thought he heard a creak from the tower stair. He rose quietly, made sure his door was secure. It was a massive thing of thick oak planks. Only a battering ram could break it down.

The door was fine. He turned to the window, which was sealed by heavy shutters. He had rigged them so he could fling them open if he had to make a hurried exit. They, too, were secure. He returned to his pallet.

The stair creaked again. He took hold of his sword, rested it across his chest.

Michael Trebilcock continuously amazed his friends with his lack of fear. The emotion was alien to him. He only vaguely understood what others felt because his sole touchstone with terror was stagefright. When asked to speak before a group, he choked. That was the deep-down essence of his secretiveness. He avoided uncomfortable moments by keeping his secrets and remaining unavailable.

He just plain hated explaining.

His door creaked. He lay still, waiting. Something fumbled at the outside latch. Michael smiled. That would do his visitor no good. The door had to be opened from within.

The fumbling stopped. The door creaked under tremendous pressure. Michael's eyes widened slightly. "What the hell?" The timbers crackled. Bits of adobe fell from around the door frame. The whole thing seemed ready to go. Michael rose and opened the shutters, studied the darkness outside.

Something had disturbed the animals stabled along the

south wall. Caravaneers with lamps and torches were calming them. Elsewhere, the compound was as peaceful as a graveyard.

He had a grim suspicion. He went to the door. The pressure had withdrawn. He sniffed, caught a hint of animal odor. A thin smile crossed his pale lips.

He had put it together right. There *was* a Lord North and his true name was Magden Norath. The Escalonian renegade *had* survived Palmisano.

Trebilcock had smelled that odor at Palmisano and a dozen other battles. It was the scent of *savan dalage*, a monster of the night, created in the laboratories of Ehelebe by Magden Norath. They were almost indestructable, and incredibly savage and powerful.

He backed away from the door, mind whirling. This news had to be gotten to the King. It cast light on half the mysteries plaguing Kavelin. Megelin was under the spell of the Escalonian. Only Norath could have created the men who had attacked Liakopulos.

Why? a little voice asked. And that he could not say. There was nothing between the general and the sorcerer to warrant murder. There was nothing between Megelin and Liakopulos.

He could guess, but he dared not guess aloud. His friends would not want to hear his suspicions. And the suspected would try to kill him if they thought him too knowledgeable.

Whatever, the King had to be alerted to the darkness lurking in Al Rhemish.

The caravan would not leave the holy city for another week. Could he survive that long? With the *savan dalage* stalking him? With someone sufficiently irked by his presence to want him destroyed? He doubted it. He had to make other arrangements.

He looked into the compound again. The caravaneers had gotten the horses settled down. They were standing around scratching their heads and cussing.

Something hit Michael's door. The oak planks exploded inward. He glimpsed a dark shape wriggling through. He swung his sword in a two-handed stroke, felt it bite deep.

He hurled himself backward, over the sill of his window.

As he fell, the building reverberated to a shriek like that of a tiger-sized tomcat. Trebilcock twisted, managed to land on his feet and one hand. He twisted an ankle, but not severely. He hobbled toward the astonished caravaneers. "Torches!" he gasped. "Get those torches up. They hate the light."

He heard the whump of a great weight hitting ground behind him. He did not look back. Nor did he turn when he heard claws tearing the compound soil, gaining fast. He seized an oil lantern, whirled, and flung it at a darkness streaking out of the darkness.

The *savan dalage* twisted aside. The lantern missed its snout, smashed against its shoulder. Michael seized a torch.

The caravaneers scattered—except those rooted in fear.

Trebilcock flung himself forward, reached for the turning beast, touched it with the torch.

The oil caught. Fire spread along a lean, ebony flank. The beast howled. The stables turned riot. The horses began kicking down their stalls.

The *savan dalage* forgot its mission. A third of its long, hard body ablaze, it streaked across the compound. It reached the roof of the stables with a single powerful bound. It vanished over the wall.

Michael sat in the dirt with head bowed, panting. He felt around for his sword. A thin smile crossed his lips. "Well, you survived their first try, me boy."

The caravaneers gathered round him. "What the hell was that?" one asked.

Michael looked up into eyes grown huge and faces grown waxy with fear. "Where were you during the wars?"

Another whispered the name. "*Savan dalage.* Here."

Michael raised his left hand. Someone helped him up. "Let's get those horses settled. It's gone. It shouldn't be back tonight."

He might not have to worry about it again, he thought. Norath might take another approach next time. The most logical would be to arrest him.

He had to get the message out quick. There was only one way. He would have to contact one of his local agents, a man no longer reliable. Obviously, Norath had found him and turned him, and had used him to send soothing reports to

Vorgreberg. The man would have to be turned back, if only for a minute.

Darkness still ruled Al Rhemish when Michael roused his former agent. Dawn was barely a threat when he killed the man and took to the streets again, hoping he could swim the lake and vanish into the desert before Norath found his trail.

Survival was a wan hope, he thought as he eased into the cold water. It depended on his message getting through, and his remaining at large long enough for his friends to invent a way to save him.

The air was hot already. It would be a miserable day to be afoot in the desert. He drank all the water his stomach would hold, and filled the wineskin he had taken from the agent he had retired. Then he started up the slope of the valley, picking a few ripe fruits as he went. His boots sloshed with every step. He was going to develop one hell of a crop of blisters.

9

Year 1016 AFE;
Rising Tide

RAGNARSON, PRATAXIS, EANREDSON, and Varthlokkur argued for two hours, while waiting for Dahl Haas to collect the Chatelaine Mist. Ragnarson ducked out once to order more chairs. Then, twenty-five minutes before Mist was expected, Slugbait came to the door. Ragnarson stepped outside.

"What is it, Slug?"

"There's a woman down to the gate says she needs to see you. Ordinarily, we just send them away, but this one maybe you should see."

"Who is she? Do you know?"

"I seen her around. She said tell you her name is Sherilee."

Ragnarson stiffened. "What's she want?"

"I don't know. She didn't make sense. You know women when they're scared."

"Scared?"

"Petrified. She's worked up about something that happened out to Lieneke Lane."

"Let's go." Bragi leaned back into the room for his sword. Slugbait had spoken the magic words. Ragnarson seldom showed it in any demonstrative way, but his children meant more to him than Kavelin or his crown. If anything had happened to them. . . . They were all he had left.

Slug was puffing when they reached the gate. Bragi told him, "Send her to the guardroom. I'll clear it out. Thanks, Slug. You thought right this time. I won't forget."

"Thank you, Sire. Just doing my job."

"Right. Keep at it and you'll make sergeant. Bustle her in here."

The girl was half-hysterical. She threw herself at him. He did a little hugging and shoulder-patting. He soon realized that half her hysteria was intentional.

Little by little, he got her talking. She and Kristen had seen Aral Dantice and another man go to Mist's house. They had worked one another up with dares. Before she knew it, she was sneaking across Lieneke Lane, through Mist's hedge, and crouching beside the house under a window that had been covered by bookshelves inside.

"Why you?"

"I'm smaller. Nobody could see me over the hedge. Anyway, there were four people in there. They were doing some kind of sorcery. After a while I knew they were spying on you. From what they said. Then they got all excited. Then one of them started talking who didn't talk before. One we didn't see go in or come out. But he left somehow, because they said he was gone. They talked about him, and that's when I figured out he was a Tervola."

She started crying again.

"Tervola, eh?" He was not entirely surprised.

"Yes! Here in Vorgreberg. You believe me, don't you?"

He sighed thoughtfully, took her hand and led her to a chair. "Sit down. I've got to think." He sat facing her. He did not release her hand. She stared at their joined fingers with a kind of awe. After a few minutes he grunted and stood again, pulling her up.

"Mist is coming. Stay out of sight till she's inside. Otherwise you might meet her and give her an idea how I know what I know. I think Slug will enjoy looking after you."

She turned on the tears. "I'm so scared." She moved against him, pushing her arms around him. He felt the fear in her, the animal quivering. It was real enough. Its object was the question.

He sighed, thinking he had seen bigger twelve year olds. He patted her shoulders again. After a moment of closed eyes and another fatalistic sigh, he held her shoulders and pushed her away. "I'm scared too, little girl." He let go and raised her chin till she looked him in the eye. "And not of Tervola. You go looking for trouble and you're liable to find more than either one of us can handle."

Her jaw trembled. She opened her mouth slightly and closed it, twice. Her gaze kept darting to one side, then she would force it back.

Ragnarson shifted subject. "I want you and Kristen to stop playing spy. This isn't any game." Then, "Do you know what we're getting into?"

She did not reply. She sniffled once.

Her chin still rested on his hand. He drew her toward him. Her jaw trembled more. Her eyes narrowed and glazed. Her lips parted and puffed as she turned her face up to meet his kiss.

Oh, gods, he thought. The fire raced through him. It was just what he had thought it would be. He pushed gently. She clung for an instant, then stood there downcast, eyes still closed.

"I want you to think about it some more," he whispered. "Please?"

She folded her lower lip between her teeth and nodded like a child receiving a scolding.

"Everything is against it. . . ." Enough of this, he thought. "Go back to Kristen after Mist gets here. And stop playing spy." He whirled and got out of there. He ran up the steps to the battlements overlooking the gate, trying to distract himself. Looking out, he spied a carriage turning into the road through the park. "Mist?" The outriders might be Dahl and Aral. He raced back down and hurried to the chamber, quickly clued the others to Sherilee's report.

Mist arrived ten minutes later, accompanied by Dantice. "Sit down," Ragnarson said. He studied the couple. There was a new shyness between them. Damn! It must be catching. "I've been cooped up here all day, so I don't feel like playing games. We made a decision. You know what it is. Let's decide what I can do to help. But first I want to know who the Tervola was and why he was in Kavelin without my permission."

Dantice made a sound like a cross between a belch and mouse's squeak. His eyes widened. And Mist, for one of the few times Ragnarson remembered, was taken completely off guard.

"I have my resources too. The Tervola is important. Call it a gesture of good faith. You've been playing your game behind my back. I don't want that in Kavelin. I've got trouble enough with my enemies, without having to watch my friends."

Mist recovered her aplomb. She spoke at length.

Ragnarson decided she was being forthright. "Sounds good overall. Assuming Kuo isn't in on the planning. What's your timing?"

"That's the other iffy part. We move when Lord Ch'ien thinks the Matayangan attack has peaked and Lord Kuo is completely distracted. We seize the key points of the empire. We leave Southern Army alone till the Matayangan attack ebbs. Then we relieve Lord Kuo himself."

"Right," Ragnarson said. "If he lets you." He stared at a point above and behind Mist's head, seeing a blonde-ringed face. . . . Damn! He had to get her out of his head. "What happens if Matayanga doesn't attack? I hear Kuo's people are talking a blue streak trying to stop them."

"The plan isn't perfect. If he talks them down, we lose. Without him knowing how much he's won."

"You wouldn't try to force that war, would you?"

"No! No more than Lord Kuo is. But why not take advantage of the inevitable? Our best recruiting argument is that there's been too much fighting lately. Shinsan can't take much more."

"Sometimes I think. . . . Never mind. What can we contribute?"

"You're doing it. Giving us a safe place to plan. The only other thing might be some shock troops for the strike against Lord Kuo himself."

"Work it out with Sir Gjerdrum."

A door opened down the hallway. Josiah Gales stepped out. He hurried to his quarters, where he secured another despatch case. Two minutes later he joined Sergeant Wortel, the man he was due to relieve. "Jack, I need you to cover for me. I got to take this upstairs."

Wortel scowled at the hourglass. "The wife is having company, Gales."

"I'm sorry, Jack. That's the truth. I ain't trying to screw you. Yeah. I won't take long. I'll pay you back. Yeah. Gales is good for his debts. That ain't no lie. You know me."

Wortel sighed. "All right. Just don't waste no time."

"Back again, Sarge?" Toby was still at the Queen's door. Gales cursed himself for not having had the foresight to await the changing of the guard.

"Yeah. Ain't this some shit? Another one, Toby. And me due to go on watch. Yeah. Ain't this a bitch?"

Toby knocked. Gales shifted from foot to foot, muttering. She would not be happy about this second visit. She would be less pleased when she heard what he had to say.

Ragnarson swore he was getting calluses on his behind. And he could not get that girl out of his head. There was only one cure. "I'm leaving, Derel. Show Mist that treaty we whipped up the other day."

He strolled into the hallway wondering what Inger would think of his sudden interest. It had been, what? Close to two years since he had dropped everything for a daytime visit.

The guard outside the meeting room stood at a rigid attention. He was new. "What time is it, soldier?"

"Getting close to seven, Sire."

"Thank you." Bragi strode away, fantasies of Sherilee mixing with visions of Inger. I didn't handle the girl right, he thought. Should have shown more self-restraint. Now she'll turn up everywhere. . . . Unless I'm imagining that I'm irresistible.

He felt a twinge of nostalgia for a time when it had not mattered whether he tumbled a willing wench, a time when he had been able to fall in love three times a week without having to consider whose lives would be affected. Those had been the days! He and Mocker and Haroun had been young. Politics had been a game for sour old farts who had lost their zest for the rest of life. . . .

He shied from those thoughts like a stallion spooked. He had had to kill his best friend. His second-best friend had gone into the Dread Empire and been heard from no more. He had had his differences with Haroun, but, damn, he missed the man now. If Haroun were around, there would be no trouble in Hammad al Nakir. If the father were king instead of the son, Lord Hsung would not think of stealing chunks of the desert state. Haroun had the temper of a sour-bellied hawk and not enough sense not to punch back.

He halted suddenly, flung himself into the shadow of a pillar. He was a hundred feet from Inger's door.

Someone was taking his leave. And, somehow, Ragnarson

was not surprised to see who the someone was, though the man should have been on duty for an hour. "Gales, I'm damned well starting to wonder about you."

He waited fifteen minutes, no longer eager to see his wife. He went through with it as much for diplomacy's sake as for desire.

The world began to twitch and shrug like a moribund giant slowly returning to life. Two days after Ragnarson's meeting with Mist, one of Dantice's smugglers brought word of a ferocious skirmish between Throyes and Hammad al Nakir.

Hammad al Nakir's rich coastal provinces were the one area of the kingdom still controlled by El Murid. Outside observers believed Megelin's Royalists would reclaim the littoral once the kingdom's heartland had been pacified. The Disciple was a toothless tiger. He hadn't the backing to withstand the Royalist tide.

So the world thought.

When the Throyens initiated the incident the old war cries of the Invincibles rocked the disputed plain. The Disciple's white-robed Chosen seemed to materialize out of times gone by. They fell upon the would-be invaders. The Throyen commanders panicked. They threw in troops held nearby, against creation of a *causus belli* with which to justify a major invasion. What could have been contained as an embarrassment diplomatically forgettable became a major and patriotically unforgivable invasion of the Fatherland. When the sun set and the dust cleared, more than a thousand Throyens had fallen. Their comrades were in headlong flight.

When Ragnarson heard, he laughed. "There'll be some red faces in Throyes," he crowed. "I bet Hsung is having kittens."

Mist was less cheerful. "They'll twist this around. They'll claim El Murid started it. They'll launch their invasion. I think we've just heard about the last hurrah of the Invincibles."

Ragnarson sobered. "Maybe so. Sad to say. The Disciple can't have much left."

Prataxis said, "Don't overlook the nationalist aspect.

People on the littoral aren't enchanted with El Murid or Megelin, but they'll follow anybody fighting a Throyen encroachment. They know the cost of yielding."

Bragi observed, "Wouldn't hurt my feelings if Hsung's stooges got bogged down there."

Next day Credence Abaca was the bearer of news. The wiry little Marena Dimura came to the office where Ragnarson was arguing finances with members of the Thing.

Irked by the obdurate committeemen, Ragnarson barked, "What is it, Credence?"

Abaca was direct. "Three men tried to kill me. In the park. I thought your tame witchdoctor might want the bodies. They're the same breed as tried to kill General Liakopulos."

Ragnarson cursed softly. Twenty minutes later he was part of the crowd standing round the bodies. For the first time in his reign he had provided himself with bodyguards.

"You're right, Credence. They are the same." He sent a message to Varthlokkur saying the bodies were on their way. He expected to learn nothing, but the effort had to be made.

"You dropped all three?"

"They weren't very fast," Abaca replied.

"Three of them," Bragi muttered. "Again. That's the Pracchia style, all right. A nine divided into three threes. Means there might be another try. Tell Sir Gjerdrum not to travel without guards till I tell him different."

"As you command, Sire." Abaca trotted toward the palace. Ragnarson soon followed, and joined Varthlokkur. As expected, the wizard learned nothing from the bodies.

"I'm still thinking Magden Norath," Varthlokkur said.

"Maybe Norath had students."

"Possible. Not probable. The man's character speaks against it. He was too secretive."

"This attack suggest anything?"

"Only that your list is valid."

"Who made it? Not Norath. He never came in contact with any of my officers."

"So he was hired."

Ragnarson's face hardened. "By who?"

The wizard started to say something, changed his mind. Ultimately, he observed, "We all have enemies. The more successful we are, the more numerous they become. Like throwing a stone in the air. It goes up and up and up. It slows down all the time. Finally, it comes to rest."

"And then it comes down."

"True. Sad but true."

"Is that an oracle?"

"No. Just a bad metaphor. I suggest you guard everyone on that list. Especially Gjerdrum. I'd guess he's next."

"It's done already. How about you?"

"I can take care of myself."

"Liakopulos probably thought so too. Never mind. You don't want a bodyguard, you don't get one. I have to cancel a Captures match because of this. And make myself unpopular with extra duty assignments. Did you find Michael?"

Ragnarson was worried. Trebilcock had been gone longer before, but never at a time so critical. And his name had been on that list.

"Aral found a cold trail. A friend of his saw Michael in Delhagen a few days after the attack on Liakopulos."

"Strange."

"Everything is, these days."

"How long till Nepanthe's time?"

"Two weeks. Three."

"Nervous?"

"Of course." The wizard smiled weakly.

"Don't worry about it. She didn't have any trouble with Ethrian."

The wizard's shoulders tightened. "Don't mention that name."

Ragnarson did not like his tone. "There you go getting goofy again. What the hell is it with you and Ethrian?"

Varthlokkur looked like he was counting to ten. "Nepanthe has a bee in her bonnet about him lately. I don't know why, but she's decided he's still alive. She thinks we should be trying to find him."

"And you don't? *Is* he alive?"

"I don't know."

It might not make a lot of sense to anyone else, but Ethrian being alive might explain the wizard's bizarre behavior of late. Might there be some connection with the Deliverer, about whom he had refused to talk? "A couple of weeks ago you told me. . . ."

"I know." The wizard's lips were tight. He was controlling himself visibly. "This isn't the time to worry about it. We've got a baby to get born."

"I think you're hiding from something. You, of all people, ought to know how much good that does. Are you even going to bother to look? Or just stall and hope she forgets about it?"

"Ragnarson! . . ."

"You don't add up. You're making your own trouble. Forget it. I'll check back later and see if you've gotten an attack of the reasonables and bothered to see if you can find something."

"There's nothing to find."

Ragnarson walked away convinced there *was* something, and it must not be good. It might pay to try twisting Mist's arm a little. She'd at least have to suspect why Varthlokkur was so spooky.

That evening Ragnarson received a note written in his son Gundar's crabbed hand. It asked him to come to his brother Ainjar's birthday party, day after tomorrow.

Sherilee flashed through his mind. She would find a reason to be there. He returned the note saying he would try.

Next day one of Trebilcock's lieutenants burst into another appropriations session. "Sire," he gasped. "Word from Captain Trebilcock."

Ragnarson sprang away from the table. The delegates watched with wide eyes. Wild rumors surrounded Trebilcock's disappearance. One suggested that the King himself had done away with his chief spy. "What? What is it?"

"A pigeon, Sire." The man still clutched a ragged bird. Michael's message dangled from his other hand.

"Pigeon? I didn't know we used them." He grabbed the message tissue.

"We don't have very many. Just for our farthest stations. They can fly farther in an hour than a rider can cover in a day."

"I doubt that." Ragnarson knew a little about carrier

pigeons. "But only witchcraft is faster." He fumbled Michael's message twice before he read it.

"By damn! The wizard was right. Guard! Find Varthlokkur. Tell him to get the Unborn. Say it's an emergency." He waited impatiently.

When Varthlokkur arrived he showed him Michael's message.

"What now?" Bragi asked.

"Now we wait. If you know any reliable deities, call them in."

Ragnarson chuckled. He was an uncommonly irreligious man. "If I knew any reliable gods," he said, "they'd be running Kavelin. I'd have them whipping thunderbolts on anyone who interfered around here. I'd keep one of them squatting in Hsung's bedchamber."

A nervous orderly tapped at the door. "Sire?"

"Come in."

"Message from Mr. Dantice, Sire. He said it's important."

"Let me see it. Come on! The man don't bite."

The orderly sidled across the room, eying Varthlokkur carefully. A gesture would set him running. The wizard donned a pained expression. Thus it had been for centuries.

Bragi read the note, passed it to Varthlokkur. The wizard chuckled humorlessly. "Lord Hsung must have been mightily impressed by the Invincibles."

Dantice had heard from his smuggler friends. Military debacle had rattled Hsung and his puppets. Throyen officers had been stripped of their commands. Soldiers had been executed for cowardice. Hsung had postponed southward expansion. The appearance of Invincibles had been unanticipated. Their gathering had gone unnoted by Hsung's intelligence people, people who had the skills of the Tervola to supplement their more prosaic resources. Rumor said there would be a shakeup in Western Army's staff. Hsung suspected the existence of a traitor.

"Think that means trouble?" Ragnarson asked. "One of his people belongs to Mist."

"They've covered themselves."

"What about Norath?"

"Uhm?"

"We don't know why, but we know who, and we know

where the son of a bitch is."

"One thing at a time. We have too many irons in the fire. We don't need a war with Megelin."

"Who said Megelin? I'm talking about Norath."

"And suppose he's got control of Megelin? Suppose we failed first try? He's a first-rate wizard. He wouldn't have survived the destruction of the Pracchia if he weren't."

"Megelin wouldn't declare war. We're supposed to be friends."

"Supposed to be. They say he's gone crazy. And now we know why."

"He can't. El Murid would climb his back."

"Let Norath ride. We're committed on this thing with Mist. And I've got a baby coming. You don't want to get embroiled with Norath if I can't be there. When it comes to chosing between helping you or being with my wife, you lose."

"Should've known better than to argue with you. I hope your critter gets this over with. If I don't watch them, the Thing will slip me an appropriation I'll cry about for years."

"Let Prataxis handle it."

"Crap. He don't bully as good as me. Hell, this whole business is his damned fault. He designed this stupid government."

"It works pretty good."

"Works great, long as I don't need something done before next month. I want to give one lousy damned medal to somebody, every son of a bitch in the Thing has to have his say."

"I haven't noticed you not getting your way."

"Yeah. But Derel's experiment with democracy is a damned nuisance."

"Strictly a matter of viewpoint. How about something to eat? Maybe tip a beer or two? It might be a long wait."

That night, in Throyes, Commander Western Army received an informational brief from a friend in Kavelin's capital. Lord Hsung was unmasked at the time. His subordinates thought him a humorless man, but he smiled and laughed a great deal while he read. His good humor lasted till he learned that he could not contact Lord Kuo Wenchin.

10

Year 1016 AFE;
Homecomings and Birthdays

MICHAEL WATCHED THE latest band of hunters fade into the distance. They were searching hard. He gave them that. They were covering ground not logically within a fugitive's reach. He had amazed himself with the distance he had covered.

The stolen horse had been a good one. He had run her till she collapsed. He guessed he had made fifty miles. He had crossed the truly bad desert immediately north of Al Rhemish. Now he was in the arid southern foothills of the Kapenrungs. He had a slim chance of making it on his own, whether or not his pigeon got through.

He glanced westward. Still two hours till dark. Eight miles for a man on foot. And the *savan dalage* could not start after him before nightfall.

How long for them to catch up? He wished he knew more about them. Did he dare keep going through the night?

No. Too risky. Better fortify a position instead, before it got too dark to find firewood.

Scraggly plants covered the uninhabited hills. There was plenty of wood. The problem would be to find a place where the *savan dalage* could come at him from but one direction. Where a fire could bar that approach.

He spent an hour locating a marginally acceptable hole in the side of a stony wadi, or dry wash. It had been used as a shelter before. There were stick figures etched in the soft stone walls. They had a runic look. He supposed they were graffiti left by Jan Iron-Hand's proto-Trolledyngjans at the time of the Fall.

He gathered brush and wood till he could barely crowd himself in behind his fire line. He built a small fire from which to light his larger protector when the hunters came.

"The trick, friend Michael, will be to stay awake."

He amused himself with games he had not played since his Rebsamen days. He made up dirty limericks. He tried to remember each of the women he had loved. The list was shorter than his friends suspected. As that wore thin, the moon rose. He imagined characters in its blotchy face. Then he tried cataloging the constellations. . . .

He wakened suddenly, totally alert. Without thinking he tossed brush onto the embers of his fire. He puffed frantically. The sounds of claws on stone came ever closer.

The moon stood high. Had he looked into the wadi, he might have seen shadows moving among shadows.

He had slept for three hours.

The dry brush caught. He spread the fire fast. In moments ramparts of flame sealed his hiding place.

"Damn!" The heat was miserable. The back of the depression reflected it forward again. He lay on his stomach in his fuel pile and hoped he would not cook himself.

The first flare caused a chorus of angry snarls. Trebilcock thought there were four hunters. Their claws clicked. Angry ruby eyes glared through gaps in the flames. "I hope you're patient, boys."

They were. Till dawn threatened. Then they became ever more restless. Trebilcock wondered how intelligent they were. Would they realize that he could play this game almost forever?

Now they made sounds like none he had heard before, deep-throated sounds of rage. He pictured four oversized black tigers slowly losing their tempers, though he knew any resemblance to big cats was coincidental.

A pair of eyes drifted toward the fire. Though the beast was just beyond the fire, Michael could discern nothing of its size or shape. Norath meant them to be creatures of darkness, and they faded in perfectly.

What might have been a paw lightninged through the flames. It ripped air a finger's breadth from Michael's nose. He was tempted to throw rocks and taunt the beast, the way monkeys torment a leopard. He thought better of it. Sometimes the leopard got even.

Another beast reached in. This time Michael laid his blade along the flashing paw. The thing yelped, but Trebilcock knew he had not injured it seriously. Wounds bothered them very little. During the Great Eastern Wars only one means of handling them had been found. That required burying them too deep for escape.

The things growled among themselves and paced.

"Michael, old friend, I think you miscalculated. You should have kept going. They wouldn't have caught you before dawn. They're working themselves up to jump in here now."

Though the heat was murderous, he built his fires higher.

He was not afraid of death, but the pointlessness of its occurring here irked him. He had always expected a more useful end.

The growling and spitting hit a new note. They were ready. He braced himself, his sword poised to skewer the first monster through the fire.

The caterwauling changed tone. Michael could see nothing through the intensified flames, but would have sworn that one beast's howls were fading into the distance.

The others were not pleased.

A second monster voice hurtled away. Then another. But one remained, and he could read its thoughts from its low, soft sounds of rage. It was coming.

He burrowed into his brush pile and waited.

The thing roared. Its claws cut stone. Michael's eyes widened as a darkness blotted his wall of flame. He thrust, every ounce of strength behind his pitiful toothpick of a blade.

The monster halted in mid-leap. Trebilcock's stroke fell short. He gaped as the *savan dalage* hurtled back through the fire, screaming and writhing. "What the hell?" he murmured. "Just what in the hell?"

Claws scraped stone. Michael crouched. Another was coming.

The angry protests began.

Three repeats and then there was no sound in the wilderness. Michael Trebilcock seated himself cross-legged and faced his fire, sword across his lap, his forehead puckered in a frown.

The fire suddenly died. And Michael said, "You. Of course. I should have guessed."

* * *

Ragnarson and Varthlokkur had taken turns dozing. Now Bragi wakened as a bar of sunlight slipped over the east wall and smacked his face. He moved a few feet to the right, cracked one eyelid.

The wizard was awake too, and as groggy as he. Bragi asked, "Think we ought to give up? It's got to be too late now."

"Not necessarily. Radeachar will bring him back."

"In pieces, maybe."

"If it comes to that."

"That pigeon restored my faith. I'd hate to lose him just when he turned me around. Wouldn't hardly be fair, would it?"

Irritably, the wizard said, "Do we have to talk? I'm a little old for these vigils. Give me a break."

"You got it." Ragnarson leaned back, closed his eyes, let the torpor steal over him. Damn, but it was hard to sleep on a stairstep.

Next thing he knew, someone was shaking him. He grabbed his sword.

"Take it easy," Michael said. "We're all friends."

Ragnarson looked round quickly. The sun had risen to the ten o'clock position. Varthlokkur was trying to wake up too.

The wizard asked, "Michael, will you crack my neck for me? I think I popped it out, leaning against this damned wall."

Trebilcock placed one hand on the side of the wizard's head, the other under his chin. "Don't everybody get excited at once." He rolled Varthlokkur's head a few times, yanked. The courtyard walls echoed the pop.

"Ey! Don't break it!"

"Yes sir, Mister Crab-Ass Wizard, sir. Maybe I should fly back and keep walking. Give you time to organize the parades."

Bragi grumbled, "Glad you're back, Michael. Glad you're alive. Where the hell have you been? We waited up all night."

"The Unborn didn't find me till almost sunrise. Then he wanted to play with the *savan dalage*. Flying is something! I've got to try it again. You can see half the world. You look down and it's like seeing a perfect map."

Varthlokkur rubbed his neck. "Next time you feel one of these mysterious jaunts coming on, tell somebody. Save us some time and grief."

Ragnarson growled, "I want to talk to you about that, Michael. Somehow, I got to get the word through to you. Stop being so damned secretive. You were lucky this time. Your pigeon beat the odds. But what if it hadn't? Your whole damned outfit would have died with you. Nobody else knows what the hell is going on."

Michael sighed. He turned to the Unborn. "How about taking me back? Let's try this homecoming again tomorrow."

Varthlokkur asked, "What did you mean about the *savan dalage*?"

"He kept them off me till the sun came up. Then he plopped me on top of a pillar of sandstone. Then he dragged one out of hiding, backed off about ten miles, and came at me so fast I wouldn't have seen him if he wasn't coming right at me. I had to lay down so the wind wouldn't blow me off when he went over.

"Just before he got there, he dropped the *savan dalage*. It hit the rock so hard I thought the whole pillar would go down. And. . . ."

"And?" Varthlokkur prompted.

"Those things are tough. Not tough enough to take that, but you know what? It didn't die. It was smashed up, but it kept trying to get into the shade."

"Norath invests his monsters with a certain vitality. The thing will mend and be back in business in a few months. But congratulations, Radeachar. An effective expedient. Better than anything we thought of during the war."

Groaning, Bragi climbed to his feet. "What say let's go have breakfast? Maybe full stomachs will make us more enthusiastic about your return, Michael. And you can tell the story from the beginning. I mean the beginning where you got the notion that Al Rhemish was the place to dig."

Michael developed a sour expression. He looked as though he might have been happier back in the desert.

* * *

Ragnarson had gotten in a solid six hours of dreamless sleep. He was feeling good. He barely cursed Dahl for having wakened him. "You're sure Nepanthe's in labor? It's awful early yet, isn't it?"

Haas shrugged. "I don't know, Sire. I did hear that they thought it might be another two weeks."

"That's pretty close. Elana always came in a little early. Happens with big babies. Mine were all whoppers. That reminds me. Today is Ainjar's birthday. They're giving him a party tonight. See if you can find something he'd like. I don't know if I'll go yet. If I don't, we'll send it out."

"Of course, Sire. I know just the thing."

"Don't make it clothes. Kids hate getting clothes. One time, when we still had the place in Itaskia, Elana gave Ragnar a suit in cloth. Beautiful blue cloth. Expensive as hell. Specially tailored in the city. Know what he said?"

Dahl looked nostalgic. "Those were happy days, weren't they? Oh. Excuse me, Sire. No. What did he say?"

" 'But Mom, I already *have* a pair of pants!' " Ragnarson guffawed. "He already had a pair of pants! He was right, too, far as he went. He wouldn't have changed them before they fell off if his mother hadn't made him."

"You miss them, don't you, Sire?"

Ragnarson went cold. "Yeah, Dahl. I miss them awful. All of them. Your mom and dad as much as any of them."

"There's hardly any of us left."

"But this is a new life. That's what I tell myself. That we've been lucky enough to have two lives. What do you do, Dahl?"

"Try not to remember too much, Sire."

"Ever met my daughter-in-law, Dahl?"

"I know her, Sire. Just to speak to."

"Want to come along if I go out there tonight? Take a closer look?" It had struck him that, while Kavelin suffered a shortage of bachelors, he was surrounded by unattached males. Dahl. Gjerdrum. Aral Dantice. Michael. Even Derel. Of the lot only Gjerdrum had a regular girl, and that was a doomed relationship.

"I don't think so, Sire. That would be inappropriate."

"Inappropriate? She's female and alive. . . . Dahl, sometimes you beat hell out of me."

"I'm sorry to distress you, Sire."

"Shit. Distress me? Hell. Never mind. Go tell the Queen I'm on my way over. That I have a favor to ask."

Haas bowed slightly, stiffly, and backed out. Bragi muttered, "Well, I got to him for a minute. There's somebody inside there."

Ten minutes later he was at Inger's door. "Hello, Toby. Want to tell them I'm here?"

"Yes, Sire." The guard knocked, spoke to a woman. "Just a minute, Sire."

"How's life treating you, Toby?"

"Good enough, Sire. Uh. . . . Do we have to forfeit if we miss our next match?" He was an alternate on the Guards team.

"I still have to talk to the judges. Maybe they'll give us a postponement. We don't want to chance somebody getting killed just so we don't miss a match, do we?"

Toby looked dubious. Captures was important. The Guards had lost just the one match so far. They were in contention. "But if we did forfeit, we'd be one down. We'd never catch those Charygin Hall bravos."

"That's life, Toby. Sometimes you have to make the hard choices."

The door opened. Ragnarson stepped past the guard. In seconds he was crossing a room to take Inger's extended hands. She wore one of her more dazzling smiles.

"I must be doing something right. This's the second time this week. In broad daylight."

He kissed her cheeks, surprised her with a strong smack on the lips. "That green does things for you. Randiness didn't bring me here, but maybe I'll change my mind."

"Thelma, go away before you find out how human royalty is." Inger raised an eyebrow. "What, pray, did bring you?"

"Nepanthe's water broke. I thought it would be a nice gesture if you offered to help."

Inger frowned. She abhorred the birthing process. "What could I do?"

"Moral support. It would mean something to her."

"I see. Another installment on your debt."

He winced. "Maybe. And maybe because I wish you could be friends."

"All right. Maybe it'll do me some good too."

"You're okay, you know that?"

Her eyes recovered their twinkle. "It's rumored that I'm good in bed, too."

"Who could've told you that?"

"A man I went to bed with in a hospital in Itaskia."

"I remember him. Soldier fellow. Wounded. Maybe the fever clouded his judgment."

"I could always prove it."

Bragi latched the door. "You're talking yourself into trouble, woman."

"Oh, no." She rose. "You're the one who's got trouble, old man."

"Old man?" He lunged. She squealed as he threw her over his shoulder.

After supper Ragnarson joined Varthlokkur in his sitting room. "You have a classic gait to your pacing."

"Should I be in there?"

"Does she want you?"

"I don't know. Wachtel doesn't."

"I see his point. How's she doing?"

"All right, they say."

On cue, Wachtel and Inger came from the bedroom. "Well?" Varthlokkur demanded.

"She has a long way to go. It'll come around midnight, I'd guess."

Inger slipped her arms around Bragi. "It's not as bad as I expected. She's braver than I was."

"You did all right."

"I acted like a spoiled kid. I'm ashamed whenever I remember the things I said."

Bragi shrugged. "Women do that. They don't really mean it. If they did, the race would die out. No woman would have more than one baby."

"It's changed her. She's out of her shell. She's interesting."

"All my friends are interesting. Maybe not very nice, or

couth, but interesting. I've got to go. It's Ainjar's birthday. I promised I'd go to his party."

"Tell him happy birthday from me."

"Sure. Look at that."

Varthlokkur was furiously busy. "I forgot to cast horoscopes for the child." He flung books and charts, pens and inkwells onto a table. "Midnight. Damn."

Ragnarson grinned. "That'll keep him out of the way. Bye, Love."

She squeezed his hand. "Be good."

Ragnarson went to the stables wondering what was happening to them. A refreshing warmth had crept into their relationship.

He could not count the children at the house in Lieneke Lane. They would not hold still. When he arrived they seemed to be playing Captures with the ground floor serving as field. Gundar made a lordly referee. Ainjar and his sister yelled, "Hi, Dad," as they hurtled past.

From a seat on the stair Kristen looked at him in mute appeal. "The barbarians are here," she said.

"And they're our children, eh? Sounds like Prataxis. Don't you have any help?"

"Mist, of all people. She's showing the cook how to make some kind of punch. Julie was supposed to come, but her little boy took sick."

"That's all?"

She flashed a knowing smile. "You were expecting someone else?"

"No. Why?"

"I hear you took personal delivery of the message I sent the other day."

"Oh." More to himself than to Kristen, he mumbled, "Women are worse at kiss and tell than men."

"Kiss? Oh, my. I didn't hear about that. Tell me all about it."

"In a manner of speaking. Kristen, don't pull a stunt like that again. Next time it might be somebody nasty. And you might get caught."

"Fooey. I'm grown up."

"And we live in a world filled with beartraps. Don't go

sticking your fingers in them."

"I'll be careful."

"Promise?"

"Promise. What did you get Ainjar?"

The package rested on the stair beside him. "I don't know. I had Dahl get it. I was running all day. Nepanthe went into labor. That threw everything out of kilter."

"Then you'll both be surprised. I shouldn't tease you, but. . . . Well, Sherilee didn't come because she isn't ready."

"What?"

"She's thinking about what you said."

His heartbeat quickened. He had a sinking feeling. He was surprised at how disappointed he felt. He stared into nothing and asked, "Honestly, Kristen, what would you think if something did happen? I mean, I'm a married man. She's your friend. And half my age."

"I wouldn't think less of either of you. I think I'd be happy for her. The only thing is. . . . Well, you are married. And she isn't. Both of you could get hurt. I wouldn't want that."

"That's why I said what I said the other day. Guess I'm mellowing. Fifteen years ago I would've said damn the consequences."

"And I think it's that caring that attracts her. She's been through it with the 'damn-the-consequences' type. They're also the 'the-hell-with-you' type when the consequences close in."

"Sometimes you scare me, Kristen. You give me the feeling there's a wise old woman behind those good looks."

"Don't stop now. I take my compliments where I can get them."

Mist entered the room. Ragnarson was amazed. She wore an apron. She looked matronly as she settled the thundering herd. She also looked more radiant than she had since Valther's demise. Bragi observed, "I guess Aral had the cure for what ails her."

"The way he comes and goes, you'd think they were kids having their first affair."

"You never get too old for that magic. Especially if it's a

long time between loves."

Kristen looked bleak. She asked, "Are you solving any of your problems?"

"I know who tried to kill Liakopulos and Abaca. Magden Norath. A sorcerer. I don't know why. Varthlokkur thinks he did it for hire. He doesn't have any emotional connection with anybody here."

"How do you hire a wizard?"

"Everybody has some kind of price. Somebody offered him something he wanted."

Kristen's doorman approached the stair. "Sire, there's an officer here who wants to speak with you. Captain Haas."

"Send him in."

"He didn't want to intrude, Sire."

"He wouldn't be. He's like part of the family." Haas's mother had been Kristen's housekeeper till her death last year. "Get him."

Dahl stopped at the foot of the stairs. "Report from Throyes, Sire. Through Captain Trebilcock's people. By pigeon, I understand. Supposedly a final message from Trebilcock's agent there. He says Lord Hsung received a message from somebody inside Castle Krief. He says he couldn't obtain access to the text, but that Lord Hsung was pleased. Trebilcock's contact says he thought the news that there's an eastern agent here would itself be of inestimable value."

"As indeed it is," Ragnarson replied, aping the younger man's style. "I'd be amazed if my enemies didn't have people here. But I am surprised Hsung got his hooks into someone. I don't want to loose the Unborn. . . . Bad for morale. But it's time I winnowed out the dangerous ones. Maybe Michael can turn them around. Any word on the wizard's wife?"

"Still in labor, Sire. Still guessing midnight."

"Get some punch and join the party, Dahl."

"I have work at the palace, Sire." Haas's gaze became shifty. He kept sneaking shy glances at Kristen.

"So do I. The hell with it. Take a night off. It won't go anywhere. I'll make it an order if you'll feel more comfortable."

Haas hazarded a half-smile. "That won't be necessary, Sire."

Ragnarson eyed his adjutant's back. "Shy? Dahl? That never occurred to me."

11

Year 1016 AFE;
Interlude

THE MONTHLY COURIER had come in from the south. The
Duke's advisers were all in the castle. He gathered them for
a progress report.

"... in Kavelin our hand remains unsuspected. They do
know something is going on. Norath delivered per agreement. Our people used the merchandise twice, causing
considerable excitement. We've made valuable friends
there, especially in the Thing. We're doing pretty well."

"It's going too damned slow."

The Duke glanced at the speaker. Old Carmin. He wanted
results before he died.

"It'll pick up."

Another offered, "From the look of this report, we ought
to get the Colonel a tutor. His penmanship and spelling are
atrocious."

The Duke replied, "He's a soldier. He's done a fine job,
except with the attacks on Ragnarson's cronies. And that's
more Norath's fault than his."

Carmin demanded, "Something has gone wrong?"

"Attacks on Liakopulos and Abaca failed, in each case
because the target outfought his assailants. Liakopulos,
despite being wounded in the first rush, slew one attacker
and left the other two in such bad shape they had to be
destroyed. Abaca took his three without getting scratched."

"Maybe Norath gave us second-rate assassins. Maybe we
ought to complain."

"I did. I went over his head. I was told it wasn't Norath's
fault, that the deployment of the assassins was unimagina-
tive, that we should have taken into account the fact that the
targets were superb fighters."

"That means we've wasted two-thirds of them without
knocking a name off our list. How the hell do we isolate

Ragnarson if we can't get rid of his confederates?"

"A point I brought up myself. I was told appropriate support will be forthcoming—*if* we can show ourselves capable of making headway on our own. In some quarters this is considered a high risk enterprise. The potential gain doesn't yet offset the probable cost of premature exposure. If we want help our people on the scene will have to provide a dramatic coup."

The Duke rose and opened a side door. A short, balding, dumpy man stepped inside. He wore a black cassock with a rope belt from which hung numerous small skulls. He had an unhealthy yellow cast. His smile revealed rotten teeth.

The Duke said, "I asked Babeltausque to sit in. His remote observations may be of interest. Take a seat, Babeltausque. Anything to add here?"

The wizard fingered what looked like a baby's skull. "Uhm. The woman. She seems a little reluctant." His raspy voice raised the hackles of everyone who heard it. "The Colonel has his reservations, too, but he hasn't let them affect his performance. Contrary to your opinion, Dane, Ragnarson, Trebilcock, and Varthlokkur are all suspicious. They're not quite sure of what, though, so they're keeping their own counsel. If they put their heads together they might have enough between them to know."

The Duke grunted, disappointed. He surveyed his advisers. "Gentlemen?"

No one responded.

"Babeltausque? Anything else?"

"Someone in Vorgreberg is in contact with the commander of Shinsan's Western Army."

"Who?"

"I don't know. The shielding around Castle Krief is oppressive. I did come up with one related piece of intelligence. Ragnarson will back an attempt by Mist at overthrowing Kuo Wen-chin."

"That is worth knowing. Do you think? . . . The Colonel didn't mention that or the eastern agent. Of course, he might not know."

The wizard said, "It takes time for messages to get here, Dane. His reports only tell you what he knew when the courier left."

The Duke pursed his lips. Babeltausque was getting presumptuous. "Should we warn Lord Kuo? Should the Colonel push harder while Ragnarson is distracted?"

Babeltausque said, "No. The attacks on Liakopulos and Abaca will have them looking for trouble. Stop the attacks. We're dealing with Varthlokkur and the Unborn here. One slip could ruin everything. Tell him to keep his head down unless he can grab off a major victory."

Already Babeltausque's rasping had so irritated the Duke that he was considering eliminating the wizard once the dust settled.

"And don't contact Kuo. Let the cards fall as they may. It won't matter in the long run. You don't want to form an association that might haunt you later."

"That will be all, Babeltausque," the Duke said. "Return to your work." Privately, Dane agreed. The family had enough troublesome alliances now.

The wizard departed. There was a hitch in his step which suggested that he was offended by his dismissal.

Definitely have to get rid of him, the Duke thought. He's ambitious. That makes him a liability.

Someone agreed. "He's getting ideas, Dane. Watch him."

"Of course. One thing more. Our people in the City say the King is wondering about us. We've been too quiet. Mortin, you're down there more often than anyone else. Give him something to keep him happy. That's it for today, then, gentlemen."

He remained seated as they filed out. Things were going about right. That worried him. He wasn't accustomed to the family luck running favorably. It gave him the feeling fate was storing up something nasty.

12

Year 1016 AFE;
On the Move

RAGNARSON WAS PASSING through the park surrounding Castle Krief when the sky erupted with pink fireworks. Big, bold letters formed. They proclaimed: IT IS A GIRL.

He laughed till his sides ached. "Wizard, that's carrying the proud papa routine too far." But he understood. This birth culminated a star-crossed love centuries in the waiting.

Ragnarson dragged his weary carcass to the wizard's apartment. A grinning Varthlokkur was accepting congratulations from all and sundry. He shook hands with people who had never dared approach him before.

"Make way for the King!" someone shouted.

Bragi extended his meaty sword hand. "It was a long time coming, wasn't it? How's Nepanthe?"

"Perfect. Happy as anyone could be."

"Good. Good." Bragi joined Inger. She leaned against a wall, drooping in exhaustion. "Why don't you go to bed now, love?"

"I will. In a few minutes. Just doing some thinking. About how her whole attitude was different from mine while she was in labor."

"Hey, don't worry about it. Sleep. You'll have a better perspective in the morning."

"You look like you could use some sleep yourself."

"About a week's worth, and I'm starting in five minutes."

"Wrong."

"Hunh?"

Inger pointed. Dahl Haas was pushing his way toward them, immaculate as ever, face taut.

"What is it, Dahl?"

"You'd have to see to understand, sire. If you'll follow me?"

Just then a pallid Varthlokkur grabbed Bragi's hand. "Come on."

"What the hell?"

"Just come on. You'll see." The wizard hurried to the east wall.

Horrendous flashes back-lighted the Mountains of M'Hand, making their peaks look like the teeth of a rusty saw. "Gods," Bragi said. "I've never seen anything like that." The barrage rolled on. It couldn't be lightning. There wasn't a cloud in the sky. The stars stared down with cool indifference. "What is it?"

Varthlokkur did not reply.

"Can you read those, Dahl?" The signal fires which carried night messages from the Savernake Gap were all ablaze. "Has Hsung attacked Maisak?"

"No, Sire."

Varthlokkur whispered, "It's begun. Matayangan has attacked Shinsan. A god wouldn't dare those battlefields this morning."

"I wonder," Bragi said. "Did Baxendala and Palmisano look that hairy from this far away?"

"Maybe. What are the Matayangans doing? They're wholly unprepossessing at thaumaturgy."

Haas murmured, "Is he speaking Wesson?"

More and more people came to see the display. Bragi studied them. Seldom had he seen them so subdued.

Horns sounded outside the castle gate. Hooves clattered on cobblestone. "That will be Mist," Varthlokkur said. "She'd have been alerted before we were."

"Dahl, find Colonel Abaca, Sir Gjerdrum, and General Liakopulos. There'll be an alert, just in case. Have them meet me in the War Room. Get Captain Trebilcock, too, and send somebody after Mr. Dantice. And find Baron Hardle. We don't want the Estates to feel slighted."

"Of course, Sire." Haas departed at a run.

Mist appeared a few minutes later. "It's started. The reports started coming in after the birthday party. The Matayangans have conscripted everyone over fifteen. Those without arms are supposed to take their weapons from the dead."

"Will they break through?" Varthlokkur asked.

"I don't know."

"When will you move?" Bragi asked.

"Too early to decide. I want to see what's happening first."

"I've already got Dahl setting up in the War Room."

"Go to my place instead. I'm in touch with my people out there. And I'm already set up."

And, Bragi thought, somebody here in the castle writes love letters to Lord Hsung. "Expect us in two hours." He took another look at the fire gutting the eastern sky, shook his head. "Varthlokkur, are we backing the wrong horse?"

"We're tempting fate."

"I meant to tell you. We've got a traitor in the castle. Not one of those minnows who spy for the Estates. A real shark. Working for Hsung."

The wizard whistled through his teeth.

"Yeah. So far only four of us know we're backing Mist. That's probably safe. But what else has leaked?"

"Time for Radeachar to interview people," Varthlokkur said. "Maybe we should cull them more often."

"Why do they turn on me when they know there's no chance to get away with it?"

"Because they think they're different. That the odds can't catch up. The same reasons any of us play the long odds. The big payoff. Don't question that. Ask about their secret motives."

"Eh?"

"You want the truth? Most people don't believe in what you're doing. Not even those who benefit most."

They entered the War Room. Liakopulos, Abaca, and Sir Gjerdrum were waiting. So was Derel Prataxis, whom Bragi had not remembered to invite. The secretary gave him an accusing look. He ignored it. Trebilcock appeared a moment later. Then Dahl Haas, who said, "I'm going after Dantice now."

"Get the Baron instead. We're moving to Mist's place. Ride out with us." Baron Hardle's townhouse was not far from Mist's.

Ragnarson told his officers, "Before we leave, put all the regular units on full alert. Move the Briedenbachers up to Baxendala. Hsung shouldn't try anything, but let's not take chances. Assemble the other regiments. Derel, have the Thing keep me an hour open. I may want to make a speech."

"Are you going to drop it on them cold?"

"No. Hotter than a rivet. After we're committed. General, can you ride?"

Liakopulos nodded. "I'm almost completely recovered, Sire."

"Good. Credence, you're squirming."

"Why don't I know what's going on?"

"I'll explain when we get to Mist's house."

Abaca muttered something about not trusting that Shinsaner witch.

"Let's move." Ragnarson stepped out of the War Room, found a crew of bodyguards listening raptly to Sergeant Gales. "Gales."

"Sire?"

"Find Sergeant Wortel. Tell him I said to trade duty with you." He surveyed the others. One more Itaskian. "Take Hunsicker with you."

Gales looked as doleful as a freshly kicked puppy. "Yes, Sire. Hunsicker."

"What's that about?" Prataxis whispered, dismissing a messenger.

"I've started wondering about the sergeant. He's getting *too* strange."

"The man barely has the brains to get out of the rain."

"Maybe. I've been spooky since my best friend tried to murder me. Maybe that's why I'm alive. 'A Prince durst trust no man. Trust least of all him thou needs most trust.'"

"Radetic? He felt justified at the time. Overall, though, *Advice to the Prince* speaks in extremes. I didn't know you'd read him."

"I try to surprise everybody, Derel. Anybody sent word to the stables?" Messengers were coming and going in gaggles.

Dahl Haas materialized. "Horses should be waiting when we get there, Sire."

"You boggle me with your efficiency, Dahl. Let's move."

They made a fair-sized parade. The city was up early, roused by the eastern display. People made nuisances of themselves, asking what was happening.

There were guards behind the hedges at Mist's home.

They wore no uniforms, but to the trained eye it was obvious they were soldiers of the Dread Empire. Bragi said, "I don't want to hear a word from anybody. That clear? Dismount." Mist's people took their animals to the stables behind the house.

Ragnarson hastened inside. "Mist, better replace your friends with our bodyguards. We'll draw enough attention without orientals parading around out there."

Mist agreed. "I'll see to it."

"Dahl, take charge of the guard detail. Nobody in or out without my permission. If you need more men, send Wortel to the King's Own barracks."

Mist said, "I'm up on the third floor. Come on."

As he climbed the stairs, Ragnarson said, "You sound disturbed."

"I am. You'll see in a minute."

He was amazed. He had not visited Mist's third floor in years. It had changed dramatically. The partitions were gone. The windows were masked by heavy drapes. An elevated tier of seats ran along the nearer and side walls. Some were occupied. Ragnarson met the snakelike eyes of maskless Tervola. The far wall was bare and shadowed.

A man stepped out of thin air there. He conferred with the gentleman in charge of the room's awesome centerpiece. "I'd give an arm for a map like that in my War Room," Bragi murmured. The map represented Shinsan and its tributaries. A red splash defined the Matayangan advance. It looked too orderly to be credible. The miles and numbers involved belittled any expectation of order.

"Let's move over here and sit," Mist said. Another messenger popped into existence. A tableman spread red sand. Mist said, "My people are doing better than I expected. I'm getting first-rate information."

Ragnarson kept staring at that unnatural orderliness. He glanced at his commanders. They were equally impressed. It was against this sort of discipline they had succeeded during the Great Eastern Wars.

"How is Southern Army doing?"

"You can see the map. Maintaining the integrity of its lines. That's all you could expect against the odds." A messenger appeared. Mist leaned to eavesdrop on his report. The table chief began moving unit markers at the map's easternmost edge.

"What's all that?" Bragi asked.

"Eastern Army is under attack."

"Matayanga caught them with a surprise ally?"

"This has been going on a while."

"A whole separate war?"

"Yes. Not large, but.... Something awful is going on there."

Ragnarson glanced at the representation of the Matayangan front, rose. "I see. Come with me." He headed for the door to the stairs.

Mist gave him a hard look that faded to bland. After a moment, she followed. Varthlokkur's eyes tracked them, his face tight. Outside, safe from other ears, Mist asked, "What?"

"Would you guess I know you and Varthlokkur fairly well? Considering the years I've had to watch you? Would you guess I'm moderately able to estimate the thinking of Tervola in general?"

"I suppose. It's been your career."

"Then how long do you think you can put me off by skipping over, glossing over, subject changing, whenever Shinsan's far eastern situation comes up?"

"What are you? . . ."

"Point. You would not risk what you're about to hazard without a damned good idea of the local situation everywhere in the Dread Empire. Nor would your allies. I know you and I know Tervola that well. Either what's happening out there is of small consequence, and can be safely ignored while you're carrying out your coup, or it is of great consequence and you'll use it to keep your political enemies preoccupied. I know Tervola well enough to know they'll defend the empire before they'll abandon the frontier to play politics. I favor the latter view. Comments?"

Mist shrugged.

"I'm ignorant by your standards but not stupid, Mist. I can add up the odds and ends. Something big and nasty in the far east. Somebody called the Deliverer. You and Varthlokkur not willing to say anything about it even though you *have* to know what's happening. Varthlokkur not even willing to hear the name of Nepanthe's son, let alone make any effort to learn what became of him. Nepanthe becoming almost obsessed with the idea of finding him, and she with the witchy blood of her family. To me all that says Ethrian is alive, up to his ears in whatever's happening out there, Nepanthe senses it, Varthlokkur knows what it is and wants to shield her from it for whatever reason, and has twisted your arm somehow so you won't tell anyone what you know, either. For fear it will get back to Nepanthe. Knowing Varthlokkur, I'd guess he's decided whatever it is will break her heart and maybe cost him her. And he is obsessed with hanging onto her now that he's got her. Comments?"

"No."

"You expect me to jump into something blind, then. Without being in any position to compel me. Bad tactics, Mist. Bad tactics. I'm the kid that owns the ball. I can pick it up and go home. And leave you twisting in the breeze. You're almost completely committed already. But I'm not. It won't cost me to walk away."

Still Mist would not speak.

"I don't plan to run through the streets of Vorgreberg screaming out the secret. No matter, I guess. You're going to call my bluff. The old man always told me, the best way to bluff is not to be kidding. I wish you luck with your scheme. If it falls through, come back. I'll always need somebody tough to hold Maisak." He started to move around her, to the door to her situation room.

She eyed him, estimating, and concluded that he was not bluffing. "Wait."

He paused. After a few seconds, he asked, "Well?"

"He'll be furious. Maybe he'll back out on me himself. But all right. You're basically right. About the situation out east. It's very tight, very dangerous, and with the war with Matayanga having broken out, doubly so. I'm not as familiar with it as I should be. Almost no one but the general commanding really knows what's going on, and he's too busy to gossip. But large armies employing the most grim necromantic sorceries having been attacking the empire viciously, ceaselessly, and mostly winning. They are led by someone who calls himself the Deliverer. What that is supposed to mean no one really knows. But it has been determined that the Deliverer was the son of Nepanthe and your friend Mocker."

"Was?"

"He underwent some dramatic changes between the time the agents of the Pracchia abducted him and when he reappeared in our easternmost territories with his armies. He is not the child Ethrian anymore. He may not even recall that child. He is an instrument of destruction. He is a thing that would make you look kindly upon the most despised of my people. He is a creature completely of shadow. And I believe Varthlokkur is right. If Nepanthe saw Ethrian as he is now it would, at the very least, shatter their marriage. She would blame him for not having salvaged her child from the darkness."

Bragi leaned against the doorframe, considering. Half a minute passed. "I think you underestimate Nepanthe. Both of you. But I could be wrong. Let's go back to work."

"Are you satisfied?"

"For the moment. I think later I'll want more details."

"You know as much as I do now."

"I doubt that." Ragnarson pushed inside. Varthlokkur's iron gaze tracked him from doorway to table. He ignored the wizard. Mist joined him in examining the Matayangan front. He asked, "Have you decided when to move yet?" He surveyed his people. They knew the truth of the situation now. Abaca looked ready to explode in indignation. "Michael. Can you get a message to Throyes fast?"

"If I have to."

"You might suggest that your friends there give Lord Hsung a hard time."

Michael laughed. "They need me to tell them that? Go teach your grandmother to suck eggs, boss. This is what they've been waiting for. By now the whole middle east is aflame."

"And Hsung probably expected it."

"He isn't a fool."

Bragi returned to his seat. "Michael says Hsung might be in for a bad time."

Mist's smile was a hard, sharp, brittle thing. It was the uncompromising smile of an empress. This wasn't the woman who had made punch the night before. "There were a few riots. They're under control, except in Throyes. Those will die out once the ringleaders have been crucified."

Ragnarson made a nasty face. "Crucified?"

"Lord Hsung can't afford to be gentle." After a moment's reflection, "We have to be concerned about him. He isn't political, but. . . ."

"Heard he's Kuo's brother-in-law."

"Not relevant. He's always stood with established authority till the Council of Tervola acknowledged change. His allegiance goes with the vote. He'll be a bitter opponent. We may use your men against him, too."

"That's all you need?"

"We have the strength we need elsewhere."

"Why involve Dantice and Mundwiller?"

"We thought we'd have to hire mercenaries. Somebody had to collect them. Merchants use them all the time. Who'd be suspicious if the Delhagen syndics organized a big expedition now that the Gap is open?"

Ragnarson considered the map. Nothing obvious was happening. The tablemen occasionally added red sand.

"I'd better make arrangements for my people," he said. "I'll keep them at my place." He eased off his chair. He told Michael, "Keep an eye out. I don't want Hsung getting any more letters."

Trebilcock nodded. "I should help Haas. There isn't anything I can do in here."

"Right." Ragnarson collected Abaca, Liakopulos, and Sir Gjerdrum. "Take turns watching that map. See if you can spot something they don't."

Abaca whispered, "May I ask a question, Sire?"

"Go ahead."

"Do you trust this woman?"

Ragnarson snorted. "What do you think?"

Abaca smiled, satisfied.

An astounded Baron Hardle lumbered in. "What in the world?" he gobbled.

Ragnarson slid an arm around his shoulders. "It's our shot at castrating Shinsan. We're going to overthrow Lord Kuo. The Chatelaine goes home."

Hardle gulped air. "Isn't that risky, Sire?"

"Very. Consider the stakes, though. Swinging it would

solve half of Kavelin's problems. I apologize for keeping you in the dark, by the way. We had to keep it tight. Hsung has a spy in the palace. Have Sir Gjerdrum fill you in. I'm going to need your help."

"But . . . Sire . . . Who'll keep the Thing in line?"

"They'll manage. Probably just squabble. We'll be done by the weekend, I hope. Derel, you coming or staying?"

"Staying, Sire. These people intrigue me. One seldom sees this level of sophistication outside Hellin Daimiel."

"No doubt," Ragnarson muttered as he descended the stairs. "No doubt. One of these days I'll show you the real Hellin Daimiel, outside your university compound."

Gawkers were collecting already. Dahl kept them across the lane. Ragnarson chose a pair of bodyguards and walked to his house. He found Kristen on the porch. She asked, "What's going on over there?"

"Can't tell you. We'll be at it a few days. Think you can put up a mob of soldiers?"

"Depends."

"Me. Michael. Dahl Haas. Liakopulos. Derel. Baron Hardle. Sir Gjerdrum. Maybe a few bodyguards. You don't have to do anything fancy. Just feed us and give us a place to sleep."

"I'll have to get groceries. And somebody to help."

"Go through the commissary at King's Own barracks. Careful who you hire to help. They shouldn't ask questions, answer questions, or remember anything they accidentally hear."

"I know exactly who to get." She grinned.

"I thought you might. All those bachelors. What did Ainjar think of the crossbow?"

"I took it away from him. He shot out a window. He hates me forever now."

Bragi smiled. Ainjar was always hating someone forever, or ten minutes, whichever came first. "Did you see the sky this morning?"

"Yes. What was all that?"

"Matayanga and Shinsan."

"Oh. I didn't think they would . . . I didn't think anybody had that much nerve. Except maybe you. Does what's going on at Mist's have something to do with it?"

"Something."

"I can take a hint. When do you want the beds?"

"Me and Varthlokkur will need them pretty soon. We haven't gotten much sleep lately."

"What was it, anyway?"

"What was what?"

"The baby."

"Oh. Didn't you see his fireworks? No? A girl. He's crazy-happy. Baby and momma doing fine."

"They decide on a name?"

"Not yet. They want to wait a couple days."

Kristen mused, "You know, it's funny."

"What is?"

"Life. So much is going on. Men are killing each other over there, and I'm more interested in what somebody is going to name their baby. Doesn't that have a kind of horrible moral smell?"

"That's life, girl. We don't know those men. Hell, for all we know, they don't really exist. It might all be a big lie. If we was to decide to go watch the war, the gods might get in a panic trying to get the props set up before we got there."

"You going a little strange on me, Father-in-law?"

"Could be. Spend too much time in strange company. Mainly my own." There was little force to his chuckle. He did wonder about himself.

He wrote a note to the quartermaster of the King's Own regiment, then returned to Mist's house. There was no change in the situation map.

13

Year 1016 AFE;
At the Ready

THE INTERMINABLE WAIT had become a deathwatch. The Matayangan thing went on and on and on, and still Mist insisted the time was not ripe. Vorgreberg's rumor mill churned a thousand wild speculations. They trickled into the provinces, where they became wilder still.

Ragnarson asked Mist, "How long before Hsung's agent puts it all together?"

"I know. I know. Pretty soon we'll *have* to assume he knows. Damn the man!" she snapped. "Lord Kuo, I mean. Why doesn't he move?"

The red sand now thrust deep into Shinsan. Mist's informants said Southern Army scarcely existed anymore. There was a huge gap in its line.

Ragnarson was tempted to back out. Why risk his people in a coup attempt when Matayanga threatened to crush Kavelin's enemies for him?

Baron Hardle said something. Bragi swore at him, then apologized. Everyone wanted a minute off. He did himself. But rules were rules. There would be no leaks.

Inger had sent a dozen messages. He had ignored them. The tone of the latest was strident.

Mist said, "Fifty hours. If Lord Kuo hasn't moved, I will myself."

"In the dark?"

"In the dark. I can't keep my people under control much longer. If one defects, they'll stampede. It would take ten years to put it together again."

Dantice concealed his hurt.

"It's late," Ragnarson observed. "I'm going to get some sleep."

He was leaving when Haas called, "Sire, would you remind Captain Trebilcock that he was supposed to relieve me half an hour ago?"

"All right. Sir Gjerdrum, too. He's supposed to have relieved General Liakopulos." He walked down the lane muttering. Kristen had brought in her friends. Now Gjerdrum, Dahl, and Michael were dodging their watches.

He spat into the dust beside the road. "Sure as hell miss Inger." Why didn't he feel that way when they were separated within the palace?

Human contrariness, he supposed. A month ago he was upset because he wasn't interested in women. Now he was going crazy thinking about Inger and Sherilee.

He kicked a pebble. It hit a cobblestone, ricocheted straight up. He grabbed it on the fly. "Good reflexes, old-timer."

He'd really fixed himself with Sherilee. Talked himself right out of it. Kristen hadn't heard from her all week.

He eyed a distant tree trunk, snapped the stone. It hit ground short and to the right. "Damn! I can throw better than that." He collected a fist full of pebbles, quickly discovered that he didn't have a twenty year old arm anymore. Remembering when set him to recalling lost opportunities.

He had a whole catalog. It did not just include women he had failed to tumble. More and more, lately, he found himself irritated about every wasted moment.

Derel declared it was a normal life stage. He said most men Ragnarson's age went through it. Varthlokkur claimed it never ended. He claimed he could not count the times he had determined not to let opportunity escape, only to let it get away almost immediately. The trouble was, a man seldom recognized opportunity till it departed.

Something popped in Ragnarson's elbow. It left a dull ache. His next throw went nowhere.

"Damn it all, anyway!" He selected another stone, threw with his whole body. And thought his arm would fall off.

But he hit the damned tree. A glancing shot, eight feet above his point of aim, but he hit it.

"Just got to admit old time is catching up. It's a damned shame you don't get more." He kicked another pebble. It rolled ten feet. "Even better would be to live the same life over, four or five times, trying it different ways."

Was he too preoccupied with his own mortality? He had some good years left. He should worry about getting the most out of them, not how he had squandered those already gone. "Whining won't get them back, Ragnarson."

Michael was seated on the front steps, beside Julie. They eyed one another with an unmistakable intensity.

"Trebilcock!" Ragnarson snapped. "Knock it off! You're late for your watch."

Michael sprang up. He looked like a child caught red-handed at some mischief.

"Sorry, Sire. It won't happen again."

Kristen opened the door. "Saw you coming," she said. Bragi eased inside. "Little short, weren't you?"

"Probably. I'm getting worried."

"No progress?"

"No. Where's Gjerdrum? He's late too."

"In the pantry with Tilde."

"Figured it'd be something like that. You sure know the right friends. They all set their hooks, didn't they?"

"Just about." She put on a brave smile. "I could always go after Derel." A tear escaped her eye. She buried her face in his chest.

"Hey! What's all this?"

"Always a bridesmaid, never a bride, I guess."

"One of them steal the guy you were eyeballing?"

"No. Not really. None of them are my type. It's just the idea. Suddenly, all of my friends have friends, and here I am, still in the audience."

"Yeah, well. Be patient. Your day will come."

"I keep telling myself that. You want to eat now?"

"I guess. Though what I really need is some sleep."

"Go on upstairs. I'll send your supper up."

"What's wrong with the kitchen?"

"It's full of Guardsmen. You don't look like you're in the mood for them."

"You're right. Well, let's see if I've got enough energy to make it to the third floor."

"Want some stretcher-bearers?"

"Smart mouth."

He was using the room that had belonged to his brother

Haaken before his death. Kristen had wanted to put him in the room he had shared with Elana. He would not so much as look through the doorway, though the room had changed since his wife had died there.

Haaken's was the one room which held no ghosts. He had visited it rarely. Haaken had used it only occasionally. He had commanded the Vorgreberger Regiment, and had made his home at their city barracks.

It was a tiny room, about seven by ten, with the bed shoved to one end, beneath a window. There was a chair and a small table that Haaken had used as a desk, and a few mementoes. One was a locket their mother had given them before their flight from Trolledyngja. Bragi opened it. It contained a curl of his mother's hair. Where was Helga now? Long dead, probably. He felt a vague guilt. He ought to go home, to see.

He shut the locket, dropped onto the bed, began remembering. There were a lot of years to review.

He fell into a half-sleep, recalling the bad times after the El Murid Wars. He, Mocker, and Haroun would have sold their souls for a hundredth of what he had today. They nearly had for less. If a god had told him he would become a king, he would have collapsed in sad laughter.

Funny. He wasn't happier now than he had been then.

A soft, tentative tapping came from the door. "Bring it in," he mumbled. Hinges squeaked as the door opened and closed. "Put it on the table." Feet went tap-tap.

He and Mocker and Haroun. The intrepid trio. The darers of any damned foolishness. The inseparable comrades who hadn't trusted one another farther than a dwarf could throw a bull elephant. They had had their moments, and no other lives to worry them in their games of forfeits.

I guess that's what I really miss, he thought. The absence of pressure. The freedom from responsibility.

He hadn't heard the footsteps depart. . . .

He rolled, quick as a cat. His dagger sprang into his hand. He crouched, ready to spring. . . .

Sherilee clapped a hand to her mouth, backed toward the door.

"Hah!" he snorted. "That's hard on a man's heart, woman." He reversed the knife, flipped it. It stuck in the doorframe. "What're you doing here?"

"I brought your supper. Kris said you were hungry."

She was pale as a sheet, and shaking.

"Sorry. Didn't mean to scare you. Sit down. What did you bring?"

In a voice as tiny as she, Sherilee replied, "Chicken."

"Should've known. Chicken. I don't think there's a hog or cow in this whole benighted kingdom. The sheep must have died during the winter. I've eaten enough chicken to fill four coops this month."

"I could get something else." She met his eye for a second.

"No you couldn't. One trip up those stairs is enough. We haven't seen you all week."

She stared at her hands. She was wringing them. "I couldn't come right away. I had things to do."

"But now you're here."

She met his eye again, smiled nervously before tucking her lower lip between her teeth. She nodded. He stared at her while tension bred butterflies the size of vultures.

There was but one subject which was safe. "Are you hungry? I'll share, if there's enough." Talking about the weather seemed idiotic.

"Oh. All right." She lifted the cloth covering the tray. It was buried in victuals and drink.

"Kris fixed the tray. I didn't see it before."

"She has a high opinion of my appetite."

With a trace of sauciness, Sherilee suggested, "Maybe she didn't expect me to come back down."

"Maybe she didn't." He selected a drumstick, looked at her over it. She pretended an intense interest in the food.

"Am I going?" she asked, voice tiny again.

At almost the same instant, he croaked, "Are you staying?"

"The chicken would get cold."

"Yes. It would." He returned the drumstick to the tray. "Do you care?"

"No. Sometimes I like it cold."

Slowly, he extended a hand. Just as tentatively, Sherilee left the chair. Her lower lip folded in between her teeth again. She no longer avoided his eyes. She blushed as they joined hands.

He knew it would be fireworks. It would be as wild as it had been with Fiana. It might consume him. And he didn't give a damn.

The tapping at the door wouldn't stop. The voice kept insisting, "Father! Wake up!" He grunted, raised his head. Light leaked through the curtains. They'd slept that long? He yanked the fabric aside.

The east was aflame once more. The skies over the Mountains of M'Hand burned in dreadful lemons and limes, shot with savors of blood.

Gently, he disentangled himself and went to the door. "Who's there?"

"Kristen."

He opened it a crack.

She asked, "Did you see the sky?"

"Just now. It's started again." He wasn't ready for it. It meant he had to rejoin Mist. He had to abandon this idyll.

"Is this what you were waiting for?"

"Probably."

"I thought so. That's why I came up."

"Any word from Mist?"

"Not yet."

"I'll get dressed." He got started. "What're you doing up, this time of night?"

"Couldn't sleep. Conscience, I guess."

So. Her teasing and matchmaking had stopped being a game. "Let the sinner atone for his sins. El Murid said that. He did produce a few gems."

She understood. He donned the light mail shirt he almost always wore, thinking, Kris reads me as easy as Elana did. Is there a little witch in her blood? Ragnar was lucky to have her.

He strapped on his sword. He was ready.

He looked down at delicate features shifting under the terrible lemon light. He bent, kissed Sherilee lightly, murmured, "It was more marvelous than I expected, Little Bit." He glanced out the window. Bloody lightning sabred a background of yellow and green. "But what have I given you?" He touched her hair, turned away.

He stepped into the hallway. "Anybody else up?"

"It's a cemetery." They went downstairs quietly. Kristen was right. Not a soul was stirring. She followed him onto the porch. "Don't worry about Sherry. All right? She did what she wanted."

"What do you mean?"

"I know you. You've got the morning after guilts. Taking advantage of the poor girl. Like that. Don't. Concentrate on what you're doing. And come back when you can. She'll be waiting." And, as Ragnarson stepped into the lane, she murmured, "She's got what she wants, Father. And how I envy her."

She went inside wondering how she meant that.

The lane was awakening. People were gathering to watch the skyshow. Ragnarson watched over his shoulder, awed. He almost annihilated Derel Prataxis in their collision.

"Sire. Good. The Chatelaine sent me. You've seen it, then?"

"I could miss it, Derel? It's flashier than last week. I keep wondering why the earth isn't shaking. Is this it? Is Kuo out of hiding?"

"So she says." Prataxis glanced round furtively.

"Expecting spies in the bushes?"

"Colonel Abaca alerted the attack teams, Sire. They'll muster in the park."

"Fine. Has she regained contact with her people in Kuo's outfit?"

"You'll have to ask her, Sire. I know she contacted Eastern Army briefly."

"What's going on there?"

"I don't know, Sire. I can tell you it's worrying her, and Varthlokkur seems quite distressed."

They reached Mist's gate. Ragnarson said, "Tell Kristen to get everybody up and fed."

"I was about to suggest that, Sire."

Ragnarson joined Mist. "Is this it?"

"Lord Kuo counterattacked." She seemed ecstatic. It could have been her own pet ambush, so enthused was she.

She also had a relaxed quality that Bragi hadn't seen for days. He glanced at Aral Dantice. Aral, too, had a sleepy, satiated look. Ha!

He felt more comfortable with the woman immediately.

He did not trust anyone with total self-control. Those were the people who would turn in an instant, without remorse, for the moment's advantage. That was why he was often uncomfortable with Michael. And with Inger, who remained an ice maiden till she consciously elected to let go.

"How soon do we go?"

"I'll need more information. But I think later today."

Ragnarson eased around the Tervola reconstructing Lord Kuo's counterstroke, studied the table's nether end. He had noticed Varthlokkur perched over the area and suspected the man might be ready to open up. "What's this business?"

The wizard reflected a moment before saying, "We're still not sure."

"Why so interested?"

"Northern and Eastern Armies have said they'll support Mist. But they're too busy with the Deliverer to lend any real help."

"The Deliverer?"

"He's decimated Eastern Army. Northern Army is trying to plug the gap."

Bragi risked looking at the wizard directly. "You have a special interest in the Deliverer?"

Varthlokkur nodded. His body language, usually so carefully controlled, screamed of an intense inner struggle.

"So?"

"It's Ethrian. He's out there somewhere."

"He's alive, then?" They were going to pretend that he had not spoken with Mist and that the wizard was not aware of the fact that he had. That was all right with him.

"Intuition says yes. I'm not sure he is. Not the Ethrian we knew."

"That's great for Nepanthe, though. First a new daughter, then her lost son found."

"If what I sense is Ethrian she won't want him back."

"Oh?" Seldom had Bragi seen the wizard so bleak. "Why is that?"

"I want to extract a promise from you. If it turns out to be what I fear, I want you to forget you heard me mention Ethrian's name. Nepanthe has had too much hurt from life already."

"But. . . ."

"She doesn't need this pain. She couldn't endure seeing her child grown into a monster. I will do anything to spare her."

"But. . . ."

"I will do anything to spare her. Tell her about this and you forfeit my help forever."

"Take it easy, man. I don't intend telling her anything. I think you're wrong, but it's not my place to horn in."

"Sorry. I'm scared and worried. But I do mean it. I don't want her bothered."

The tenants of Kristen's house were drifting in. Some brought their breakfasts with them. A sleepy-eyed Michael Trebilcock singled Ragnarson out. "Sire?"

"What, Michael?"

"Got a note from my staff. Lord Hsung has eradicated the Throyen rebels. That's the word our contact used. Eradicated. He's also interned our caravan people. Claims they were smuggling weapons to the rebels."

"Were they?"

"Not likely. Too early in the honeymoon to break the rules. He's getting ready to pull something."

"The bastard. Anything we can do about it?"

"Not much. I don't think we'd better try, either. My guess is, it's mostly a warning not to get frisky during the Matayangan crisis. He'll probably release them in a few weeks."

"Are they in trouble if we go ahead here?"

"It's too late to back down now, isn't it?"

"I suppose it is. . . ."

There was a disturbance at the door. Gjerdrum burst in. Indignantly, he shouted, "Sire, three men just tried to kill me! Right in front of your house."

"Are you hurt?"

"No. We got two of them. The other one ran."

"All right. Calm down. Tell it quick." He beckoned Varthlokkur. "Think the Unborn can trail the one that got away?"

"He can try."

Gjerdrum hadn't much to tell. He and a bodyguard left the house. Would-be killers charged out of the park. Two assassins went down. The bodyguard was injured. The third assassin fled.

"Which way did he go?" Varthlokkur asked.

"Toward town."

The wizard assumed an air of concentration. Ragnarson climbed into a chair. He watched the map while he waited.

The splitting of Shinsan's Southern Army had allowed a long red arm to reach deep inside her. Countless Matayangans crowded that limb. Now Lord Kuo was amputating it at its root. A huge army would be cut off in hostile territory.

Ragnarson summoned Abaca. "Think they can pull it off, Credence?"

"Like the Chatelaine says, Sire, it's too early to tell. Sire," Abaca whispered, "We should be rooting for the Matayangans, shouldn't we? Maybe be doing something to help?"

"We are, in a way. We're keeping Western Army tied up. Matayanga can't win anyway. Not in any final sense. Shinsan is too damned big. All I want is to make sure what's left is friendlier."

Abaca glanced at Mist. His expression betrayed his belief that changing rulers wouldn't change anything else.

Varthlokkur said, "Radeachar is following him. He's headed toward the city. He's injured."

"Gjerdrum. Did you wound your third man?"

"I don't know. It got pretty brisk."

Ragnarson turned to Varthlokkur. "Norath didn't do much good, did he? Three failures. Someone is going to be pissed."

"Let's hope Someone does something stupid enough to give himself away."

Bragi watched the map till he grew bored with its miniscule changes. He went to watch the troops muster in the park. "Dahl, run those spectators off. Have the team sergeants over for briefing when they're ready."

The briefing killed two hours. Two hours closer to. . . . to what? Solution to Kavelin's biggest problem? He wondered.

He kept recalling a dreamy-eyed face surrounded by tangled blonde hair. A night of reality hadn't murdered the

fantasy. Scant minutes had done so in other, similar en-
counters. This time, he was hungrier after than before. He
wanted Sherilee, wanted her bad, wanted her now. He
started down the lane.

"Sire!" Prataxis shouted. "Sire, the Chatelaine wants
you."

Ragnarson sighed. "Kavelin, you're a jealous bitch." He
clomped up to the map room.

Mist indicated the pincers nipping the Matayangan arm.
"We're going to go when the prongs are ten miles apart.
About four hours. We'll need three assault teams from you.
Most of the Tervola here will accompany and support you."

Her tone was imperious. Bragi found it irritating. "You
ain't number one yet. You're Chatelaine of Maisak till the
dust settles." He glanced at Varthlokkur, who observed
blandly. Damn me, he thought. I wish I weren't dependent
on him. If I lost him, the wolves would be all over me. He
turned. "Credence. Want to lead a commando team?"

"I'd be delighted, Sire."

"That's two. Who takes the third?"

"Two, Sire?" Prataxis scribbled madly, occasionally cursing as his overworked pen spattered ink.

"I'm taking one team."

"Sire!"

"I know the arguments, Derel. Save your breath. I'm
going. Credence? Who's the best man?"

Abaca pursed his lips.

Sir Gjerdrum volunteered. Ragnarson said, "Not you.
I'm taking Derel and Varthlokkur. That means you stay to
keep them honest here. Not you either, General," he told
Liakopulos. "Somebody has to run the army while
Gjerdrum runs the country."

Gjerdrum protested, "Damn it, you do this every
time. . . ."

"The price of being trustworthy. Be quiet. Credence?"

"Perhaps Captain Haas?" He smiled thinly.

There was little warmth between Haas and Abaca.
Ragnarson suspected the Colonel wished Dahl the opportunity to prove himself incompetent.

Michael pushed past Gjerdrum and Liakopulos. "I'd be
honored, Sire. Could I take my old sidekick, Aral?"

Ragnarson glimpsed a pudgy hand waving behind the others. He grinned. Finally. Baron Hardle was politically perfect. King's flanks guarded by officers from the social extremes. He liked flashy gimmicks. "Make room for the Baron, men. Baron, I accept. You take the third team."

Hardle looked nonplussed. He hadn't expected to be taken seriously.

Abaca grumbled. Ragnarson smiled. Abaca always grumbled.

"He's a leader, Credence. As you'll recall."

"I guess. Like it or not. He saved my ass at the Battle of the Fords. I can put up with him if he can put up with me."

Bemused, Hardle offered Abaca his hand.

Bragi exchanged glances with a triumphant Prataxis. By damn! There were tears in Derel's eyes. He understood the thoughtless symbolism. The ideal had taken root. Nordmen and Marena Dimura, shaking hands! They had no idea how far that gesture said they had come.

Ragnarson studied the Baron. He no longer seemed small and fat and ineffectual. He had a new dignity, a new air of self-worth. His class had lost much of both after, in the main, serving the wrong cause during Kavelin's civil war.

"Let's see what our friends need," Ragnarson suggested. A vision of blonde, insatiable perfection ghosted through his thoughts. He pushed her away. The question persisted. Would he taste those delights again? Or would he leave his bones in an enemy land?

The hell with Varthlokkur's divination. He was scared. The wizard guessed wrong sometimes.

14

Year 1016 AFE;
There and Back Again

A SOLDIER PLOWED into Bragi from behind. He staggered forward, collided with a Tervola, instantly decked the man. His troops spread out. The enemy began to react, baring weapons and preparing spells. Varthlokkur hurled a spell of his own. Chaos spread like a plague. Wild spells rampaged through the headquarters, ignoring allegiances.

In a quarter hour the place was secure. Baron Hardle reported having secured his objective too. But Credence Abaca was in trouble. He had fallen into the headquarters Lord Kuo was currently using. The defense was stiffer. "Let's get there before they close the transfer portals," Ragnarson growled. He herded his men through. Baron Hardle's troops joined them.

For a half hour Bragi knew nothing but the continuous clang of sword on sword, the smash of shield against Tervola armor, the hair-raising instant when a spell had been loosed and he feared it might lash his way. He was battling an excellent swordsman, and weakening, when Lord Ch'ien, Mist's leading Tervola, ended hostilities by announcing the enemy's surrender.

It was over. The coup was a success. Lord Kuo Wen-chin had fallen. Kavelin had placed a friend on Shinsan's throne.

Bragi made the rounds. The cost! He'd lost a third of his men. The rest had taken their nicks. He had a few shallow wounds himself.

Baron Hardle turned up sporting a grin, a bloody blade, and a fine collection of bruises. "By god, Sire. we pulled it off. We pulled it off."

"We sure did, Baron. Get set for the counterattack. Where's Colonel Abaca?"

Hardle went pale. "Counterattack? Uh. . . . Of course. Credence is in yon corner, Sire."

Tervola spilled from an unsecured portal. The battle was on again. Spell met spell. Blade smacked blade. A friendly Tervola shouted, "They're from Western Army."

Western Army? Bragi thought. Mist was supposed to neutralize Hsung's bunch.

The counterattack faded. "We haven't been as successful as you'd hoped."

Bragi turned. Varthlokkur stood behind him, staring at the portals. "How so?"

"Lord Hsung recaptured the other two headquarters."

"Damn! More men lost."

"This is too pat. It stinks of trap. Lord Hsung knew we were coming."

"I told you there was a traitor in the palace."

"Luckily, Hsung didn't get word to Kuo in time. Let's get out now. We're no longer useful."

Bragi was startled. "What?"

"I've opened a portal to Kavelin."

"I've got you. Derel. Shuttle the wounded through that rabbit hole. Varthlokkur, did you look Credence over? How is he?"

"Not good. I did what I could. I can't guarantee he'll make it."

Bragi glanced around. Already captive Tervola were being paroled to war duty. He wished it were that easy at home. His rebels went to the gallows unrepentant. Why did he bother?

"Sire?"

"Oh. Baron. What?" He'd been on the edge of a reverie about Sherilee.

"The coup was successful except where Lord Hsung intervened. Lord Kuo is out. Probably dead. The Council of Tervola will declare their position once the war situation stabilizes. Mist is negotiating with Lord Hsung."

"Lord Ch'ien know?"

"Not yet."

"Don't tell him. He'd slap us in irons. Let's get out of here." He caught Prataxis's eye, pumped his fist. It was a field signal for hurry up. Derel nodded. The Tervola paid no attention. They had problems of their own. The distraction of the coup had allowed Matayanga to seize a more favorable position in several places. "Think we rate a chanson, Baron?"

"Sire?"

"Little kingdom doesn't like the management in a big empire, so it puts somebody else in charge."

The Baron sneered. "Your tame Daimiellian might write it so people on the coast would believe it. *We* know they used *us*." Hardle had donned his political persona. Bragi liked him better as a bumbling captain.

"We used them too."

"I wonder, Sire. You're too trusting. The Chatelaine of Maisak was your friend. You're dealing with the mistress of Shinsan now."

"Her fate isn't out of my hands." He moved to the portal. "I'm going back, Derel. Get the men out fast. Varthlokkur, come with me." He stepped into the transfer.

He found Mist arguing with several unfamiliar Tervola. He located Dahl Haas. "Dahl, pick some good fighting men and get them up here." He scanned the room. He had a little help. . . . The big map table was gone. Wounded carpeted the floor where it had stood.

Varthlokkur joined him. "I'm calling Radeachar."

"Good."

Mist noticed them. She seemed puzzled.

"The Baron was right," Bragi muttered. He sent guards to the portals, told Varthlokkur, "I get the feeling we weren't expected."

The woman said something to her companions, came their way. "I see you made it back."

"Some of us. A lot of my men died out there. Hsung laid a trap. It almost worked."

"My people were hit hard too. The trickster who almost stopped us wants to meet you."

"Hsung?"

"*Lord* Hsung."

"Ain't Lord Nothing to me, Mist. Don't go taking yourself too seriously. Not in my territory."

"Of course. I'm sorry. It's been an emotional day."

Lord Hsung introduced himself. "Keeping your job?" Ragnarson asked. "Still going to be boss of the occupation?"

"Her Highness has chosen to entrust me with our western provinces."

"Guess I can expect the same old crap then, eh?" Lord Hsung stiffened. Ragnarson did not relent. "My turn to do a little arm-twisting. I won't cry about Hammad al Nakir. I won't even whine about you putting spies in my palace. All part of the game, right? But I am irked about my caravan people. A whole lot irked."

Glass shattered behind Ragnarson. A chill crawled his spine. Help was here. The Unborn had come. It had forced one of the blocked windows.

"You know how much good glass costs?" Mist shrieked. "We're on the same side, remember?"

"We weren't first to forget," Varthlokkur countered. "I can't prove it, but I'm morally certain the King and I weren't supposed to return from the raid."

Bragi said, "I get mean when people mess with me. You're going to be a guest of the Crown for a while."

Mist looked deflated. "For how long? We're involved in two desperate wars."

"Two?"

"That thing in the east."

"Ask me how much I care. The worse the whipping you take, the more weight off my back."

"This thing has big nightmares, Bragi. It hates the world."

Varthlokkur made a warning gesture. Why? And why was he so pale all of a sudden?

Mist led Bragi aside. "I didn't have any choice, Bragi. You don't understand what you mean to those Tervola who survived the Great Eastern Wars. They want you bad. I made it a soft trap, hoping your famous luck would hold. It did. We all got what we wanted, didn't we? Can we go on being friends?"

"Okay." But I won't forget, he thought. I'll get my turn. "But don't screw around with me. All I ask is that you deal with me straight. I'll hurt you if you don't. What does he want?"

Varthlokkur was gesturing excitedly. He called, "Radeachar got it!"

"Got what?"

"He found our man. He followed the assassin into the city and watched him make contact. In the park. His control is one of the Queen's men. Radeachar couldn't tell which. He has an identity shield."

Ragnarson cursed. "We'd better stake him out. An Itaskian, eh? I figured some of them were spies, but. . . . Let's go."

"Home at last," the wizard mumbled. "You realize I haven't seen my daughter since she was born?"

"I haven't seen Inger."

"Why the long face?"

"Thinking about our other problems. Dahl! Get us a couple horses. Tell Sir Gjerdrum he's in charge. He can let Mist's people go."

Dahl clicked his heels and bowed stiffly, imitating Itaskian military fashions. Ragnarson sent a disgusted look after him. "He's getting carried away with the etiquette and honors."

"He means well," Varthlokkur observed. "A little more of that and the Estates might take you seriously."

"The Estates can put it where the moon don't shine. Hurry up, Dahl."

"You're changeable today, aren't you?"

"In and out of an 'is-it-worth-it' mood."

Haas brought the horses. Ragnarson started toward town. Varthlokkur cantered up beside him. "I've been through it a hundred times. You always end up going on. You have to. Too many people are keeping your wagon in its ruts."

"Just as many are trying to push it off the road."

"No. That's another rut." Later, Varthlokkur said, "Might better keep your eyes open. We left our bodyguards."

"Think Norath sent more than one nine?"

"No. Somebody else might try. The somebody who paid Norath. It's a good time to strike. The country is confused. It's ready for bad news." The wizard glanced up. The Unborn drifted overhead, high enough to attract little attention. "There's Radeachar, of course, but crossbow bolts strike quickly. Especially if the assassin has a shielded mind."

Rowdy drunks howled just inside the city gate. The

streets seethed with mobs trundling about shrieking the victory song of the Charygin Hall Panthers.

"Damn it all!" Ragnarson swore after hearing the news. "They beat Cynith's Bears by three goals. The Bears were supposed to be better than the Guards. Smart money went with them when we held the Panthers close in the second game."

"I could put a curse on them." Varthlokkur chuckled at Ragnarson's reaction. "Thought creative cheating was part of the game?"

"There's cheating and cheating."

"Pity. Radeachar would make a hell of a striker. He'd give the game a new dimension."

"Get thee behind me."

The wizard chuckled again.

Bragi listened to the chatter in the streets. Most people were too busy to notice him. He seldom dressed more elegantly than his soldiers.

"Going to be dusk when we get there," Bragi observed.

"Uhm. I'll have Radeachar scout ahead."

"Right."

It was dusk when they reached the park. Ragnarson was saying, "You don't realize how much you miss, sometimes. Out of town one week and it turns into a foreign city."

"Quiet. Ah. I thought so. Swordplay. Over there. Where Radeachar said the assassin was hiding." He looked up. The Unborn drifted above the trees.

"Let's go." Ragnarson dismounted, hastened into the orchard with ready sword. "Uhm," he muttered. "Getting stiff." His wounds weren't bad, but they ached abominably.

The wizard was a step behind him, running with a lightness remarkable for an old man.

The clang of swordplay grew louder. A man cried out, mortally wounded. Blades met again. Ragnarson panted, "Can you stop them?"

"I can try." Varthlokkur stopped, closed his eyes. Bragi ran on.

A second death cry howled among the fruit trees.

Ragnarson found Josiah Gales panting over two dead men. One was the assassin. The other was an Itaskian stonecutter named Thom Callison.

"Drop the sword and back off, Gales."

The sergeant spun, came to guard, took a step forward. He looked panicky.

That faded. He composed himself, deposited his weapon on the trampled earth, backed away. He seated himself, hugged his knees.

Ragnarson rested his swordtip on the earth. "Start talking." He wished there were more light. Gales' shadowed face could not be read.

Gales did not hesitate. "Callison acted strange all day. He was supposed to work on the dolphin fountain. This morning he asked for a pass so he could pick up a tool he'd had made. I gave him the token. He went and came back. I didn't see any tools. Next watch he gave Beckett the same story. I didn't find out till a little while ago, by accident. I went to see how he was doing on the fountain. He hadn't hit a lick. I talked to a couple men from back home. They told me he was acting spooky. I went looking for him. And I'll be damned, there he was, heading out the gate. Carrying a sword. I hadn't seen Thom Callison wear a sword in ten years. I asked at the gate. They said he was going to town to pick up a tool. How come the sword, I asked. They said he said he was worried about getting jumped. It would be dark before he got back.

"I did some thinking. Known Thom how long? Soldiered together. Maybe the tool was almost ready and the smith kept saying come back. Then I realized it wasn't like Thom to go fetch. He'd have the smith deliver. So I said to myself, why don't we just check this out?

"What he was doing was coming out here to see that critter there. I recognized it straight off. Same as went after the General and Colonel. They talked some. I couldn't hear them. All of a sudden, it looked like Thom was getting ready to kill the guy. Getting rid of evidence. I couldn't believe it. Thom running a bunch of assassins? He's a stonecutter. Then I remembered he acted strange the day they jumped the General, too.

"I couldn't let Thom kill that thing. I jumped out and told them to drop their swords. Thom looked at me and got a real sad look. He said, 'Gales . . . why the hell did you have to follow me?' Then he said something foreign. The other guy came after me. Thom jumped in too. It was rough. Getting dark. I had the advantage 'cause I didn't have to worry about who I cut. I got one of them. Then there got to be a little more light." Gales looked up. Ragnarson did not follow his glance.

"Then Thom came after me like he'd gone crazy. He turned into a wild man. I didn't want to hurt him. Maybe he got himself into a bind somehow, you know? Like somebody had something on him. Maybe the Queen, she could square it if I could get him to talk to her.

"But Thom wouldn't let it happen that way. He used to be good. A little rusty. Maybe he forgot we used to practice together. He tried one of the old tricks. Before I knew what I was doing, I took him out. Then you jumped out from behind a tree and scared the shit out of me, and almost got yourself killed too, making me think there was more of them."

Ragnarson nodded. "All right, Gales. I'll buy it. Go get somebody to clean up. Don't forget your sword."

Gales disappeared quickly. Varthlokkur joined Ragnarson, who asked, "What do you think?"

"Could be the truth. Fits the visible evidence."

"And he could be a glib liar. Maybe Callison followed him."

"Why?"

"Gales is acting peculiar lately. And the way he talked. Clear. Direct. Hardly wasting any words. Not your usual Gales. Like maybe he was too busy thinking fast to have time for his act."

"He was shielded."

"Aha! Maybe he and I should have a little chat in the dungeon."

"Callison was shielded too. I suspect all the Itaskians are. Only two or three would need it. . . . If you only masked the traitors, they'd be marked men anyway."

"I'll keep an eye on him. Call it a hunch. He strikes a big wrong note. Inger's whole crowd seems offkey sometimes." The look he gave Varthlokkur half-dared the wizard to comment.

"You would be wise to take a closer look."

"What do you mean? I don't like the way you said that."

"I meant exactly what I said. Nothing more, nothing less. It's been said before. They're not your people. Their first loyalty lies elsewhere. Maybe one, ten, or a hundred came here to do something that isn't in your interest."

"You know something you're not saying?"

"No. Just pursuing a logical chain. Neither Gales nor Callison is the sort who could hire a Magden Norath."

"There's a depth to it. . . ."

"We've known that all along. The stumper is, who profits?"

"Where's the sense? Take out Liakopulos, Abaca, and Gjerdrum. What happens? I promote somebody. The regimental commanders are just as trustworthy."

"It'll come in time." Varthlokkur gazed toward the castle. "Can you run out of need for me for a while? My wife has needs too."

"Mine too, I guess." Bragi's thoughts drifted toward Lieneke Lane. "Later, then."

The wizard waited till the King had vanished among the plum trees. His eyes closed. The Unborn descended. Thom Callison, stonecutter, got to his feet.

The wizard asked questions. Callison answered. The wizard departed the death-ground wearing the expression of a man who had seen a vision of darkness. He could no longer tell himself that his suspicions were the result of a hyperactive, black imagination.

15

RAGNARSON ROLLED OUT of bed gently, careful not to disturb Inger. He went to the window, stared out at mist-shrouded Vorgreberg.

He had come to Inger with the best of intentions, then had put her off, pleading wounds and weariness. She had accepted his claims. Yet the story would have been different had he been with Sherilee, he was sure.

There was something wrong between them. Something getting wronger. Sherilee was the latest symptom.

Why was it going bad? It had seemed so right when they met, during the war.

No, he told himself. You had your reservations when you sent your proposal. You had doubts and suspicions. You just weren't sure. She'd been good to you in your exile. You were vulnerable.

She's been trying, hasn't she?

Maybe she has mixed feelings too.

He couldn't shake a conviction that he was missing out. That there had to be something more to life. Would Sherilee give it to him? Probably not. Her best gift would be a last illusion of youth.

It couldn't last. He was twice her age. He was on the downhill side. It would catch up. But, gods! how alive he had felt that night. Inger hadn't done that for him, ever. Neither had Elana, despite all their years together, though he had loved her deeply and did still. Fiana . . . *she* had had the knack.

How much was emotion? How much physical? "Damn!" he growled. He could analyze forever and never unmask the whole problem. Some of the mental parts were quite clear. The physical . . . was it simply a matter of more approximate physical templating, where the needs of one pairing

159

simply meshed better than another?

"Gods," he muttered. "This is Prataxis-thinking. Maybe that's why he never married. Maybe he analyzes too damned much."

The bed creaked. He didn't turn. Inger began kneading his shoulders. "What is it?"

He stared across the misty city. Morning birds winged above the carpet of wool. He watched a brace of blackbirds harass a crow who wanted nothing more than to pursue his corvine business. There I go, he thought. Only there's a whole flock after me, with half of them invisible.

"Brooding," he replied.

"Can I help?"

"I don't know. I have to find out the problem before I figure what to do about it. I feel kind of hemmed in, kind of guilty about maybe not caring enough about things, lonely, like I've wasted half my life, and maybe plain restless. Yesterday I scored a big coup. If it turns out, it could be one of the big dates in Kavelin's history. And I'm not excited. I don't feel any sense of accomplishment."

"Talk to Derel."

"I have. All he does is give me a scholarly explanation. That doesn't help."

"Maybe part of you doesn't believe you gained anything."

"What?"

"Maybe your heart knows something your head doesn't. Your intuition is spooky. How many times have I seen you guess right without any apparent evidence?"

That talent was contributing to his nervousness and indecision. He wanted desperately to still its dark whispering. He had ideas and suspicions even Derel had not heard. There are things in each man's life he tries to make untrue by virtue of concerted disbelief.

"Maybe that's my mother's witch blood."

"Maybe it's saying there's still something wrong."

"In Kavelin?" Stop pushing, woman. Don't make me face these thoughts. You might be sorry. "I don't need witch blood to know that. I'm bailing a goddamned sinking boat. Sharks are chomping holes in the bottom while the rats squabble among themselves. My friends may be more dangerous than my enemies. I've been too successful.

Kavelin isn't in any imminent peril. People are grinding their own axes. I'm halfway tempted to ride away. If I had somebody like Mocker or Haroun to go with, I'd be gone."

"Don't be silly. You can't. Too many people are dependent on you."

"That's one of my worries. Another is I can't depend on anybody. Like the palace . . . I feed people, clothe them, pay them, give them important work, and what's my reward? One becomes an agent for Lord Hsung. Others try to kill Liakopulos, Abaca, and Gjerdrum. Your people. It just baffles me. I can't figure why they'd do it."

"What do you mean, my people?"

He told her about Gales and the stonecutter and the assassin who had died in the park.

"I'll talk to him," she said. "He's been with me since I was little. Sort of my personal bodyguard. He saved me from getting raped once."

"What?"

"I was fifteen. Pretty romantic. A band of brigands were hiding in the forest near our manor. My father told me not to go riding till they were hunted down. Being young and stupid, I naturally disobeyed. I went looking for them. I had the idea they would be romantic foresters. They turned out to be . . . it was bad. Josiah nearly died of his wounds, but he got me out before they hurt me. I owe him. . . . He's embarrassed to be around me now because they had me unclothed before he saved me. He's a dear, sweet man, Bragi. He wouldn't do anything to hurt me."

"I never said he would. We're talking about what he might do to *me*. Or maybe not him. But somebody from Itaskia."

"I'll find out. I don't like it, but if you say it, it's true. You don't talk till you *know*." She continued rubbing his shoulders. He began to relax. After a pause, she said, "This really bothers me. If we can't trust them, who *can* we trust?"

He closed his eyes momentarily, controlling his tongue. "I count their names on my fingers. And I don't know if they'll be trustworthy tomorrow."

She laughed.

"I'm serious."

"I had a vision of you and me here, holding off the world.

And doing it, because you're so damned stubborn. We weren't fighting with swords. We were using ideas. Ours were better than theirs, and, oh, how they were howling! Like the Panthers when you beat them."

"I didn't know you'd noticed. Thought you hated Captures."

"I do. That doesn't stop me from betting. I won two hundred nobles that day."

"Well, son of a bitch. What do you know about that?"

Outside, the mists had begun to clear. Mist. Best double-check that woman. Have Varthlokkur sniff out her backtrail. "Damn!"

"What now?"

"Nothing. Just seeing enemies under every bed." And in a few, too. He strolled to the nursery door. A startled nurse faced him when he stepped through. He did not visit often.

Fulk lay on his stomach with his knees drawn up. Beautiful. Precious little things, babies. Made a man philosophical. "We all started this way," he told Inger. "Ever think about that?"

"What do you mean?"

"That's everybody, a long time ago. You. Me. Magden Norath. Varthlokkur. High lords of the Dread Empire. All helpless like Fulk. All cuddle, giggle, wet, and squall. What happens? How come we start cutting each other's throats when we get up on our hind legs?"

"You are in a mood, aren't you? Take that one to Derel. It's beyond me."

"Uhm." Ragnarson bent, kissed his son. Fulk opened one eye, closed it again. "Better get to work. Still got to clean up after ourselves." Sherilee crossed his mind. Business would take him out Lieneke Lane, wouldn't it?

His breakfast consisted of scrambled eggs and fried chicken. Chicken again. Idly, he wondered if his enemies weren't attacking through his palate.

First order of business? he wondered, leaning against the table.

Slugbait wandered through without noticing his monarch. He was arguing with another Guardsman. "We got to come up with a gimmick. Can't let this match go. After yesterday, we could win a fortune."

"Could, Slug. That's the problem. We ain't going to beat the Panthers again."

"I say we can, if we got the King and we don't have to go against them for a couple weeks."

"How you going to get the match delayed? No. No way I'm going to lose any money on you guys."

"Well, shit. Be that way. More for the rest of us."

Ragnarson ignored the rest. He had found a place to start his day. He would see the judges. How could he get the match with the Panthers set back?

He encountered Varthlokkur at the stables. "Headed for town too?" The wizard grunted affirmatively. "How's Nepanthe?"

"Fine."

"The baby? Decided on a name?"

"Perfect. No."

"Something bothering you?"

The wizard looked at him as if noticing him for the first time. "Oh. Still thinking about Norath's assassins. Radeachar winnowed the castle last night. The Itaskians are all shielded."

Ragnarson stared at a sentry atop the wall. "All?"

"Every one."

It came up like a fist to the solar plexis. He grunted, faked a stumble to cover his distress. "Anyone besides the dowrymen?"

"A few. Mostly wives and children."

"Babies? Even the babies?"

"Even the babies. Babies can hear. It's not as bad as it looks. It's mostly smokescreen."

"Smokescreen." Ragnarson looked back at the citadel. "Smokescreen." One lay between himself and the wizard. They were avoiding what they had tucked into the backs of their minds. "What's in town, anyway?"

"I had Radeachar search the city. He found the place where Norath's killers hid out."

"Need help?"

Varthlokkur shook his head.

"Might still be a couple around. We never accounted for all of them that attacked Liakopulos."

"I'll be all right. What're you up to?"

Bragi explained about having to delay the match with the Panthers. Varthlokkur gave him an odd look. It asked why he was fiddling with trivialities. Bragi did not justify himself.

They departed the castle in silence. Finally, Bragi said, "These shieldings. Those people were checked before. How come we're just noticing now?"

"They weren't shielded before, possibly. Or we didn't notice because we weren't looking for it."

"Or the plot's growing?"

"Uhm."

"Can't you just break through?"

"There was a time. . . . The shields are too strong."

Bragi sped the wizard a puzzled look. "How come?"

"Not sure I can explain. Not sure I understand myself. Negative entropy."

"Huh?"

"Know what entropy is? The tendency of a system to run down, like a fire burning out?"

"You can always throw more wood on a fire."

"Only till you run out of wood. The wise believe the universe itself is a woodpile that will be gone one day."

"What's that got to do with shielded minds?"

"The classical view of sorcery has been that the Power is entropic. That there's only so much. Each time a spell is cast, a little is used up. When it's gone, it's gone. I now believe recent events have proven that viewpoint false."

"I still don't see. . . ."

"Consider everything that's happened in your lifetime. Back to the El Murid Wars. Sorcery, but nothing really startling. Come forward. Here, there, a bigger thing or two. Then Shinsan's war with Escalon. The biggest release of thaumaturgic energies since the Fall. Then the Great Eastern Wars. Bigger still. And now this war with Matayanga. Even bigger. Part of it is increased know-how, but more is because spells are getting easier to cast. Less talented people are using the Power with greater effect.

"We're chewing holes in the fabric of reality. Our spells are like worms gnawing through timbers. Each one lets a little raw Power leak away and float free. Just like the air. Next time someone tries a magick, it's a hair easier, a hair stronger, and more Power leaks free. I think it's that free-floating energy that powers my Winterstorm. And Radeachar."

"Then he'd be getting stronger too, wouldn't he?"

"He is. That's what started me thinking."

"Is it important?" Ragnarson saw shadows. Black shadows. More shadows that he did not want to see.

"It could be. I don't know. I hope it doesn't mean something is beginning to unravel. . . . I don't know what it means." The wizard seemed to be talking to someone else, to be arguing. "There're too many distractions. I don't get time to think, to study, the way I once did. What I need is a year locked up in Fangdred."

"The older you get, the more the world closes in," Bragi observed, for want of a better response.

They were several blocks into the city. "Here's where I leave you," the wizard said. "Place is a couple blocks that way."

"Take care." Ragnarson resumed trying to invent an excuse that would impress the judges.

The wizard stood in the street with his eyes closed. Passers-by looked at him askance, recognized him, hastened away. Most made signs against the evil eye. Often as not, the sign was repeated, interposed between signer and palace. There was a distinct fear of the darknesses the King had enlisted as allies.

The wizard listened to his creature, Radeachar. He scanned the building with his own powers. He was a cautious man.

Nothing. No trap. But still he was nervous. Not a half mile away lay a castle filled with people he could not read. He prepared a bitter spell. Any ambusher would receive a nasty surprise.

He need not have wasted his time. Nothing moved inside save the ubiquitous roaches. The men who had occupied the flat would threaten no one ever again.

For a long time he could not look at the bodies. He had seen his horrors over the centuries, but. . . .

The flat was barren save for blankets ranged as pallets along the walls. The dust was thick. A few sausages hung from a beam. Gnawed, moldy cheeses lay piled in one corner. A scatter of crumbs marked the site of a bread stack.

He glanced at the bodies. The rats had been at them. Tiny red eyes stared at him through a tangle of dry hair. He shuddered.

He prowled restlessly, sneezing as he stirred up the dust. There was no stink of corruption. Norath's creatures seemed immune.

He began searching, wizard's senses probing. Nothing. What had they done here, these created assassins? Sat in silence, eating when the flesh demanded? No games to while the time?

He murmured, "Norath, you scare me more than my old enemies in Shinsan."

Searching as if these had been true men, likely to conceal damning evidence, he nearly overlooked the paper. He looked for loose boards and secret compartments till by chance he noted the tattered, wadded scrap behind the cheeses, perhaps thrown there before the food was laid in.

A long, lazy hand, full of arrogance, declared, "Milady: The appearance of the bearer will assure you of the completion of my half of our agreement. Norath." The ink had faded to sepia

Varthlokkur eased toward the door, an unhappy man. This scrap could hang. Should he pass it to the King? The assassins had failed, after all.

The message was less important for content than for the language in which it was written. Itaskian.

Ragnarson found himself passing through Vorgreberg's west gate. His mount seemed to be taking him to Lieneke Lane without conscious guidance.

"Sire?" the voice called a second time, breaking his self-enchantment, startling him with its concern. "Are you all right?" Sir Gjerdrum and Aral Dantice were staring at him.

"Just daydreaming." He flashed a grin. "Tell Slugbait I got the Panthers match set back. Put your money on the Guards. We're going to win."

Dantice responded with a dubious scowl.

"Well, don't bet the deed to the old family farm. I'm

headed out Lieneke Lane. Come from there?"

Gjerdrum nodded. He looked grim.

"Something wrong, Gjerdrum? Trouble?"

"No. It's personal. Going to tell Gwenie it's over. Can't think how to say it. Julie and me . . . there might be a wedding."

"Congratulations. I guess. Seen Mist, Aral? She pull out yet?"

"She's gone." Dantice fumbled inside his shirt. "Left you a letter." He was not a happy man.

Ragnarson accepted the envelope, opened it after leaving the younger men.

Mist merely repeated her apologies, saying he had been a friend good and true throughout her exile. As a gesture, she would leave her children with him. He grinned. Crafty witch. They would be less hostages to fortune here. She wasn't making a gesture. She was shielding them from the politics of the Dread Empire.

He'd have to hand them over to his daughter-in-law. How would Kris take that? Two more mouths, two more little bodies to cuddle and mend, another two hearts to keep unbroken. . . . "She's going to raise merry hell."

Lieneke Lane was quiet. His own house seemed silent, moody, withdrawn. Down the lane, Mist's place already looked deserted.

Kristen stepped out as he dismounted. She placed hands on hips, glared. "Just what makes you think I'm going to take care of Mist's brats too? What is this? An orphanage?"

"What?" He threw up his hands in faked bewilderment.

"Don't try to con me . . ."

Bragi's face drooped into an idiot grin. Sherilee was leaning out an upstairs window. Kristen shrugged, defeated by chemistry.

The old doorman collected Ragnarson's horse. Bragi gave Kristen a hasty peck on the forehead, charged upstairs. Sherilee squealed when he swept her into his arms.

Varthlokkur cradled his daughter with his right forearm. His left hand lay folded within his wife's fingers. He stared out the window. "Looks like rain tomorrow."

"What's the matter?" Nepanthe asked.

"Trouble."

"Always trouble. Ours?"

"The King's. Looks like Inger bought those assassins."

"Inger? She's so nice. I don't believe it."

"It wouldn't be a historical precedent. I think Bragi knows, too. He's trying to lie to himself. Like maybe if he ignores it long enough, Inger will come to her senses."

"Talk to him."

"Too much like telling a man his wife is cheating. He don't want to hear it. Puts him in a vise. He has to do something. Like as not, he takes a whack at you instead of the woman." He didn't want the King taking a poke his way. He might say something Nepanthe shouldn't hear.

How much did Bragi know about the east? And Mist? She would soon be intimate with the situation.

"Talk to Prataxis. Bragi will put up with anything from him."

"That might do it." But he was thinking Michael Trebilcock, not Derel Prataxis. Michael would *do* something.

The sun plunged into the clouds of the west. Derel and Baron Hardle reined in before the King's suburban home. They made a mixed pair, those two, yet were as alike as pod-mate peas today. Two more sour, embittered faces could hardly be imagined. They did not speak as they stalked toward the house.

Kristen answered their knock. The pandemonium of a small herd of children echoed behind her. "Yes?" Her smile faded as she saw their grim faces. "What's happened?"

"Is His Majesty here?" Prataxis asked.

"Come in. I'll get him. Strangle a few kids if they bother you."

Prataxis watched her bustle upstairs. He muttered, "More complications. He couldn't have picked a worse time."

"Uhm." Hardle, too, had seen enough to guess what was going on. "Can't say as I blame him. A delectable morsel."

Prataxis snorted. He was a man perpetually baffled by the power woman exercised over others of his sex. He just could not comprehend how an otherwise sensible man could be knocked cuckoo by a skirt, though he had seen countless such devastations.

The more he thought, the more irate he became. He was in a positive frenzy when Ragnarson appeared. "Where the hell have you been?" he demanded. "We did everything but call out the Vorgrebergers."

"What's happened?" It had to be bad to make Prataxis stand on his hind legs and howl.

Prataxis retreated, awed by his own temerity. "It's too late now."

Sourly, the Baron added, "Too late for anything but the weeping."

"What are we talking about?"

"We needed you in the Thing. To stand witness for yourself. We couldn't find you, and couldn't argue for you because you never told us. . . ."

"To the point. What did those idiots do?"

"They passed a succession law," Prataxis said. "Seems they started on it when we locked ourselves up out here. It went through today. The Estates bought enough votes. . . ."

"Succession law? The Estates?" Red crept through the King's beard. Prataxis handed him a rolled copy. He did not read it immediately. Derel would not be here, in this mood, were its terms acceptable. "Where the hell were you? Why didn't you stop them?"

"We were here till today," the Baron reminded him. "Along with Sir Gjerdrum, Colonel Abaca, and everybody else who might have made a difference. Mundwiller couldn't beat them alone."

Ragnarson ripped the roll open, read, hurled it away. He sat on the stairsteps, folded his fists before his face, gnawed the knuckle of a thumb.

Kristen retrieved the copy. She scanned it, stiffened. It fell from her hand. She glared at the men, flung herself from the hallway.

Ragnarson muttered, "Fulk. With Inger Regent. That's not what I wanted. Definitely not what I wanted."

Derel refrained from saying I told you so. "That's why I scrambled so hard trying to find you. Never occurred to me to look here till Gjerdrum mentioned meeting you at the gate."

"All right. We blew it. They slipped one past us. How do we undo it?"

"Lawfully, we can't," Hardle said. "They made a good job of it."

"Laws can be unpassed, can't they?"

"We could change it if we muster the votes. What the Baron wants to say is, we can't."

"Why the hell not? Get all our people here and ram it through."

"We've been deserted. On this, not in general. There's a lot of relief about having everything settled. Some of our people don't want the question reopened. They want a defined succession."

"But. . . ."

"The future is enemy territory," Prataxis said. "Most people don't have your take-what-comes attitude. They want it scouted out."

"Damn! Hand me that thing, Derel. Maybe there's a hole in it somewhere."

Prataxis retrieved the document. "No loopholes, Sire. Some good men shaped it up."

He saw that. Fulk was his successor, with Inger Regent should the throne come vacant before Fulk achieved his majority. Which, without doubt, the Estates hoped fervently. Next came any other children Inger might bear, then Inger herself in a twistback counter to all tradition. Only then did the line leave Inger's control. It swung to Bragi's grandson, and from the younger Bragi to Ragnarson's sons. A complex document and, as Prataxis said, without loophole or leeway.

"Well. Damn my eyes. This'll learn me, won't it? Guess we have to live with it." Again he stared at the floor. After a time, "Thanks for coming round. I'll be along. Strategy session. Got to talk to Kristen first."

Derel and Baron Hardle bowed slightly, departed. Their faces were greyer than ever.

One day's victory had segued into another's defeat. The old ways were threatening a return.

Ragnarson continued reflecting on what that document meant beyond what it said. It constituted a quiet, gentlemanly declaration that the Estates had returned to the field.

It was a letter of marque for anyone who cared to take his head. From now on he had better be damned careful, damned quick on his feet.

Michael's face crossed his mind. He smiled. It was not a pleasant smile. It was wicked. "Kristen. Let's talk now."

Michael strode into Arsen Street, stopped. "What the hell?"

He had not visited Arsen Street since that infamous night of the coronation. In those days it had been the heart of the underworld, the city's vice center. It had had a more than shopworn look, and had been both dark and dangerous.

The buildings had received facelifts. Lamps illuminated the pavement. Armed watchmen stood at each corner. A lady of quality passed Trebilcock, unafraid of the night. "What the hell?"

The Fat Man's was as changed within as without. That screaming, ramshackle dive had gone elegant. The doorman wore livery, and was mannered. "Are you a member, sir?"

"A guest. Of Aral Dantice. Where's Gus?" The former bouncer/doorman had been seven feet tall, nearly as wide, and as mean as his place of employment.

This doorman was offended. "The gentleman hasn't been here for some time."

"The gentleman hasn't. There've been some changes."

"Indeed. If you'll follow me. Mr. Dantice has his own booth."

Some changes, Michael thought. A neighborhood had clawed its way up to respectability and he hadn't known. He did not like that. He wanted to know what was happening everywhere, all the time.

Maybe he was too outward-directed, paying too much attention to the provinces and Kavelin's neighbors. Vorgreberg was, after all, the kingdom's heart.

Aral was waiting. "You look puzzled, Michael."

"It's changed."

"Not as much as you think. We're just trying to reach a class with more money."

"We?"

"Me and the Fat Man. We're the bosses down here. Though he's out front."

"You?"

"I sort of decided to diversify when my Dad died."

"I knew you were into smuggling, but . . . Hell, all traders are smugglers."

Aral laughed softly. "Don't look so shocked, Michael."

"It's not shock. It's old-fashioned surprise. I'm supposed to know things. I didn't know about this."

"Why should you? You're supposed to watch the King's enemies. He doesn't have any down here."

A waiter appeared. He offered Aral a bottle of wine. Dantice sniffed, nodded. The waiter went for glasses. Real glasses, not the hardy stoneware taverns used to lessen breakage. Aral awaited Michael's reaction. Trebilcock had been raised in genteel circumstances.

Michael ignored him. He compared customer faces to the file in his mind. Known hoodlums? A few. Merchants. Minor nobility. . . .

Aral grumbled, "Hang up your hat. Relax."

"In a minute."

"What is it?"

"I need your help."

"I'll do what I can. You know that. What is it? Business or personal?"

"Business. I need to know what's going on in Throyes and Al Rhemish. I've lost my assets there."

Dantice nodded. He sipped his wine. "I see."

"I want to watch Hsung close. He'll be trickier than ever. And Norath. . . ."

"Norath?"

Michael had not told Aral about his visit to Al Rhemish. He did so now. "Somehow, he got out of Palmisano alive. He's back in business. In Al Rhemish. Running Megelin."

"Another one?" Dantice looked worried. "Mike, how many of them got away? Are they all out there laughing at us?"

"What do you mean?"

"I don't know for sure. Some hints out of the north Basin. Strange doings. Sound like the Old Meddler."

"Couldn't be. The King killed him. Norath is the problem. I need information from Al Rhemish. Please."

"I'll do what I can. It won't be easy. The desert run is

dangerous. Now I know why. Come on. Let's enjoy."

They strove valiantly, but the evening failed. They were not the men of years before. Michael had too much on his mind. Dantice kept letting a lost love's face get in his way.

Josiah Gales shivered continuously, though the apartment was warm enough. He felt the cold breath of Death.

"You think he suspects?" Inger asked.

"No, My Lady. I think he *knows.* I think he has for some time. I think the wizard does too. And Trebilcock has a strong suspicion."

Inger shivered too. "Damn," she said softly. "We'd better be careful."

"Damned careful. It could be worth our heads. I have a feeling he's giving me the rope to hang myself now."

"Back off. Stay away from everything. Be the ideal soldier."

"I suggest we all take that approach. My Lady, not even you are untouchable."

"Josiah?"

"Your husband is slow to anger, but he's a hard man. He killed his best friend. You're not immune. Not if he decides it's in Kavelin's interest."

Gently, almost unconsciously, Inger made a sign against the evil eye. "Josiah, I think you're right. It's a filthy game we're playing. Why did I let them push me into it?"

Gales shrugged.

"Back to your quarters. Pass the word. No operations without my personal approval. Don't approach me unless it's an emergency."

Gales bowed, slipped out of the apartment.

Only Radeachar noted his going. The Unborn could not put a face to him. Gales was shielded from its probings.

16

Year 1016 AFE;
A Plea from the East

RAGNARSON DISMOUNTED OUTSIDE Mist's home in Lieneke Lane, greeted the guard seated on the steps. The man's head popped up off his chest. He snapped to attention. "Good morning, Sire."

"Are you keeping the vandals and thieves out?"

The soldier's face reddened. "It won't happen again, Sire."

"I know."

"The wizard arrived a half hour ago, Sire."

"Uhm. Upstairs?"

"I suppose. Want me to take your horse, Sire?"

"Just loosen his cinch. Take him over to the park." Ragnarson entered the house. "Varthlokkur?"

"In the cellar. Be right up." Seconds later he came from the kitchen. "I found two portals besides the obvious one on the third floor."

"Leave the one up top. She'll want to visit her kids."

"I did. I shut the others down. Radeachar is out looking for more."

"What about Maisak?"

"Took care of it last night. Found four."

"Think she was planning something?"

The wizard shrugged. "I'd guess they were for communication while she was getting her plot together. Not that she wouldn't use them later if they were still there."

"How's the baby?"

"Perfect. Nepanthe is up and around, too. We decided to call her Smyrena."

"That's an unusual name."

"It was my mother's. Nepanthe's idea."

"What about Ethrian? Anything?" Ragnarson stopped, startled by the wizard's sudden dark, dangerous look.

"I said let sleeping dogs lie. I've finally gotten Nepanthe off the subject."

Ragnarson decided to forget it. "I've got one problem you could help with. Mist's kids. Kristen has work enough with mine."

"Nepanthe mentioned them this morning. They're her brother's children. We'll take them as soon as she can handle them." He didn't sound enthusiastic.

"All right. What are your plans now?"

"There's Norath. And the treachery here. How I long for the peace of Fangdred."

"So go. Leave it to Michael. Once we cleanse the palace, Norath becomes moot. His interest should have ended when he delivered his assassins."

"I can give Michael a few hints. What about Hammad al Nakir?"

"Michael and I can handle that. My big worry is still Shinsan."

"Uhm. I'm done. Nothing to do but wait for Radeachar."

"Had breakfast? Come on over to Kristen's."

"Thanks. No. I'll get back to Nepanthe."

"See you later, then."

Varthlokkur nodded curtly, a gesture of dismissal. Irked, Ragnarson stamped outside. The guard exploded off the steps, raced to retrieve his king's horse. Bragi growled and grumbled and cursed till he was in the saddle.

Kristen waved from her porch. He turned in. "How're you this morning?"

"So-so. Weren't you going to stop?"

"Hadn't made up my mind."

"Somebody here you might want to see." She gave him a saucy smile.

"She's still here?"

"Sure."

"Isn't that a little . . . ?"

"I'm going to complain? She helps with the kids, helps with the house, and lends me a crying shoulder. I need one lately."

"I've got Derel and the Baron working on the succession thing, but don't get your hopes up. It doesn't look good. Think you could give the old man breakfast?"

"In bed?"

"I'm not in the mood."

"Figured you for a good mood. Look out there. Is that a morning for grouchy?"

Bragi admitted that it was a beautiful day. A change. It had rained most of yesterday.

"Sausage and eggs do you?"

"With fresh bread, butter, and honey on the side? You've got a deal."

"I'll start cooking."

"Cooking? What do I pay servants for?"

"I like to. I want to. This may not last. I have to keep in practice."

"Humph. I'd think you'd enjoy it while you can."

"Come on. You can break the eggs."

Sherilee found them in the kitchen. "I've got them playing out back, Kris. Bunch of savages." She looked at Bragi with a twinkling question in her eye.

"Morning," he said.

"He's doing his cranky bear imitation this morning," Kristen explained.

"I know a cure for that."

"What's happening to young people today?" Bragi demanded. "Women weren't this bold when I was your age."

"They probably were," Kristen said. "You probably were shy."

"Come on. . . ."

"Want to see the kids?" Sherilee asked. "I'll call them."

"Later. We have things to talk about."

"Give me those eggs," Kristen snapped. "Playtime after you eat."

Ragnarson returned to the palace feeling sated and self-satisfied. What a morning! What a man. Who'd believe he had that much left?

Gales had the duty. "Ho! Majesty. Your man Trebilcock is looking for you. Yeah. Trebilcock."

"Where is he?"

"His offices. Yeah. His offices."

Ragnarson scowled at the Itaskian. His response was gratifyingly nervous. He had been the messenger between palace and Thing while the Estates were pushing their succession law. Josiah Gales was one semi-plausible excuse short of the mercies of Trebilcock's questioners. He knew he was gone if he strayed far from the Queen's protection.

Ragnarson encountered Dahl Haas a minute later. Haas relayed the same message. "Dahl, what do you think of Sergeant Gales?"

"Crude, Sire. But a first-class field soldier."

"Not what I was wondering. More like how deep do you think his treachery runs?"

"Sire?"

"Never mind. Have the kitchen send up lunch. And a quart of apple juice. I'm dying of thirst."

"Yes, Sire. Will you need me there?"

"Not today." Bragi strode down the hall. After a half-dozen paces he halted, looked back. Something wrong with Dahl. . . . because he wasn't allowed into the inner councils? That seemed to upset him. Why? He was not that senior. Maybe it was time he gave Dahl something more. He was a man now, not just the child of an old follower. And King's adjutant *was* supposed to lead to better things.

"Mention it to Michael," he muttered. "We could send him to back-check Inger's people."

Michael was conferring with aides when Bragi arrived. He dismissed them immediately. "You look like hell," Ragnarson said. "What have you been up to?"

"Two days drunk. Aral talked me into visiting some of our old haunts the other night. I'm not as young as I used to be."

"None of us are."

"Did you know he's a big wheel in the underworld?"

"Smuggling. The difference between trader and smuggler is a matter of viewpoint."

"Not just smuggling. The whole spectrum. People on Arsen Street call him sir. People who wouldn't do that for us."

"Interesting."

"Certainly worth remembering."

"Don't let friendship put you in a compromising position."

"No problem. Aral's more concerned about that than we

are. He's really got his life divided into compartments."

"People say you want to see me."

"Yeah. Got an interesting report out of Sebil el Selib."

"So? Go ahead."

"El Murid has abdicated. Yasmid has taken over. The Throyes thing did him in. Yasmid came in with a roar. Big purge. Military reorganization. Stepped-up attacks against the Royalists. She reformed the Invincibles, disbanded the Harish, and started a cult of her own called Al Dawa. Means The Call. As in call to arms, Derel says. He says she's ignited a fundamentalist resurgence."

"That sounds like Derel. I thought they'd had that pounded out of them."

"A new generation. You can sell the same old snake oil forever if you change the label once in a while. My contact says Al Dawa will eventually replace the Invincibles."

"What'll it mean to us?"

"You've got a bond with Yasmid. Stronger than that with Megelin, now Norath is in Al Rhemish. Derel and I think it should be nurtured."

Ragnarson thought a moment. "All right. Send her everything we know about Norath, Megelin, and Throyes. Any luck getting somebody back into Throyes?"

"Aral will cover it. Some of my sources survived the riots, but I want to husband them. They could get more important."

"Sleepers?"

"Yeah. I don't want to waste them. Hammad al Nakir is our main interest now anyway. Right? Shinsan should be no trouble till they settle accounts with Matayanga."

"You're doing better, Michael. I'm more comfortable with you this way. Try to relay that package through Habibullah. He's a friend of Kavelin, more or less."

"Sure. Sire?"

"What?"

"Never mind."

"What is it?"

"Nothing. Forget it."

The match with the Panthers had been on Ragnarson's mind since he'd conned the judges into a postponement. "What're they saying about the Guards-Panthers match?"

Trebilcock was baffled by the switch. "People are mad about the delay."

"How about the betting?"

"What betting? Nobody will go Guards. Not unless you give them three goals."

"How about to win?"

Michael looked more baffled. "Name your odds. You could get ten to one anywhere."

"How come?"

"The word is, Charygin Hall took steps. I hear they've paid off some of your players."

Bragi grinned. "Aral into gambling?"

"It looked like it."

"Here's what I want. I'll have Derel release a hundred thousand from the treasury. Sneak it to Aral. Have him pass it to his people and get all the bets he can against us. Have him hold the bets. None of this word of honor I'll pay if I lose. I want him to go after the high rollers in the Estates and get every crown he can."

"Are you sure? Our finances are so bad . . . the whole Thing would turn on you. That's betting the longest shot. . . ."

"If he needs more to cover all the bets, let me know. I'll even make loans if I have to."

"Why? Why risk everything on a ball game?"

"We're going to win, Michael. The take will retire a few debts. We owe almost two hundred thousand nobles. If we average five to one return on a hundred thousand crowns, less say five percent to Aral as commission, we'd retire a quarter of it. If we drive it higher, and get the barons to bet big, we can strip them of a lot of their wealth. And wealth is power."

"In other words, you're going to backstab them for what they pulled when we weren't looking."

"There. You're starting to see it. Another debt we're going to pay."

"How can you be so sure you'll win? The experts say you'll be lucky to score two goals. The Panthers are taking this one like it's the match of the century."

"I'll win because I have to."

"Suppose word gets out and the odds plunge?"

"That's what Aral gets his commission for. If we win. The more we win, the more he makes. Right?"

Michael smiled. "I like it. Basically. I'll work on it. Though it hardly seems meet work for a secret service."

Ragnarson scribbled a note. "Give this to Derel. Your first hundred thousand. And authorization to draw more. Tell Aral to keep his pigeons from talking to each other. I want to hit those bastards *hard*."

He was angry. He hoped some deep-seated, unrealized rage was not compelling him to undertake totally foolish risks. There was no guarantee his plan for winning was not subject to prior detection.

"One more thing, Michael. Find out who was paid off."

"You'd better believe. I'm riding this one with you."

Prataxis read the note a fourth time. "He's out of his mind."

"I want to talk about that," Michael said. Derel gave him a hard look. "Really. He's getting weird. Playing too many long shots."

Prataxis leaned back in his chair, folded spidery fingers under his chin. "Tell me about it."

"Look. The thing with Mist. We lucked out."

"He's a lucky man."

"He's been a lucky man. Luck turns. Then there's this girl. He's making no secret of her. She's staying at his country house."

"An ancient and revered custom."

"I know. I'm a little prudish. But so are these Kaveliners. They won't care that he's got a leman. Who doesn't that can afford one? What'll shock them is, he's keeping her there where his kids can see it. That's a big deal here. We're from farther west. We don't see it that way. But. . . ."

"Enough. I agree. I've dropped a few hints. He doesn't listen anymore."

"Now there's this. Betting the whole treasury on a ball game. It's plain crazy. There's no way he can win. It's like he's trying to destroy himself."

"He's cagey. Some ways, he has fewer scruples than a Tervola. Captures is for cheaters. My guess is, he'll outcheat the Panthers."

"Oh, he'll win on the field. I'm talking about off it. We can't keep this quiet. Suppose he does fleece the Estates? They're going to smile about it? What'll people say about him risking public moneys?"

"So don't do it."

"You kidding?"

"Actually, yes. I do hope to get out of Kavelin with a whole skin once my work is done."

"So what do I do?"

"I can't help you." Prataxis pursed his lips thoughtfully. "You're right. He's getting strange. We have to rein him in. We have to convince him, first, that he's not favored of the gods, and, second, that he can't keep laughing in the face of fate. What's happening is, he's got a touch of that old royal megalomania. Since he wasn't raised to it, it's taking some odd twists."

"*Can* we educate him? He hasn't learned from his lapse with the succession."

"Uhm." Prataxis rose. "Let's get you that money."

"That's it? Go ahead?"

"What can we do?" As they neared the doorway, Prataxis mused, "His biggest error may be the way he's handling his wife." He looked Trebilcock directly in the eye.

"You're onto that too, eh?"

"It's pretty obvious. It's just as obvious that he knows. And he's doing nothing. Nothing."

"Think somebody should act for him?"

"That would be between a man and his conscience. Maybe. If the somebody could be sufficiently circumspect. But not right away. Let it ride a while."

Michael nodded. He respected Prataxis's political sense. Timing was everything.

Since returning from Al Rhemish he had been trying to come up with a way to carve out this cancer without getting carved himself. Maybe Varthlokkur would help. . . .

Bragi was having dinner when Dahl intruded, apologizing profusely. He bore a note. Bragi read it, frowned.

"What is it?" Inger asked.

"Mist is back. Wants to see me. All right. Bring her up, Dahl." The woman arrived a few minutes later. She looked older by a decade. "Been rough?" Bragi asked.

She nodded. "Could you spare a meal for a tired old woman?"

Inger gestured. A maid departed. Bragi eyed Mist uncertainly. He'd planned on a heart-to-heart with Inger. Mist's appearance had killed the chance. Something always got in the way.

Or was he just finding excuses?

Mist sagged into a chair uninvited. "I'm exhausted."

"You asked for it." Ragnarson frowned. This was out of character. What was she up to? "Excuse me if I'm blunt. What're you doing here?"

"Looking for help. Again."

"I thought you got what you wanted."

"It's that mess in the east, Bragi. I didn't know how bad it was till I got a closer look. Now I know why the Tervola are spooked. It could mean the end of the world."

"Come on!" Inger said. "That's too much to swallow."

"You haven't seen it. I have."

"Start at the beginning," Ragnarson suggested. "All I know is what you've already told me. All Varthlokkur will do is threaten me about shooting my mouth off to Nepanthe."

So Mist told a tale about her predecessor, Lord Kuo, having had a presentiment about the great desert east of Shinsan. He had sent men to investigate. They had wakened some force terrible and ancient, that acted through a creature who called himself the Deliverer.

"Armies of dead men?" Ragnarson murmured in horror. "It raises up the dead against the living?"

That was the heart of it. The force behind the Deliverer empowered him to raise the recently dead to lead in battle. Those fighting him had to do more than battle: they had to keep their own fallen from coming under the Deliverer's sway and had to burn his casualties too, lest they be reanimated again and again. To Bragi it sounded like a struggle that could not be won by the living. A parable of the inexorability of death.

"It's a Trolledyngjan draug tale come true," he said. "Terrible. But why do you come to me?"

"Because when he's done with the empire the Deliverer will come for you."

"I don't understand," Inger said. "I missed something. You two know what you're talking about. . . ."

Bragi said, "Mist claims this warlord of the dead is Ethrian. Mocker's missing son. Nepanthe's son."

Mist said, "And you killed his father, Bragi. The real power that makes the Deliverer run is his obsession with revenge. First the empire, then you. Then the rest of the world."

"I think I understand why Varthlokkur doesn't want Nepanthe to find out. If what you say is true."

"It's true. Something in the east saved Ethrian from the Pracchia, made him over, and gave him immense power. I think it lost control. I saw him, Bragi. There is no describing him in words. He's like a natural force gone made. And if he isn't stopped it'll be the end of the world."

Inger croaked something. Bragi groaned. "I believe it. I don't want to, but I do. Look at Mist. She's scared silly. A princess of the Dread Empire terrified."

Mist admitted it. "You're right. It's got me so scared I can't think."

"And Varthlokkur knows all this."

"Probably. There is little that escapes his notice."

"Uhm. He knows. Maybe even more than you. But he wants to stick his head in the sand because Nepanthe might be upset. I can't put up with that. Let's go see him."

They found Varthlokkur in the castle library, reading an ancient book he closed too quickly when he noted Bragi's approach. He looked dismayed when he noticed Mist. "What is it? What do you want?" His voice threatened to squeak.

"I think you know. Tell him, Mist."

Mist repeated her story. The wizard's expression grew more and more distressed, then gradually hardened. Before she finished, he interrupted. "The answer is no. Find another way. I've finally gotten Nepanthe satisfied that her son is dead. As he is, in his way. Leave him in the grave."

"How about sending the Unborn?" Bragi asked.

"No. Aren't you listening? I won't help. Neither will Nepanthe. You deal with it yourself, woman. Bragi, I've warned you. You tell Nepanthe about this. . . ."

"I don't plan to. You're going to do it."

"You're not thinking rationally," Mist said. "What if I can't stop it? And the Council tells me there's a good chance I can't with the resources available. Then what? Where do you go to hide when the bulwark of Shinsan is gone? The Deliverer will find you in the Dragon's Teeth themselves."

Varthlokkur spat, shocking Ragnarson. "I'm going to protect my wife. . . ."

"I think that's what she's asking you to do," Bragi said.

"My way. Ragnarson, recall what the Thing did. With that law in place you're a dead man if you don't have me."

"Damned stubborn ass. What the hell is it with you? You *want* trouble with me? You know I don't stand still when people try to twist my arm."

"You'd better."

"I got along without you before I met you. I can live without you now." Ragnarson was getting heated. The wizard had been from the beginning.

"Stay away from my wife. Mist, the Deliverer is your damned problem. Ethrian is dead. And I'm going to keep it that way."

Mist smashed a fist into a stack of bookshelves so hard a dozen volumes tumbled to the floor. "You're not only being bullheaded, you're being stupid. Don't you understand? He won't stop with Shinsan."

Bragi took her arm. "Come on. We're wasting our time. He's gone goofy." He headed for the door. Over his shoulder, he said, "I'll remember this."

For a moment it almost seemed Varthlokkur would stick out his tongue.

Outside, Mist asked, "What now? There's not much hope without him."

"You and me, I guess. Maybe I can do something to reach the boy inside this Deliverer. Come on. I'll have to explain to Gjerdrum and Derel so they can cover my ass while I'm gone."

Mist's fright had lessened. She looked at him appraisingly. "In more ways than one, no doubt."

"Eh?"

"Why do I have a feeling my children are sudden hostages, just in case this is a scheme to separate you from your base of safety?"

"Because you're a practical woman familiar with the way politics work. You're my friend, but what does that have to do with the course of kingdoms and empires?"

"It could be a nicer world."

"Derel and I have been trying. Nobody wants one. Unless they are in charge."

"Josiah, I asked you to lay low. You'll get us all hung, coming here."

"My Lady, this was too important to ignore." He told her of the confrontation in the library. "So now he's going off to Shinsan to confront this Deliverer personally. They're with Prataxis now. You needed to know."

"Maybe. Probably. Thank you. Now get back to your post before you're missed."

Gales bowed slightly, departed. He could not conceal his injured feelings.

Inger was scared. This looked like a gods-given opportunity. . . . It was too soon after the victory in the Thing. That wound had not scabbed yet.

She paced, trying to balance risk against gain. "Damn it! All right! You can't win if you don't play." She seized a cloak, pulled it tight around her, concealed her hair and face inside its hood. She slipped out unnoticed by her servants, hurried toward Nepanthe's apartment.

Varthlokkur eased into his quarters. He lighted a candle, sat, tried to continue his research. The calligraphy kept slipping out of focus. It had been an hour since the scene with Bragi and Mist. He remained shaky, and a little embarrassed, a little ashamed. And a whole lot torn. Part of him insisted they had been right. That he was being foolishly selfish.

A shadow fell across his lap. "Nepanthe! How come you're out of bed?" Fear hit hard. She had dressed herself for travel. She had the baby bundled. "Oh, no," he murmured. "Why?"

"You lied to me, Varth. Ethrian is alive. He's at a place called Lioantung, in Shinsan. And something has been done to hurt him. Mist was here today about him. I'm going with her when she goes back."

She had her stubborn face on. The wizard knew there would be no dissuading her.

"Did they tell you what your son is now?"

"Did who tell me? What?"

"Ragnarson and that Shinsaner witch."

"I haven't seen either of them. What have they got to do with it?" Anger fed anger. "You can come or stay as you please. But don't try stopping me."

"All right! We'll go!" Varthlokkur shouted. There was an hysterical edge to his voice. "Bragi, you cut your own damned throat. I'll sit back and laugh when the wolves pull you down."

Mist's shoulders slumped. Her beauty seemed to have deserted her. "It seemed the best hope, confronting him with his mother. He's still a child. The shock of having her see him the way he is. . . . I thought it might bring him out of it."

Ragnarson grunted. He ran a whetstone along the edge of his sword. "Maybe. And maybe if he's got the big hate on for me I can do it my own way. What happens if I kill him? Will he rise up again, too?"

"I don't know." She tinkered with the portal she was preparing. "Five minutes."

Ragnarson grunted again. Outwardly, he was calm, a soldier about to enter battle for the thousandth time. Inside, he was in turmoil. Self-doubt raged. He was not sure he could do the necessary if the Deliverer could not be shocked out of his madness. Guilt about having slain the father still nagged him. Could he strike the son? Especially when the threat was less immediate and apparent?

Mist still had some convincing to do.

"Look."

He looked. He saw Varthlokkur and Nepanthe approaching. The woman was determined. Varthlokkur moved jerkily, like a marionette, lost within himself, face angry stone.

Nepanthe said, "We're going with you." The wizard said nothing at all. To him they did not exist.

"Just in time," Mist replied. "The gateway will open in a minute."

Bragi tried cracking a joke. Mist looked at him oddly. Nepanthe and Varthlokkur kept their eyes fixed on the portal. Bragi tried again. He could not get a smile. Not even from himself. "The hell with you all, then."

Nepanthe twitched. Varthlokkur did not respond that much.

"Time," Mist said. "I'll go first. You second, Nepanthe. Then Bragi and Varthlokkur and *that*." The Unborn had drifted into the room, its infant face alert and diabolic. Mist stepped forward and disappeared.

Ragnarson paced. *Was* this some grand trap meant to eliminate himself and Varthlokkur, Shinsan's dearest foes?

Nepanthe tightened her grip on Smyrena and stepped into the portal. Fighting butterflies, Bragi pocketed his whetstone, raised his sword, and stepped up to the mark. I'll charge through, he thought. They won't expect that.

He jumped.

Mist and a single Tervola waited on the far side. Ragnarson flew across the room, tripped over rubble, plunged headlong. His sword slipped out of his hand. He scrambled after it, conscious of stares, feeling sheepish. "Better safe than sorry."

Mist smiled and shook her head. The Tervola's face was concealed behind his mask, but his stance betrayed patronizing amusement.

Varthlokkur came through the gateway. He looked around intently but said nothing. He joined Nepanthe. The Unborn popped through seconds behind him.

The Tervola nearly jumped out of his boots. Bragi chuckled. Mist said, "Easy now. It's all right." The Tervola had his fingers up twisting the initial gestures of a spell. "Take us to Lord Ssu-ma."

Bragi walked through the city in a state approaching shock. Lioantung, Mist called it. Dead Lioantung, he thought. Never had he seen such destruction. Fire had gutted everything. In some places brick and stone had burned, or melted like candle wax. The remains were strewn as if by an earthquake. Bones and fragments of corrupt flesh were thoroughly mixed with the rubble. The stench was overwhelming. Twice their guide used a minor spell to destroy particularly noxious clouds of flies.

"About time somebody used the Power for something practical," Bragi joked. Mist looked at him askance. He muttered, "Gods, this place is depressing. What the hell happened?"

"Ethrian happened, that's what. Varthlokkur. Do you believe me now?"

The wizard ignored Mist.

"What's that?" Bragi asked, indicating a pillar of smoke to the south.

"The legions burning their dead so Ethrian can't use them against us. Come on. We have to hurry."

The meeting with Eastern Army's staff was exactly what Ragnarson expected. The Tervola nearly exploded when they learned who he was. Only the calming presence of the army commander, a Lord Ssu-ma Shih-ka'i, kept their fury leashed.

Bragi responded positively to Shih-ka'i. The man didn't belong with the usual run of Tervola. Short and wide where they were lean and tall, he had a mischievous sense of humor. His mask represented an enraged boar. Mist said he sprang from peasant pig farmer stock. "Tell him he looks like an honest soldier," Bragi told Mist.

She translated. Shih-ka'i responded. Mist said, "He says you'd find him more stubborn than Lord Ko Feng." The woman and army commander engaged in a long exchange which betrayed occasional flashes of heat. Bragi guessed Shih-ka'i was dubious about her plan to bring Ethrian face to face with his mother. Mist apparently convinced him. Shih-ka'i led them back into the tortured streets.

Bragi watched Nepanthe closely. She drifted through the ruins with gaze firmly fixed, her face pallid. But near Lioantung's north gate she got the shakes. She paused to retch into the gutter. When Varthlokkur tried to comfort her, she waved him off. "I can stand it. I always could. I'm a real grown up person."

Rebuked, the wizard resumed his air of aloofness. His inner turmoil was reflected only in the agitation of the Unborn, which bobbed and flitted like a moth with indigestion.

Lioantung was enough to gag a maggot, Bragi reflected. "Mist, this should be frozen in time. Made a memorial. Bring every would-be warlord in here and make him live with it for a week."

Mist answered with a weak smile. "It wouldn't do any good."

"Probably not. Human nature."

Shih-ka'i took a white flag from a soldier and headed out the gate. He set a brisk pace. Bragi hurried to stay close, so as not to seem less determined. These dread creatures in black had to be shown he was fearless. He laughed at himself. Human nature.

Ahead, an emaciated creature in rags rose atop a hummock, ran his hand through his hair. A woman in white, who seemed fuzzy around the edges, helped him stand. He gestured. A panther, a bear, and a forest buffalo quickly joined him, assuming guardian stances. Mist and Shih-ka'i exchanged a few words. Mist told Nepanthe, "There he is."

That derelict is my godson? Bragi thought. That's the monster who wasted Shinsan's eastern provinces?

The boy looked ghastly, looked almost as dead as the corpses which supposedly fought for him.

Shih-ka'i halted. Bragi stopped beside him. Mist and the wizard stopped too. Nepanthe never slowed.

"Ethrian?" she said. "Look. See? This is your sister. Her name is Smyrena."

Bragi almost exploded from tension laughter. The incongruity of it! And yet, how better to shock Ethrian back to reality?

Torment filled the boy's eyes. He started blubbering. "Mama. I thought they killed you. I thought they killed you."

Nepanthe held the baby in one arm, put the other around her son. "It's all right. It's over now, Ethrian. It's all right. You can come home."

The air was still, but . . . something was wrong, Bragi

thought. The woman in white . . . her clothing fluttered as if
stirred by a rising wind.

Suddenly, the beasts rose and loped away. Ragnarson
sighed. He hadn't relished facing them.

Mother and son started toward the city.

Ethrian hurled his mother aside. A dark nimbus formed
around him. The air crackled. Shih-ka'i bellowed.
Varthlokkur caught Nepanthe before she fell. Ragnarson
drew his sword, crouched, growled like a cornered beast.

Nepanthe shrieked at Ethrian. The Tervola tackled the
boy, clamped fingers round his throat. From the corner of
his eye Bragi saw movement on Lioantung's wall. He
whirled, saw a long shaft arcing across the sky. Timing! he
thought. His sword hammered the air above Shih-ka'i.

The Tervola bounced to his feet as Bragi pulled the
broken spear from the earth. He said something which must
have been a thank you, turned to the boy.

It all became confused, Bragi couldn't tell what was real
and what was illusion: The woman in white apparently
didn't exist in the flesh. Something equally fleshless apparently possessed the boy. Mist and Shih-ka'i did a lot of
yelling at one another. Ethrian kept trying to shout and
Shih-ka'i kept stopping him. The woman in white kept
helping her partner's enemies. At one point Varthlokkur
spoke at length in the language of Shinsan. Then a great
black cloud exploded from Ethrian, rushed upward in an
oily pillar. At its base a glistening dome formed. And Mist
said, "The devil in him has been forced out."

Baffled, Bragi stared up the pillar of black smoke-stuff. "I
don't understand what's going on."

"We've won. We've conquered the Deliverer."

"I still don't understand. You said that before."

"I didn't. . . ."

The earth trembled beneath them. Maybe he couldn't
understand everything, but he could sense that great forces
were contending. He would have to be content to take Mist's
word for the importance of the confrontation.

"It's over," she said. "Let's leave Nepanthe alone for a
while. It was a slim hope, but she lost. Hell." She started
toward the city. The Tervola was hurrying thither already,

probably to find out about the shaft that had come within a whisker of killing him. Bragi walked beside Mist. She tried to explain.

Varthlokkur hovered uncertainly between his wife and Mist, finally halted two hundred yards from the site of Ethrian's fall. Bragi glanced back once, saw the woman in white fade away, saw Nepanthe standing tall and brave beside the gleaming dome. "I hope it comes out for them," he said.

"Who knows? He's too damned stiff-necked for his own good. And she has to learn. . . ."

Nepanthe shrieked. Bragi whirled. The dome had vanished. Nepanthe was down on the earth, clutching a body, shouting for Varthlokkur. The wizard raced toward her.

"Good gods," Mist murmured. "He's alive. He survived. I don't believe it. He survived the exorcism."

"What exorcism?"

"The ghost woman did it while. . . ."

"She never made a sound."

Mist chuckled weakly. "You didn't hear her? Then your witch blood isn't as thick as you claim. Come on. They need to be alone for a while."

"You can be halfway decent when you want, you know that?"

"Is that a compliment? Don't kick it around where the Tervola can hear it. I'm a princess of Shinsan now."

"Speaking of which . . . well, I was supposed to get my caravan people turned loose. Remember? Hsung hasn't come through. Michael says he's gone back to his old ways. We were supposed to get along, I thought."

"Lord Hsung is something of a problem. I'll straighten him out. Or get rid of him." She indicated the wall over the gate. Lord Ssu-ma was up there. "A dead man under Ethrian's control shot that spear. I have to run back to the war with Matayanga. Stay close to Lord Ssu-ma. Some of his staff would love to stick a knife in you. I'll see you in a few hours."

But Ragnarson didn't see her again. She went on to be Princess of the Dread Empire, and he went back to being King of Kavelin. To being King of a Kingdom where the news of his falling out with Varthlokkur quickly spread. To being King of a troublesome witch's cauldron almost eager to boil.

He never did understand everything that had happened before the walls of Lioantung. But he did understand what it had cost him.

The threat he never fully appreciated had been removed at the price of Varthlokkur's support. He sometimes wondered if ever he would be sure he had gotten a bargain.

17

Year 1016 AFE;
The Great Championship Match

DANTICE LEANED BACK in a plush chair. His feet rested atop a table. To his right a mousey Siluro totalled columns of figures. Opposite him sat a man who weighed over three hundred pounds. Aral said, "The King can't cover any more bets."

The Fat Man rumbled, "I can draw another fifty thousand easy. Since you let it out he was betting heavy, Nordmen have been inventing money. They all want a piece of him. They'd be lined up outside if it wasn't for the weather." Thunder crashed. The building shook.

"Fifty thousand?"

"Minimum. Maybe a hundred."

"Tolliver. What're we carrying now?"

The clerk yanked a paper from the rat's nest atop the table. "King's money, a hundred ninety-six thousand, two hundred forty-three. All others, forty-three thousand, four hundred seventy-two."

"We get a commission on that?"

"Only on the King's money."

"How much belongs to Michael Trebilcock?"

"Forty thousand."

"Meaning three thousand and something is all anybody else would risk. Can you still get odds?"

"They're getting nervous. But still a good two to one."

Dantice tapped his front teeth with a fingernail. "What's the game look like?"

"The King's going to lose 'less there's a miracle. Charygin Hall reached eight Guards that I know about."

"Can we offset that?"

"Bribes? No way. This much money on the line,

Charygin Hall ain't taking no chances. They've got their boys locked up so tight even their mothers can't see them."

"Then if they lose, nobody will accuse anybody of anything."

"Be hard to make a case."

"How would you reach them?"

"Don't think I could."

"Uhm." Dantice dropped his feet, leaned elbows on the table. "But somebody goes in and out. They've got to eat."

"Top officers of the Hall. Nobody we can touch."

"None of them owe us?"

"Nope. I checked."

"Who does the cooking?"

"Got an idea?"

"A silly little notion. Been knocking it around a couple days. Suppose the night before the game they ate something that would give them the back door trots next morning. Could you keep your mind on Captures when you had the drizzling shits?"

The Fat Man cackled like a hen laying square eggs. "Oh! Beautiful. But it'd be obvious, wouldn't it? Forty guys don't come down with the runs sudden like."

"Okay. Not everybody. Ten or fifteen. One pot of bad food. Happens all the time, right?"

"They'll suspect."

"Naturally. They're crying foul about the last two games. So are the Guards. Handle it so nobody can prove anything later."

"You saying do it?"

"And cover the rest of those bets."

"What about the money?"

"Get some that's already bet and bet it again."

"Damn, are they going to howl."

"Ask me if I care. What can they do about it?"

The Fat Man grinned a lopsided, evil grin. He hated as only a former Nordmen victim could hate. "All right. Death to the Panthers, and all that crap."

"Good. Tolliver. What's headed for Throyes?"

* * *

Ten soldiers stood at attention in Michael Trebilcock's office. Trebilcock wore his seldom-seen uniform. It gleamed. Inside it, he was a cold, pale, angry devil. The soldiers did not know why they had been summoned. He paced up and down, delaying the telling, making the waiting an exquisite agony.

They were terrified. They had heard the stories about Captain Trebilcock's cruel way with those who displeased him. The rumble of the storm fed their dread.

Michael stepped back. "Gentlemen."

One said, "Sir?"

"I can't hear you, Corporal."

They knew this formula well. "Sir?" ten throats thundered.

"Good." For half a minute Trebilcock fumbled through the notes and gewgaws upon his desk. Then he stared each man in the eye. "The Palace Guard. An elite unit. Hand-picked men. Absolutely loyal to His Majesty. Its men ready to lay down their lives." He settled his rump on the desk's edge. A scrap of paper dangled from his fingers. "A plush posting. Easy duty. Pretty uniforms. Top pay. No field maneuvers. Envy of everybody in the Army. That right, Corporal Nikkles?"

"Yes sir."

"And at the opposite extreme might be the Briedenbacher Light. Border duty in Loncaric and the Galmiches. The regiment for bad boys. Right?"

"Yes sir."

"And then there's Cargo, where the bad boys send their bad boys. One light horse troop right in the heart of bandit country."

"Sir?"

"Nikkles, this piece of paper says you're going to become second stableboy with the Cargo troop."

"Sir?"

"Why? What did you do? Nothing. Yet. If you do, it's Cargo for the lot of you."

"But sir. . . ."

"Six days ago Corporal Kalsy Nikkles was paid a sum of forty crowns silver. Twenty-five crowns each were paid to Willem Fletcher and his brother Clete. Next day, twenty crowns each to Arman Sartella, Marles Bowyer . . . need I continue?"

Nikkles said, "Captain, I. . . ." and stopped.

"Not much you can say, is there? Here's the choice. Cargo or the palace. If you want to stay here, make sure the Guards beat the Panthers."

"Sir, we can't. The only reason I took the money is everybody said they're going to pound us anyway."

"If they do, you're gone."

Someone grumbled, "That's not fair."

"Fair doesn't interest me. Winning does. You do have a third option. Desertion. That puts you on my shit list. I'll catch up eventually." Trebilcock surveyed their ten grey faces. "Nikkles, have I made myself clear?"

"Yes sir."

"Good. We'll see you on the Captures field. Dismissed."

"Thelma, find Sergeant Gales."

"My Lady?"

"Are you deaf, woman? Move!" Inger marched to a window, stared into the storm lashing the city. The thunder had declined in violence, but the rain had not. She shivered.

"My Lady?"

She turned. Gales. How long had she been lost in the cruel storm? "Josiah. What's happening?"

"Happening? Nothing."

"Something's in the wind. Where's the King?"

"I hear he went out to the cemetery."

Lightning flashed. Thunder cracked. "That was close. On a day like this?"

"Sometimes he does strange things."

"I don't like it. Whenever he's going to start something, he goes and talks to his dead Queen."

"Maybe she tells him what he wants to hear."

"Don't joke. I'm scared. He could start on *us* now. Send somebody to watch him."

"In this weather?"

"In this weather, Josiah."

"As you wish." He was trying to remain detached. He didn't need any more heartaches.

"Let me know what you find out."

"Of course." He departed before she became any more unreasonable.

Inger received Gales' note five hours later. He had been unable to locate the King. Ragnarson had not gone to the cemetery. Her level of fright rose a notch. "At least the wizard is out of the way."

Ragnarson wore a heavy, waterproof cape. He leaned low over the neck of his horse. Nevertheless, he was soaked to the skin. He shivered in the chill wind. "Got to be a damned fool to be out here." His words vanished in the wind.

Lightning slammed down. Chunks of an old oak flung through the air. A shattered, steaming branch hit mud a dozen feet behind him. "That could've been me. How bad do I want to win this thing?"

He peered into the downpour ahead. Was that it? Yes. The boundary marker. "Git up," he growled. "Almost there."

His mare maintained her desolate pace. The footing in the woods was treacherous.

A quarter hour later he swung down, tied the mare, took a trenching tool from behind his saddle. He looked for a specific rock. "What a day. But it has to be today." The storm would wipe the evidence away.

The rock was flat, twenty inches across and six thick. He tried to move it, slipped on the slick leaves. He tumbled downhill, into six inches of galloping runoff. The rush tried to drag him away. Sputtering, he took his anger back to the rock.

Once he moved it, he dug. The earth flew into the water. The surge carried it away. Then the hole was big enough. He reinforced it with a few small stones, slid the flat rock back into place, considered his handiwork. "Guess it'll do."

That was one. Four to go. And already his hands hurt. He was going to have blisters on his blisters.

He and his mare were covered with mud before he finished. He was cold and miserable and ached in every muscle. He patted the mare's neck. "Let's go home, Lady." Headed south, she set a more ambitious pace.

* * *

"Never seen you this glum, Derel," Ragnarson said. "Got your stuff all packed?"

"Sire?"

"Ready to run for it if we lose today?"

"I'm more afraid of what they'll do if you win."

"Scream and yell and cuss like you ain't never heard."

"That too."

"Buck up. We'll come up smelling like roses."

"Better start dividing the money," Dantice told the Fat Man.

"We don't know who's going to win."

"Let's assume it'll go our way. Get the King's share ready. We'll have to move it out fast."

"Damned big temptation."

"No shit. Only it's *too* big. You could never disappear with that much."

"What if the King loses?"

"We have Tolliver start paying off. We run like hell before anybody finds out we bet money we don't have."

Michael did a few jumping jacks to loosen up. He told his mirror, "Rich or broke tonight, son. You fool."

Dahl Haas dismounted before the King's house in Lieneke Lane. Three carriages rolled to a stop behind him. He dashed to the door. "Ready, My Lady?"

"Yes. What's it all about?"

"Just a precaution. Come on, men. Get these chests loaded."

"Precaution against what, Dahl?"

"Against losing the Captures match. If the Guards go down, we're all done for."

"I don't understand. That sounds too melodramatic."

"I'll explain when we're rolling."

Sherilee herded the children onto the porch. Dahl could not conceal his disapproval.

"The road to where?" Kristen asked.

"Sedlmayr first. Out of the country if the news is bad."

* * *

Inger summoned her maid. "Thelma, what's going on? Has everybody gone crazy?"

"It's the Captures match, My Lady."

"Captures? People are acting like it's the end of the world."

"It might be for some, My Lady. The King is way out on a limb, they say."

"You mean all the mystery is over a damned game?"

"Yes, My Lady."

Inger dropped into a chair, laughing. "A Captures match! All because of a damned Captures match." The relief drove her to the edge of hysteria.

Thelma decided she was as mad as her husband.

Bragi called, "Slug. Over here. You too, Michael."

The whole team milled around outside the castle gate. Trebilcock kept a hard eye on his teammates. They responded satisfactorily.

"Sire?" Slugbait asked.

"Game plan."

They talked all the way out. At the field Ragnarson tried to give a rousing speech about this being the most critical game of all time, claiming much more than a championship was at stake.

"We going to put this off another day?" one of the judges hollered.

Ragnarson snarled, "Blow your damned horns." His gut knotted in fear. This was it. The big one. The do or die.

Bragi sprawled atop the moist leaves. There was barely enough daylight to see Michael's face. He panted, "Even my hair hurts."

"Oh," Michael groaned. "I'm a thousand years too old for this." He rolled onto his stomach, reached over, grabbed the King's hand. "We did it. We really did it. I don't believe it. I really don't believe it."

"Come on. Let's go. I want to see that much money all in one place. Ach!"

"What?"

"Cramp." He laughed. "Know something? Nothing hurts when you win."

"Yeah. Let's go before the wind shifts." He cackled.

"Wonder what happened to those guys, anyway?"

"Who cares? Lucky for us. Oh! Give me a hand. I won't walk right for a week."

The news reached Vorgreberg before the teams. Messengers had gone galloping after each score. With the sounding of the second Guards capture a rider had gone to Sir Gjerdrum and General Liakopulos. They scattered the King's Own and Vorgrebergers through the city, both to prevent disorder and the flight of losing bettors. The third Guards capture had elicited a great cry of rage and agony from the gallery. All the spread bettors had lost.

Despite manipulations on behalf of the Guards, the game had been in doubt till the last. Somebody stayed bought. The Guards tallied their final capture only seconds before the Panthers.

"Help me get on this critter," Ragnarson growled. "I'm too stiff to swing my leg."

"Who's going to help me?" Michael asked.

Most of their teammates were mounted already, whooping and bragging and galloping in circles. They shouted insults at friends slow to leave the field. They were eager to howl their triumph through the streets.

"Man," Slugbait bellowed, "they're going to go crazy in town."

"If they don't lynch us," Snakeman grumped.

Ragnarson kept suffering uncontrollable fits of laughter. They were pure, explosive relief. Never had he played a longer chance and won.

Wagons lined the inner court of the treasury. "Just empty those sacks on the floor in there," Ragnarson told the men unloading. It was the morning after the upset victory. Vorgreberg remained in shock.

"Sire?" Derel asked.

"Just do it. You'll see."

"Humph." Prataxis resumed counting.

Michael Trebilcock arrived. "Riots and fights all night," he reported. "Couple of cases of arson. Gjerdrum had to escort the Charygin Hall boys out of town. There was talk of a lynching. Liakopulos closed down the taverns at midnight.

Starting to settle down now. Oh! I've never seen the Nordmen so shocked. They can't believe they got taken. They're like zombies this morning."

Ragnarson's grin faded. "Now we get to the hard part, don't we?"

"Baron Khelra is going to make it."

"Make it? What happened?"

Prataxis spat, "I forgot to tell you. What's wrong with me?"

"He was the biggest loser," Michael said. "You took him for two hundred thousand. Aral got him for another hundred fifty. A hundred fifty on the pay-you-when-you-catch-me. He wouldn't come across. Somebody got into his place this morning and left him with a lot of broken bones."

"Aral did that to a Lord of the Realm?"

"Maybe Aral. Maybe somebody else who saw a chance to get in a free hit."

"Your friend from the woods," Prataxis suggested.

"Who?"

"Colonel Abaca. You see what's happening? The breakdown of standards has begun."

"Wasn't Khelra the one who started that business at the Victory Day wingding?"

"The same. He holds a lot of our notes. One of the richest men in Kavelin. Sire, if you want to keep the armistice with the Estates, you'd better get to the bottom of that assault fast. Bring his attackers to justice. No matter who they are."

"The hell I will. He earned every lump."

"Sire, the law belongs to all men. The baron isn't outside its protection. Neither Abaca nor Dantice are immune. And you're not above it. Your mission is to enforce it."

Ragnarson smiled nastily. "Michael, get Khelra's people. And Aral. I want to pay them what we owe them, then watch Aral take it away."

"That's not wise," Prataxis said, exasperated. "Don't rub salt in the wound."

"Why the hell not? They do it to me all the time. Give Michael your record of what and who we owe. We've got enough here to pay almost everybody. I never dreamed we'd clean up like this."

"That's because you underestimate the depth of the

hatred the Estates feel for you, Sire."

"It's mutual. Ha! Now they can't *afford* to stir any shit."

"Some even bet their estates," Michael said. "Aral's stuck with the property."

"Hope he makes tenant farmers out of them."

"Vindictive today, aren't we?" Prataxis said, with far more meaning than his employer caught.

"Merciless." A guard brought a whispered message. "Let him in. Mundwiller's here, men."

"Now it starts," Derel said. "You'll never sell what you did. It wasn't an acceptable risk."

"We won, didn't we?"

"That's all that'll save you. In the end, you'll find the loss of trust more important than the monetary gain. . . ."

"Enough. Just damned well enough, Derel."

"Derel is right," Mundwiller said. "That's what I came over to tell you. Your friends in the Thing are about to skedaddle like a flushed covey. They're asking if you've lost touch with your sense of responsibility."

"They'll get over it. Nothing succeeds like success."

"Last bag, sir," one of the porters told Prataxis.

"Come on," Bragi said. Inside, "Humph. The pile is smaller than I thought. Hell. Watch this. Something I've always wanted to do." He dived in head first.

Inger met Sergeant Gales well away from her apartment. Shadows masked their identities. "What's their temper, Josiah?"

"Pure rage, My Lady. They think they've been robbed."

"Have they?"

"Not really. They walked in with their eyes open."

"They just resent not being the robbers, eh?"

"You might say."

"It doesn't matter if the anger is righteous. It's useful. I think it's time you summoned our friends from back home."

Gales nodded. "I think so. He's not likely to get much weaker."

Ragnarson kept sitting in the money pile while Kavelin's readily available creditors received what the Crown owed them. He made a mockery of the process. He once laughed outright when Aral Dantice and his thugs collected immediately after a payment.

Dahl Haas found him there. The adjutant was a tired man. He had not slept all night. "They're safely off, Sire. I rode with them as far as Tewsbury. Should I have someone go bring them back now?"

Ragnarson eyed the grim-faced Nordmen baron accepting repayment of a loan. He was not as blind as he pretended. "Give it a few weeks. Let's see what crawls out if the rocks roll over."

"Sir Gjerdrum told me where to find you. He said to tell you that that Habibullah who used to be El Murid's ambassador is here. He won't talk to anybody but you."

Ragnarson's malicious humor evaporated completely. "I'll be there in half an hour." He rose from the dwindling pile. "Get somebody to wrap it up here, Derel. Make the right kind of apologies for me. Tell them I was off my oats, or something. Then collect Michael and wait in the War Room till you hear from me."

What does Yasmid have in mind? he wondered. Will there be a respite? Will there be time for me to put my own house in order before we start on hers?

This being King wasn't all it was cracked up to be.

18

Year 1016 AFE;
Tightening Screws

HABIBULLAH AWAITED RAGNARSON in the chamber where so many conferences had taken place recently. Bragi stepped in, quickly noted, "You may think you're dressed local, but you won't fool anyone."

Habibullah shrugged. "Speed was of more essence than secrecy. I received the material from Trebilcock. I speak for the Lady Yasmid as well as myself when I express my gratitude."

"Glad to help."

"A cunning maneuver, that Captures match. I expect it will be more appreciated outside Kavelin, though."

Bragi was having his own second and third thoughts. Somehow, in winning, he had lost something, and he just didn't understand what or why. If some Nordmen baron had pulled the same stunt, nobody would have thought anything about it. There would have been no whining in the streets if the Panthers had won.

Was he supposed to be too good for that kind of stuff? Was it because he'd dipped his hands into too many strongboxes? Or did he just have a thin skin?

He shrugged. "I guess congratulations are due, Habibullah. That whipping you gave the Throyens. That was beautiful. I split a side laughing."

"A grand victory, but more symbolic than practical. It wakened our enemies. They won't underestimate us again."

Soberly, Bragi observed, "You're probably right."

"Megelin is pressing us from the desert side. He's using a lot of sorcery. We can't stand up to the *savan dalage*. And the Faithful in Throyes say Lord Hsung is preparing a major push into the littoral. He'll use the legions from Throyes and Gog-Ahlan to give his Throyen puppets backbone. That means thirty to thirty-five thousand invaders, twelve thousand of them soldiers of the Dread Empire. Too much for us to handle."

Bragi sat quietly for half a minute. "Mind if I bring Prataxis and Trebilcock in here?"

"Do you really need to?"

"I think so. They're familiar with more aspects of the situation." He rose, stepped into the corridor, looked around. He saw no one but the guard. "Get Prataxis and Captain Trebilcock. They're waiting down in the War Room."

"Yes, Sire. But who'll stand watch?"

"I'll be all right. Go on."

"Yes, Sire."

Rather than return to Habibullah, Bragi poked around the corridor. Curiosity took him to the door of the room he'd seen Gales exit. He stepped inside, looked around. The room appeared as innocent as ever.

What the devil had Gales been doing that day? He started looking around. Minutes tripped past. "Here. What's this?" He fingered a scratch in the wainscotting below hip level on the wall facing the conference chamber. A decorative boar's head was loose. It had been moved often enough to have gouged the panelling. He fiddled with it.

Something clicked. The next panel left eased back an inch. He prodded it with a toe. It swung back. He hunkered down, scrambled through, found himself in one of the innumerable hidden passageways which networked the palace. "I thought I knew them all," he muttered.

A moment later he was looking through a peephole at Habibullah, who was waiting patiently, arms folded and eyes halfway closed. He looked older and more tired when he didn't know he was being observed. Trebilcock and Prataxis entered the room. Michael asked, "Where's the King?"

Bragi didn't stay for Habibullah's answer. He returned the way he had come, muttering, "Gales, you belong to Michael now." He couldn't put it off any longer. No matter what Michael uncovered.

A part of him wanted to cry. He had tried hard to convince himself that he was wrong, but his intuition had scored again. He glanced in the direction of his wife's apartment. "I guess blood *will* tell."

His expression was bland, mild, and friendly when he returned to the conference room. "So. They beat me back. Michael, Habibullah has been telling me some things. I want you and Derel to hear him out, then add anything you can."

Habibullah started over. When he mentioned Hsung's intentions, Michael added, "My contacts say he can't take Mist seriously because she's a woman. He's treating Western Army's area of operations like it was his own personal empire. He seems to think Mist can't touch him before the Matayangan crisis is settled."

Prataxis said, "Sire, he's one of your worst enemies among the Tervola. Breaking you is an obsession with some of them."

"So Mist kept telling me."

"He respected Lord Kuo's wishes, but I suspect he never intended to honor the commitments we made during our negotiations. He may have been playing me along to keep his superiors happy. Lately, his treatment of our caravan people has been more indicative of his thinking than anything he's said."

Bragi said, "Mist promised to straighten him out."

"What if she doesn't?" Habibullah asked.

Derel replied, "There isn't a thing we could do. Our people are at his mercy. Yours are too." To Bragi, Derel added, "Michael says it's probably only a matter of weeks till he invades the littoral. Apparently the decision to go has been made."

Michael nodded. "That's the word I get out of Throyes."

Habibullah said, "That agrees with what we've heard. And we won't be able to put up much of a fight."

"What have you got?" Bragi asked.

"Maybe ten thousand old, tired, worn-out men led by Invincibles past their primes. We couldn't engage except on the best terms. We expect to get a lot of local guerrilla support, and help from the Faithful who live in Throyen territory, but that's not enough. We've decided our strategy will be wholly partisan. Our main force has to be kept intact in case Megelin hits Sebil el Selib. The Lady Yasmid has ordered increased guerrilla activity west of the mountains, to make it more difficult for Megelin to approach the pass. But he has Beloul, el Senoussi, and Rahman. There isn't much we can do to stop them."

Bragi knew the three Royalist generals. They were smart and tough and unlikely to be deterred by partisans. Especially not with Magden Norath backing them.

Varthlokkur, why did you have to be such a pigheaded fool? I need you now.

"Derel, maneuvers are supposed to start next month. Can we move them up? Use them to bluff Hsung?" The planned operation was a rush by regular units to Baxendala, in the Savernake Gap, to see how quickly they could respond to a sudden eastern threat.

"Moving them up would be difficult. Credence isn't well enough to take part. Sir Gjerdrum would have to carry the whole load. And I don't think Lord Hsung would be particularly impressed anyway."

"Once the regiments are assembled, we could move up to Maisak any time he threatened to invade Hammad al Nakir. Make it look like we'll jump on his backside if he goes in. In his shoes I don't think I'd call our bluff."

"Why not?" Michael asked.

"If he gets us stirred up he'll get too far on Mist's bad side. She doesn't want him starting new wars while the Matayangan thing is so iffy. He didn't make army commander doing stupid things."

Sourly, Prataxis observed, "The only way to run a bluff is not to be bluffing. We can't do that. Our home situation is too precarious. And Lord Hsung knows it."

"Michael?"

"Derel is right. The Captures match polarized everybody. We're not very strong right now. There would be rioting if it looked like most of the army was moving through the Gap."

Ragnarson sighed. "You'll just have to increase your efforts, Michael."

"There are more of them than there are of me. Without the Unborn to ferret them out. . . ."

"Do your best. Habibullah, I'm sorry you had to hear all our woes. You've got problems of your own."

"We all have troubles, Sire. You and the Lady Yasmid are fighting for the survival of ideals. The struggle has used up most of your resources, but you can't let yourselves betray your beliefs. That's why the Lady is proposing we share resources."

Bragi grunted noncommittally. Yasmid was no more enthusiastic about this than he. His participation, such as it was, was an acquiescence to necessity.

Someone tapped on the door. The guard leaned in. "Sire, Captain Haas wants a word with you."

"Excuse me." Bragi stepped into the corridor. "What is it, Dahl?"

"Trouble in the Thing, Sire. Mundwiller says the Estates are pushing a motion of censure. He says you'd better show up to defend yourself."

"What do you think, Dahl?"

"I think he's right, Sire. They're in a mean mood."

Bragi sighed dramatically. "All right. Give me a minute here." He stepped inside. "I have to go over to the Thing. Derel, you and Michael go ahead and talk to Habibullah. Habibullah, I trust them completely. Hammer out your deal. Michael, I have a job for you. Gales. He's been listening in." He tapped the wall. "Hidden passageway."

Trebilcock looked unhappy. "I'll take care of it." He exchanged glances with Prataxis.

Bragi stepped into the corridor. "Let's go give them hell, Dahl."

Trebilcock stared at Habibullah for half a minute. "Tell me what we can do for you. Really. Other than make gestures, I don't see much myself."

"You could provide weapons. You have a considerable stockpile taken during the Great Eastern Wars. You could share intelligence. You have other assets we don't. Especially the wizard."

Michael concealed his surprise. Habibullah hadn't heard about the big split? Interesting. But then, the match was all the talk in the streets these days.

"I do, yes. As to the weapons, the army has those."

Derel said, "The King would let us deal them. Can you deliver them, Michael?"

Trebilcock nodded. Aral's smugglers could handle that end. For a price, of course.

Prataxis went on. "There's no problem, then. Let's say arms for five thousand men. What can you do for us, Habibullah?"

"The Lady Yasmid has suggested a loan of the Harish."

Trebilcock met Derel's eye. Each man wore an expression so blank the other knew it was studied. "The Harish?" Michael asked.

"The cult has dwindled. There are fewer than a hundred left. The survivors are an occasional embarrassment. The Lady would like them used up profitably. Preferably away from home. They could do you a lot of good."

Trebilcock recalled the long lists his people had assembled. They grew longer daily. In that he saw the hand of the enemy within the palace, the enemy the King wouldn't admit existed. "All right. But we'd have to share this with Credence Abaca. His people would have to provide the bases for that big an operation."

Derel protested. "You're talking about wholesale murder."

"Assassinating a few hundred is better than getting thousands killed in a civil war, isn't it? We're headed for one, Derel. Unless. . . ." Michael turned to Habibullah. "You don't want those men coming home?"

Habibullah winced. "I didn't mean that. We just want them out of our hair while we reorganize."

"Where do you want the weapons delivered?"

"Michael," Derel said, "I really don't like this."

"It's egg-breaking time, Derel. The day of nice is over. Habibullah, I'll see Abaca right away. I'll let you know where he wants your people to go. Where are you staying?"

Habibullah told him.

"That's good. Lot of foreigners there. Don't come back here. If you need to contact me, see a man named Harry at the Three Candles in Tintner's Lane." Michael rose. "I'd better find Gales, Derel."

"Wait for me." Prataxis took a courteous leave of Habibullah, hurried after Trebilcock. "Michael. . . ."

"Wait till we're outside. Walls with ears."

They stopped at the fountain the stonecutter Callison had been building. Someone had started it flowing, though it remained unfinished. Its babble masked their whispers.

Prataxis said, "The King seems ready to face the truth."

"Yeah. But will he take steps?"

"He has too much ego and sentiment invested. I hate the proposition, but I think it's time for a strong prejudicial action."

Michael chuckled. "Strong prejudicial action? That's what drove me crazy at the Rebsamen. You dons couldn't say anything straight out."

Derel stared into the dancing waters. His face was pale. This was his first murder plot.

Michael told him, "It's set up. But I won't say the word without your go-ahead."

Prataxis chewed a fingernail. Emotional torment distorted his features. He had come to Kavelin to be Ragnarson's secretary. His intention had been to write a history that would make him famous in scholastic circles. Somehow, he had lost his objectivity and become one of the King's chief lieutenants. And now he had to decide whether or not someone should die. . . .

He'd been round and round with his conscience since Michael had come to him after his last conference with Varthlokkur. The idea was his own, not Michael's. He was ashamed of himself. He had told Michael to see what he could do. And Michael had found a way. Damn him.

"I'm sorry, Derel. I know how you feel. I don't like it either. But the decision has to be made, and it's not one I can take on my head."

"I know. I know."

Trebilcock saw Sergeant Wortel passing. "Wortel. Come here."

The sergeant trotted over. "Sir?"

"Seen Sergeant Gales? I need to talk to him."

"Funny you should ask, sir."

"Funny? Why?"

"He's missed his last two watches. Nobody can find him."

"Damn! When was he last seen?"

"Last night. He rode out about an hour before he was supposed to go on duty. He didn't come back."

"All right. There's probably no point, but I want to talk to the men who were on the gate."

"Yes, sir." Wortel hurried off.

"Derel?"

Prataxis sighed. "Go with it, Michael. We don't have a choice." They started walking. "You know he'll know what happened, no matter how good you make it look."

"Probably. And he'll probably guess who did it. Let's hope he's in a forgiving mood when he hears about it."

They interviewed the men who had been on guard duty while Gales was making his exit. "Sounds like he was planning a long trip," Michael said.

"Sounds like," Derel agreed. "Think he was running while the running was good?"

"We couldn't be that lucky. He was here doing a job. He's still working."

Dahl said, "Sire, that was the finest speech I've heard you make. Powerful. Loaded with emotion."

Cham Mundwiller agreed. "He's right. But I don't think it changed any minds."

"Why are they so determined to get to me? I haven't done anything those Nordmen bastards wouldn't have done if they'd had the chance."

"I guess it's just that time again. It goes in cycles. For a while everybody is behind the Crown one hundred percent, then they all turn. That's Kavelin's history."

Bragi sighed. "At least the Marena Dimura and most of the Wessons stuck with me."

Dahl startled him by observing, "Watch the Wessons, Sire. They're getting so some of them are having aristocratic ideas."

"Is that true, Cham?"

Mundwiller turned red. "More or less. I wouldn't put it in those words. But some of my colleagues are starting to identify more with the Estates than with their own people."

"Could we replace them with more responsive souls?"

"If they weren't secure they wouldn't have gotten fat."

"I see. Yech! What's this?" Prataxis and Trebilcock were approaching. Derel looked terrible.

"The man you wanted me to see?" Michael said. "He deserted. Rode out last night equipped for a long trip."

"Must have felt fate's breath on his neck. Cham, can I see you later?"

"Surely, Sire." Mundwiller excused himself.

"Do you feel up to a long ride, Dahl?" Bragi asked.

Haas didn't look as surprised as Bragi thought he should. "Yes, Sire."

"I've been pushing you pretty hard lately. And not really using all your abilities."

Haas shrugged. "I'm a soldier. It's not my place to ask."

Ragnarson smiled. The lad did feel slighted. "I'm going to give you a special job. When we finish this we'll find you something better than adjutant. Your own field command sound good?"

"Yes, Sire."

"All right. Go after Gales."

"Sire?" Haas sounded disappointed.

Michael caught on. "I'll be damned. He thought you were going to send him to Sedlmayr." He punched Dahl's bicep. "You rake, you."

Haas reddened. He stammered unintelligibly. "Lay off," Bragi said. "Do you want to do it, Dahl? I can send someone else." Amazing. Dahl with a crush on Kristen. When did that get started?

"I'm not clear on what you want, Sire."

"Get on Gales' trail. See where he goes. See who he reports to. I have a hunch he's headed for Itaskia. While you're there, check on the rest of this crowd. Derel will give you letters of introduction to friends of mine up there. People in high places who can help you."

"Yes, Sire. All right. It's an opportunity I can't refuse. I have relatives there I haven't seen since I was fourteen. Should I visit the old steading?"

Ragnarson still owned property in Itaskia, where he had lived before coming to Kavelin. "If you have time. It's not important."

"I'll make time, Sire. I have roots there."

"All right. Whatever."

"When should I leave?"

"As soon as you can. Gales won't waste time. Stay close or you might miss something."

"I'm on my way. If you'll excuse me, Sire?"

"Go." Bragi watched Haas hurry away. "A good man, Dahl. Wish I had a few thousand more of him."

"He does seem eager to prove himself," Derel said. "What did you work out with Habibullah?"

Inger stood at a window, staring out at the city. The sun was setting. Long shadows stretched behind the spires of taller buildings. Each shadow seemed to be a grasping hand reaching for her. "Have you heard anything, Thelma?"

"Not a word, My Lady. Something is happening, though. People won't answer my questions. The Guards are acting funny around our people. It's scary."

Scary? It was terrifying, that was what it was. Josiah, Josiah, did you get away clean?

They had messed it up somehow. Right now she was balanced on a razor's edge, kept from falling only by Bragi's feeling for her. . . . He did know, didn't he? He had to know. "Why did I let Dane push me into this? We could have been happy if it weren't for him. I don't really *care* about family vengeance."

"Yes, Mistress."

She'd been thinking aloud. Dangerous habit. Bragi was right when he said the walls had ears. That damned Michael Trebilcock . . . Thelma had seen him skulking down the hall a few hours ago.

The shadows were longer. Sunset on a crazy dream, she thought. It's hell being scared all the time. Will the Estates really protect us? They've broken so many vows. It's impossible to trust them.

Nordmen conspirators had helped her get her law of succession. Most of them would go when Dane got here. Out Death's door behind Abaca, Trebilcock, and that lot. Otherwise they would turn again.

She understood Bragi's frustration. The Nordmen were a bunch of snakes.

"My Lady, your supper is getting cold," Thelma said. She'd been dithering around the table trying to keep things warm.

Inger waved a hand in a go away motion. "No. No. I can't. I'm not hungry."

"My Lady, you have to eat. You haven't had a decent meal since yesterday."

"Take it away, Thelma. Maybe I'll be hungry tomorrow."

Thelma looked disgusted. "As you wish, My Lady." She rang a bell. Her helpers appeared. Thelma began hustling the food out. Inger smiled. Wanted to get to it herself before it got cold, probably.

Inger snuffed the candles and sat in the gathering darkness watching lights come alive in the city.

A girl named Carol burst into the room. "My Lady," she gasped.

Inger stared at her silhouette in the doorway. The girl was shaking. "What is it?"

"It's Thelma. And Martha and Zeal. Something's wrong. You'd better come see."

Inger rose, a fatalistic haze gathering her into itself. What now?

All three women were in Thelma's little cubicle. Inger pushed through the women crowding the doorway. Inside, someone moaned horribly. Inger understood after one glimpse.

Thelma had brought the meal to her quarters to share with her friends. Half-empty plates lay on the floor. One was overturned, another was broken. All three women were curled up, clutching their stomachs.

Someone said, "Thelma is vomiting blood, Lady."

Inger covered her face with her hands. She felt the sting of Death's cold breath, started shaking. The sounds made by the poisoned women didn't help her nerves. "Did you send for Doctor Wachtel?" she croaked.

"Yes, Lady."

There wasn't much point. They would die. The meal must have been half poison. What was this nasty? Arsenic? Whatever, the poisoner hadn't tried to be subtle. He—or she—had wanted to make a point in no uncertain terms. She started shaking again. It wasn't a point someone was trying to make. Somebody wanted her dead. That was *her* supper.

The doctor came in, shooed everyone away save Inger. He examined the three women. "Nothing I can do for them now. And you? Did you get any of it?"

She shook her head. She didn't trust herself to speak. She

might not stop talking. All her fears and regrets were clamoring to get out.

"Just rattled?"

She nodded.

"I'll give you a little something for the nerves." He mixed something in a tall mug. "Drink."

She drank. It tasted awful. Horrified, she dropped the mug. It didn't break. She stared at it as if it were a venomous spider.

Wachtel guided her into her own chamber, settled her on her bed. "Starting to feel better?"

She felt lazy, languorous, and a little sleepy. "Yes."

"Want to tell me about it?"

She shook her head. "It *was* poison, wasn't it?"

"Yes. A massive amount. Meant for you, wasn't it?"

She shuddered. "How did you know?"

"The way you reacted when I gave you the sedative."

"Yes. It was meant for me. What can I do?"

"Watch what you eat and drink. Patch it up with whoever you've offended. Ask your husband to turn Michael loose."

"Michael?" She laughed giddily. "No. Not Michael. I'll take care of it myself."

"You've made female enemies here?"

"Female?"

"Poison is usually a woman's weapon. These days, anyway. In Imperial times sorcerers used poison, but prided themselves on their subtlety. There was nothing subtle about this. This was like using a battle-ax to swat a fly. How do you feel now?"

"Relaxed. Sleepy."

"Good. You need sleep. But first, what should I do with your women?"

"They're really going to die?"

"They're dead," Wachtel said. He was usually less blunt. Tonight he was upset. He didn't like murder.

"Bury them. I'll assume the expense. And don't tell anyone what's happened." The room began spinning. She felt a feather touch of fear. Darkness descended.

19

Year 1016 AFE;
Born to Trouble

PRATAXIS TRACKED MICHAEL down in the palace library. He found Trebilcock whispering with one of the Guards. "Michael, it didn't work."

Trebilcock told the Guard, "You can go, Snake." He waited a few seconds. "I know. The kind of screwup called an act of fate."

"I don't mind saying I'm nervous, Michael. What's the King going to do?"

"Maybe he won't find out. He hasn't heard yet. They've got that apartment sewed up tight. Itaskians standing guard inside and out. Far as I know, Wachtel is the only one who knows. He got rid of the bodies, but it's not in his nature to get involved. He's probably the only apolitical creature in the kingdom."

"That won't stop him from complaining to the King."

"Maybe not. I'm not concerned."

"Wachtel is old. Nobody would be surprised if. . . ."

Michael was surprised. "No, Derel. Not Wachtel. There isn't a good enough reason. You really are scared, aren't you?"

"Ragnarson is funny about women, Michael. Never quite rational. And there are so many women involved this time that I can't pretend to predict his behavior."

Michael leaned back, frowned. He'd always suspected Derel of misogynism. "Go on."

"Every focus of action the past few months has been a woman. Nepanthe. Mist. Inger. Kristen. This Sherilee creature. Each pulling him a different direction, and each a danger. Nepanthe cost us Varthlokkur's help. Mist nearly killed him, then went away, taking that source of support. Inger has turned like a mad dog. Kristen, in her eagerness to have her son designated crown prince, may have been involved in schemes which worked to our detriment. There's no way she could have been as innocent as she pretended. And this Sherilee thing has him completely distracted from statecraft at a time when every minute has to be devoted to keeping the kingdom on a steady course."

Michael nodded. "And now there's Yasmid, pulling him yet another way."

Having vented some of his tension, Derel dropped into a chair. "What are we going to do?"

"If he finds out? Claim we didn't have anything to do with it. He might not believe me, but he'll believe you. It's not your style. You don't get that involved." Trebilcock chuckled.

"I'm too involved. I should get out. I've been here too long. I don't even pretend to be objective anymore."

"Meaning?"

"Damn it, I like him. I want to see what he's trying to do work. It's part my baby. I want to see it grow up."

"And?"

Derel glared. "And my whole life is here now. Hellin Daimiel isn't home anymore. I've been gone too long."

"Me too."

"Eh?"

"I came out with Gjerdrum after we graduated from the Rebsamen. Just for a while, while I got my bearings before I took over the family business. And now I'm as much a part of Kavelin as the King is."

Prataxis snorted. "Who is another foreigner bewitched. Strange, isn't it? The people who love this country most are people who came from somewhere else and got caught up in it."

"It's a spider's web," Michael agreed. "Question. Do I take another stab at it?"

"I want to say no. . . . Do you think she's neutralized?"

"That's what I was talking to Snake about. He don't know what's going on, but his post is up that way. He says Inger's people are scared to death. Meaning she is. He says her apartment is locked up tight. Long as it stays that way, we can't get in and she can't get out where she can cause any more trouble."

"Good. Can we help her isolation along? Like prevent any contact?"

"I plan to give orders to that effect, Derel. So she'll have to come out if she wants to visit with her accomplices."

"Yes. Good. Keep track of anyone who wants to see her. I'm telling you your job? Look. Keep her scared. Keep her locked up. Don't let her talk to anybody unless it's somebody we can't keep away." He meant the King. "Her friends in the Estates will get nervous fast. The King's trick with the Captures match had one positive effect. It showed the Estates that he's still tough and tricky, and he won't put up with any crap."

"It also showed them that there're people around who aren't afraid to break their bones if they don't behave according to rules that are good enough for the rest of us."

"Dantice? He might become a liability. Look. I'll give the orders to keep people away. We'll let it out that she's bad sick. Nobody will believe that, but the orders will have more weight if they're mine. And from you they'd cause too much talk."

Michael raised an eyebrow.

"You're a living devil, you know. People think you're something almost supernatural. You scare them. Scared people do dangerous things."

"Come on. . . ."

"Take my word for it, Michael."

Kristen arrived in Sedlmayr about the time Derel and Michael went their separate ways. The house to which her escort delivered her was simple to the point of being plebeian. There was room enough only if she and Sherilee shared one room and the children all bunked together in another. An old couple named Shastain managed the place. They were friends of Michael Trebilcock.

A courier from Vorgreberg had reached the Shastains hours earlier, having passed Kristen's party on the road. Elma Shastain told her, "Our orders are to keep you inside all the time. No contact with the locals. We haven't been told who you are, and Mr. Trebilcock doesn't want the neighbors to find out."

Kristen was irritated. Cooped up in a small house with

four children, day after day? "For how long?"

"Until we hear differently. Three weeks at the least."

"Three weeks?" Kristen groaned. "I'd rather do three months in the Scuttarian galleys."

"I'm sure it's for our safety," Sherilee said. "I'll help with the kids."

"You don't know Michael. Mrs. Shastain, was there a message for me?"

"There's a sealed pouch. Maykin will get it for you when he's gotten rid of your drivers."

"Let's get the children settled in, Sherry."

Upstairs, Sherilee asked, "You think there'll be a letter for me?"

"I don't know. He's not good at writing letters. Don't be upset if there isn't. He said a lot more by sending you here with me."

Children whined and fussed. They had throughout the journey. Sherilee snapped, "Gundar, act your age. And help your sister."

Maykin Shastain was a cherry-cheeked, fat little fellow with a tonsure of white hair and a cherubic smile. He brought the letter pouch. "Mrs. Shastain explained the rules?" he asked.

"Yes." Kristen broke a nail trying to unbuckle the pouch. "Why do we have to stay locked up?"

"You'd understand that better than I, Mistress. I have no idea who you are or who might be looking for you. I don't want to know. It's not my job to know. My job is to look after you."

"I guess Michael knows what he's doing."

"He usually does, Mistress. He usually does."

"There is one for you, Sherry." And three for her, one each from her father-in-law, Michael Trebilcock, and Dahl Haas. Her eyebrows rose when she saw the latter. She smiled, opened that letter first.

"A month down here," Sherilee said. "He wants us to stay a month. Just in case. I can't not see him for a whole month. What's the matter with you?"

"They're sending Dahl to Itaskia."

"Oh. I guess I shouldn't complain, then, should I?"

"No."

"You decided you like him, huh?"

"Maybe. Maybe it's just because he doesn't care that I was married to the King's son."

"I wonder how Julie is doing."

"Julie? What made you think of her?"

"Talking about men. She's going to marry Sir Gjerdrum."

"He's engaged to that Gwendolyn creature."

"That will change." Sherilee grinned. "She hasn't told him yet. But she decided."

"I see. One of those situations."

"One of those. I wish I knew what was going on in the city."

"They won the match."

"Then why do we have to stay?"

"Because they think somebody might try to hurt them through us. A lot of people lost a lot of money, I guess."

"Well, I hope it blows over fast. I miss him already."

Kristen shook her head and went to check on the children. Sherilee was getting strange. Acting too possessive. That might cause trouble. . . .

Well, that was what she'd wanted when she'd pushed them together, wasn't it? A gimmick to pry her father-in-law away from Inger and make the path wider for Ragnar. . . . I guess I just won't ever be satisfied, she thought.

Michael eased his mount nearer Derel Prataxis. He leaned, watching the King's back. "He said anything? Let on at all?"

"No. I don't think he's been up to see her. He doesn't even know she's locked herself in."

"No time?"

"No. He hasn't been that busy. Last night he had time to do some reading. I guess he just doesn't want to see her."

"That's fine with me."

Ragnarson growled, "You want to listen up back there? Derel? Michael? You need a special invitation?"

Ragnarson scanned his henchmen. Those who were going along looked ready to go. Those who were staying looked impatient. Good. Everything as it should be. "Sergeant, get with the pipes and drums. Let's get the crap over so we can hit the road."

Drums boomed. Pipes tootled. The castle gate swung open. Outside, trumpets sounded. Bragi glanced up at the window of Inger's bedroom. He saw a face barely visible in the pre-dawn light. It jerked out of sight. He looked through the gate and tried to put her out of his mind.

For most of an hour the Vorgrebergers and King's Own passed in review. Those of Ragnarson's intimates who were to stay in the city fretted. Some wanted to be about their own business. Others, like Credence Abaca, chafed at being left behind. Finally, the last troop filed past.

Ragnarson turned. "Credence, Michael, Cham, I'm counting on you to keep things quiet. Derel, rap them on the knuckles if they don't." He chuckled. It was difficult to picture Prataxis physically chastising anyone.

Prataxis scowled and grumbled. Then he scowled some more. He was thoroughly disgruntled. Never before had he been denied the chance to accompany Ragnarson when something important was going on. But he understood. His pretense to be an historian had evaporated. He would be of more value here, overseeing the palace and mediating between Cham, Credence, and Michael.

"Be good, people." Ragnarson nudged his mount into a walk. His staff and bodyguards formed around him. At last, he thought. After three years, back in the field. Away from the endless bickering and backbiting. Away from all the insoluble problems. Back to doing what he knew best. Soldiering. It felt good.

One battalion each of Vorgrebergers and King's Own swung out of the parade and returned to barracks. Ragnarson didn't expect trouble during his absence, but Vorgreberg could be volatile. He couldn't deny Credence the tools needed to control it.

He didn't look back. He didn't want to see the palace till he returned. He was tempted to stretch the maneuvers just as an excuse to stay away.

Sherilee drifted across his mind. One good reason for

hurrying back. Maybe he could bring her home by then. "Miss you, little girl," he whispered.

Inger jerked back from the window. He had seen her. And he hadn't made a sign. He hadn't come all week, and now he hadn't bothered to say good-bye. She could no longer doubt the estrangement.

For a while she'd hoped he would come see her and they could talk it out. The mess wasn't insoluble. With Josiah gone she felt less constrained to stay with the program. But he hadn't come. He hadn't even inquired about the poisoning attempt.

She was sure he'd had no part in it. It wasn't his style. If he had wanted her out of the way, he would have done something very direct. No, someone else was responsible. He probably didn't know.

She could think of only two candidates. Michael Trebilcock and Bragi's daughter-in-law. She was inclined to suspect the girl. The grasping little witch was determined to have her son installed as crown prince.

She looked out the window again. She saw pennons dip and sway as troops passed in review outside the wall.

He was leaving, they said. Going up to Baxendala with the troops. He would be gone for a month.

For a month there would be no one between her and the person who wanted her dead. Fear clawed at her guts. Again she told herself, "I was a fool to let Dane get me into this." She was living like she was besieged, making friends taste everything before she touched it herself, sweating whenever there was a knock. The fact that none of Bragi's people knocked didn't soothe her nerves. She had this paranoid certainty that they were biding their time, drawing the noose tighter, before they kicked her feet from beneath her.

She was getting cabin fever. And there was no end in sight. Unless they were starved out. Just like a regular siege.

Maybe they hadn't thought of that yet. "Sally. Janey. I need men for a bodyguard. We're going out to market."

"My Lady? Do you think that's wise?"

"No. I don't, really. But with the King gone we're going to be in worse danger. We won't dare go out. But if we don't, we'll starve. So before it occurs to our enemies to watch for it, we're going to stock up on provisions."

The response to her coming forth was baffling. No one seemed to notice, care, or react. The palace people, all devoted to Bragi, ignored her, but did nothing to hamper her. The guards at the gate let her go without comment. "Hunsicker."

"My Lady?"

"I thought they wanted us to stay locked up."

The soldier shrugged. "Maybe they changed their minds."

It was a bright, warm, windy day. Birds sang in the park. Some of the trees bent their shoulders under the weight of early-ripening fruit. It was not a day belonging to Inger's troubled world. She wanted clouds and gloom and drizzling, chilly rain.

Should she run for it now? Ride right through the city to the estate of one of her friends? She liked the notion. . . .

"We have company, My Lady," Hunsicker said. Inger glanced over her shoulder. Three riders were following them. "Shall we try to lose them?" Hunsicker asked.

"No. We don't want any more trouble than we have." Her heart sank. So much for running away.

All day long she sensed the presence of watchers. She recognized only one man. In the market she once found Michael Trebilcock staring at her through the crowd. The cold pallor of him sent tremors up her spine.

She was glad when it was over and she could retreat to her apartment.

"I've been studying it for three days," Michael told Prataxis. "There's no way in except by force. And her people are loyal enough to fight."

"Why?" Derel asked. "She wasn't that important before she came here. She shouldn't command that much devotion."

"Your guess is as good as mine. Maybe Haas will find the answer."

Dahl Haas had driven himself to exhaustion. His quarry was older than he, and more easily wearied, but he had ridden hard too. It had taken Dahl a long time to overtake

Gales. They were in northern Ruderin at the time. Dahl was satisfied that Gales was headed home. To reach Itaskia the man would have to cross the Great Bridge over the River Silverbind at the City. He decided to race ahead, rest, and be fresh when Gales hit town.

Baxendala was refreshingly friendly after Vorgreberg. The townspeople came out cheering when the troops marched in. They lined the road up to Karak Strabger, the castle overlooking the town, and cheered their King as he passed.

Sir Gjerdrum said, "They figure we'll spend a lot of money."

"Cynic."

"I can't argue that. This damned country makes you cynical. I should have listened to my father. He never wanted me to come back." Sir Gjerdrum's father, Eanred Tarlson, had been Marshall when Ragnarson had arrived in Kavelin. He had died during the civil war. Ragnarson had replaced him.

Bragi stopped the column. "Gjerdrum, look out there." He pointed west. It was a fine, clear day. They could see all the way down the Gap to the more level lands. The view was tremendous. Snowcapped peaks framed it.

Gjerdrum looked for more than a minute. Finally, he said, "All right. I can't say it isn't worth it. If you can go on after all you've lost, so can I."

An hour later, looking at the same view from the higher vantage of Karak Strabger's watchtower, Sir Gjerdrum said, "Sire . . . Bragi . . . I need a big favor."

"Anything within reason."

"It's Julie."

"Julie? What happened to Gwendolyn?"

"She's ancient history. Anyway, Julie's whole family died during the wars. She's all alone."

"So I've heard. Wasn't her father with the Damhorsters?"

"She had brothers and uncles and cousins in the South Bows, the Sedlmayr Light, and the Damhorsters. But yes, her father was with the Damhorsters. He's buried over there." Gjerdrum indicated a sprawling memorial cemetery filled with the dead of the battles fought here. "She wants me to lay a wreath."

For a moment Ragnarson stared up the quiet, bright pass and recalled the sound and fury and gloom and fear of days gone by. He pictured the air aswarm with dragons, the slopes dark with the eastern hordes, the earth trembling under the thundering contest of rival sorceries. This soil was rich with the blood of good men. Of too many good men, on both sides, driven by the ambitions of their captains. "We'll lay wreaths for them all, Gjerdrum. For them all. What was it you wanted?"

"For you to stand up for Julie. She doesn't have anyone to do it."

They're all dead, and they died for me, Bragi thought. "All right. Getting married, eh?"

Shyly, Gjerdrum said, "Once winter sets in and the pressure is off us for this year." During winter Kavelin was safe from her enemies. The little kingdom's people dared get domestic then.

"Yeah," Ragnarson said. "All right."

"What's the matter? You sound a little strange."

"Nothing." Bragi smiled. "Just never thought of you as the marrying kind."

"I'm getting older. And I found the right woman."

"Can't argue with that. They ought to be about ready downstairs. What say we go get this thing rolling? Those people from Maisak here yet?"

"No. But they should be in before sundown." Two flights downward, Gjerdrum asked, "You think Hsung really is pulling the garrison out of Gog-Ahlan?"

Bragi shrugged. "It'll be interesting to find out. That's all I can say. Interesting to find out."

Aral Dantice eased up out of a sleep haunted by dreams of a woman he would never again see. "Damn," he said. "Why won't she go away? How is she different from any other woman?"

A sleepy voice muttered, "Hunh? What's that, Honey?"

"Nothing. Nothing. Go back to sleep," he whispered. He eased out of bed, went to a window. Heart of the night. He couldn't have slept more than an hour. Shouldn't have fallen asleep at all.

"Damn," he said again. "Got to get back before they steal

me blind." He dressed quickly and hurried downstairs.

The place was three-quarters empty, and this was usually its busiest hour. He ambled over, took hold of the Fat Man's elbow. "Still bad?"

"It's terrible." Their upper-class customers were staying away in retribution for their suspected part in the Captures match fleecing.

"It'll pick up. Here or one of the other places. People need their vices."

"No doubt. No doubt. You get those boxes shipped for your friend yet?"

"Seventy percent. Takes a lot of men to move that much stuff."

"You ever find out what it was?"

"Sure. Weapons. The gamut. But mostly swords."

"Weapons? That many? Your friend equipping an army?"

"Must be." Aral had made Michael explain before asking his smuggler friends to do the job. He didn't like it. Supplying weapons to El Murid's Chosen. Seemed suicidal. But what did he know about foreign policy? He hoped the Fat Man didn't find out. The Fat Man had a big hatred for anything that smelled of the Disciple. He'd lost a brother in the El Murid Wars.

"Going to go out and prowl," Aral told the Fat Man. "See what's happening around the neighborhood."

The whole district was as quiet as their home place. Aral hoped he was right about business improving with time.

Time to go back, get some sleep. He was supposed to ride with Michael in the morning.

Mist had an appointment with Lord Ch'ien Kao E, the man most responsible for her restoration. She faced it nervously. Lord Ch'ien had spent the day representing her before the Council of Tervola. He would bear good tidings or bad.

He came in with a nod. They had decided to back her! She was Princess in fact as well as name. The empire was hers again, and this time without dispute. There was no O Shing in the outlands gathering armies to challenge her claim. She bounced off the throne and threw her arms around Lord Ch'ien. "We did it. We did it, Kao E. All the way home."

Kao E actually hugged her back, lightly, tentatively, in the first affectionate gesture she'd ever seen from him. Behind his rigorously proper demeanor, he was excited too.

She backed away. "What did it? What convinced them?" She had expected them to temporize because of her long association with enemies of the empire.

"Your swift stabilization of the southern front coupled with your success in the east. Lord Ssu-ma spoke for you, and spoke well. He was a great admirer of Lord Kuo Wen-chin. He tipped the balance. I think we can look forward to a long and tranquil reign. There isn't a hint of a plot to come back at you. The Tervola are tired of coup and counter-coup. They've seen the cost of disunity. In all the realm there is just one potential troublemaker."

"Lord Hsung?"

"Exactly. I haven't had time to watch him. What's he done lately?"

"Nothing new. He just hasn't cancelled his plan to attack Hammad al Nakir."

"I think it's time you replaced him, Princess."

"He has a lot of friends. And many of the Tervola share his ideas about the western problem." She smiled gently. She had decided what to do about Lord Hsung long ago. "We can't move him out till he does something incontestably insubordinate."

"At which point we'll be at war with El Murid. He's not a heavyweight anymore, but we don't need more enemies of any sort."

"Did you make the arrangements in Lord Hsung's headquarters?"

"Exactly as you directed."

"Good."

"I don't like doing that to a brother, Mistress. If I may say so."

"I don't either. But there are limits. He'll damn himself out of his own mouth—and become an example."

"As you say, Mistress."

"As I say. One more thing. Ask Lord Ssu-ma to see me tomorrow. I want to thank him personally."

"Of course."

Thank him? Mist thought. He's been thanked already.

But only he and I know, Lord Ch'ien. I'm sorry, old friend, but I'm going to disappoint your secret ambition. Lord Ssu-ma is a better man for the job. But your turn will come. I promise you that. You've served me long and well. Be patient. I never forget my friends.

She reflected on old friends in the west, friends who would be ill-served if Lord Hsung had his way. She hoped Bragi would interpret her gesture positively.

20

CREDENCE ABACA FOLDED his hands, closed his eyes. "Read the last part again." His aide went back to the report delivered by Michael Trebilcock's messenger. "Tonight, eh? Here's what you do. Have the carpenters rig a sixteen-man gibbet. Send Blakely's company down there in civilian clothes. Tell him to grab the shit disturbers the minute they start sounding off. Give them to Trebilcock." Michael's report predicted rioting in the Arsen Street area.

"You know what this is, don't you?" Abaca asked. "A diversion set up by the Estates. The main show will take place somewhere else. They want to test me. Send that back to Trebilcock. Have Adam pass the word to stay alert. Oh. Ask Trebilcock where else we might expect trouble."

The riots began exactly as Michael predicted. Abaca was quick and merciless. His gibbet collapsed under an overload. Bodies were left lying in the streets. People were appalled and intimidated when they had time to reflect.

Abaca's prophecy proved correct. The rioting was a diversion for a band of men who tried to raid Castle Krief. They were supposed to free the Queen and spirit her into hiding in western Kavelin. They perished in the attempt.

"Perfect end to an ill-conceived plot," Abaca observed next morning. "We win the first test of strength. Next time they won't underestimate me. What's holding up breakfast?"

Dahl picked up Gales coming off the Great Bridge into the Wharf Street South district of Itaskia. Gales was a day later than Haas expected. He had had time to contact his king's friends in the Itaskian government.

He had been surprised to find them eager to help. The man assigned to aid him was a Colonel from the War

Ministry staff. He brought a team of thirty men with him. He took one look at Gales and told Dahl, "That's no infantry sergeant, Captain."

"Sir?"

"The name is right. Josiah Gales. But he's a colonel in the Greyfells family forces. One of the Duke's top men. We thought he'd been eliminated. He's been missing for several years. Let's get back to the Ministry and review what you remember about his friends."

"He's a Greyfells agent, then?"

"Yes. A good man, too. He's wasted on them. The rumor is, he sticks with them because he's in love with Inger, and because he thinks he owes them for a lapse of his while guarding her when she was young."

Dahl said, "I think you've answered most of the King's questions already."

"You sound happy."

"I was afraid I'd have to hang around for months. I left a lady friend. . . ." Dahl blushed.

"I see. Before you run back to her, give us a few days. With your help maybe we can scuttle this thing from this end. Chop off the dragon's head, as it were. We knew the Greyfells lot were up to something, but we couldn't pin it down. We expected it to be something here. Can you stay?"

"Of course. I want to ride up north while I'm here. King Bragi has some property up the river. I have relatives there."

"I know the place. We used to have troops garrisoned there. It's abandoned now, except for a few farmers. Your relatives farmer types?"

Dahl nodded. "My father gave them his share of the property. You sure your men will keep track of Gales?"

"Better than you could. Let's go over what you know today. Go see your relatives tomorrow. I'll give you a full report when you get back. We can go over any new questions, then you can head home."

"Sounds good to me." Dahl was eager to see the old place. He'd been happy there. He hoped he could recapture the feel of the past.

The news Bragi was awaiting finally came from Maisak. The Dread Empire legion stationed at Gog-Ahlan, a ruined city at the eastern mouth of the Savernake Gap, was pulling out. "We move in the morning," he announced. "Up to Maisak."

Sir Gjerdrum looked at him askance. Baron Hardle asked, "Why the hurry?"

"Even a fast rider needs a week to get from Gog-Ahlan to Baxendala. We want to make some noise while there's still somebody to see us."

"I have a bad feeling about this," Gjerdrum said. "Something doesn't smell right."

"What?"

"Just a hunch. Nothing I can put a finger on."

"Ahead of us or behind us?" Ragnarson had the same feeling, but his intuition hadn't told him which way to jump.

"Can't say. There were those riots the other day."

The news had arrived quickly, via the watchfire telegraph running from Maisak to the capital.

"That don't seem like a problem. Credence cleaned up on them."

"Maybe it's because there are too many variables. The factionalism at home. Megelin and Norath. Yasmid. Hsung. Mist. Too many people pulling too many directions."

"That may be. Even so, we move up tomorrow. Try to look fierce, eh?"

Aral cantered to where Michael awaited him. This would be their first ride since last week's riots. "Long time no see," Michael said cheerfully. Aral scowled and grumped. "What's the matter? It's a beautiful day. Was the storm yesterday more your style?"

"I was up late last night."

"You have a partner. Let him run things. You're supposed to be staying respectable, anyway."

"Wasn't that. I was talking to some smugglers. Some back from delivering your weapons, some in from Throyes."

"And?"

"They say it's going to blow up out there. Hsung has his mind made up. He's going ahead despite orders and good sense."

"Not a lot we can do about that, is there? So why the long face?"

"I'm scared the King will get another wild hair."

"Come on."

"He's changed, Mike. He's making the long bets without thinking. He's getting arrogant about his luck. Taking chances when he doesn't have to. Maybe being King has gone to his head."

Michael couldn't disagree. "He does tend to ignore advice when it isn't what he wants to hear."

"I'll let you in on something, Mike. Our organization isn't betting on him. We're moving our money out of Kavelin. We don't think he's going to last."

"Why not? Everything is under control. I have the troublemakers spotted. In a month or so. . . ." He dropped it. Aral didn't need to know about the Harish.

"I'm saying that one more long bet and a lot of people are going to give up on him. And a lot more will try to make something out of it. He needs to take a more realistic approach to dealing with people, too. He's got to make them *want* to work with him. He did that while he was Marshall."

"The mess isn't all his fault. There are some people sabotaging everything they can. They're doing their damnedest to make him look bad."

"I can guess who. There's a lot of Itaskian gold floating around my part of town. But I say that's his fault. He should have stopped it before it got out of hand."

"That's partly my fault, Aral. I was suspicious a long time ago. I didn't tell him. I figured he'd do something when he was ready. I didn't want to hurt him. He's already lost almost everybody who ever meant anything to him. That's probably part of his problem. He's sublimating it all into a devotion to Kavelin that's becoming pathologically unrealistic."

"Hey, Michael."

"What?"

"Look here. Look at me. This is Aral Dantice, the caravan outfitter's son. Not your roommate at the Rebsamen."

Michael laughed. "Sorry."

"I know what you're saying even if you don't say it in words ordinary mortals can understand. And you're probably partly right. But only partly."

"Well, damn. We're around already. And that's all the

time I have for today."

"You'll pass the word about Hsung?"

"Of course."

"Mike? Just an idea."

"What?"

"Go see the Queen while you've still got her scared."

"What for?"

"To negotiate. Let her buy her safety by getting out of Kavelin."

"Ooh. That's dangerous, Aral. The King would have a fit."

"Even if you and Prataxis and Mundwiller were all in on it?"

"I don't know."

"You'd better do something before the hammer falls. Because like I said, I've got a hunch he'll try the long odds one more time."

"I'll think about it, Aral. I'll talk to Prataxis. That's all I can promise."

It was pure fate. Gales was at the Ministry visiting an old friend and happened to be looking out a window. He spied someone familiar marching toward the building. "Dahl Haas. What the hell are you doing here?"

"Josiah?" his friend asked.

"Uhm?"

"You look green around the gills."

"Must be coming down with something." He tried to be entertaining, amusing, whatever, to buy time, but failed. So he simply overstayed his welcome till Haas left the building.

The young Captain wasn't alone. His companion was one of Itaskia's top agents. "I'll stop boring you now," he said. He hit the street as quickly as he could. Mortin of Greyfells was at his town villa. He headed that way.

He became aware that he was being followed. He realized that some of the faces he now noticed had been around for days. Well, let them follow. He wasn't doing anything extraordinary. Extraordinary procedures would begin once he reached the villa and was able to command the Greyfells resources.

How had the kid managed to track him? . . . No. The

important question was, how had he become intimate with someone high in the King's favor here? How much had he passed on? Was the Kavelin operation compromised?

That, Gales supposed, depended on how much Haas had been told before departing Vorgreberg.

I should have expected this, he thought. I should have made more effort to see if I was followed.

Mist examined Lord Ssu-ma's field charts. "They're up-to-date?"

"Unless he's cleverer than we think. The Throyens are massed for the attack. He has one legion in line behind them and the other trickling in from Gog-Ahlan. He's going to do it."

"How soon?"

"Tomorrow? The next day? It won't be long."

"What kind of reaction can we expect?"

"His assessment is that the Disciple's troops will collapse. He expects residual partisan activity, and some trouble in Throyen territory with followers of the Disciple. He expects his Aspirators to clear that up within two weeks. He intends to push south to Souk al Arba, establish a line, then drive into the Sebil el Selib Pass. The Disciple will be captured there or will flee westward, to be captured by Royalist forces."

"I recall a previous assessment of his going sour. What are the chances this time?"

"He might carry it off. In spite of himself."

Mist tapped the map where the Savernake Gap snaked through the Mountains of M'Hand.

Lord Ssu-ma nodded. "Ragnarson is at Maisak with the bulk of his army. He's posturing. He won't move."

Mist agreed, but asked, "Why not?"

"He has severe problems at home. He hasn't called anyone to the colors except a few militia units in outlying areas. If he were serious he would have ordered a full call-up. He'd want his rear protected from his enemies at home."

"Why is he making the gesture? Is there a connection with El Murid's people?"

"There must be. Obviously not an alliance. That's politi-

cally unfeasible. But some sort of cooperation. Else how
would he be alert to Lord Hsung's activities?"

"Michael Trebilcock. In his way Michael is as dangerous
as Varthlokkur. He's deadly. He's afraid of nothing. And he
has hundreds of friends in unusual places. He seems to
know everything."

"I've seen estimates from Lord Hsung's staff which say
otherwise. His reputation is bigger within Kavelin than
without. Most of his coups relied on Varthlokkur's help. He
doesn't have that anymore."

"That was my reason for thinking Ragnarson wouldn't
attack. He doesn't have the wizard to cover him anymore."

"What are your plans for Lord Hsung?"

"Let him run free. Let him damn himself so thoroughly
the Council will unanimously censure him. The Matayangan thing has them scared enough to be very short-
tempered with disciplinary lapses."

"How goes the war?"

"Well enough. The encircled armies should collapse soon.
Once they do, we'll be able to take the offensive."

"The situation is no longer critical?"

"No. Just serious. But it could go bad again."

"Give Lord Hsung another week, eh? Even if he goes?"

"At least. Maybe longer."

In the high, wild mountains called the Dragon's Teeth,
Varthlokkur turned away from a mirror which could reflect
images of anything anywhere. He sighed. He had predicted
it, but had hoped he would be wrong. He no longer had that
hope.

"What's wrong, Varth?" Nepanthe asked.

"I was right. The wolves are going to pull Bragi down,
unless the apparently stupid things he's done are part of a
plan I can't fathom."

"You'll help him, won't you?"

"I won't. And don't argue. The break is complete. No
matter what happens."

"You're a stubborn old man. And you're just as foolish as
he is."

"Maybe." Privately, he agreed. But his pride wouldn't let
him make peace with Ragnarson.

Children's voices echoed up from below. Nepanthe said, "I'd better settle them down before they waken Smyrena."

"Send Ethrian up. I'll work on him some more." He sighed again. Mist's children were driving him to distraction. Sometimes he wished they were as vacant as Ethrian had become.

The boy had survived, but his mind was gone, lost in the shadows of his brain. He drifted around in a dream, able to communicate only the simplest wants. He was as helpless as his sister.

There had to be a way to free him. There was a way, damn it. Somewhere in these old books.

He glanced at the mirror. "Damn. There it goes. Don't the fools ever learn?"

A puzzled soldier told Inger, "My Lady, Captain Trebilcock is here to see you."

Her heart jumped. Trebilcock? Here? What was it? A trick to get close enough to kill her? "He's alone? Did he say what he wanted?"

"No, My Lady. He didn't. Yes, he's by himself. And he's not armed."

She debated sending him away with a few defiant words. But that wasn't wise. Seeing him might at least buy time.

She had to buy time. Time for Dane. Time for Bragi to get back from the mountains. Especially time for that. His intercession was her only real hope.

Maybe a reconciliation wasn't impossible. She could break with her family and try to win him all over again. She was the mother of his son.

Don't be a fool. You've completely destroyed his trust.

She peeped into the sitting room where the soldier would bring Trebilcock, hoping to get some sense of Michael before he saw her.

He was the same old Michael, sans weapons. Tall and pale and cool, unacquainted with fear. She considered the mad notion of having him killed. He scared her so much. He was like Dane, especially in his lack of conscience.

She screwed up her courage and stepped into the chamber. Guards snapped to attention. Michael bowed. He pursued the courtesies due her station. "Your Majesty. You look well. We'd heard you were ill." He acted like there was no enmity between them.

"I'm recovering." Was this going to be a play of double meanings and pretense? No. She wouldn't allow it. "What're you doing here?"

Michael didn't respond as she expected. He simply replied, "I have a proposition for you. A way to break this deadlock and avoid its unpleasant potential."

She sat down, studied him. He didn't react to her scrutiny. He said, "You look unhappy. I've always thought that your most endearing quality was your ability to smile no matter the circumstances. I've always envied you that. I'm sorry to see you in a position so tight the smile has died."

She was taken aback. "Stick to the proposition."

A smile flickered across Trebilcock's lips. "All right. One. You yield your claim to Kavelin's throne. Two. Fulk surrenders his claim to succeed. Three. The marriage is annulled. Four. You return to Itaskia, with all your people, and forget Kavelin exists. In return, we'll see that you get away safely and compensate you for any properties you've acquired here."

"That isn't a very exciting proposal, Michael. I'd have to give up everything I've lived for."

"It means you'll live."

"What?"

"In plain words, Your Majesty, it's the only chance you and Fulk have of getting out alive. I would hate it if it came to the other extremity. I wouldn't want to face my conscience afterward. Fool that I am, I've always had a soft place in my heart for the King's unattainable lady. I'd hate to be forced to make a choice between my heart and my duty."

Inger sprang up. "What?"

"You do have the most marvellous smile."

Inger strode to the nearest window and stared out without seeing the roofs and spires of Vorgreberg. What was this? She couldn't have been more confused had Derel Prataxis come courting. It had to be a lie. Some part of their plan.

"Your Majesty," Michael said, "there was a rumor that

somebody tried to poison you. I got Doctor Wachtel to tell me about it. Unfortunately, I haven't been able to find the party responsible. I do know that you've made a lot of enemies among the King's friends. I know that if the Estates try to instigate another riot, your life won't be worth a farthing. I barely restrained Colonel Abaca last time."

She turned, stared at him, totally baffled.

"Your absence from the picture would simplify everything. It would draw the teeth of the Estates. They wouldn't have a figurehead behind which to rally. You see? So I'd rather have you safely out of Kavelin than dead here."

She opened her mouth, closed it again. What could she say?

Michael moved toward the door, then paused. "My people can get you out. We can pretend that you're here till you're safely away. But if you don't fulfill the other three points, they'll keep after you. I'm not the only man in Vorgreberg who has a long reach."

Again she opened her mouth and closed it.

"Let me know soon? Please?" The emotion in his voice sounded genuine.

He stepped out. A soldier closed the door. Inger returned to her chair and the wild turmoil rampaging through her mind.

Fortress Maisak, which guarded Kavelin against encroachment from the east, clung to the side of the mountains in the narrowest section of the Savernake Gap. At that point the pass was a steep-sided, twisting canyon, and Maisak commanded all movement through it. The fortress itself was nearly invulnerable. Only Shinsan had ever been able to reduce it.

Ragnarson had completed a thorough inspection brought on by boredom. Sir Gjerdrum and Baron Hardle stood by nodding as he observed, "The place is in first class condition. I can't see a thing that needs improvement."

The garrison commander beamed. Ragnarson turned, looked out at the canyon. His army was camped on the canyon floor, facing the first eastern checkpoint, which lay just a few miles east of Maisak. He felt a tingly eagerness to be doing something, an almost suicidal impulse to charge ahead.

A messenger appeared. He looked pallid. "Signal from Vorgreberg, Sire. From Captain Trebilcock."

"Well?"

"Throyen troops have entered Hammad al Nakir. The fighting is savage. Lord Hsung had to commit his own troops to effect the initial breakthrough."

That tingle grew to a buzzing in Ragnarson's bones. Damn! His bluff hadn't worked. He said, "We've been sitting here for nothing. Mist. . . . Mist. . . ." He didn't know quite what to say about her. "Messenger. Did Captain Trebilcock say how old his news is?"

"No, Sire."

Bragi stared into the canyon. Assume Michael had gotten the word through Aral's smugglers. That meant it had been hand-carried across the mountains along rugged game trails. At least a week in transit. Meaning Hsung had been rolling at least that long.

"Gjerdrum. Send a recon party down to that checkpoint. See how they react."

Sir Gjerdrum looked worried. "You want me to engage them, Sire?"

"Yes. Push them good. I want to see what happens."

Gjerdrum looked at him askance.

"Go on. I want to know before dark."

"Yes, Sire." Gjerdrum's voice was taut. And Baron Hardle had gotten an odd look.

Bragi said, "Not to worry. Border skirmishes happen all the time. Nobody gets excited about them."

"We're supposed to have a deal with Lord Hsung," Hardle said.

"Supposed to have. He didn't live up to it. He's imprisoned five hundred of our people. So we should feel guilty?"

Hardle kept looking at him strangely. Irritated, he went down to his quarters. He tried to eat, to nap, and could do neither. His nerves were aflame. He prowled restlessly.

Gjerdrum returned. "The post was abandoned," he said. "They were down there four days ago. I sent scouts on down the canyon."

"Good. What do you think?"

"About what?"

"The situation."

"I don't want to think about it. I get bad feelings."

"Suppose we moved up again? Just enough to rattle Hsung."

"I don't think you can shake him. He doesn't care what you do."

"No. I think he decided I was bluffing. If we went down and occupied Gog-Ahlan. . . ."

"He's committed, Sire. He's Tervola. He isn't going to back down. Not from us."

"You're probably right. Should just pack up and go home. But damnit, the man makes me mad. I'd like to give him a good kick in the ass."

"You don't want him down on us."

"No? He's already as down on us as anybody can be."

Michael's next report said Hsung's move had inspired more guerrilla activity than even the Disciple's commanders had hoped. Yasmid's troops, too, were fighting more stubbornly than expected.

Bragi wondered, "How long before Megelin starts moving? That's when Yasmid will have real problems. She'll be hopping like a one-legged fireman. Gjerdrum, keep moving down the pass. Don't stop till somebody gets in your way."

"Yes, Sire." Gjerdrum looked sour.

"Caught between the Tervola and Magden Norath," Bragi mused. "I don't envy her."

The pass proved to be clear all the way to Gog-Ahlan.

Michael sent another message. Hsung was stalled. His Throyen puppets had suffered severe losses. Throyes itself was in flames. Hsung had had to move his headquarters out of the city. He had called for reinforcements from his legions at Necremnos and Argon.

"That does it," Bragi said. He assembled his captains. "We can tip the balance. We're going ahead. Into Throyes."

The arguing grew loud and bitter. Ragnarson ended the debate, at last, by thundering, "I'm not asking. I'm telling you what we're going to do. Just like the raid on Argon at the beginning of the Great Eastern Wars. We're marching. First light tomorrow. And I'll have the head of any man who sends word back to Vorgreberg. Understood?"

The meeting broke up in anger and disaffection. Bragi watched his captains nervously. Would they stick it out? They'd better.

Hsung was going to be one surprised son of a bitch.

21

DAHL DOUBLE-CHECKED his document case, made sure his gear was secure, swung into the saddle. There was a lot he wanted to say, but he wasn't good with people. He just said, "Good-bye, Colonel. Thanks for everything."

"Godspeed, son. Tell your King we'll try to break it up at this end."

"Right." Dahl urged his mount into the street. Dawn hadn't yet broken. He had Kristen in his eyes. He was in a hurry to get home.

Home? he thought. I always thought of the stead as home. The old saw was right.

Introspective, wondering what would become of himself and Kristen, he wasn't alert. It wasn't till he had begun riding through farmland south of the Silverbind that he suddenly realized the three men behind him had been there for some time. He increased his pace. They did the same.

He was in trouble.

What to do? He couldn't fight. Could he outrun them? Not likely. They were travelling light. His mount was loaded for a long journey. Lose them somehow? How? This was open country. It was a good fifteen miles before the road entered wooded ground. . . . They didn't seem eager to catch up, though. Why rush it? If they were just following him, let them. He could outlast them. His horse was a tireless beast. His own stamina was superb. He could keep on till they couldn't stay with him anymore.

Good thinking. It would have worked, too, had they not been herding him toward confederates waiting in the woods.

The trap closed neatly. Dahl found himself surrounded by tough-looking men. Their captain was Josiah Gales.

They looked at one another. Dahl knew there was no lie he could tell that would explain his presence. Gales knew exactly what he was doing, just as he knew about Gales. He sighed. "What now, Colonel?"

"You come see a man who wants to talk to you."

Haas shook his head, smiled weakly. "Nine women in one day," he said.

Gales scowled. "Not here, Haas. That game is over." He wheeled his mount. The others followed, Dahl tucked neatly in amongst them.

Got to get rid of those despatches, he thought. Can't let them get hold of those. He racked his brain. Nothing came to him. No opportunity arose. His escort remained close and watchful.

They took him to a small hunting lodge. Gales politely asked him to accompany him inside. Dahl decided to make no fuss over his possessions. They might decide to dig through them.

They would be expecting him to be carrying something, of course. Maybe they could be distracted with the smaller courier's case strapped to his side.

He studied the lodge as he moved through it. It hadn't been designed as a fortress or prison. Get out of sight of his captors for a few minutes and he could be gone.

Gales took him to a bone-thin old man eating pheasant in a small, comfortable room off the kitchen. "Sir Mortin, this is Captain Dahl Haas. Dahl, Sir Mortin."

Dahl knew the name. He had learned a lot about the Greyfells family during his stay. "Good morning, sir. Why have your men waylaid me?"

Mortin smiled. "You might ask that, young fellow, but why bother? You know perfectly well why, and you know I know. Let's not bluff each other. Sit down." He indicated the chair opposite him by pointing with his knife. "Reeves. Bring another setting for our guest."

Dahl decided to cooperate for now, to disarm them with his amenability. "Thank you, sir. And, sir, I really don't see why your men have waylaid me."

"Young man! Do you take me for a fool? Because you're carrying information to Kavelin."

"Nothing the King doesn't already know. Stopping me is

meaningless. I'm just going home. The important information went south by courier the day Gales arrived in Itaskia.
He was recognized by people from the Ministry."

Mortin looked up at Gales. "Josiah?"

"He could be right, sir. That's the sensible thing to have
done."

"Yes indeed. Yes indeed. Young fellow, you present me
with a quandry."

"Sir?"

"Evidently we shouldn't have bothered intercepting you.
But we have. So what do we do with you? Go ahead. Eat. It's
a fine bird. It'll just go to waste. Let's see, then. Assuming
that courier did go out, you're no longer of any significance.
No use to us, and of insufficient value to our enemies to
make it worth killing you. Yet the idea of just turning you
loose again grates. Josiah? Do you have a suggestion?"

"Well, sir, we might try talking him around to our side."

Dahl was astounded. He wanted to spit out a defiant
curse. Common sense made him keep his mouth shut.

"Why didn't I think of that? What could be more useful
than having the King's adjutant on our payroll? There's a
problem, though. From what you've told me about this lad,
we'd have to invent some leverage. He wouldn't turn for
money, and certainly wouldn't for love of our Duke or his
Queen."

Gales smiled. "No. But we'll have time to consider it
along the way, wouldn't you say?"

Dahl looked up sharply, a string of pheasant flesh trailing
from his lips.

"Ah, yes, Dahl. We're headed for Kavelin. This mob
and a lot more, as you'd surely learn being around here.
If for no other reason than that, we can't let you go. Sir
Mortin?"

"Definitely. His courier couldn't have known that. Well,
son, we'll have to keep you with us. I'll be a good host as
long as you're a good guest. But I can't guarantee your
health if you do something dramatic. We do have to protect
ourselves. Josiah, I'd say the pantry would be the best place
to keep him."

"Yes, sir. When you're finished, Dahl."

Haas ate slowly. His mind raced. He seemed to be in no

immediate danger. But his chances of getting away with his documents, and warning the King that the whole damned Greyfells clan was about to descend on him, looked slim.

He wondered what they were doing back at the Ministry. Had they caught on yet? Would someone be coming after them?

It looked like time for a prayer.

22

Year 1016 AFE

MICHAEL WATCHED CREDENCE Abaca limp into his office. He leaned toward Aral. "Looks like that limp is going to be permanent."

Aral whispered, "I heard they cut him up pretty bad."

"Sit down, Credence. Derel should be here any minute." He eyed Abaca. Maybe they should recall Liakopulos from Karak Strabger, where he was training the year's recruits. Credence's wounds were awfully slow healing. Perhaps he had fallen foul of a poisoned Tervola blade.

They might need a garrison commander who could get around fast. Liakopulos could turn his trainees over to someone else.

Derel came in. He looked exhausted. "Hard day in the Thing. The Estates are trying to revoke the weapons act again. We barely defeated them. Mundwiller almost had apoplexy. Two of his people deserted him. We've got to get Hardle back here to whip the Nordmen into line."

The weapons act had given freemen the right and obligation to keep and bear arms. It was the single most effective constraint on the power of the nobility, who no longer dared ride roughshod over their tenants. Another law enacted about the same time had virtually eliminated serfdom, freeing peasants from their bonds to the land they worked. They could now desert an unjust liege. That law, too, was unpopular with the Estates.

Prataxis sagged into a chair. "So what is it now, Michael? Your message sounded desperate."

"Could be. Is Cham coming?"

"No. He's planning tomorrow's counterattack. He's on his last legs, though. If the King doesn't get back soon. . . . What is it? You look grim."

"I'll let Aral tell you. That's why he's here."

Dantice hemmed and hawed. He felt out of place.

"Get on with it," Michael said. "Just tell them what you told me."

"This came in this afternoon," Aral said. "From a friend who just got back from Throyes."

Prataxis said, "I was becoming concerned. We hadn't heard anything for so long."

"You have reason," Michael said. "Aral?"

"Hsung was assassinated."

"What? The guerrillas?" Prataxis was shocked. How did an assassin reach a Lord Hsung?

"No. His own people did it," Aral said. "I didn't get many details. Just that he was killed, and another Tervola stepped right in. Sent by Mist."

Michael interjected, "Meaning she was behind the assassination."

Prataxis nodded. "Lord Hsung was way out of line. I'm surprised the Council would authorize that vigorous a sanction, though."

"All very interesting," Abaca said. "But why are you in a panic? This Tervola or that, what's the difference?"

"This one has stopped the invasion of Hammad al Nakir," Aral said. "He ordered the troops to stop where they were, and not to fight unless they were attacked. He's trying to negotiate with Yasmid, hoping she'll make peace."

"And she will," Michael opined. "Word I get out of Al Rhemish, also courtesy of friend Aral, is that Megelin has sent Rahman, Norath and five thousand men to attack Sebil el Selib."

"So the fighting has stopped. So what?" Abaca asked.

Prataxis replied, "So we've had no contact with the King for eight days. Right, Michael?"

"Exactly. When I send a message to Maisak I get evasive replies. Nothing from the King. I queried Liakopulos. He's in the dark too. What it suggests is, the King got a wild hair and moved on down to Gog-Ahlan. Maybe even decided to attack Hsung from the rear."

"We're in trouble," Prataxis said.

"Maybe big trouble," Aral agreed. "There's already rumors saying he went east. Right now they're just bull put out by the Estates, but in a few days people are going to be asking serious questions. And we won't have the answers. Michael, I told you he would shoot the long odds again."

Trebilcock closed his eyes. "I sent Aral's news to Maisak right away. I demanded a direct response from the King. They acknowledged receipt. I haven't heard anything else. I'm praying I do get something from him. If I don't pretty soon, though, I'll assume he went on through the pass."

"Stupid," Abaca muttered. "Stupid, stupid, stupid. I'd better call in reinforcements."

Prataxis suggested, "Better warn the garrisons in Damhorst, Breidenbach, Forsberg, and Sedlmayr too. If there's trouble it'll spread from city to city fast. I'd recommend a general alert. Better do something about Kristen, too, Michael."

Michael asked, "I take it we all expect the worst?"

"Maybe not expect it," Prataxis said. "But plan for it. Be ready for it. Damn. I wish we could send the Thing home. Get them scattered around so it would take them longer to cause trouble."

Michael said, "Let's get to it. We may not have much time."

Abaca grumbled, "I'm beginning to wonder if it's worth it anymore. We never seem to make any headway."

"I hear you," Derel replied, and stumbled wearily out of the room.

Michael growled, "I feel the same way sometimes, Credence. Like right now."

Inger had gathered those of her dowrymen who were party to the family plot. She was ready to accept Michael's offer. "Anyone have anything to tell me?" They knew what was on her mind. The King's people had mounted a harsh psychological offensive. "Trebilcock asked to see me tomorrow. He wants my answer. My mind is pretty much made up. Karl?"

"Stall him if you can. We've finally established communication with the outside. The Estates say you should hang on. Ragnarson may have overstepped himself and gone on through the Gap. Let's find out if that's true. Could be the break we need."

Inger asked, "That's a rumor, right? What's the source?

The Estates? Or someone less likely to be making it up?"

"Can't tell for sure. Estates agents are spreading it, but they claim they picked it up in the streets. You know the King better than anyone. Would he go off like that?"

"Yes and no." Yes, he would do something like that. He'd done so before. But no, not under today's conditions. He'd had half the wizards of the west with him during his raid on Argon. He had no wizard now, and faced one of the top dozen Tervola of Shinsan. Bragi wouldn't attack in those circumstances.

"He wouldn't do it," she decided. "He might let everybody *think* he was doing it. Then he could see what we'd do if we thought he was off doing something insane. No. He's up there in the Gap where nobody can see what he's doing. He's waiting, studying the news. At the right time he'll swoop down like an eagle. And anyone who's fool enough to believe the rumors and try to profit will get snatched up like some hapless rabbit."

Her advisers looked thoughtful. One observed, "This morning Abaca ordered a new gibbet put up. A big one. Might mean he's expecting something."

Inger's stomach tightened. "The Estates aren't planning another riot?"

"No. The last one went so badly. . . ."

"Find out for sure. Trebilcock said the next one would kill us. Abaca could be building that gibbet for us."

The man added, "Abaca also sent secret orders to all the major military commands. He's called some units into Vorgreberg. He must know what's going on."

Another said, "Sounds to me like he's part of what the Queen was saying. That buzzard is sitting up there laughing at us. The way things were going, he couldn't do anything that didn't make him look bad. But if we do anything now, it'll look like treason. Nobody would much complain if something happened to us."

Inger said, "There are a lot who would cheer. A lot who resent the fact that there are so many foreigners in the palace. They like us less than they like my husband."

"That raises a question that's never been adequately answered, My Lady. What do we do with the man? Assuming we ever do take over?"

"That's a moot question." And one I want to avoid, Inger thought. "Our taking power isn't even a pipe dream anymore. Survival is the question here. We have to decide what I'm going to tell Trebilcock tomorrow."

"Stall him."

"Put him off."

"What if he won't be stalled?" She didn't want to stall. She was tired of this dreary little kingdom and its plague of selfish nobles, tired of the role her family had thrust upon her. She was tired of being afraid, and tired of being in continuous danger. She was ready to meet Michael's conditions. She just wanted to get away, to go home, to raise her son and be free of the vicissitudes of politics.

She wished she could ride away the way Bragi had described, drifting off into history, Kavelin's crown left for whoever wanted it. Maybe she should have offered to ride away with him. It might have been interesting, living with him the way his first wife had, with every day an honest struggle for honest pay. . . .

"My Lady?"

"Yes? Sorry. I was daydreaming. All right. I'll try to stall him. Meantime, find out what's going on. Try to contact the Estates again. If there's anything I should know, tell me before Trebilcock shows up. Now go somewhere. I need to think."

What she needed was time alone, time not so much to think as to weep for everything that might have been, everything she had hoped for in the few hours between her receipt of Bragi's proposal and her having gone to Dane for advice.

Dreams die hard.

Ragnarson gave the signal. The light horse company surged forward, swept round the flank of the hill, hurtled toward the shanty trading center built alongside the ruins of Gog-Ahlan. "Drums," he shouted. "Double cadence, forward."

Drums began grumbling. The troops picked up the beat and double-timed forward. The heavy horse rolled along at their flanks. "They look good," Ragnarson told Baron Hardle. "Very good indeed."

Sourly, Hardle replied, "They've had good leadership. And they believe in their supreme commander."

Ragnarson scowled. Hardle was worse than Gjerdrum. But give the man his due, he wasn't sabotaging anything. He was performing his tasks to the limits of his capacity.

"Back with your men. Septien!" he shouted at the commander of his Marena Dimura scouts. "Move out. If anybody gets by you I'll have your scalp."

The scouts galloped off to interdict the road to Throyes. They were to stop anyone who escaped the light horse.

Ragnarson spurred his mount, hastened to the head of the column. He rounded the flank of the hill and looked out on the plain where the ruins lay. "What the hell?"

There was nothing there. At least, nothing to compare with what had been there last time he'd come this way. The trading town had been a city then, wild and colorful and ramshackle. Now there was nothing but a neat geometric layout. A barracks city with only a few non-standard buildings off to one side. The barracks and the low curtain wall surrounding them seemed to have been assembled from stone salvaged from the ruins.

"That makes sense," he muttered. "Use the materials at hand. And why would the traders stay after trade was cut off?"

Ragnarson pointed at a trumpeter, beckoned, charged toward the town. He was certain he would find it wholly abandoned. All this energy expended for nothing. But it would be good for the men. It would get them used to moving when it was time to move.

The light horse were almost upon the barracks, their wings sweeping forward to surround the buildings, when a lone horseman appeared among the ramshackle civilian structures to the right. He whipped his animal into a gallop. A squadron of horsemen turned after him. Ragnarson did the same. In the distance Septien swung back as he spotted the horsemen too.

The man turned this way, that, and saw all escape fade away. He pulled up and waited. In moments he was surrounded.

Bragi reined in, looked the man over. "Throyen. Anyone speak the language?" Most Kaveliners spoke several tongues, if only because there were four languages current in Kavelin itself. Many more spoke the tongue of one or another of the kingdom's trading partners. Of those Throyes had been the most important.

"Here, Sire," one soldier said, and another raised his hand.

"Ask him questions. The kind of things we're interested in."

The soldiers asked when the legion had withdrawn, where the civilians had gone, what this one man had been doing there alone. They asked about the surrounding territory, and about what lay between Gog-Ahlan and Throyes. Bragi occasionally suggested additional questions. The prisoner was moderately cooperative.

He had been left to watch the pass. Insofar as he knew, there were no armed forces between Gog-Ahlan and Throyes. "Things have gone bad wrong," he said. "El Murid has a new general. Better than the Scourge of God, the old people say. I know we lost a couple of big battles. They've been sending everyone to the fighting."

Ragnarson exchanged glances with Hardle and Gjerdrum. "Better than the Scourge of God, eh?" Bragi muttered.

Hardle said, "He must be if he's making a showing against everything Lord Hsung's thrown in."

And Gjerdrum, "You think Habibullah exaggerated Yasmid's weakness?"

"No. He believed the story he was telling. Those people are funny. They'll fight like devils for a leader they believe in. You're not old enough to remember the things Nassef and el Kader did. Have the Baron tell you sometime. They damned near conquered the world."

The army made camp thirty miles southeast of Gog-Ahlan. Ragnarson kept his captains up late. It was obvious from his picking of nits that he wasn't comfortable with what he was doing. He went walking the camp perimeter after sending the others to bed.

It was a cool night, boding the approach of autumn. The stars were crisp and cold in the black felt sky. The encampment was orderly, and the cooking fires were low and shielded from the casual, distant eye.

These are good men, he thought. The best I've ever led. Perfectly honed, well-disciplined, and positively motivated. Were it not for the sorcery, they would stand up well to Shinsan.

What is the matter with me? Why am I doubting myself?

Why am I doing this? Logic weighs against it, as Gjerdrum and Hardle remind me with every look. Even if I do swoop in, and pull off the biggest coup of my life, what's really been gained? What drives me? Why do I *have* to do this? Because so much has gone badly at home? Am I trying to balance my failure as King with success at the one thing I *can* do well?

He stopped at the point of camp farthest south, stared toward where Throyes lay. His intuition had nothing to say. Instead, ghosts from his past hemmed him in. He remembered the friends and loved ones lost, the triumphs and defeats, the good times and bad. "I'm here because I don't know any better," he whispered. "I've been hurrying toward a fight, or running away from one, since I was fifteen years old. This peace since the end of the wars is the longest I've ever gone through. Maybe helping Mist woke something inside me."

A shooting star arced across the sky. "A man's life. One bright moment in the darkness. Am I looking for a flashy exit?"

When you got down to it, this raid had suicidal aspects. Hsung might be a renegade defying his Princess, but he was Tervola. If he were destroyed, or severely embarrassed, his brethren would be that much more incensed, that much more determined to settle scores. . . . Ragnarson jumped.

"Sire?"

"You startled me, soldier."

"I didn't mean to, Sire. I was being quiet on account of you might be thinking about something important."

Bragi chuckled. "Who can say?"

The soldier saluted and started to move on.

"Hold on a second."

"Sire?"

"What do you think about this?"

"This, Sire?"

"This march on Throyes. What do you think? What do

the men think? Honestly, now. I was a soldier myself once."

"Well, Sire, I don't think anybody is happy about it. Nobody understands. But for the most part they figure you know what you're doing, and it must be important or we wouldn't be out here."

Curious, Bragi thought. They still trust me. "Not that much grumbling and second-guessing?" Every soldier was a general, figuring he knew better than the people up top.

"No, Sire. Like I said, a lot of wondering why, but the only bitching is about the food."

"Some things never change. Thanks, son. On about your rounds now." He fixed his gaze on distant Throyes once more.

Four days, he thought. A hard, fast march. Into the city. Capture Hsung's headquarters. Wipe out his puppets. Give the pro-western and faithful Throyens a chance to organize, then scuttle back home.

I hope we take Hsung alive. . . . Ought to put him in a zoo and charge admission.

Four days. Will my nerves hold out?

Day dawned brisk and clear. Bragi bounced out of his tent and did a few jumping jacks. "What's that?" he yelled to his cook. "Smells damned good." He felt fantastic. He'd had a restful night, with no troubling dreams. The morning was one of those when everything seemed right, when he felt ready to whip the world.

He walked around behind his tent, which stood atop a hummock, stared off in the direction of Throyes. Can't be more than sixty miles now, he thought. Push hard today, rest well tonight, and hit them tomorrow.

It was going to go right. He knew it. All that soul-searching and worry had been for nothing. Throyes would fall easily. If it went well enough he might push on south, help Yasmid wrap Hsung's army in a pocket where it could be destroyed.

Wouldn't that frost the Tervola? More of their legions casually crushed by the western bane? Ha! And Mist? He'd love to see her face when she got the news. Serve her right for not keeping Hsung on a shorter leash.

He was sure Hsung didn't have Mist's sanction. She must

be having trouble getting the Tervola into line. Nobility could be restless, as well he knew.

"Good morning, Baron," he said cheerfully, as Hardle came up the slope to join him. "Isn't it a glorious day?"

Hardle smiled. "It is indeed, Sire. There's a magic in the air, isn't there?"

"I don't know what it is, but I feel great. I hope it's not just you and me."

It was not. The feeling infected everyone, though nerves should have been bowstring tight. But there are those mornings when things just seem ideal, and the world appears a beautiful place to all but the most sour of heart.

Even Sir Gjerdrum was cheerful. He hadn't smiled since Maisak. In private, he said, "I've been thinking, Bragi. You may be right about this. We might pull it off. And if we do, it might be the coup we need. It might get Shinsan off our backs for our lifetimes. It might be the stroke that silences our enemies at home. And they can't wait a lifetime. It's only the old Nordmen who want to get rid of us. There won't be many to replace them when they die off."

Bragi punched Gjerdrum's bicep. "Now you're getting it. This looked like a long shot when we started, but now I think we'll manage it. Wizard or no wizard." For days he had been looking over his shoulder, expecting Varthlokkur to appear. He assumed that the wizard would relent before the army reached Throyes.

"You think he'll show?"

"I'm confident. He's stubborn, so he'll try to make me worry, but he'll be here in time."

Breakfast finished, Ragnarson got the army moving. He had his scouts range far ahead. It wouldn't be long before they encountered some of the outlying farmsteads and manors orbiting Throyes. They were only seventy or eighty miles from the sea now. Though it was sparse, there was enough rainfall to support some cereal crops.

The night chill burned off fast. The day turned warm, though it never really became hot. The sky remained a clear, incredible cerulean blue. Bragi continued to marvel at how grand a world surrounded him. The hours slipped by.

"Look there, Klaus," he told one of his bodyguards. "That bird. It's a gull. We slide over the top of that range of hills and, if it stays this clear, you'll be able to see the sea."

The hills came closer. They were all rounded, humpy things, very old, carpeted with sere grass which gave them a tawny appearance. Off to the east there was a long black swath where a grass fire had run wild.

"Yo, Sire," a man shouted, pointing. "Riders coming in from the van."

Bragi stood in his stirrups, watched the men approach. They weren't hurrying. A routine report. He sat down, urged his mount forward.

"Sire," one scout said, "we've found a small watchpost." He indicated a hill slightly off the line of march. "Looks out over most of the plain. It wasn't manned, but there's a garrison in an adobe fort behind the hill. Twenty men, near as we could judge. Shinsan. They didn't act like they knew we were here."

"Uhm," Bragi grunted. He glanced back. The column was raising a lot of dust. "Is it that hill standing alone, out this way from the rest of the range?"

"Yes, Sire."

"Uhm. Did you see if there were any Tervola or Aspirators there?"

"No sign of any, Sire."

"You left somebody to watch? To keep them off that hill?"

"Yes, Sire."

"Good. Messenger. Get me Captain Tompkin." Back to the scout. "That fort very tough? Any reason a light horse company couldn't take it?"

"It's not really a fort, Sire. More like an adobe blockhouse with a four foot curtain wall around it. The gate was off its hinges."

"Good enough. Show Tompkin where it's at. Give him a look from the top of the hill. He can decide what's the best way to take it."

The attack went smoothly. Tompkin returned to report that the garrison of eighteen, taken by surprise, had fought well but in vain.

"They should have been on their toes," Bragi said. "When you've got a war going you've got to watch your back as close as your front."

The column began skirting the hill during the afternoon.

Bragi remained cheerful. Twenty miles of hills and ten of flatland and he would be pounding on the gates of Throyes. He would camp in the hills tonight, and swoop down in the morning.

"Sire."

Bragi looked where the man was pointing, to his left and the column's rear. Riders were coming in fast. The screen of outriders was folding in behind them.

"That doesn't look good. Halt the column. Trumpets, blow commanders to me."

Gjerdrum arrived first. Bragi told him, "Get up that hill and see what you can see."

The knight wheeled away. Five minutes later the scouts arrived, their horses lathered and winded and stumbling. Their leader swung down and began babbling excitedly in Marena Dimura.

"Hold on, son. Slow down. I can't follow when you talk that fast."

The man jumped up and down and pointed. Bragi still didn't get what he said, but his meaning was obvious enough. There was trouble out that way.

Captain Septien arrived, listened, went grey. "Sire," he said, "there's a Shinsaner cohort headed this way."

"They seen us?"

The chief scout asked, listened. "He doesn't know."

"All right. Damn it all anyway. Baron, take charge here. Get the outriders in. Get the column behind the hill. I'm going up top to watch. You. You. You." He indicated messengers. "Come with me."

He met Gjerdrum halfway up. The knight looked greyer than Septien had. "What is it, Gjerdrum?"

Gjerdrum swallowed, said, "You'd better go see for yourself."

"Bad, eh?"

"Yes."

Bragi ascended to the watchpost. The scout had been right. Five or six hundred men formed a dark stain moving his way. No problem, really, except . . . except that that was just one of four such stains moving in from different directions.

"Gjerdrum. Think there's more of them?"

"Yes. In the hills. That's where I'd have put them."

"Right. No doubt that they know we're here? That they're coming after us?"

"Not in my mind."

"How did they know? And where did they come from? They're supposed to be tied up down south."

"What will we do?"

"We have the interior advantage. They're scattered. Get down there, take the horse out and smash . . . that bunch. They're the closest." The armies of the Dread Empire seldom used mounted warriors. Against western heavy cavalry they hadn't ever shown well. "Then come across after this bunch due east of us. Then that bunch there. Knock us a hole we can run out."

"You're going to run for it?"

"Damned right. No point in going ahead when they know we're coming. We won't fight any more than we have to to get away. We get through the gap, we should be able to stay ahead. We're in as good a condition, and they'll have to break through the horse to reach the rest of us."

Bragi scanned the plains again. He was disappointed but not upset. The mood of the day persisted. The trap did not look inescapeable. "You bastard, Hsung, you won a round. But I'll get you one of these days. Get going, Gjerdrum. Runner. Message to Baron Hardle. We're going to dig in on this hill till Sir Gjerdrum clears us a way out. Go tell him."

Bragi looked at the approaching enemy again, then elevated his eyes to the sky. There was one small trouble with his scheme. There might not be enough light left for Gjerdrum to open a wide enough gap.

Gjerdrum did crush two of the enemy units before the seeing became poor. But four more groups appeared. No hole big enough opened. "A whole damned legion, must be," Ragnarson murmured. Meaning the force he faced was at least as strong as his own. And, overall, better trained, armed, and disciplined. His men were good, but the soldiers of the Dread Empire were better.

"Well, Baron, looks like I did it this time," he said over a cold evening meal, against a background of grumbling eastern drums. "I put us in a good fix."

Hardle nodded, then surprised Ragnarson by saying,

"But you'll get us out. You always do."

The man's faith was touching. "Maybe. We've got the South Bows and the high ground. We get dug in good tonight and we'll be all right."

He hoped.

Silently, he thought, Varthlokkur, where the hell are you? I'm up to my ass in Tervola. I need a little help here. It's time to quit fooling around.

23

Year 1016 AFE

NEPANTHE LOOKED OVER her husband's shoulder, into a mirror where ghost-shapes on a southern hill dug ditches and erected earthen barriers. Other men moved into positions surrounding the hill, creating barriers of their own.

"You are going to help him now, aren't you?" Nepanthe asked.

Her son Ethrian stood behind her, a specter of a youth, his eyes dull. He made a strange whimpering sound whenever his gaze crossed the mirror. The baby fussed whenever she heard that sound. Nepanthe crooned to her.

Varthlokkur did not answer her.

Mist's children trooped into the room, leaned on the back of the wizard's chair. "What's that, Uncle Varth?" one asked.

"A battle. In the south."

"Can we watch?"

"You should be in bed. Besides, nothing will happen till tomorrow."

Ragnarson's men launched nuisance strikes all around their perimeter. Their enemies did nothing but drive them off. Nepanthe observed, "It looks like Hsung doesn't really want to fight."

Varthlokkur replied, "He'll unleash his Tervola in the morning. Why fight when the Power can deliver an inexpensive victory?"

"And you won't be there. Will you? You're going to let those men die just because your pride was hurt. You're a fool. Sometimes you disgust me."

"Put the children to bed."

Nepanthe left in a huff, herding the children before her. Varthlokkur stared into the mirror for an hour. His face reflected a bitter inner struggle. Finally, he swore, "Damn it!" and rose.

He took a small case off a nearby shelf and sat at a table. Within the case lay a bow eighteen inches long and four black arrows half that length. The arrows had silver heads and beaten gold fletching. Their shafts were inlaid with red and white traceries so fine they were barely discernable. The wizard strung the bow with a string of virgin's hair, stared at it for a long time.

He swore again, took up a pen and thin piece of paper. He scribbled something, sanded the message, wrapped it round the shaft of an arrow, touched it lightly with spittle and said a few words. The paper clung tightly.

He rose, bow and arrow in hand, and descended the long stair spiralling down the inside of the tower atop which his workshop perched. He went outside the castle keep, crossed a courtyard, mounted a wall overlooking a two thousand foot drop. His home, Fangdred, crowned the highest mountain in that savage range called the Dragon's Teeth.

He considered the naked stars. They seemed to mock him. Fool, they called him, just as his woman had done. Stubborn fool.

He stared across the ivory-tipped peaks, spoke a few words in the tongue of his youth. He visualized Mist. In moments her face seemed to be floating before him. He laid arrow across bow, let fly at the snickering stars. The shaft vanished into the night, pursued by a deep-voiced moan.

Radeachar drifted down out of the darkness, hovered above the wizard, sensing his inner conflict, sensing that Varthlokkur needed something, not knowing what to do. The wizard touched the Unborn's protective globe. "My one true, unquestioning friend. Let's go inside. My bones are old. I'll take my death of chill out here."

"P'u Hsiu says they've finished encircling his legion, Mistress," an Aspirator reported.

Mist slid back from the table and map she'd been studying, gestured. The Aspirator placed another map before her, smoothed it out. He used a marking crayon to draw a kidney-shaped enclosure, then some fragmentary lines indicating the approximate positions of neighboring legions.

Mist nodded. "What do we have in reserve down there?"

"One cohort without Tervola or Aspirators, commanded by Leading Centurion Ki Mo-Jo. They were taken out yesterday for rest. Little more than half normal strength."

"Have Mo-Jo attack to the left and plug that gap."

"The right is a narrower break, Mistress."

"That's where they'll expect the counter. Tell Mo-Jo he can have shaft support if he needs it, but not to waste them. Budget him a dozen."

"As you command, Mistress." The Aspirator removed the map and went about his business.

Mist stared at the smaller scale map revealed once more. It portrayed a sad situation. The counteroffensive had bogged down in the sheer mass of the Matayangan foe. She was consuming her reserves in a struggle to maintain the integrity of her front. Still, fracture lines appeared faster than they could be patched. She leaned back, sighed in exhaustion and disappointment.

Never before had the empire been faced with the possibility of having to negotiate from a position of weakness. If the Matayangans didn't crack soon, her own armies would. Their resources were almost exhausted. Soon she would have to start stripping Western Army and the training legions.

Something touched her lightly, like a spiderweb encountered on a lonely woodland path. It enfolded her, seemed to pull at her.

She sat bolt upright. Somewhere some master of the Power was concentrating on her. She'd better ready her defenses.

A window burst inward. A low moan filled the room. There was a *whump* as something smashed into her table. Maps flew. Dust motes danced in the candlelight. A small arrow stood quivering in the tabletop. A piece of paper encircled its shaft.

She studied the arrow, sensed only the spells that had propelled it. She licked a finger, touched it to the paper. It let go of the arrow. She picked it up gingerly, read it. "Humph! Lord Lun-yu. Do we have a portal connecting us with Commander Western Army?"

"We did this morning, Mistress. I'll check."

She read the note again. So. Varthlokkur knew what was happening in the Throyen theater. Knew more than she, evidently. Lord Shih-ka'i had Bragi surrounded.

What damnfool notion had brought Bragi out of the mountains? Why hadn't he stayed there? The idiot!

Lord Lun-yu reappeared. "We do have an open portal, Mistress."

"Good. You know Lord Shih-ka'i. Go tell him to complete his present operation without resorting to the Power."

"Mistress?"

"He's encircled Ragnarson."

Lord Lun-yu very nearly danced. Mist nodded gently. "Yes. But I've just had a message from Varthlokkur. If Lord Shih-ka'i uses the Power, he'll intercede. With all the might at his beck."

"So?"

"I'm aware of the emotion involved in this, Lord Lun-yu. I'm also aware that it would be easier to take Ragnarson using the Power. But risking the wrath of Varthlokkur and the Unborn is far more dangerous than risking meeting Ragnarson in normal combat. Do you see?"

Reluctantly, Lord Lun-yu admitted, "I did see the Unborn in action during the wars, Mistress. I suppose we'd better give the wizard his way."

"Tell Lord Shih-ka'i to free up as many men as he can, too. Our reserve situation is desperate."

"Yes, Mistress. Mistress, can we trust the wizard to stay out of it now?"

"I think so. His word is usually good. Get going. The night is nearly gone. Lord Shih-ka'i will need time to adjust his plans."

"As you command, Mistress."

Mist gathered her maps. She began studying one which showed the debacle growing around the Argonese incursion along the Matayangan seacoast. "It was a good idea, Lord Kuo," she whispered to the ghost of her predecessor, "but you grossly overestimated the Argonese army."

* * *

"Officers and noncoms will take the last watch," Bragi said. "Let the men rest." He looked down at the encircling enemy camp. It was past midnight. His positions were as strong as they could be made.

Baron Hardle suggested, "You'd better get some sleep yourself. You look a bit hollow-eyed."

"Uhm. Maybe." He rubbed his eyes, knew there would be little sleep for him. He would be wrestling his conscience all night.

It was he the Tervola wanted.

He scanned the enemy again. One legion, he guessed. One legion that had been cut up some already. He had to get them to attack him. His bowmen could carve them up. Then a counterattack down the long flank, there, to open enough room for Gjerdrum to mount a charge. They couldn't keep Gjerdrum from breaking through if he got a run at them. Then the knights could hit them from the rear.

He snorted in self-derision. It sounded good, but it wouldn't work. The Tervola were going to use their power, and there was no way he could stop them. Unless. . . . He stared northward, toward the far Dragon's Teeth.

He was worried. Could the wizard really let him go down? "Don't be negative," he told himself. "The situation is never impossible."

"Sire?"

"Nothing." He sketched his thoughts about pulling the enemy under his bows.

"Did Lord Hsung serve in the west during the wars?" Hardle asked.

"I don't think so. Why?"

"Toward the end they pretty well learned how to handle massed arrow fire."

"What do you think of negotiating, then?"

"Sire?"

"Hsung wants me. Suppose we could get him to let the army go if I turned myself over?"

"No," Gjerdrum said.

Hardle shook his head. "Not even in extremity. We rose together, we'll go down together."

"I want to do what's best for Kavelin. What happens if Kavelin loses two thirds of its best soldiers?"

"What happens if Kavelin loses a King who cares?" Sir Gjerdrum demanded. "You know who takes over. The Estates. Inger will be like a peasant girl trying to ride a wild stallion. They suckered her on that succession business."

Bragi smiled a thin, hard smile. "Don't be so sure. The Estates might find they were suckered. That's one tough lady when she makes up her mind. And she has some nasty friends."

"Norath," Gjerdrum said. "I nearly forgot."

"Norath. Among others. I want you to get some rest. Win or lose, it'll be a hard tomorrow."

Ragnarson slept, but just for a few hours. He was up watching the enemy encampment long before the stars began to fade. He wakened the cooks early, had food distributed to the men. He had the company commanders double-check weapons and equipment. He had his forces in position long before the morning breeze brought the sun ballooning up over the eastern horizon.

His enemy was as ready as he. The growing light revealed black armored soldiers drawn up in order of battle, behind a trench which entirely encircled the base of the hill. "So much for sending Gjerdrum in," he growled. "At least till we're able to counter-fill those ditches. Messenger. Tell Sir Gjerdrum I want the animals brought to the top of the hill. Everyone will fight on foot."

He peered down at the tent where the standard of Western Army stood. The standards of two legions flanked it. He scowled. Two legions? There weren't that many men out there. . . . Maybe it was elements of two legions, survivors of the fighting in the south.

He began pacing round the hilltop, studying the enemy lines. They were extended temptingly thin. A captain less familiar with the legions would not have been able to resist.

He put temptation aside. "They have to come to me. Pray they don't try to do it the easy way by starving us out." Idly, he wondered if there were some way he could get a message to Yasmid asking her to step up her activities. Put Hsung under pressure to finish here, and. . . . Had Hsung beaten her already? But the way that prisoner had talked, Hsung's people had gotten the worst of it down there.

He shuddered. The legion drums had been pounding constantly since their arrival. The ceaseless rumble was getting on his nerves.

What was going on? Hsung being here had to have some meaning he couldn't fathom. Had to have. Something had happened. He looked north. "How much longer are you going to let me roast, wizard?"

The tenor of the eastern drums changed as the sun's lower limb cleared the horizon. Enemy troops began crossing their ditches and assembling facing the hill.

"Five cohorts," Bragi muttered. "Sending in almost half his men, like the five rays of a star. Just to test our stubbornness." But he wondered. Hsung hadn't even made a pretense of negotiation. That suggested both an intent to destroy Kavelin's army, and a supreme confidence in his ability to do so.

Why? Ragnarson wondered. He doesn't have the manpower to be that confident. . . . The sorcery. Of course. They have it and I don't.

Any minute the first smashing blow would fall. The air would scream with the torment of deadly spells.

The beat of the drums changed again. Five cohorts surged forward.

Ragnarson pointed at a trumpeter. The man blew till his eyes bugged, a screaming sound new to Kavelin's signal repertoire.

The army's drums began pounding out a beat which partially drowned that of the eastern drums. Somewhere on the flanks of the hill the attackers would reach a point where they could no longer be sure of their own signals. Hopefully, they would become confused.

The first arrows arced into the sky, rained down on the enemy. A few men went down, but, as Hardle had feared, they had adjusted their shieldwork to cope. "Come on, Talison," Bragi muttered. "Get those arbalasts down low. Let them get their shields up, then cut them off at the knees."

He paced, circled the hill, watched each enemy force for a moment before moving on to watch another. On the lee of the hill he cussed a regimental commander who was a little slow. Almost immediately smoke rose from the dry grass.

Flames leapt to life, began running before the breeze.

"Good. That ought to slow that bunch." He moved on.

The combination of confusing drums, flames, plunging arrow fire, and crossbow fire low had its effect. The attacking forces were growing ragged. But they came on. They approached the first ditch.

The real test would take place there.

Bragi paused to stare at the enemy headquarters. "When are you going to come with the witchery?" he wondered aloud. "You're overdue." Unconsciously, he hunched his shoulders against his neck.

The blow didn't come. Instead, more troops crossed the ditches below, advanced up the aisles unused by forces already climbing the hill.

"So. You're going to go for it all first try."

The first wave reached his first ditch. The clangor drowned the sound of the drums.

After a while, Bragi muttered, "Yes, going for it all first time." Hsung had kept just two cohorts in reserve. Ragnarson guessed that six thousand men were trying to fight their way up the hill. The defenders of the first ditch began to waver. Only on the grassfire side had the assault broken down.

He selected an average-looking section of slope and tried counting bodies. "Not bad," he grumbled. "But it could have been better. A whole hell of a lot better." His bowmen weren't doing nearly well enough. He had no way to estimate his own losses.

The long, bloody day dragged on. Eventually the first ditch had to be abandoned. Casualties nearly filled it. His men had given a good account of themselves. The tentativeness of the advance on the second ditch proved that.

Bragi glanced at the sun. A quarter of the day gone. Already. While time seemed to drag so slowly. He wished he had a taller hill and more trenches. Three had seemed enough when he had thought the bowmen would massacre whole formations.

Where was the sorcery? Why was Hsung wasting all those lives? Did he have something especially nasty waiting for just the right moment?

Noon. The second trench had fallen. The enemy seemed

to have left half his number lying on the hillside. But now the arrows and crossbow bolts were spent. Now it would be strictly sword and spear, hammer and dagger and maul. Does it come now? Bragi thought. The great nasty blow?

No. The legionnaires just stood there, this side of the second ditch, resting behind their shields, daring him to mount a counterattack. He did not. He would not. Not till they compressed his forces a good deal more. Not till they had taken more casualties and were even more tired.

The casualty ratio favored Kavelin. The battle was a bloodbath, but Shinsan was doing more of the bleeding.

Sir Gjerdrum took advantage of the lull. "We're doing good over my way," he reported. "Considering who we're up against. I'd swear we're taking three of them down for every one we lose."

"That good? Maybe we'll go your way when we try the breakout."

"Think the third line will hold?"

"Can't say. They'll have to come against mostly fresh men. They'll show just how good they are if they do break it."

"Something stirring down there. I'd better get back."

Hsung's reserves crossed the trenches. A thousand men, Bragi estimated. Would they lead the next assault?

Where was the damned witchery?

Shinsan's drums altered their beat. The battle resumed.

The third line proved less stout than Ragnarson had hoped. Soon he was rushing reserves here and there to shore up weak spots. "Messenger!" he finally howled. "Get me Sir Gjerdrum." He scowled in the direction of the Dragon's Teeth. "Wizard, you'd better hope I don't get out of this. Because if I do, I'll get you." Then he laughed at himself. "Fool. Blaming it on somebody else. All your own fault, you know."

Sir Gjerdrum found him readying himself for battle. His bodyguard had formed the drummers, trumpeters, cooks, and least badly injured into a final reserve pool. "Sire? You wanted me?"

"Damned right. Start extricating your horsemen. It's time to try a breakout."

Gjerdrum scanned the action. "That would weaken the

lines too much, wouldn't it?"

"Maybe. I'm taking this crowd down to stiffen them."

"Is that wise? If you're injured the men will lose heart."

"They'd collapse right now if they could. Half of them would run if there was anywhere to go. Gjerdrum, we're going to go down unless we do something. I know there's no room to launch a decent charge, but give it a try."

"What about the ditches?"

"What about them?"

Gjerdrum held his tongue. The ditches would kill men and animals. "Nothing, Sire. I understand." The situation was worse than he had thought. The hour of desperation had come.

"Varthlokkur may still show, Gjerdrum. Hang onto that." Ragnarson glared at the enemy headquarters. A handful of Tervola stood watching the hill. "Why haven't they used the Power?"

"I don't know, Sire. I almost wish they would."

"Do it when you're ready, Gjerdrum. I'll be too busy to give orders."

"As you command, Sire." Gjerdrum strode away.

Bragi ducked into his tent, collected his personal bow and arrows, signalled his bodyguard to follow him. He marched down the hill, selected a good vantage, loosed shafts carefully. Each found a mark. The damage stalled the enemy in that sector. During the disorganization he forced his way into the battle line. A ragged cheer arose. It rolled round the line and came back, and began rolling again. "Remember Baxendala! Remember Palmisano!" The enemy troops wouldn't know what the shout of defiance meant, but the Tervola below would hear it and be piqued.

Shield smashed against shield. Swords clanged. Bragi used every vile trick he knew. He sent an eastern soldier to his knees. Another took his place. The tides pushed them apart. Bragi faced a third opponent. The man on his right fell with a cry. Another bodyguard took his place.

The shout went up again. "Remember Palmisano!"

Bragi hardly noticed. His mind had gone on pure automatic. Stroke. Heave shield. Kick. Parry. Stab. Howl. Curse. Sweat. Especially sweat. Curse again as a vicious blow hit his shield so hard his arm went numb.

He had been here a thousand times. All the battles of his life melded into this one. He no longer knew or cared whom he fought. Time stood still.

But time hadn't stood still for his flesh. He was a man in his forties. He didn't have the stamina of decades past. His legs were pillars of stone, his arms limp bars of lead. Sweat ran into his eyes, stinging. And still he fought, lost in the dust and stink and bang and clang.

He did not hear the trumpets sound Sir Gjerdrum's charge. He did not witness it, either. Sir Gjerdrum led his charge down the nether face of the hill. He did respond when neighboring companies began backpedaling, drifting toward the opening Gjerdrum rent.

The shouting and cursing redoubled. Horses without riders screamed and reared and tried to flee through the press. Wounded men and animals carpeted the earth.

Bragi's bodyguards shouted at him to back off, to let them surround him. He flung a wild stroke at an enemy soldier, ducked back.

Something like a god's hammer hit his ribs on his left side. The breath exploded out of him. He couldn't groan. He felt his broken ribs grating. His bodyguards seized him, kept him upright. Red swirled around him, became blackness.

Gjerdrum was disappointed. Too many of the horsemen had fallen already, and he'd been able to extricate only a portion of the survivors. He guessed he had at most five hundred with which to attempt the breakout. He formed them with knights at the shock point, light horse behind and on the flanks, charged with keeping the aisle open once the knights broke through.

"Ready?" he asked.

"Ready, sir," the officers replied. They were pale, unsure. They too knew the ditches would be bad.

Gjerdrum scanned the fighting. The lines were holding. The ragged Palmisano cheer ran round and round the circle. Maybe it would be better to stand here. He had his orders. "Sound the advance."

Horns blared. Gjerdrum started forward at a walk. The

infantry had been warned. He hoped they were paying attention.

They were. They began forming aisles. Gjerdrum spurred his mount.

There wasn't much room, but he did get up a little speed. He drove his lance into the eye of an enemy, yanked it free, struck at another. His mount ploughed into the line. Enemy soldiers flew away. His lance snapped. He drew his sword, flailed about himself. His companions pressed from behind, driving him through. His animal lurched forward, toward the ditch.

He glanced back. A rent a hundred yards wide had been torn through the circle. Already the army was pouring through.

He looked forward again, estimating the ditch, trying to decide where to form up once he reached the plain. He had to hit the enemy headquarters. . . .

A shadow caught his eye. He glanced up. Already the crows were circling.

The ditch! He reined in frantically. He could negotiate it by walking his mount.

Someone ploughed into him from behind. His mount tripped over a corpse, went down in front. He tumbled forward.

"Oh, damn!" The earth came up to meet him. The wind burst out of him. Feebly, he fought to regain his feet. The weight of his armor was too much for his weakened muscles.

He did make it to his knees.

A knight plowed into him. He went over backward, tumbling into the ditch. His helmet flew off. He lost his sword. He came to rest on his back.

He saw a screaming horse and flailing rider falling sideways toward him. A wild, ironshod hoof drove toward his face. He flung up an arm. Too late.

There was but an instant of pain before the Dark Lady gathered him to her bosom.

When consciousness returned Ragnarson found himself at the top of the hill, supported between two bodyguards, in plain view of friend and foe. The battle continued, but the third line had broken. The enemy had forced a melee. He swore. Bloody spittle dribbled into his beard. "Sir Gjerdrum?" he croaked.

"Dead," a bodyguard replied. "Some of them broke out, Sire. Eight hundred or a thousand. Most just ran for it. A few tried to attack Hsung. He drove them off." The man's voice was shaky. His face was pale and sweaty. He was terrified.

Bragi tried to support his own weight. Pain stabbed through his left side. He nearly went down.

"Stand up, Sire. Stand up. You have to stay up. They'll keep fighting as long as you're standing."

"No," he gasped. "Let them stop. Don't let them throw their lives away."

"They're taking no prisoners, Sire. No prisoners. They're killing anybody who tries to surrender."

"That's stupid." Ragnarson tried to curse Varthlokkur, Hsung, Mist and himself. Especially himself. No words would come. Not till, looking one bodyguard in the eye, he managed to gasp, "I'm sorry."

"Stand up, Sire," the man said as he sagged again. "You have to stand up."

A remote spark of will forced stiffness into his legs. He stood, ignoring the pain, closing his eyes to what was happening to the finest army the west had ever produced.

From far, far away he heard the clang of sword upon sword as eastern soldiers reached the ring of men surrounding him. He lost consciousness.

A soldier heaved at Baron Hardle's shoulder, trying to obtain his attention. "My Lord. My Lord!"

Hardle whirled, blade slashing. The soldier ducked, having anticipated the stroke. Hardle recognized him. "Sorry, man. What is it?"

"We need you up top. The King is down. Sir Gjerdrum is dead."

Hardle eased out of the fighting, looked uphill. The royal guard had formed for a last stand. He saw the King sagging in the arms of his men. "How bad is he?"

"Smashed up, but not mortally. He passed out. Ribs stove in."

Hardle strode uphill. "Get that standard straightened up, soldier," he bellowed. "Let's see some pride." He attained the crown of the hill, surveyed the situation.

It did not look good. Those who had managed to break out were still running, not turning to help their comrades. "A curse on the lot of you," Hardle thundered. "May your cowardice be remembered forever. May they write songs of scorn naming your infamous names. May your children spit upon your graves." He almost enjoyed himself once he got going.

"A pity Prataxis isn't here to record this," he muttered. "The great last words of the rogue Nordmen. Talison! You yellow-livered son of a bitch, get back down there with your men and get a line formed." In a softer voice, "Got to break this melee somehow. You. You. You. Get over there and spook the rest of those horses. Run them down the hill."

"My Lord, if we run them off, how will we. . . ."

"Don't worry your pretty head about how you're going to get away, darling. You're not going to. Not unless we whip these bastards. If you try, I'll cut you down myself. I make myself clear? Anyone else in the dark?"

In fifteen minutes of frenzied order-giving he almost regained control. Almost. The absence of the men who had run made the difference. Once he was certain it was too late, he looked down on the enemy headquarters and murmured, "You know not what all you kill today, Tervola. Kavelin, we mourn thee before thy passing." He punched the men nearest him, demanding their attention. "You. You. All of you. Start chanting. Baxendala. Palmisano. So they never forget."

The end came slowly but inexorably. The madness of their overlords drove the eastern soldiers to needless death. Those great fools wanted so much more than victory. Nothing could satisfy them.

One by one, Kavelin's best went down.

Hardle was among the last. He died with a curse upon his lips, not for his enemies but for his brethren, those of his own class who would now have a free hand with the kingdom.

24

THE SHORT, WIDE Tervola in the boar mask walked slowly round the hilltop, stepping over torn bodies and mangled limbs. The setting sun cast long shadows across the battleground. Crows leapt up swearing as he disturbed them. Flies buzzed, rising and falling in dense clouds. They masked the eyes of the dead, filling them with their eggs. "Where do they come from?" he murmured. "Why doesn't the wind blow them away?"

"Lord Ssu-ma?"

"Nothing, Lord Lun-yu. Nothing. Tell me. Will you report this as a great day in the history of imperial arms?"

"You sound displeased, Lord Ssu-ma."

Lord Ssu-ma Shih-ka'i was displeased. "This shouldn't have been. It was a criminal waste of lives."

"But we saw the end of Ragnarson." Lord Lun-yu made that sound like *the* crucial event of recent history.

"Did we, now? Quite a few of them got away."

"Not he. He stood here on the hilltop till the end. Let's find the body. We'll parade it before the assembled Tervola."

"We will not."

"Lord?"

"There are limits, Lord Lun-yu. While I don't share your feelings about Ragnarson, I understand them. But I won't allow his corpse to be made a showpiece. He was a great foeman. He deserves honorable treatment. Moreover, I'm in his debt. He saved my life the day we finished the Deliverer. As you well know. You were watching from Lioantung's wall."

Lord Lun-yu scowled behind his mask but did not protest. Lord Ssu-ma was in high favor.

"I pity his kingdom without him," Shih-ka'i said. "Re-

274

turn to the Princess. We're finished here. Report a great victory if you dare tell the lie. Tell her I'll send as many men to the Matayangan front as I can."

"Lord . . ."

"Please go, Lord Lun-yu. As you noted, I'm not pleased. I wish to be alone."

"As you command, Lord." Lord Lun-yu withdrew.

Shih-ka'i slowly advanced to the hilltop, stepping around and over the fallen. Here and there men still breathed raggedly, moaned softly, cried out. They begged for water in a half dozen tongues. Below, his men were starting to clean up. They were finishing the western wounded. Their own they were carrying to headquarters. The Tervola there would decide which could be saved. Most who had survived this long would be. The Tervola had the Power to aid them in healing.

Shih-ka'i stared northward, toward the home of the wizard Varthlokkur. He shook his head. He did not understand. A man didn't abandon his friends.

He reached the circle where the royal guard had made its stand. Kavelin's army had fought well. On this hill the heart and guts had been carved out of two legions. Shih-ka'i thought real winners and losers were hard to discern.

What madness had brought Ragnarson through the Gap? He had walked into the trap with his eyes open. . . . No. He hadn't. He'd believed Lord Hsung to be in command. He wouldn't have come had he known otherwise. And had Lord Hsung been here still, Ragnarson's crazy gamble would have paid. Western Army would have been swallowed by disaster.

"I have salvaged the east, and now the west. And I feel nothing. Not even a little pride." He looked eastward. "Will she throw me at Matayanga next?"

He circled the heap of bodies marking the westerners's last stand. "This one. His name was Hardle? A great warrior, the Princess said. Sad. Ragnarson's champions went down with him. His kingdom will become a madhouse when those fugitives return." He looked across the plain. Columns of dust marked the whereabouts of fleeing westerners. "You could have won," he told their distant backs.

"You could have won. But you broke discipline when you needed it most."

His own men would have died to the last if never given the order to flee.

He spied the fallen King beneath several of his guards. "And that was the difference, my friend. That was the difference." He rolled one of the dead men off. "Maybe I'll raise you a monument. We shouldn't forget our great enemies." He heaved another dead man aside.

The King groaned.

"Well," said Shih-ka'i. "Well now. You're not completely dead, are you? Which, I suppose, means I have to repay my debt." He knelt, felt Ragnarson's pulse. It was strong. He heaved the last corpse off and examined the man. "Broken ribs. Punctured lung. Cuts and bruises. Otherwise, you're in good shape, my friend. They say you're extraordinarily lucky. And maybe they're right. Maybe your luck didn't turn all the way." He stood, faced his encampment, concentrated on the mask worn by his best life magician. His fingers wove subtle patterns in the air. "Come," he whispered. "Come here."

Kristen unsealed the letter from Vorgreberg. Sherilee hovered over her shoulder. The messenger remained at the door, one eye on the street. A dozen troopers from the Palace Guard waited there. They were restless, troubled

"What is it, Kris?"

"Michael thinks there might be a big uprising. He wants us to leave the country. He's sending us to a friend in Tamerice."

Elma and Maykin entered carrying a heavy trunk. The messenger called outside, "Bring those carriages up, Slug."

"What are you doing?" Kristen asked.

Maykin replied, "We were told to go with you."

"Why should we go anywhere? I haven't seen any sign of trouble."

"You haven't been out, either, Lady. The kingdom is rushing toward civil war. The Queen has been putting ideas into the heads of the Lords of the Estates."

"That bitch. I'll cut her heart out."

"Calm down," Sherilee said. "Kris, we'd better go. If

there is trouble, and she's behind it, it will find us first. You
know that. She's doing this for Fulk. We'd better be someplace else."

"What's the King doing?" Kristen asked plaintively.
"Why doesn't he come back and stop it?"

"He will," Sherilee said. "When he's ready. And he'll get
rid of Inger, too. You watch."

Kristen folded the letter and rose. "This is scary, Sherry.
Really scary. You're right. We'd better go."

An hour later they were in flight again, closely guarded by
Slugbait and his squad. Unknown to anyone but Slug
himself, and Trebilcock and Prataxis back in Vorgreberg,
most of the royal treasury was concealed in false bottoms in
the carriages.

"Are you satisfied now?" Nepanthe demanded. Tinkering
with the far-seeing mirror, she had learned what had
happened in the south. "Gjerdrum never did anything to
you, did he? He was always a good friend to me. And Baron
Hardle. . . . He was the only one who could keep the Estates
in line."

Varthlokkur stared at his dry old hands, not responding at
all. He needed no outside torturer to rack him.

"You've done it again. Destroyed another kingdom. This
time by inaction."

He rose and walked away, went out to the wind-swept
wall and stared into the canyon's deeps. Radeachar hovered
over his shoulder. Had the Unborn possessed a voice, it
would have whined.

Dahl sat his horse apathetically. He had given up on
escaping. These men watched him too closely. They kept
him at the heart of their company. There were almost four
hundred of them now, all hard veterans, managed by their
Duke himself.

"Gales is coming," Sir Mortin called.

Dahl looked up. Gales and a half dozen scouts had
returned from the checkpoint where the road left Altea for
Kavelin. Gales reined in before the Duke. He looked
puzzled.

"Well, Colonel? Can we cross?"

"Yes, Your Lordship. Easily."

"Why the long face?"

"Because there's no one at the checkpoint. The Alteans say they left day before yesterday."

"That's unusual?"

"Very. It's alarming. I'd guess it means all the troops are being gathered in anticipation of fighting farther east."

"There was no threat of war when you left?"

"None, Your Lordship. The King had irons in the fire, but the only reason I can imagine for mobilization would be internal."

"We'd better join Inger as fast as we can. Damn, but I wish we'd heard something. This silence is ominous."

Gales nodded. "Absolutely."

Dahl's heart quickened during the conversation. Fighting between the King's men and the Queen's? Kristen would be in danger. He had to get away. Somehow, anyhow, he had to elude these men.

Gales turned and rode ahead once more. The Duke spurred after him.

Gales turned when the Duke called after him. "Your Lordship?"

"I wondered if you'd noticed our guest's reaction to your news."

"I'm sorry. I didn't."

"He was thoroughly distressed. You haven't been able to enlist him?"

"He won't even listen."

"Pity."

"Ragnarson's people are that way. He inspires them with loyalty."

"You sound like you admire him. Eh. No matter. Save the excuses. Maybe Haas can help anyway. Without being on our side."

"Your Lordship?"

"He's quite taken with Ragnarson's daughter-in-law, right? You said she was sent into hiding before the Captures match."

"She was, yes."

"Think he knows where she is?"

"It's possible."

"Let him escape. Have him followed. If he goes to her, we're that much ahead. If he doesn't, we're out nothing. He isn't that important."

Gales nodded, concealing his disgust. "Eliminating potential pretenders would make things a lot easier."

"That's what I was thinking."

"He'll get away tonight. Someone will make a stupid mistake."

"Good, Colonel. Good. And this is the border? Yonder lies the fabulous kingdom of Kavelin?"

"That's it, Your Lordship. Not much different from any other kingdom, just to look at." Gales nudged his mount forward. Not much different, he thought. But sweeter than most. He felt like he was coming home.

Trebilcock dropped into a chair in Prataxis's office. "She's still stalling," he said. "I gave her a deadline. Told her I couldn't hold Credence longer than tomorrow. I think I'll have to throw in a little something extra, just to get her off the pot."

Derel nodded. He didn't look up. He flipped a sheet of paper across. "Look at that."

Michael read it. "Where'd it come from?"

"Your friend Dantice. Along with a good-bye. Said he'll see you someday, maybe down Tamerice way. Thought he was making a funny poem."

"Uhm. So. He was right all along. Bragi did do it. Six days ago?"

"He'll be in Throyes by now." Derel pointed. A small, crude map lay before him. He was using a compass to estimate distances. "And maybe done."

"Done?"

"Or done for. Is Credence ready? If Dantice knows, it won't be long before the whole country does. I'd guess we don't have much more than twenty-four hours."

Michael strained, grunted as he got to his feet. "I'll tell Credence. He'll want to up the level of alert. Then I'll get to work on the Queen. Maybe we can get her out before the news breaks."

* * *

A young signalman burst into Liakopulos's chambers unannounced. "Sir . . . Sir . . . You'd better come to the tower, sir."

"What's wrong, lad? You look like you've seen a ghost."

The youth gulped several times before saying, "It . . . it may be . . . it may be worse. Sir, the King may be dead."

Liakopulos surged up. "What?"

"The message wasn't all in when Sergeant Tipke sent me, sir. But Maisak says there was a battle. Some of the men just got back. They claimed everyone else was dead."

"All right." Liakopulos grabbed his swordbelt and cloak. "Let's go. And calm down. There must be some mistake."

There wasn't. Liakopulos had the message repeated. It didn't tell him much more, or anything different the second time round, though it did so at some length. It added that survivors of the battle were just beginning to trickle in.

"That's a hopeful sign. Message to the commander of the Maisak garrison," Liakopulos told the signals sergeant. "Hold all survivors there till the whole story is clear. And don't relay anything to Vorgreberg without my personal okay. And Sergeant, I want you and your men to go into seclusion. I don't want any wild stories getting out before we know exactly what's happened. Understood?"

The sergeant was a veteran of both the civil and Great Eastern Wars. He understood. "I'll see to it, sir."

"Who has the next watch?"

"Romin, sir."

"That the Marena Dimura fellow?"

"Yes, sir."

"Very good. Carry on, then." Liakopulos returned to his quarters, tormented. Suppose the King *was* dead? His legal responsibility was clear. He had to inform Vorgreberg, facilitate an orderly transition. But what was his moral responsibility? As the law stood, power would pass to people bitterly opposed to everything Ragnarson, Fiana, and the old Krief had tried to build.

Where did he stand in the equation? Assuming Ragnarson had gone down, and Sir Gjerdrum and Baron Hardle with him, he now controlled the army. He and Credence Abaca. And the army, even weakened by defeat, could be a kingmaker.

He did not want that responsibility. He had come to Kavelin to repay a debt to Ragnarson, not to juggle its crown. "Ye Gods above and below, attend me. If that message be true, make it false. Take this off my shoulders."

Inger couldn't tear her gaze away from the body. Cold sweat covered her. She began shaking. Ladies-in-waiting guided her to a chair well away from the window. Very, very softly, huskily, she said, "That could have been me. If Karl hadn't stepped in front of the window when he did, that could have been me."

Hunsicker ducked away from the window, came to her. He was pale. "The man who loosed that shaft was one hell of an archer, My Lady. It had to come all the way from Fiana's Tower."

"I don't care where it came from, Hunsicker. I don't care if the bowman was skilled or lucky. What I care about is that a man is dead, and it would have been me but for fate's intercession." She strained for control. Her shakes subsided. "I've had enough. They win. Send for Trebilcock."

"But My Lady. . . ."

"No more arguments. No more stalling. Karl is the last sacrifice to my cousin's ambitions. I want Trebilcock here within the hour, and you not being able to find him won't be an acceptable excuse."

"She gave in," Michael told Derel. "She's in a panic. And just in time. Gales is back. He's in Damhorst, along with another four hundred Itaskians."

"And still no sign of Haas?"

"None. I'm worried for him. But maybe we don't need him to learn what we wanted to know. The Duke of Greyfells is Gales' travelling companion."

"Greyfells? *The* Greyfells? The King's old enemy?"

"Not the same man, but probably of the same philosophy."

"Then she hasn't just been acting for herself."

"I've doubted that for some time. But actually, I think if she'd had her way she would've been satisfied having Fulk declared crown prince."

"These little *tête-à-têtes* you and she are having haven't

softened you, have they?"

Michael chuckled. "Hardly. But I know a little more
about her. She isn't the villain we've tried to tell ourselves."

"Who is? We all like things black or white. Makes it easier
on our consciences. How are you going to work this so she
don't get wind of Gales?"

"Thought I'd move her to the old Dalthin manor tonight,
then north through Anstokin and Volstokin later. We'll need
to let Volstokin and Anstokin know she's coming. State trip
home to see her family, and such."

"All right. I'll contact their ambassadors. You get her out
of the castle. Damn, but I wish the King would get back."

"Better figure it'll take at least another three weeks.
Probably longer. It'll depend on how much he fools around
over there."

"Three weeks. A month. Can we hang on that long?"

"Credence has everything sewed up. Anybody tries anything, he'll be all over them. And they know it. Cham says
the Thing has gotten as still as death. We get Inger to sign
away her rights, the worst will be over."

"Well, do it, man."

"Easy, Derel. I'm on your side."

"Nerves. Lack of rest and nerves, Michael."

"Back to let you know as soon as I can."

Inger greeted Trebilcock at the door. He said, "I understand you've finally decided."

"I have. I'm packing now. You convinced me this time."

"How was that? You were still stalling yesterday."

"The arrow, Michael. Don't kid me. Nothing happens
without you knowing, without your approval. Not in
Vorgreberg."

"Ah, Inger, if you only knew. Hell, you do know. One
whole hell of a lot goes on without me knowing. Wouldn't
you say? What about an arrow?"

"Come here. Look at this and lie to me." She led him into
another room.

A dead man lay on the floor. Michael knelt beside him.
"Karl. How the hell? . . ."

"Through the window. The arrow was meant for me. Karl

stepped in the way at the wrong time."

Michael went to the window. He looked out, toward Fiana's Tower. The arrow hadn't been meant for anyone. "I don't know anything about it, Inger. I will say this. The man who killed Karl was a hell of a bowman."

Inger hissed, exasperated. "So Hunsicker told me. I don't care. I do care about my life and the lives of my people. I didn't bring them here to be murdered."

"I'll find out who did it. He'll hang. Rest assured."

Uncertainly, she asked, "What if it was Abaca? You're always warning me about him."

"Assassination isn't his style. If he wanted you dead, he'd trump up some way to declare martial law, then bust in here and hang you before anybody could get in his way. It's something like that that he's been setting up. That's why I wanted you out. No, I don't think Credence did this."

Confused, Inger said, "That little bitch Kristen, then. She hates me because of Fulk."

"Maybe. Whoever, we've got to get you out of here. As soon as it's completely dark I'll take you to an abandoned manor north of the city. My own people will come in and pretend you're still here. As soon as I make the arrangements, we'll send you north, through Anstokin and Volstokin."

"Why north?"

"Because the people trying to kill you won't expect you to go that way. Because Credence won't expect it. I've tried to make it clear I wish you no harm. Don't force me to state my feelings any more openly. That wouldn't be fitting in a servant of your husband."

Inger gave him a confused look. She sat down. "How soon?"

Michael glanced out the window. "Have to let the night settle in. Say two hours?"

"Won't all these people attract attention anyway?"

"They would if they all went. They're not going to. Pick four or five. The rest stay and keep up the pretense."

She gave him a hard look. "You sure you're not trying to get me out where you can . . . ?"

"Don't be silly. If I wanted you destroyed I could do it

right here. Credence would be glad to help."

"Then why leave my people behind?"

"The attention. And, bluntly, as hostages. You mean much to me, Lady, but so does my duty to Kavelin."

Inger's face soured. "Duty. To Kavelin. I wish you knew how sick I am of hearing that."

Michael shrugged. "The King believes in what he's trying to do. Till he changes course, is succeeded, or I quit, my duty is to carry out his wishes."

"I take it you don't always agree with him."

Michael looked out the window, at a bloody sunset. "Not always. But he makes policy. The rest of us execute it."

"Prataxis makes policy. His pipe dreams are where Bragi gets his crazy ideas."

"Sometimes. Sometimes." *You're walking a thin line here, Michael,* Trebilcock told himself. *Be very, very careful.*

Dahl Haas knocked on the door of the house in Sedlmayr. No one responded. He kept pounding. After a long time the door opened. Haas slipped inside.

"This must be the place," said the sergeant commanding the squad tracking Haas. He assembled his men. "You three go round back and see if there's another way out. Two of you cover it if there is. The other one come back and tell me." He faced the house, studied, waited.

One of his men asked, "Do we really have to do them all?"

"Duke's orders."

"But kids. Sarge, I never killed a kid."

"Knock it off. Just do your damned job." The sergeant was bitter and curt. He didn't like his orders either. But orders were orders.

One of the men he'd sent out returned. "There's a back door."

"Can two men cover it?"

"No problem."

"All right, gents. It's that time. And remember. Nobody out alive. Nobody. Or the Duke might shorten our necks. Let's go."

There was one survivor. Dahl Haas fought his way out the

back door, leaving the men there with spilled guts. He lost his pursuers in the shadows of Sedlmayr's alleys.

General Liakopulos and four companions, clad as hunters, entered Vorgreberg unnoticed. The General hurried to his quarters, shifted into military dress, and sent a flurry of messages.

Prataxis arrived first. He had a grey look. "What are you doing here?" he demanded.

"Wait. I'll go through it for everyone at once. I've sent for Trebilcock and Abaca too."

Abaca arrived only minutes later. Trebilcock showed right behind him. Liakopulos's mere presence had alarmed them.

"Sit," Liakopulos said. "I need help making a decision."

"What's going on?" Prataxis asked. He was aquiver with nervous energy. Abaca remained standing. Trebilcock betrayed no emotion at all.

"The King is dead," Liakopulos said. "Be quiet!" he snapped as all three men babbled questions. "There was a battle. The King was surrounded. Only a fifth of our men escaped, apparently because they ran when they were supposed to attack from the rear. I don't have the details. We'll look into it and apply discipline where needed. That's neither here nor there at the moment. The fact is, most of the army were slain. Including the King, Sir Gjerdrum, and Baron Hardle. The news began filtering in several days ago. I waited till I was sure it wasn't hysteria. I ordered the garrison commander at Maisak to hold the returnees there. I interrupted the telegraph so word wouldn't get through. Once I was sure I rode down to consult you all."

Abaca growled, "Kill her before the word gets out."

"You want to kill Fulk too?" Michael asked.

"Goes without saying."

"I don't kill babies."

"I'll do it."

Liakopulos said, "No you won't, Credence. That's no defense of the crown. That's murder. That's regicide. Fulk became King the moment Ragnarson died."

"A sound legal point," Prataxis said. He still shook. "You're suggesting treason, Credence. And yet. . . ."

"You see my quandry," said Liakopulos. "If we don't

violate the law, the new masters of the law will rape what we've worked so hard to nurture."

"Two dead," Abaca snarled. "End of problems."

"If we ourselves scoff at the law, can we reasonably expect anyone else to respect it?" Prataxis demanded.

Liakopulos interjected, "I've been over these arguments with myself. It's a no-win situation. I've decided what I'll do. Your courses are up to you and your consciences."

Abaca inquired, "What are you going to do, sir?"

"I came here because the Guild owed Ragnarson. No Ragnarson, no debt. I'm going back to High Crag. If you three decide to obey the law, I'll stay to help insure an orderly transition. If you chose rebellion, I'll get out now. I can't join you, but I won't oppose you either."

Prataxis and Abaca nodded. That would give Credence sole command of the army. Abaca said, "The King's daughter-in-law is more sympathetic than Inger. Would she be regent for young Bragi?"

Prataxis replied, "The King's first choices were Mundwiller, Sir Gjerdrum, and Baron Hardle."

"Mundwiller, eh? I could work with him."

Liakopulos said, "We can talk forever, but talk isn't what's needed. We have to act. The people at Maisak can't keep the news quiet forever. Some of the survivors are sure to return over the smugglers' trails."

Prataxis said, "Michael, Kristen and the children will be in danger once the news breaks."

"I moved them out of the country already. With the money."

Abaca and Liakopulos looked askance. Neither Prataxis nor Trebilcock explained. Abaca asked, "Where do you stand, Trebilcock?"

"Right in the middle. Like all of us. I'll probably follow the General's example."

Prataxis said, "Same here."

"You three have somewhere else to go. I don't. This is my homeland." Abaca rose. "So be it, I guess. If I'm outvoted, I'm outvoted." He strode toward the door.

Liakopulos rose, said, "We'll have to see the Queen before the news breaks. Get her braced for the shock when it hits."

Michael said, "I'll take you to her, General. I'll meet you

here in an hour. I have some things to do first. Derel, you bring Credence and Cham."

Abaca asked, "Why not just tell us where she is and we'll all meet there?"

"I don't think so," Michael replied. "The fewer who know, the less chance of trouble."

Abaca gave Trebilcock a hard look. "All right. Whatever you think." He departed.

"He's going to cause trouble," Prataxis said.

"Maybe," Michael admitted. "General, look for me within the hour."

Liakopulos extended a hand. "Trebilcock, it's been nice. We had something here. I'm sorry it has to die this way. Prataxis, you too."

Derel shook hands and muttered, "Why did he do it? There was no sane reason for him to attack them."

Liakopulos said, "He had his neurotic streak, same as the Tervola. Let's hope he didn't die in vain, that the Tervola are satisfied for now."

Trebilcock grumbled, "That's all we need. Shinsan starting a push. Well, later."

Prataxis said, "I'd better find Mundwiller," and followed Michael.

Liakopulos sat down again, closed his eyes, and tried to imagine what Kavelin might have become had the King not gone after his wild goose. He ended up shedding tears.

25

Year 1016 AFE

IN THEIR DRAGON'S Teeth fastness Nepanthe and Varthlokkur followed events in Vorgreberg without speaking. They saw the first small riots blossom, fertilized by a wildfire rumor that Inger and Fulk had been murdered by the King's cabal. They saw Abaca give too harsh orders for suppressing the riots, and witnessed the flight of the Marena Dimura members of the army.

Varthlokkur turned his back on the mirror. Choked, he said, "You were right. I was wrong. I was a fool."

"What are you going to do about it?"

"Now? I can't do anything. It's too late. It has to run its course."

"A lot of people will get hurt."

"I know. That's the way of these things. All I could do is make it worse. It'll be a purging of the national spirit. Every nation goes through them. They're horrible for individuals, but the kingdom comes through tempered and unified."

"Spare me."

"All right. Just understand, I admit my culpability. And it's now too late for me to contribute anything positive."

"If you say so."

One large tear dribbled down the wizard's cheek. He thought, don't tear at me now, woman. I have trouble enough living with myself.

Mist had been so long without sleep she was seeing double. "Lord Ssu-ma?"

"Report on affairs in Kavelin, Princess. If you're interested."

"Of course I am. Go ahead."

"I'll be brief. I know you're pressed. Basically, the old order is doomed. Ragnarson's people have very little sup-

288

port left. Looks like civil war coming."

"So. The noble experiment dies. And not the brave death, but ignominiously, with ghouls and jackals squabbling over the corpse. A sad ending."

"Sad indeed, Princess. May I return to my duties?"

"Please do, Lord Ssu-ma. And thank you for having humored my orders out there."

Shih-ka'i did not respond. Mist turned her attention to Matayanga once more, Kavelin out of her mind. Shinsan would not turn westward again for a long time.

Trebilcock and Liakopulos swung into the track to the Dalthin manor. Michael looked for signs betraying the Queen's presence. He saw none, and was pleased. He said, "Gods, I hate this. And I can't see any alternative but Credence's."

"I'm resigned."

"At least she didn't wrestle it away from us. She got it by default."

"Maybe. Maybe she was the reason the King did what he did."

"It's moot now."

"You sure they're here? The place looks dead."

"It's supposed to." Michael had a vile thought. He kicked his mount forward.

"What is it?"

"Maybe Credence found out. He sent his Marena Dimura out of town as soon as he left us." He and Liakopulos had been delayed while he studied reports on the sporadic rioting. "In any case, Derel should be here now. Though I can't picture him and Cham controlling Credence if Credence doesn't want to behave."

He'd planned to arrive first, then had been too preoccupied to worry about Abaca. He reined in before the manor house, jumped down, ran.

All for naught. A perfectly healthy Inger greeted him at the door. "What're you doing here? I didn't expect you till tomorrow."

"Didn't Derel explain?"

"Derel? I haven't seen him."

Michael exchanged glances with Liakopulos. "He was

supposed to meet us here. We're way late. Some rioting. Your friends are claiming we've killed you."

"I looked over the papers. I can sign them. Why did you bring the General? I thought he was at Baxendala on maneuvers."

"He was. He came back. Let's don't worry about the papers. Damn it, Derel, where are you?"

"What's wrong?"

"Have you been comfortable enough?"

"As comfortable as one can be in a ruin. I'll be glad to get out of Kavelin. It's been nothing but heartaches. I was a fool to want to make Fulk King."

"There you go, Michael," the General said. "Antedate the papers."

Inger's eyes narrowed. "What *is* going on? Why are you here? Why is Derel coming? To give those rioters something to scream about?"

Michael laughed weakly. "Far from it. It's a big confab. You. Me. The General. Derel. Mundwiller. Abaca. Only I'm beginning to wonder if the rest are going to show. Maybe the riots turned worse, or something. General?"

Liakopulos shrugged. "The word could have gotten through. You know what that would mean."

Inger said, "Michael, you'd better get to the point."

Michael looked at Liakopulos. The General nodded. "All right. The straight of it. The King is dead. Fulk is King."

"What? How? Are you sure?" Inger became very pale. Her hands fluttered aimlessly.

"He tried to sneak up on Lord Hsung. While he was out of touch with us, Hsung was assassinated, replaced, and his invasion of Hammad al Nakir called off. When Bragi got to Throyes the legions were waiting for him. Only a few men got away. The General brought the word today."

"Let's go somewhere where I can sit down." As she led them into the house, she muttered, "He's dead? Bragi is dead? I can't believe it."

"It's true, Your Majesty," Liakopulos replied. "It was a great bloody slaughter, and he was among the last to fall."

"Spare me the gory details," she breathed, "He's dead? I don't believe it. How could that be? He was always so lucky.

I didn't even believe he'd go through the pass. I thought he was up at Maisak waiting for the Estates to do something so he could come down and hang a few Nordmen." She wheeled on Michael. "This is another of your schemes, isn't it?"

"No, Inger. No scheme. We talked it over this afternoon. It got hot, but we decided to come out as a group and tell you. Your son is King. You're Regent. We want to take you back and get the government into your hands before the news gets out and Kavelin begins tearing itself apart."

"He's not dead. I don't believe that. It's some kind of a trick." She looked at each man. "Oh. You really believe it. But it isn't possible. . . . Why are you even telling me? You were finally getting rid of me."

"That was when you were intriguing against the Crown," Michael said. "Now you *are* the Crown. What it boils down to is, we decided to stick with the law. The law was on our side then. Now it's on yours. We don't agree with you on much, but our duty is to the Crown. We came to take you back."

Inger sat down. "Michael, this is a lot to swallow. There's been nothing but bitterness. All of a sudden, now, you people are going to be on my side?"

"Only in a manner of speaking," General Laikopulos said. "Inasmuch as Sir Gjerdrum and Baron Hardle were slain with the King, I've become commander of the army and Cham Mundwiller has become principal royal spokesman in the Thing. My conscience won't let me continue in my post longer than it takes you to replace me. But continue I will, to maintain order. When you replace me I'll retire to High Crag."

Inger's eyebrows rose. "Really?"

Michael replied, "Really. Derel plans to return to the Rebsamen. I haven't spoken to Cham, but I expect he'll fight a desperate rearguard action till you can get rid of the Thing altogether. Abaca didn't say, but he'll probably go back to his people. He already ordered the Marena Dimura troops to return home."

"That little toad. He'll cause trouble. He hates me."

"You didn't do much to make him love you."

She gave him a hard look. He didn't flinch. "What about you, Michael? What do you plan to do?"

"Probably the same as the General. Help keep order till the transition is over, then leave. I don't want to see what your people are going to do to Kavelin. I have family in the west. I'll go back to the business, the way I was supposed to years back."

"You really think the people on my side are plunderers, don't you?"

"There's little evidence to the contrary, Inger. I recall only a handful of Nordmen who ever cared a whit for the kingdom or anyone but themselves. And the history of your family is common knowledge. I expect your cousin will swoop down like a bandit chieftain. When he's picked the kingdom's bones, he'll sell what's left, the Gap, to the Dread Empire, for a western vice-regalty, or something of the sort. And you and Fulk will get nothing but the short end."

"You have an altogether too narrow view. Let's not argue politics."

"Let's don't. The important thing now is to get you back to the castle before people find out about the King. If we don't, all hell will break loose. Kavelin can't survive another civil war. There're too many wolves waiting to devour it."

"You're right. Absolutely right." Inger stared into the distance. "Michael, now that it's fallen on me, I don't really want it."

"It'll be rough. Just as rough as it was for Bragi."

"He used to say he never wanted it either."

"He didn't."

Liakopulos said, "Your Majesty, when dreams come true sometimes they turn out to be nightmares."

"Nightmare or not, the kingdom is in your hands," Michael said.

"I don't want the responsibility."

"Then why all the plotting, the duplicity, the dealing with monsters like Lord Hsung and Magden Norath?" Michael demanded.

"It looked different then. I don't know if you can understand. Anyway, I just did what I thought was best for Fulk. I didn't ever want to run things myself." She paused thoughtfully. "I want you to know something. I want you to believe it. No matter what else happened, I loved him. I loved him a lot. And when the numbness wears off, I just might come apart. Stick with me that long, will you?"

"I'll stay as long as you want. The General too. And Derel. I know you don't much like us, but we're willing to help because. . . ."

"I know. I know. For Kavelin." She rose and began pacing. "Damned pimple of a kingdom. It's gotten to me, too, a little. I find myself caring. Hating it, but caring. At the same time."

Michael raised an eyebrow. The General said, "It does seem infectious."

One of the Queen's handful of companions slipped in. He was clad as a squatter. "Milady, there's a man outside shouting for Captain Trebilcock. One of the Palace Guard."

"Michael?"

"I don't know. I'll see what he wants." He went out the back and round the side of the house while the others went to the front to watch through the ruined windows.

The man was one of the trusted handful who had spirited Inger out of the castle. Michael slipped up close, asked, "What is it, Mark?"

The man jumped. "Sir! I didn't hear you coming."

"You look awful. What's happened?"

"The riots. . . . Sir, Colonel Abaca announced that the King had been killed trying to attack Throyes. People just went crazy."

"Oh, damn him! Damn him to hell! Damn me! I should have expected that. How bad is it?"

"Awful sir. The Quarter is burning. There's looting. Wessons and Nordmen are fighting each other in the streets. They're both picking on the Siluro. They all think the Queen is dead too. The Estates have seized the Thing. They tried to break into the palace. We drove them off the first time, but who knows now?"

"Prataxis. Mundwiller. What about them? Can't they get anything organized?"

"They're dead, sir. At least, Mundwiller was dead when I left. They were ambushed in the street. We got Prataxis back inside the palace, but Doctor Wachtel said he wouldn't live long."

"What about the regular garrison?" Liakopulos demanded, stepping out of the house. "What are they doing?"

"Colonel Abaca ordered them back into barracks after his announcement, sir."

Michael said, "Bring the Queen, General. Let's get in there and try to do something."

"It's probably too late."

"Probably."

Inger stepped out of the house. She had changed dramatically. Her manner had become regal. She told her men to get their horses.

Michael smiled. "Your Majesty."

She looked at him strangely. "You've never called me that before."

"You never earned it, in my estimation. I think you're ready for it now. Let's mount up."

"One more thing, sir," Mark said. "A message. Prataxis had it. Gave it to me. Said for your eyes only." He handed it across.

Michael held the letter close, strained to make out what it said. "I hope this satisfies you, Inger."

"Michael?"

"The letter is from my agent in Sedlmayr. I sent Kristen and the King's children down there right before the big championship match. Anyway, Itaskians raided the house and killed everyone in it."

Inger shuddered. "What? How could they? I . . . I'd never allow anything like that. All my people are here, anyway."

"All your people." Michael scowled into the gathering darkness, battling his anger. "But not your cousin's. I neglected to tell you before, for obvious reasons, that Gales is back. Along with your cousin the Duke."

Inger didn't respond till everyone was mounted. "That's Dane's style. Damn him. The filthy . . . Michael, believe me, I never wanted anything like that."

"Maybe not. But it's the sort of thing you should expect from your cousin."

"There'll be an accounting. Let's ride."

* * *

The Duke and his force were thirty miles from the capital, taking their evening meal in an encampment on the estate of a Nordmen ally. Representatives of the Estates were gathering at the castle nearby. There would be a council of war.

"You look glum, Gales," the Duke observed. "Sir Mortin says you've been down since you found out Haas tracked you home."

"Your Lordship?"

"I don't want my best man unhappy. Is there anything I can do?"

Go back home, Gales thought. Leave these people alone. "No, My Lord. I'm just a little under the weather, I think. It'll work itself out."

The Duke chuckled. "You don't approve of what we're doing, do you?"

"No. But I'm a soldier. It's not my place to approve or disapprove."

The Duke nodded amiably. His hunters had returned from Sedlmayr. He was in a good mood. Inger's brat had no more competition for the throne. Inger would be the power behind the boy, and he would pull her strings. "Mortin. In this meeting tonight, pick out the ones we'll need to be rid of first."

Mortin started to reply. He stared over the Duke's shoulder. His eyes got big. Gales stared too. The Duke spun. "Norath! What the hell are you doing here?"

A huge man stepped into the light. Behind him two tall, muscular bodyguards looked on with eyes like chips of ice. "Our mutual friend asked me to drop in." Norath's voice was high and squeaky, completely at odds with his physical size. Gales tittered nervously.

"I wish he wouldn't keep trying to take things over."

"He doesn't see the alliance as on only when it's convenient for you. And he has a special interest in this country. He told me to make sure you don't screw it up, the way your family usually does."

Sir Mortin rose, snatched up a sword. One of Norath's bodyguards struck the blade from the knight's hand. Red of face, the Duke said, "Take it easy. We're supposed to be friends."

"No," Norath said. "Not friends, Dane. Allies. There's a meeting tonight. I'll attend as one of your party. You'll tell no one who I am."

"Whatever you say. But why are you here really? I thought you were tied up in Hammad al Nakir."

"The opportunities here are greater." He settled near the fire. One of his bodyguards took the best meat off the roasting spit and gave it to him.

The Duke fumed quietly, schemes of vengeance shaping in his mind. He wouldn't endure humiliation from anyone.

Gales watched from outside the center of activity, wrestling his conscience for the thousandth time. Could he remain in service to a man who dealt with Magden Norath's like? He had his debt, true, but didn't he also have a higher moral responsibility? Wasn't his debt, in fact, more to Inger than to Dane's family?

Shortly after Norath appeared a messenger arrived saying that the commander of the Vorgreberg garrison had announced that the King was dead. Chaos ruled the city.

"Perfect," the Duke said. "We can restore order and be hailed as saviors."

The messenger added, "There's also a strong rumor saying Ragnarson's cronies have murdered the Queen and her son. The people think there's no one to take over."

"I will."

"Legally, fool. Legally."

Gales chuckled. The Duke's scheme was so much dust if Inger was dead. All those years for nothing. Couldn't happen to a more deserving soul. But his humor lasted only a moment. Inger was too dear a price for Dane's embarrassment.

General Liakopulos led the way round west of Vorgreberg, to the barracks of the King's Own, which lay outside the city wall. He found the troops demoralized and confused. He instructed their commander to assemble them.

"Men," he said, "you've heard that the King is dead. You've heard the Queen was murdered. I give the lie to the latter right now. Her Majesty the Queen."

Inger stepped forward. Liakopulos had torchbearers illuminate her, so there would be no doubt. "There's been a battle in the east. The King was involved. We did lose it, and badly. But as yet we have no direct evidence that the King was killed. All we have are rumors started by people who want to profit from confusion and despair. It's just more of the same thing that goes on every day in Vorgreberg. Don't take it seriously. Don't sit around like men condemned. We're soldiers. Our job is to maintain order. It's time we got on with that."

He spoke a while longer, trying to restore morale. He did not scruple against lying. When he finished he turned the troops over to their captains, who prepared to move into the city.

"Major, they seem a little weak, number wise. What happened?"

"Desertions. We lost close to seventy men. All the Marena Dimura scouts. Most of the lads of Nordmen background. The Wessons stood up better."

"They were always a more solid lot. All right. We're going to split the force into two companies. One will accompany the Queen to the palace. The other will follow me to the Vorgreberger barracks. We'll get them stirring, then start clearing the streets."

The Major looked out his window. An orange glow illuminated the underbelly of the clouds. "It may be too big a job for the tools at hand, General."

"We'll try anyway, Major. That's our job. Don't relay your doubts to your men."

"Of course not, sir. If you'll excuse me? Your Majesty?"

"One moment," Michael said, speaking for the first time. "Where's Colonel Abaca?"

"I haven't heard anything since he ordered us into barracks."

"I see. Thank you."

Passing through the city's unguarded, deserted, open western gate, Michael told Inger, "That damned Credence wanted this. Guess he figured he wouldn't leave you much to take over. Damn. He was a good man, too."

"I never saw much good in him."

"You looked at him as Marena Dimura, not as a man. Till today he was a perfect soldier. But for Bragi."

Inger didn't respond.

"Bragi was the glue that held everything together," Michael mused. "Even the Estates respected him. His is going to be a hard act to follow."

"Don't try to sell me anything, Michael."

Shouts came from the head of the column. A squadron whooped off after a band of looters. They were rounded up, tied neck to neck, and forced to march alongside. The number of prisoners grew steadily, though Michael insisted the column keep to the quieter parts of town.

"They should be cut down where they're found," Inger complained.

"Part of the problem is Credence's savagery earlier," Michael countered. "There's a place for savagery, but not when you're trying to smooth troubled waters. If we butchered anybody now we'd just get more angry people. You can't intimidate a mob. It grows faster than you can cut it apart. When you're dealing with a more limited, planned thing, like the riots a while back, then savagery can have some value."

He glanced over. Inger wasn't really listening. Since departing the manor she had retreated ever farther into herself. She was realizing how much had settled onto her shoulders.

There was a mob at the palace gate. Nordmen agitators were trying to get them to break in. The Guard was showing admirable restraint by not firing on them. Inger snapped, "Wait! Let me try first," as the company commander began dispersing for a charge.

"Your Majesty. . . ."

"They think I'm dead. Seeing me may calm them down."

Michael nodded. "I was right. You do have courage when it counts. Let her, Captain. Fiana used to do this sort of thing and people loved her for it." Something touched his cheek coolly. He held out a hand. Sprinkles. He looked at the fire-bellied clouds over the Quarter. They seemed lower and fatter. "It may rain. Wouldn't that be lovely?"

Inger looked at him strangely. "I'm scared to death, Michael. I wasn't born without fear the way you were."

Michael felt for more raindrops and replied, "That's courage, Your Majesty. Courage is what makes you go ahead, despite your fear, and do what needs to be done. Ah. Comes the cold wind. Lovely indeed."

Inger smiled weakly. "That's supportive. A little oblique, but supportive."

"I'll go with you. Captain, how about half a dozen men, just to stay close?"

"Very well." The captain called names. Inger started forward. Michael nudged his mount, caught up, smiling into the teeth of the rising wind. The six men hurried after him.

There was enough light round the gate, from torches in the mob and lights on the wall, for Inger to be recognized. Word spread quickly. Rioters quieted, gawked. Agitators gulped and fled into the shadows. People backed out of Inger's path. A few dropped to one knee and bowed their heads. Someone atop the wall had the presence of mind to sound trumpets and add to the impact.

The mob began dispersing as the gate opened and twenty Guardsmen came forth. They began departing even faster when Michael took out a scrap of paper and nib of charcoal and pretended to be noting names. It was one moment when his reputation was a positive. As they passed beneath the wall, Trebilcock said, "They'll spread the word. Things will start calming down. If a good storm breaks, so much the better. They'll go home to get out of the rain." Distant thunder punctuated his final remark.

"I hope so, Michael. I saw enough getting here to last me a lifetime."

"Get used to it if you're going to be Queen. These things happen. I've never figured out why. It's like Vorgreberg has a fever it has to purge every so often."

A Guardsman rushed up to Michael. "Captain Trebilcock. Doctor Wachtel would like to see you immediately."

"About Prataxis?"

"Yes sir."

"How is he?"

"Still breathing, sir, but that's about all."

"I'll be right there. Captain, you know what to do. Inger, you want to start taking charge?"

"What about Fulk? Michael, it worries me, leaving him out there with only two women to watch him."

Michael smiled gently. "You might send some of your people to collect him, Your Majesty. If you'll excuse me?"

"Of course." Inger dismounted and marched across the courtyard, toward the great audience chamber. The regal hauteur came over her. Michael heard her give orders to the nearest Guardsmen. He smiled again.

"She'll do," he murmured. "She'll do. Now, if we could do something about her cousin. . . ." He hurried inside, toward Wachtel's quarters.

Prataxis was conscious when he arrived. A weak smile flickered across the old scholar's lips. "Took you long enough," he whispered. "Is she all right?"

"Fine. And taking charge. We've got the troops moving again. Looks like there'll be rain to help." Michael glanced across Prataxis, his question unspoken. Wachtel shook his head.

"I'm on my last legs, Michael," Prataxis said. "I never thought it would come to this when I came here. Who attacks dons of the Rebsamen?" He tried to chuckle. It came out a pathetic gurgle. "Stay with her, Michael. Guide her. Your organization is almost a shadow government. Use it. For Kavelin's sake."

Michael sighed. "Don't put that on me, Derel."

"Was all your work in vain? Have you spent so many years building just to walk away? You can lighten the winds of change and soften the coming night. Don't walk away. But be careful. There will be dreadful people near her."

"All right," Michael said. "All right." He didn't mean it at the moment. He was just saying what a dying man wanted to hear. But even then, way back in his mind, there was a part of him which still believed in the dream.

"Thank you, Michael. Now I feel I won't have died entirely in vain."

"Die? Who's going to die? You'll be up and around in a few days."

"Don't be a fool, Michael. I'd be dead now if I hadn't been determined to see you before I go."

Yes, Michael thought. He could see Derel's reserves going as he talked. He didn't have long.

"Michael, do one more thing for me."

"Name it."

"In my quarters. In the big cedar chest at the foot of my bed. All my notes and manuscripts. All the drawings I did with Varthlokkur . . . they're more precious than gold, Michael. Get them back to the Rebsamen." A pleading note had entered Prataxis's voice. He was begging that his life's work be preserved.

How could Michael deny him? "You've got it." And this promise he meant to keep. "They'll be gone before dawn."

"Thank you, Michael. You're a good friend. Doctor, I'm finished now."

Wachtel gestured toward the door. "He'd rather it happened privately."

Michael nodded, began retreating.

Prataxis went before Michael got out, a last, soft, "Gods save the King," drifting over his dry lips.

Michael walked alone for a long time, thinking. Prataxis had been his last friend here. He was alone in a hostile land now, surrounded by the growing might of people who hated him. He wouldn't survive long if he stayed and tried to fight the good fight.

He wasn't afraid. Death held no terrors for him. But he was lonely, and loneliness was a foe he did not know how to defeat.

Eventually he went down to Prataxis's quarters and prepared the man's manuscripts for shipment.

It was there, deep in the night, with lightning stalking the heavens and a hard rain driving into the streets, that Inger's messenger found him. "The Queen would like you to join her in the audience chamber, Captain. Planning session, she said."

Michael rose from Derel's pallet. Despite the wealth that had been at the scholar's command, he had lived a spartan life. "I'll be right there."

26

Year 1016 AFE

BRAGI CAME OUT of it suddenly, like flying through a door kicked open. One moment he was unconscious, the next wide awake. He surveyed his surroundings. He was in a large, well-furnished room. It was daytime. The air was hot and muggy. He tried to rise. Pain stabbed through his chest. His muscles refused to do more than pretend to try. He fell back.

A man stepped through the door immediately. He wore the dress uniform of a noncommissioned officer and the badges of one of the legions of Shinsan's Western Army. He stared for a moment, left without speaking.

So, Bragi thought. Captured. Must have something special planned for me.

They would, wouldn't they? Mist had warned him often enough. They didn't accept defeat gracefully.

The battle came back. All the stink and sweat and fear. All the memories of how badly it had gone, how badly it had hurt Kavelin. He sank into a morass of shame. He should have known better. But he had bet against the long odds, counting on his luck. And luck had deserted him. And that was only right. Only a fool bet his luck. A wise man accepted it when it turned his way, but he didn't count on it.

Where am I? he wondered. It's too warm to be anywhere in Shinsan.

The door opened. The noncom reappeared, followed by two maskless Tervola. A short, broad one wore the badge of an army commander. Bragi frowned. Hsung was tall and lean, like most of his breed.

The taller Tervola pulled the coverlet off Ragnarson's nude frame, prodded his left side. Bragi winced. "Still tender?"

"A little."

"Should be. You had six broken ribs and a punctured lung. Not to mention cuts, scrapes, bruises, and a concussion. A challenge to my art. He can talk, Lord Ssu-ma. Call me when he tires. I'll give him a sedative. He still needs bed rest, and he looks like the kind who climbs out too early if you let him."

The shorter Tervola nodded, gestured in dismissal. He pulled a backless stool over to Bragi's bed. "Thought we would lose you for a while," he said.

Bragi frowned. The voice was familiar.

"Ah. Lord Ssu-ma Shih-ka'i. We met at Lioantung. The day we disposed of the Deliverer."

"Now I remember. You didn't speak. . . ."

"I'm a quick study with languages. Interpreters can be troublesome."

"That's true."

"You have questions. Where are you? Argon. I have shifted Western Army's headquarters here. We are harassing Matayanga's flank. What else?"

"Why?"

"Excuse me?"

"Why am I here? Why am I alive? I've been number one on your hate list for ages."

"Perhaps for some. Not for me. You're here because you saved my life. I owe a life for a life. So you will become a guest of the empire. With the approval of the Princess."

Ragnarson struggled to get into a sitting position. His muscles betrayed him again. Shih-ka'i helped him sit, propped him with pillows. "Better?"

"Much better. What happened? I had Hsung nailed to the wall, I thought. He was making an ass of himself. I should have had Throyes in my pocket before he knew I was there."

"You didn't know? Prisoners said as much, but we didn't believe them. Lord Hsung was removed. With extreme prejudice, as some say. I was sent to replace him, apparently after you were out of contact with Maisak. I broke off the attack on Hammad al Nakir, as the Princess instructed, then detected you moving in the north. The trap I laid almost destroyed me instead of you. I hadn't given sufficient weight to your horsemen, not having served in the west during the war. Had we closed with you earlier in the day, our places would be reversed now. In fact, if your final charge hadn't succumbed to panic, the situation might be reversed."

"They ran. I vaguely remember. The finest soldiers I'd ever led, but they panicked when it counted most."

"Perhaps if their commander hadn't been killed at the beginning of the charge?"

"Gjerdrum? Yes. Now I remember somebody saying he was dead. Maybe so. If he'd stayed alive to show the way. . . . But what does it matter? It's over. It's lost. Kavelin is lost. I played the fool, and handed all my enemies what they wanted."

"We all err."

"When I do, I do it right. One thing. I'll never understand why you didn't use the Power. You had us surrounded and pinned down. All you had to do was hit us with a few nasty spells. We couldn't have done a damned thing. But you used your infantry, and almost got whipped. You must have lost a lot of men, and you need every one in Matayanga."

"Indeed." Shih-ka'i rose, began to pace. "I didn't use the Power because I was ordered not to. The Princess had been told not to."

"Who gives Mist orders?"

"She wasn't ordered. It was suggested. By your wizard friend."

"Varthlokkur?"

"He promised to remain uninvolved as long as we didn't call on the Power. I didn't understand it then, and I don't pretend to now. The man has been at your side for a decade. Why did he abandon you?"

"Personal conflict, I guess. But I don't understand either. So. Here I am. Prisoner for life, eh?"

Shih-ka'i nodded. "Your imprisonment won't be hard. You won't be treated as a trophy, or such. You'll live in comfort. You simply won't be allowed to return home."

"How about if I give my parole?" He was thinking of Sherilee now, and growing melancholy. Never to see her again? That was sad.

Shih-ka'i smiled. "I think not. It has long been the estimation of the Council that you are the empire's most dangerous enemy. Having met your army, with it at a severe disadvantage, and been thoroughly bloodied, I'm inclined to agree. I owe you a life. Don't ask for more."

Ragnarson smiled too. They understood each other, somewhat. "I was thinking of a woman. I'll miss her a lot."

"She's now Queen. And seems to be doing an unexpectedly competent job of maintaining order."

Bragi shied away from thoughts of Kavelin, except to remark, "I didn't mean Inger. She and I went our own ways before I came east. I was thinking of . . . a girl I knew. A girl I'll miss. There was something special there."

Shih-ka'i paced. After nearly a minute, he said, "Perhaps something can be arranged. We'll speak of it after I've considered. For now, rest. You have a lot of recovering to do." He removed the pillows from behind Ragnarson's back.

As Shih-ka'i was about to depart, Bragi said, "Lord Ssu-ma? You're all right."

Shih-ka'i's eyebrow rose questioningly.

"Just saying I'm pleased that there are decent men among the Tervola."

Shih-ka'i smiled. "Thank you. Though I don't think my colleagues would enjoy hearing that."

"Probably not."

The stay at Sam Chordine's home had become a grinding bore for Sherilee. She was becoming neurotic, worrying about the King and fending off the fat man. "Kris," she said one morning, "I'll go crazy if we stay here much longer."

"We may not. We may go back."

"Back? We can't do that."

"I talked to Aral again a little while ago. He's heard from the Marena Dimura. Inger still thinks we're dead. Credence wants us to come back and prove we're not. To give him a rallying point."

"He wants young Bragi for a pretender, you mean."

"Yes."

"He could be that with us still here. The kids are too young for the Marena Dimura life, and that's what they'd have to live. I could do it if I thought there was any point. . . ." She burst into tears.

"What is it?"

"Kris, I miss him. We never had that much time together, but it's like part of me has been ripped out. I just can't believe he's dead."

Kristen took the smaller woman into her arms, comforted her. "I know. I know. It's still unreal to me, too. But we're going to have to accept it."

"I don't want to accept it. I want everything I'm never going to have. I hate politics."

"Take it easy." Someone pounded on the door. "What is it?" Kristen demanded.

"It's Slugbait, Lady. I got a message from Captain Trebilcock."

Sherilee turned off the tears. Both women answered the door. Slug passed the courier case inside. "Something wrong?" he asked. "Anything I can do?"

"Get Chordine to leave Sherry alone," Kristen snapped.

"He been after her again? I'll break his legs."

"No. No. Just get him to back off. Don't hurt him. We need him too much."

"I'll talk to him." Slugbait departed looking grim.

Kristen ripped at the pouch. The enclosed letter was long, convoluted, and often confused. In part, it was a diary of recent events. Michael had included his misgivings, his dreads, his battles with his conscience. He had used the letter the way he had sometimes used Aral Dantice during their morning rides, as a vent.

"What's it all about?" Sherilee finally asked.

"Basically, just that Inger thinks we're dead, and he wants to keep her thinking that. He's going to do the same job for her that he did for the King, only his loyalty will be to the kingdom instead of a person. If he can get away with it."

"That's all he says? In all that?"

"He rambles, but it's just fears and feelings and stuff. He sounds awful lonely. And if I didn't know him better, a little afraid." Kristen spared Sherilee news of the riots and deaths of so many friends.

"So what do we do?" Sherilee asked. "Go Michael's way, or Colonel Abaca's? Do you really want Bragi to be King?"

"I don't know. I just don't know. I don't even want to think about it."

Slugbait came around again late that afternoon. "Lady,

Mr. Dantice is back." His eyes were a little buggy, as if he had seen a ghost. "He has somebody with him."

"Who?" Aral was always bringing someone around with investment opportunities. He wasn't trying to take advantage, just trying to help. He felt a little guilty about running out of Kavelin.

Slugbait smiled and shrugged.

"Send them in." She told Sherilee, "Maybe I ought to let him invest something just so he can soothe his conscience."

Sherilee shook her head. "I don't think so. Don't forget how thick he was with that Mist. He's still got the disease. She could be using him. Don't get pulled into some scheme of hers."

Someone tapped on the door. "Hush. He's here." Kristen opened up. Her jaw dropped. "Dahl. Dahl. Dahl, we thought you were dead. We thought the Itaskians got you."

Haas shifted from foot to foot. "I got away." He couldn't seem to go any farther.

Kristen pushed past Dantice, threw her arms around Haas's neck. "Dahl. It's really you." She rested her head against his chest. "Come on in. Come on in. Please? I'm so glad to see you." She grabbed his hand and dragged him inside.

Tear in eye, Sherilee left them. Dantice shrugged, smiled, gently closed the door, and returned to his underworld friends.

The rain had dispersed the rioters. The reappearance of troops had prevented further outbreaks. Rioting in Kavelin's secondary cities amounted to little, though, with the exception of Damhorst, they were reluctant to pledge fealty to the new regime. The major problem in the capital became the Quarter. Thousands had been burned out of their homes. Winter wasn't far away.

Michael and General Liakopulos were the only old faces at Inger's first formal briefing, but, to Michael's surprise, the new faces were neither Nordmen extremists nor the Duke's freebooters. Inger had made appointments outstanding for their neutrality. It might be calculated, to lull the populace till they could be disarmed, but even so Michael approved.

"The agenda," Inger said. "One, the missing treasury

funds. Two, the lack of response to our call for pledges of fealty from the army." She said that with her old mocking smile and sarcastic tone. Her brittle humor had returned. "Three, my cousin the Duke. Michael? The money?"

"I haven't had any luck finding it. Prataxis had it moved out while we were guessing about what the King was doing at Maisak. Everyone who knew anything left with the treasury. Where it went I don't know."

"Think trying a little harder and remembering a little better might help?" Inger didn't believe him and he knew it. She needed that money desperately. Her gestures toward the populace were expensive. Already she was taking loans from the Estates. "Very well. General?"

"I've applied all the persuasion I can, Your Majesty. The men in the outlying posts were selected for dedication to the King's ideals. They're stalling till your direction becomes clear. They don't want to pledge, then be embarrassed. There would be less difficulty were your cousin not so much in evidence. It's the wait-and-see attitude you find everywhere. You can't blame people, really."

"Maybe not. But meanwhile our neighbors are watching us. The Alteans may be benign, but Volstokin wouldn't mind paying back the beating they took when they interceded in the civil war. Speaking of which. Everyone predicted civil war if I took over. It's peaceful out there. What happened?"

Liakopulos replied, "The estimations were predicated on the assumption that you would take power illegally."

"Michael?"

"There *is* emotional resistance. Some army units, for instance, might rebel if there was an uprising here. What it is, nobody wants to start it. The rebel fever is out there, but it's unfocused. I'd say, right now, the main reason for lack of resistance is absence of a charismatic leader. There is no pretender, no rallying point, just an undirected dissatisfaction."

"No pretender," Inger mused. She turned to Gales. "Josiah, that brings us to my cousin." Her expression soured.

Gales's crisis of conscience had been solved for him. He was now Inger's creature heart and soul. She had accomplished the transition through the timeless expedient of seduction. He was now her agent in her cousin's camp.

Gales said, "Your Majesty, any restlessness in Kavelin is nothing to that in the Duke's camp. He's very bitter. He's carrying on like you've robbed him of his birthright. It won't be long before he and the sorcerer Norath hatch something. I expect they'll turn to me when they do. His Lordship thinks I'm his agent still."

Inger nodded. "I imagine you haven't seen a tenth of Dane's fury. He had hopes of making Kavelin a base from which he could establish a western empire. I've been a severe disappointment. Tell me more about Norath. He worries me."

"I can't, Your Majesty. No one sees him. He stays sequestered. What's he doing here? What's his relationship with your cousin? Colonel Trebilcock and I have discussed this repeatedly without reaching any conclusions."

"Michael?"

"I sent queries to Al Rhemish. There's been no response. I doubt we'll learn much anyway. Norath was Megelin's chief adviser. Suddenly, he's here. That may be all we'll ever know."

"My cousin has the answer. Perhaps I can pry it out. . . . What's that?"

Someone was tapping at the door. The guard there opened it. "Messenger for Colonel Trebilcock," he said.

"Go ahead, Michael. Maybe they found the money." Sarcastic smile.

Michael went, curious and a bit nervous. He had been out of touch with his people since yesterday. What had happened? He listened to several minutes of urgent whispers. He returned to the meeting, interrupted continued speculation about Magden Norath. "Your Majesty, there is a rebel movement after all."

"Michael?"

"Can't really give you anything hard right now. I'm told messages are pouring in. Credence Abaca apparently launched a nationwide offensive at dawn, cadred by Marena Dimura troops. Several smaller garrisons have declared for him. So have the city fathers of Sedlmayr. So far Credence has limited his attacks to your friends of the Estates. The odd thing is, he claims to be Marshall, acting on behalf of King Bragi the Second." That had shaken Michael when he had heard it. He had expected Kristen to remain in hiding.

Inger turned pale. "Kristen's brat? I thought . . ." She stopped before it became apparent she possessed guilty knowledge. "How strong are they? Why didn't you warn us this was coming?"

"I told you, there's nothing hard yet. I didn't warn you because I didn't know. I haven't been able to penetrate the Marena Dimura community. They won't have anything to do with outsiders. Numberwise, Credence can't have much, though. The Marena Dimura aren't numerous, nor are they well-armed. He's trying a coup. It'll fall apart in a few days."

"General?"

"I'd agree, Your Majesty."

"You and Michael go deal with it. Now. I'll expect a report before I turn in."

"As you wish, Your Majesty," Liakopulos said.

"He pulled a slick one," Michael observed as he and Liakopulos stalked through the castle halls.

"You should have seen it coming. It was too quiet."

"Maybe. Still, it should peak today and fall apart before the end of the week."

Michael guessed wrong. Sundown brought the second phase of Abaca's campaign. It left the nation staggered. He employed the Harish on loan from Yasmid. Michael had all but forgotten them. Half the religious fanatics struck in the vicinity of Vorgreberg. Three teams of three hurled themselves at Greyfells and Norath. Norath's sorcery saved him and the Duke, but both were gravely wounded. Most of their captains were slain. Josiah Gales missed death by sheer luck.

The Estates suffered even more grievously. Abaca's planning had been meticulous, and aimed at the heart of the opposition. He was using men who did not care if they came out alive. Their strike crippled Inger's ability to respond to the rebellion.

Almost immediately, the surviving cadre battalions of the South Bows and Sedlmayr Light regiments declared for Bragi II.

Michael and Liakopulos flanked Inger at a table on which a map of Kavelin lay. Their voices were soft, and concerned. "Count out Delhagen, Holtschlaw, Uhlmansiek, and Orthwein," Michael said. "Damn. Four provinces gone already. And half a dozen more suspect."

"General, what about the other regiments?"

"The Damhorsters will stick. The Vorgrebergers and Queen's Own are safe. And, of course, the Guard is sound."

"What about the Breidenbachers and Borderers? And the garrison in the Gap?"

"The Borderers are too dispersed to go either way. Split them according to the sentiment of the area where they're stationed. Maisak is temporizing. I haven't heard anything from the Breidenbachers."

"Do something. If they go. . . . look at the damned map. The whole east would be against us. Some of their units are within a few miles of Vorgreberg."

"You forgot the Midlands Light," Michael said. The Midlands Light hadn't taken part in the summer exercises. None of its men had gone east with Ragnarson. It remained at full strength.

"Let's not talk about them," Inger said. "About them we should pray. If they go, we're dead."

"Don't give up on them," Liakopulos said. "They're mostly Wesson, but Credence never had much influence with them."

"Find out," Inger ordered. "Find out fast. If they stick, start using them. Use them fast."

Liakopulos said, "May I remind Your Majesty that I'm due to resign? I believe Colonel Gales was supposed to replace me?"

"You're both too valuable where you are. You agreed to stay as long as I needed you, General. Your conscience won't let you fight Abaca?"

"We can fight him," Michael said. "But we won't like it. He's our friend."

"Not anymore, he isn't. *He* chose enmity. Look. I want to hit back. Hard, and soon. Before this can become a real war. Can you finagle that into your sense of duty?"

"All right," Michael replied. "All right. We've started. Redouble the palace Guard first thing. There will be more attacks by assassins." He'd never confessed that he had brought the Harish into the kingdom himself, then had let Abaca get control. Nor did he admit that he knew quite a bit about what Credence was doing. His goals were not those of either party to the fighting.

Abaca spent Harish assassins liberally. He kept the Crown's forces at a standstill. Desertions plagued both sides. Norath, repeatedly attacked and twice more wounded by the Harish, not armed with his pride of monsters, and unable to cope with Abaca's woodland guerrilla warfare, found an excuse to return to Hammad al Nakir. Megelin hadn't fared well in his absence anyway.

Winter's arrival saw the sides at a standoff. Inger controlled the cities and castles. Abaca controlled much of the countryside. Their soldiers showed little inclination to mix it up. They could see no reason to fight men with whom they had stood shoulder to shoulder during the Great Eastern Wars.

Michael became a man in the middle, playing a game with purpose and parameters known only to himself. Both sides believed he was their man. For a time. In reality he began fighting his own war, as a third force. It was touchy and dangerous, and he had to be alert every instant. Whatever he might pretend, he knew he had no real friends inside Kavelin. That cannibal bitch had eaten them all.

For the first time Michael knew fear. It was just a feather's caress, and mainly fear of failure, but it was fear nevertheless. "Damn you, Bragi," he muttered frequently, like an incantation. "Why did you have to go crazy at the end? Why did you have to run off on us?"

Sometime in the heart of winter, when neither Inger nor Credence was watching, Michael disappeared. He reappeared only rarely, at random, in unpredictable places. As Derel Prataxis had observed on his deathbed, Michael Trebilcock had his own shadow empire and shadow government. He simply slipped off into that shadow world, where his own people served with unquestioning loyalty, both to him and to the dream. They were almost everywhere, and were as spectral as he.

He became an invisible boulder in the stream of war,

unseen but felt, and feared by everyone. No one could fathom his motives, but he had to be accounted for in every plan. He remained there, like that rock. Backs had to be watched. Unwritten rules, apparently benefiting Kavelin as a whole, had to be observed. He who ignored Michael did so at his peril.

Michael's war was intended to buy time. He knew something the other principals did not. Only Kristen, Sherilee, and Ragnarson's children shared the secret.

Buying time. Awaiting a chance to wake the cruel storm that would put paid to relentless ambition and bickering for all time . . . that was what Michael called the inevitable. The cruel storm.

For in Throyes a man who was not dead had set his feet on a path to coldness of heart.